RANGER

Other Books by R. W. Turner

Grey Matter

R. W. TURNER

RANGER

FIRST EDITION

Library of Congress Control Number: 2003112060

ISBN 0-9745290-0-1

Dedicated to
Mr. Lew Wasserman
who opened the door for me
and
Mr. Harry Tatelman
who pointed the way.

ONE DAY

Hot as a flapjack on a griddle and sizzling like some bacon on the side, these southwestern flatlands were, this May day, reaching out there for those horizons like they were a bunch of beaten eggs in a cast iron skillet, all spread out even and just begging to be turned into an omelet or something.... Only this isn't a restaurant, it ain't breakfast and the order of the day is hot—blistering, oppressive heat—the kind a short order cook finds near a stove on an excessively grueling day, after eating some five-alarm hot sauce and chasing it with some Mescal. A biting, stinging, uncomfortable, sweaty feeling that accompanies humidity and an unrepentant heat.

Home to every varmint, vermin and critter you wouldn't want sneaking up and/or landing on you, these mesquite and cactus-laden wastelands housed the kind of dangers only a wildfire could appreciate—if only there was enough tinder to go around. Even then, the only thing that passed through these scorched and tortured lands with any spirit and regularity were dust devils, those free flowing bursts of wind that didn't really know any better. If raindrops didn't evaporate before impact on these blazing grounds, there might have been a discernible water chart, but nobody ever really cared to stick around long enough to find out, unless they got lost out there and died. Then again, desert wasn't an inappropriate appraisal of this territory, as nothing but weeds and cacti could take up root in an area like this and call it home. But that couldn't stop the conscience of some plants, as tumbleweeds would intentionally uproot, roll with the winds and commit a form of suicide or something, by deliberately falling off a cliff or intentionally slamming into a boulder, so it could escape the constant furnace-like temperatures.

This was a hard, bitter land on a map, and if you had the luxury, forbearance, or guidance of one, you'd know better than to try to traverse. Wasteland wasn't just a depiction on a portion of this overwhelming country, like the "Bible Belt," "Breadbasket," "Heartland," or even the "Mason-Dixon Line," as much as it was more a rendering or a warning of what lie ahead.

The mute silence of these flatlands vibrate with a thundering roar that awakens an acute sounding in the area that shakes and quakes the very foundations of the earth, until the grounds begin to tremble, sway and shake, as a meandering herd of cattle are on the march to the tune of cowboys' whistles, hoots and hollers. Though "lead" steers are generally regarded as the smartest of the group, as they have an innate ability to "lead" their followers on a drive as some sort of directional guidance counselor or something, their reward for this extraordinary intelligence is to move their breed right up to the slaughterhouse, where their comrades and companions get the last great education of their lives. They weren't called "lead steer" for nothing and if they weren't prized for their uncanny ability to lead other cattle on these trails with their base, natural instincts and intelligence, then they were greatly appreciated more on the dinner table for their good eating.

Jesse Chisholm, not to be confused with John Chisum, the New Mexico rancher, first found the Texas Longhorn free grazing in southwest Texas. Spanish monks had brought them over from Madrid to Mexico, where they were eventually let go, as they weren't easily domesticated and they didn't provide much meat on the bone. Over the years, these wild beasts capitalized off their environment and multiplied. Though they didn't have enough sense to get out of the sun on these desolate, barren lands, Chisholm was able to take advantage of their obvious disorientation and actually drive them in large herds all the way to New York City, where these brilliant beeves marched right down 5th Avenue, and onto the plates of exclusive restaurants like Delmonicos and other fine establishments in the area, thereby supplanting seafood and mutton as the main course of choice.

However, the current herd pounding this dusty, flattened trail are Hereford, a farmer's breed out of Hertfordshire, England, who might have been short of foot, but were big of weight. This accounted for more money at market, which was one of the prime reasons in ranching and raising this breed. The Hereford were no more intelligent than the average Longhorn, but they were certainly more celebrated and manageable, especially around the dinner table, where they were savored most, either, rare, medium or well done.

These destined denizens of dinner, pounding away on this overworked and burdened trail, continue a time-honored tradition that has hardened and tempered the ground from over fifty years of hard travel. Though there were other beeves that were more highly-prized and cherished, such as Kobe—a Japanese breed that was massaged, fed beer and never graced the light of day—and Angus, "beef on the hoof," as ranchers are wont to say about them, it was the red and white Hereford that became the most popular beef. Though cowboys could move them with a certain ease and self-assurance, these animals could become easily distracted or spooked and sent into a wild, uncontrollable stampede, where the smartest, most intelligent thing one could do, was get out of their way.

These bellowing bovines moving down this flattened trail in a cacophony of rhythm and tones only a ranch owner could love—bump, grind and maneuver for positions in line as if it meant something beyond being a resident member of the wrong stock exchange, and, while these critters are headed for market, it ain't to buy oats or hay, as much as it is a journey to the butcher's block—portions at a time.

Taking it all in stride is the cowboy, the leader of this three-ringed marching circus—darting in and about the crowded steers in formation after these dreadfully long, labored walk on terra firma so hardened, thick and vast, water could barely penetrate the surface. Yet, these saddle-worn warriors held their various positions in line designated either "point," "swing," "flank," or "drag" men, without much complaint, thus keeping these marching giants in a neat, orderly, formed group.

The cow ponies are a breed apart for the hard, traveled, and experienced cowboy, as these horses can dash like the wind, stop on a dime and back up for any loose change, if there's any left to be picked up. They can become a cowboy's best asset on these wide open trails, as they're soft of mouth, easy to handle, and light to the touch. They are really just an extension of the cowboy and though they carry an animal instinct the cowboy lacks, as sure as a steer can get a wild-haired notion to wander or depart for greener pastures, a good cow pony can cut them off, redirect them, and seek out other strays before they can turn another notion into a mindless whim. Despite all the many roles played out on this drive between man and beast, it all goes as well as can be expected. These creatures have a date with destiny, and it's just down the line.

Off in a distant corner of these weather-beaten flatlands, moving rapidly towards the herd, the faint trace of a dust cloud rises off the sun-drenched plains. Heat waves waver and distort the image as it approaches, bouncing and dancing like a mirage or hallucination on the horizon. Though it holds the characteristics of a small dust storm, it begins to distinguish itself as a horse and rider at full charge.

There's purpose and reason in this race, as they effortlessly glide across the thick, dust-caked surface of these unforgivingly brutal lands.

Straggling behind the procession of destined dinners of delight, rolls the ever-present chuck wagon, a veritable vessel of victuals and other varied consumables for these long open runs. "Four-in-hand," the cook doubles as covered wagon driver and chef, though cooking is generally considered a second occupation, as keeping up with the advancing drive is its primary function.

These men are generally praised for their expertise in stocking provisions, bed rolls and various other essentials on the drives, while distributing hard tack, hard biscuits and warm water throughout the day as another contribution. And while beans were the usual reward for a cowhand's hard-earned day of dust and displaced dirt out there with that rambling herd, this gastronomically challenging food was often just ladled out of a pot—generally under the cover of darkness—when other contents couldn't be so easily recognized or identified. It is considered the cook's best revenge for all the criticism they get out there on the open trail.

For all the ribbing he puts up with, he is mostly prized for his ability to identify, pick and add wild herbs and spices to his "pot-of-luck" dinners, although sometimes, bacon or wild rabbit can add some flavor and chew to a meal. Occasionally, however, as befits the occasion, a lame or dying steer is sacrificed for an open roast over a pit, where mesquite or other attainable fuels could fire up a meal, and where whatever was left over went into other meals with beans.

The cook is always suspect on these excursions for his enterprising inventiveness with food as it only validates his lack of real culinary skills. While he wasn't hired for his cooking ability as much as for his ability to supply non-perishables and trail discoveries, his most important objective is in transport and keeping up with the cattle flow plus supplying the needs of the working cowboys.

Riding near the chuck wagon is the wrangler, the crusty, trusty, trail dude who herds the many saddle horses needed for these drives. They generally pull double duty keeping an eye on the horses at night. This unappreciated job usually garnishes them the affectionate nickname of "Night Owl" because these guys wouldn't generally get much sleep, and had the unique skills and talent of being able to sing and lullaby these unusual Herefords to sleep.

While some cowboys ride the drives for fame, fortune, or adventure, some of them actually profit in other ways, such as Charles M. Russell who was able to transfer these experiences to paper, canvas and bronze. Though Frederic Remington might probably be the most famous artist of the genre and period, it was Charles M. Russell who was really most known and respected as "The Cowboy Artist."

Rising dirt and dust still trails the lone advancing horseman approaching from the distance at great speed. Driving that chestnut-colored mare to the height of its limits, the rider closes the gap between the slower-paced herd while making good time as the margin narrows. The red-haired horse blends with the rustic-colored clothing on the horse-man. The rider whips the beast from side to side with a leather lead, aggressively pushing the animal to the full extent of its abilities while racing over the sun-burned terrain. The pounding hooves and grunts of the horse show the results of the long hard continuous dash laid down by the rider as the horseman keeps whipping and stinging the steed for all it's worth. There's no question that there's a strong sense of urgency and purpose in this race that says this rider won't be denied.

Wade Boyd, the rugged, cattle-worn trail boss riding post, halts his cow pony and takes notice of the oncoming rider. He removes his black, four-corner Stetson and shades his dark brown eyes, gaining a better perspective on the oncoming rider. Wiping his brow free of sweat, he replaces his brim and settles into his saddle and reaches for a pouch of tobacco in his vest pocket. Removing a thin sheet of paper from the small muslin bag and evenly distributing the contents across the sheet then replacing the pouch after drawing the attached string tight with his teeth to close and secure it, he twists the paper and tobacco into a stubby little cigarette that he seals with a well-distributed lick. Pulling a wooden match from another vest pocket, and gripping it in his closed fist, he ignites it using his thumbnail. Cupping the match between his weather-worn fingers, he lights the funny-looking smoke and takes a deep draw off it while savoring the flavor a moment before exhaling. He blows out the match and tosses it aside as he once again settles into his saddle to await the quickly-advancing rider.

Those broad Texas skies shade towards sunset on the fading horizon, tinging the twilight into shades of purple, orange, and red as the racing horseman approaches Wade. He discards the remains of his burned-out smoke and re-fits his dusty old Stetson while steadying his mount as the lone rider pulls up in a cloud of dust and comes to a halt.

Shaking the dirt and dust free from the body with a light brown Stetson, long auburn hair falls free and loose to reveal that the rider is really a woman, a very beautiful woman, a woman who's uncharacteristically out of place, except for the fact that she's the one who is really responsible for the cattle drive and crew. Her name is Lillian Ralston and she addresses the trail boss as her employee. "Push 'em on in, Wade," continuing to slap her rust-colored chaps free of the remaining dust and grime.

Puzzled, Wade replies, "Pret near dark, Lil."

"Station master says they'll take over in Bitter Creek," she responds, unfastening the red bandanna around her neck and reaching for her canteen to water it down.

"You're the boss, Lil," Wade says, spinning his steed about. "I'll spread the word." Spurring his mount to a gallop, he rides off to join the herd and crew.

Lillian squeezes the bandanna free of excess fluid, then placing the canteen strap around the horn of her saddle to rest, while wiping her face and neck clean with the warm liquid cloth after removing her brim.

She sights her cattle, spins her horse about and looks off into the distance for the coming haul. Pulling the canteen strap up and off the saddle horn, she takes a swig of the warmed fluid, replaces the top, while tying it down to the saddle.   Turning her mare around, she slowly walks it towards the on-coming herd.

If animals are one of God's greatest creations, then the message coming out of Bitter Creek's stockyards that evening was a strong one—so strong—it reeked right on through to the next day and beyond.

The stench reached right on out there to permeate the area with a smell so heavy and pungent that it carried a humidity all its own. Coupled with the eye-tearing strain of urine and methane gasses from involuntary discharge, the word was: DO NOT SMOKE!

It is said that cattle can recognize when they're about to get slaughtered but what was this confusion and misunderstanding about trains and ramps? Sure, it was their ticket to the butcher, but what do they know? If smell is one of the five senses, then maybe God was trying to say something like, "Let my cattle go!" And they did, just about anywhere and everywhere.

While you might be able to lead the cattle to market, you obviously couldn't control their ozone! Though it is true manure can be a useful by-product, it would take weeks or months before you could get near it to profit off it. And, while this didn't appear to hinder the cowpunchers at all as they wade knee-deep in it, pushing and poking that prospective beef up the ramps to those large wooden cattle cars, where, if there was a real religious experience to be had from all this, it would be: how in holy heaven could you stand all those odors? God must have had an unusual sense of humor when it came to cattle and trains that day.

Dressed in a black business suit and Stetson, while sporting a string tie to match, Donald Prescott diligently works from a pad of inventory as cattle agent on the delivery. Elderly and experienced, he looks over stock and trade with the precision of a well-seasoned professional. His deep-set blue eyes and square jaw lend themselves to this job as an honest, forthright businessman. Standing beside him on the splintered wooden loading dock next to the cattle cars, engine and rails, stand Lillian and Wade.

Donald flips through the pages of his notebook with great concern and interest as he assesses the Herefords in the pens being marched up the ramp into the cars. Speaking to Lillian in a familiar tone, he apprises her of his findings.

"Lil, your Pa ought to be real proud of you on this here delivery," he smiles and nods.

Lillian returns the smile and nudges Wade as she expresses real credit. "Wade's the one who did most of the work."

"I don't reckon to know the particulars on how you got 'em here, but I know good stock when I see 'em," Mr. Prescott says matter-of-factly. "Why don't we retire to my office and we can fetch up some numbers on this drive."

Looking the two trail-worn cowhands over a moment, he offers some thought to the two in adding, "You know, maybe a hot bath and some sleep beforehand would do you both a little good?"

Wade takes his hat off to address the two. "'Fore I bathe and get me some shuteye, I reckon a shot or two or more of some of that redeye down at one of them thar main street saloons on down a mite, ought to take the bite out of a bath and help me rest a mite bit faster."

Topping his hat to the lady and gent he finally says, "This here is where my trail ends and my drinkin' begins....

Lil, Mr. Prescott, if you all need me, I'll be takin' the edge offen this here cotton mouth on down the street a mite." Lillian and Donald laugh as they watch the bowlegged Wade spin then walk on down the wooden platform with those spurs of his clinging like tiny chimes in the wind.

He's quite the guy, Lil. Lucky you had him along," Donald laughs.

"Pa's only choice for the job," Lillian affectionately responds.

"Well...," Donald continues, smiling, "that just leaves the two of us to count and figure the totals. You still got enough in you to finish the job?"

Lillian laughs and says, "Gettin' 'em to you was half the job—gettin' paid's the other half. I'm as ready as you are. Anyhow, Pa expects a fair price on this delivery and I don't aim to let him down."

"I'm sure he does, little lady. I'm sure he does," Mr. Prescott smiles.

Bitter Creek is a cow town located between Laredo and San Antonio near the Mexican border in the southwestern county of Texas, known as La Salle. Though it's a modest town in respect to area and overall size, it is fit with all the modern conveniences of the day, including electricity, plumbing and telephones, thereby making it one of those ideal places for cattle drive loadings minus all the glitz and fuss that seems to come with bigger cities in the general area.

Fit with rail lines heading to larger junctions, it's an excellent place to negotiate business transactions without too much interference, thereby providing for fast, easy and quick stagings for the long hauls that will carry the cattle to market. Main Street, a stretch of fifteen blocks, houses a lot of saloons, cafés and hotels to accommodate trail crews following these drives. There wasn't much call or concern over reservations or credit checks as it was all cash and carry or under the stars in a bedroll for the night.

While these aged buildings might be a tad bit old, weathered, and faded, they'd stood the test of time and though the local folk like to think of it as having its own unique sort of personality they could call their own, no matter what anyone had ever thought or said about this little town, it had weathered all the countless storms, heat and cattle drives that had dared to make it that far. And that counted a lot.

While you could call this old town a lot of things, you'd be hard-pressed to ever call it dead and gone. Beneath that rough exterior were legitimate businesses that helped this town grow and thrive, such as the livery stable, barbershop, and all those various other stores where you could almost purchase anything anyone could ever want, need, or order. While there was that old, rusted- out jail to remind some folks just how long a time they'd been civilized in this part of the country, that part of the town was generally reserved for cantankerous sorts in need of some serious sobering. While this town was certainly small, it was still a railhead, and because of that, the town couldn't easily be counted down or out.

While there might have been a one-room schoolhouse to be found around there somewhere, churches had yet to settle in and make their full impact on the populous, so, like all the other little cow towns on the Chisholm trail that carried a bawdy reputation, it was already somewhat settled and spirited in different ways.

This night finds a party atmosphere as thick as the different kinds of music that's drifting out of the many honky-tonks and saloons onto already overburdened streets. While buckboards, wagons, hansom cabs, horsemen and some of them new-fangled horseless carriages cross traffic down the gravel-lined streets; the boardwalk entertains Cowboy, Indian and Mexican alike. Bottles are passed so freely from hand to hand, it's no wonder where the town got its reputation as being free and open.

While proper ladies in mixed dresses of buttons, bows and lace pass in their floor-length Sears and Roebuck mail-order catalog attire, gaining cat calls and other aggressive advances from these trail-worn cowbusters, the real women of the night advertised their wares off the rails of a balcony at one hotel, barely catching the attention or a glance from anyone below.

While shouts and whistles flood the air in various tones and pitches that blush the ear, a group of some tough-looking Mexican *hombrés* patiently sit on a corner passing their téquila while calmly absorbing all the activity, as if it were a carnival or fair playing out before their bloodshot eyes. Hard drinking calls for some hard fighting, and these boys can be a pretty rough and tumble group at times. Few are ever killed or seriously injured anymore as the old west was believed to have been tamed not more than just sixteen years before. Nevertheless, it seemed to have marked the beginning of a whole new era.

Though it might have ushered in a new time of harmony and civility, except for where the end of these cattle trails were concerned, you could still find your common everyday thug, outlaw, flim-flam man, gambler, traveling salesman, and sometimes highwayman; and, while these might have been the best of times, a more modern time, a time for more conveniences such as indoor plumbing, electric lights, automobiles, aeroplanes, player pianos and oil strikes, this was a time when the world had come to age right there in Bitter Creek, Texas.

Undaunted by the confusion and reckless abandon displayed on the streets, Lillian and Mr. Prescott make their way down the wooden walkway somewhat startled by all the commotion and festivity. Lillian views the spectacle in astonishment, asking, "Does that happen all the time?"

"Only on Saturday nights, it seems," Donald calmly assures her. "Laredo and San Antone are pretty heavily policed these days, so everyone just comes over here to let off steam. Nobody'll hurt you if you mind your own business,"

Donald calms her, adding, "at least, that's what I've come to learn."

Lillian nods as Mr. Prescott goes on to say, "Anyhow, we've got business to attend to and money helps keep this town afloat, even if does get a little rowdy at times."

"Rowdy?" Lillian responds in question. "I'd say the whole place was plain loco," drawing a laugh from the cattle agent.

Between, beyond and betwixt the clamor of this unusual town, rides a single horseman that strongly stands out from all the rest. His smart, high-spirited Appaloosa distracts from his simple appearance as his white canvas duster and hat hide most of his features. Though his Stetson rides low on his head, he isn't an easy man to make out. Beyond that, he's old, range-worn and weather-beaten. There's a base stiffness about this cowboy that carries an edge, or something beyond, that suggests no nonsense as he meanders through the maddened pace and spectacle of this cow town. More aside and not really a part of the town, he and that smart-stepping steed continue prancing down the gravel roadway.

Lillian takes note of this curious man, as she enters the stock office to further eye his continued march through the crowded streets filled with wild pandemonium, yet immune to all the activity abounding around and about him. Lillian catches one last glimpse of this serious-looking cowboy as the door to the cattle agent's office closes.

Riding up to the Heaven's Gate Hotel, the small but orderly cowboy stiffly dismounts his high-strung mount and slightly limps towards a hitching post to tie his leather lead. With a labored, humorous kind of gait, he steps up to the boardwalk, turns to look the town over, shakes his head, steadies his hat, straightens his shoulders, spins towards the hotel entrance and begins that funny, unusual kind of walk towards the front door of the establishment.

Entering the old wooden structure, he takes note of the interior lobby, complete with some plush red chairs and couch, a small wood table and a glass vase with some flowers inside.   The weathered and worn-out wallpaper peels, shreds, and buckles towards the ceiling where a brass chandelier of dubious character dimly lights and flickers over the bright red carpeting that leads to the front desk of this ancient complex.

Shaking his head once more, he pulls his hat down and makes his way to the old wooden counter; absent of any proprietor, he studies the hotel register a moment. Glancing at the mail slots behind the counter, he turns to the rickety old stairs with frayed carpeting to begin that unusually labored walk towards the stairs, where he climbs each step slowly, grasping the bannister more for help in his ascent than leverage, as the gentle chime of spurs trail him. A poorly-lit hallway silhouettes this small but puzzling man as he makes his way down the darkened corridor looking left and right as he passes the many closed doors that line the way. Coming to one door to his left, he stops, as a certain tenseness is all at once relieved, but only for a moment, as his shoulders stiffen and his square jaw begins to tighten. He begins to remove his gloves after taking a deep breath while still staring at the door in deep concentration, as if his very glance could penetrate through the door into the room and beyond. He slowly unbuttons his duster in a manner that appears to be automatic and well-rehearsed, or something that's been staged many times before.

Opening the floor-length canvas cover, it becomes clear why he carries this labored and curious walk of his. He's wearing and carrying an arsenal of weapons: one double-barreled, sawed-off shotgun and a Winchester rifle in one deep pocket, while the other pocket sports a pump-action, single-barreled shotgun next to a Buffalo gun. He has a buscadero six-shooter rig on each hip and two holsters crisscrossing his chest housing another couple of pistols and rounds. This is one seriously well-armed individual, and if he isn't burdened by the great load he carries on his person, then he must certainly be burdened by the load of memories that must accompany such armaments.

Inside the room of this hotel is Ben Kilpatrick, the "Tall Texan" and his brother Boone, talking to Lee Wright and two other members of the Wild Bunch, all of whom are packing their saddlebags and rolls in this tightly-packed room.

Though these are some tough-looking desperados, Ben projects a different portrait as he speaks only with concern. "The way I see it, we go south, just like Butch and Sundance."

Placing his saddlebag on a bed, Lee responds nervously, "I don't care where we go as long as we get a-goin'. There's a price on all our heads and it don't make no never mind who's aimin' at us, there's bounty on our heads."

Boone turns from the bag he's packed and says, "I ain't going back to jail alive. They're going to have to carry me belly down on my saddle, with my body full of lead. The sooner we leave this place, the better I'm gonna feel. I can sense the law on us right now and I don't like it a bit."

The other two outlaws silently tie bedrolls to their saddles resting on the bed as Ben goes on, "I don't like it much myself, but the times are changing and if we don't head out tonight, there's gonna be some serious pressure on us."

Lee places his saddle on the bed and looks out the window and begins to shake his head. "All that fuss going on out there and we've fifty miles from our freedom."

The door is kicked in on the Wild Bunch in such a fury, it catches the outlaws completely by surprise. The aggressively-armed intruder sends one burst of his scatter-gun to one side of the room while sweeping the other side in an automatic motion, letting go the other barrel. The gunman drops the sawed-off shotgun while still continuing his onslaught with a Colt blazing away in his other hand. Reaching into his duster and grabbing another pistol from his buscadero, he continues the full-on assault, dropping emptied weapons, reaching for new ones, discharging, rearming, firing again and again in this devastating close range shoot-out. Weapons are juggled and barely aimed and fired, and inside the smoke-filled room, hardly anything can be seen, except gun smoke.

The echo of silence reverberates off the walls, floor and ceiling when it all comes to a sudden stop as quickly as it had all begun. While the horror of it can hardly even be seen through the haze of spent black powder, the thunder off all those booming weapons vibrates throughout the room as if it had a pulse all its own. All that remains standing now is that curious but devastating little cowboy in the floor-length canvas duster.

The attack was so swift and lethal, not one gun was used in defense, nor did any bullet answer the assault, as it was an experienced execution. Not one outlaw remains standing, sitting, or alive. Moving from the doorway with two pistols in hand, the cowboy steps into the room to examine the bodies. Picking over the dead with his guns, he searches the bodies for any signs of life.

From behind the cowboy, a young man peeks into the room from the hallway, surprising the little cowboy who instinctively bends, pivots and raises his weapons, but holds fire and pulls his revolvers back.

Standing up while eyeing the little fellow, he says, "I'm Abner Caleb, Texas Ranger. These men were wanted dead or alive by the state of Texas." Awe-struck, the young man steps forward inquisitively to assess the carnage. "Why don't you get the Marshal, boy," the Ranger says.

Main Street has stopped in its tracks from the outburst in the hotel. The gunfight wasn't a long one, but the effect is riveting. Throngs of people gravitate to the street outside the hotel, mingling and gathering in curiosity. "A Texas Ranger," and "Some outlaws...maybe the Wild Bunch," is whispered, passed and spread amongst the bystanders. When word filters down the street, it attracts even more people with a want and need to know.

Aside from the free-flowing music that has been disrupted throughout the town, the general tempo and wild abandon displayed earlier has come to a dramatic and complete halt. Tom Tucker, the town Marshal, a slightly rotund sort of man wearing a black, three-piece suit with a badge over his heart and a pistol on his hip, finally makes his way through the crowd and up the stairs into the hotel.

From across the street, Lillian and Mr. Prescott have been drawn to the front door and wooden walkway to see what all the commotion's about. The gunfight disrupted their meeting, but the crowd is further adding to the distraction as they continue to mount in numbers spreading word about the "Texas Ranger" and the "Wild Bunch."

Having reached all the way to the stockyards and train depot, people in the yard drop what they're doing to move closer to the action, as even these people have curiosity over current events. Cowpoke, engineer and mechanic alike, leave their posts to make their way down the gravel-lined streets towards the Heaven's Gate Hotel, leaving the yard and trains unattended.

The whole town has stopped in its collective tracks because of that shootout and while this kind of stuff might have happened a lot a long time ago, it had been some time since the likes of a Sam Bass or some other owl hoot passed through and felt the need to simply shoot and kill a man for something as simple or as minor as snoring too loud. Then again, this was more than one shot and it wasn't through a wall into another room to clip some old, worn-out cowboy already dead to the world at sleep. This was major gunplay and various caliber weapons were used. This was real news, on the spot type stuff, not the kind of thing that would be watered down or played out in the bi-weekly newspaper Bitter Creek distributed for a copper. If you wanted your news hot off the firing line, it was over there at the Heaven's Gate Hotel, and no matter what you were doing at the time, it could wait.

No one is more moved by the events than those Mexican hombrés sharing the téquila on that corner of the street. They seize the moment to slip into the night towards the stockyards where opportunity presents itself. Led by Major Rudolfo "The Butcher" Fierro, the bandits move on the cattle pens and trains as a well-organized team.

Sizing up one cattle train already loaded, the team quickly takes control of the engine and carefully moves it down the tracks until all the cattle cars couple up. While it might be weighted and somewhat cumbersome, the train is able to slowly make it out of town unnoticed, as the commotion at the hotel still unwinding, is distracting enough to pull off such a hijack. As the train rolls to the edge of town, one last bandit standing at a small electrical power station clips some lines in the box with some wire cutters then makes a dash for the caboose, barely able to grab the iron rail. A wave from the man in the last car to Fierro in the engine cab signals them to build up speed and exit into the night. If success is stealing the train, then they have also stolen the night. Fierro sounds the train whistle in confidence, contempt, and defiance of these gringos, inviting them, challenging them to come after him.

The train whistle splits the evening air like a knife through wet putty, catching the ear of several bystanders at the hotel. But it's only one old cowboy who responds to everyone's alarm. "The Train! Someone's stealing the train!" he shouts while pointing down the gravel-lined road.

Looking down the street in the direction of the stockyards, Lillian bites her lip as she stands there completely helpless, confused, and befuddled over the current events: a serious shootout across the street, a stolen train....

Mr. Prescott turns to Lillian somewhat perplexed and bewildered over the events as well. He shakes his head dejectedly with a frown, saying, "This can put a damper on things, Lil. I don't see how I can complete negotiations under circumstances like these."

"What?" Lillian responds.

"That train has all your cattle on it," Donald sympathizes.

"My cattle?" Lillian says. "I brought the cattle in. You counted them. What do you mean you can't negotiate business?"

Once more shaking his head and trying to apprise the little lady of the hard facts, Donald says, "Lil, I can't pay you for goods I ain't got."

"So?" Lillian replies earnestly. "What are you going to do about it?"

"Me?" Mr. Prescott surprisingly answers. "I only account for them, Lil. I don't own them till they reach market in Laredo."

Stunned, Lillian looks up at Mr. Prescott and asks, "What am I supposed to do?"

"You came into town with a crew, didn't you?" Donald reminds her. "Maybe they'll help you fetch it back?"

Shocked by such indifference and total disdain for her immediate dilemma, she can only express herself in harsh tones that can hardly even be completed. "Why, of all the...," catching herself and taking a deep breath, she stares at the agent asking, "What am I going to tell my father?"

"You tell him whatever you want," Mr. Prescott answers sorrowfully. "But until that cattle train is caught and returned, I can't pay you."

Angered even more, Lillian spins and rushes down the boardwalk in contempt for this deal-maker, as the electric street lights begin to flicker and dance in random uncertainty down the street, confusing her even more.

Entering through the butterfly doors of the Silver Dollar Saloon, Lillian views a confused and drunken crowd weighing gossip and rumor over the immediate events. These barflies and town drunks would rather nurse a shot of the type of whiskey, whose fumes have already dried out the old wooden walls and floors of this fire hazard thought to be a bar, than to settle for the real truth of the streets or that gun battle, but they can't afford to lose their place between sips and gulps of that rot gut, for while smoke, liquor and talk is equally displaced by the patrons in this rat trap of a joint on Main Street, the old barkeep has no difficulty sustaining the flow of booze from behind his counter.

Lillian is able to catch a glimpse of Wade and the crew huddled at a table in a darkened corner of this establishment. Pushing her way through the drunken crowd towards Wade's table, she sees Wade can barely pour his last shot of what is labeled "Tarantula Juice."

Tarantula Juice—a unique, rare and delicate blending of rye for taste, tea for color, and pure grain alcohol for that interesting feeling like you'd just taken a bath in a cactus patch and dried yourself off with sandpaper. While it might have looked like whiskey, felt like whiskey, and strongly resembled whiskey, you didn't want to have it drip or spill on you, and you certainly didn't want to step in it, for the general word of caution when served was, "don't smoke, don't ignite matches too close to it, and don't leave open too long near an open flame when consuming." There were some who claimed it had put hair on their chests, receded hairlines, and underarms; while others held that it had medicinal powers that not only helped clear up their eyesight and vision, but had also flat out cleaned up some perspectives they'd long held on such things as the Battle of Bull Run, Manasses, and who sank the Maine.

"Wade!" Lillian shouts at the startled trail boss who is as tipped as the bottle he's trying to pour. "You've got to help me. Someone's stolen the train with all the cattle on board!"

Drunk, dazed, and confused, Wade halfway focuses in on Lillian and beyond, more tipsy than anything else. Finally he finds some words after an unsteady start. "Lil, if I could get out of this here chair, I'd be more than happy to oblige you. But...," he looks his drunken and highly disabled crew over. "Well, we're pretty messed up here right now and I don't reckon anyone will be able to fully muster till before dawn or thereabouts. What does Mr. Prescott suggest?"

Upset, Lillian shakes her head and departs the saloon in anger as the drunken group's celebration deteriorates into the dreams and nightmares hangovers are known for.

Moving down the wooden walkway to the hotel, Lillian fights her way through the crowd of bystanders in the hotel and finally makes her way upstairs to the room where the shootout took place. Once more, she sees that curious-looking cowboy in the room with the Marshal. She pauses a moment to view the remains of the fight. Though shocked by all the blood and shattered remains of human life she sees spread out before her in the room, she looks at that cowboy in the duster a little differently—more confused and unsure of him now than when she first noticed him riding down the street. She gathers her courage and enters the room to address the Marshal.

"You've got to help me get that train back, Marshal," she pleads.

Turning from the dead bodies, the tin star looks the little lady over and says, "Can't you see I've got enough on my hands as it is, ma'am?"

"Well, what am I supposed to do then?" she puzzles out loud.

The Marshal shakes his worried head and points to Abner. "Why don't you talk to that Texas Ranger. It's his territory too. Why don't you take it up with him?" He turns back to the bodies half saying to himself, "As if I didn't have enough to do already." Looking at the Ranger and scratching his brow, he adds as he looks the room over, "Don't leave much room for questioning, do you?"

Moving through the moon-washed night, the train rides comfortably, unchallenged by any followers. Two bandits laughingly shovel coal into the engine furnace while Fierro sticks his head out the side window of the cab and looks down the tracks into the darkened night. Holding his wind-blown sombrero and turning back into the cab, the major speaks to one of his compatriots, "We must make Nuevo Laredo by dawn!"

"Can we make it?" the bandit responds.

"Can we not?" exclaims the major indignantly. Sticking his head out the window of the cab again, the major holds his hat down as he stares down the tracks towards the horizon and the star-filled sky.

Lillian watches the Texas Ranger reloading his many weapons and putting them away. He reaches into his duster and pulls some wanted posters out and tosses them on the bed next to the Marshal. When that doesn't get the Marshal's attention, he tosses a handful of empty cartridges next to the posters on the bed. The sound of metal casings ring loud enough to catch the tin star's attention and draw him from his duties. Looking firmly at the Marshal in a cold, business-like manner, he continues to load his weapons, spinning the chambers of the revolvers and holstering them.

Lillian moves towards the Ranger and inquires, "Aren't you going to do anything about the train?"

Distracted from his reloading and eye contact with the Marshal, the Ranger casually replies, "Nope." He casually goes back to reloading and readjusting his arsenal.

"You can't just let someone steal a whole train and not do anything about it," Lillian says.

Halted by the inquisitive little lady, the Ranger looks at her a moment in puzzlement and clearly lets his position be known to her. "My job's supposed to be in trackin' these men down. I don't have anything to do with trains."

Surprised, Lillian counters. "But it's your duty to uphold the law."

"Ma'am," he says, looking the room over, "that's just what I did."

Shocked, Lillian argues. "You call this the law?"

Holstering his last firearm, he looks at Lillian and says, "I call this...over!" He buttons his duster as he looks at the

Marshal with a cold stare, as if in need of some sort of lawman's code or confirmation over the event.

"Look," Lillian authoritatively asserts. "My father is a very important man in Oklahoma, and...."

"...And that ain't my territory," the Ranger says firmly, walking to the door.

Following him, Lillian continues. "He has important friends in Texas and I'll see to it he's made aware of your actions."

"Ma'am," he says, tipping his hat, "I've completed my job here. Passing through the door to the hallway, he says to the little lady, "Pardon me," and continues down the corridor in that labored, unusual walk of his. Lillian chases him down the hall as the lights begin to flash, flitter, and flutter. Sensing her behind him, the Ranger stops, turns around and confronts her. "Okay, ma'am. What do you expect me to do about it?"

Relieved, she says, "Well, first of all, call someone!"

"Like you did me?" he laughs.

Countering, Lillian says, "Can't you call someone down the line or something? We do have telephones you know."

Stumped, he shakes his head in disbelief. "Ma'am, I ain't no telephone operator and I ain't no train conductor. You seem to know a lot more about all this modern stuff than me. Look, I'm an old, weary man. You can't just expect me to go down there and lasso a danged train now, do you?"

Lillian breaks down in tears as the lights begin to flicker and fade. Uncomfortably touched by the weeping woman and the fading electricity currently going on and off, he says, "Okay, missy. What do you want me to do?"

Wiping the tears from her eyes, she sparkles for the moment, saying, "Go after them!"

"What? Who? The train? The people who stole it?" He shakes his head. "Come on now. They've got a whole bunch of miles between here and...wherever they're headed."

"I don't know who took it. I don't care. All I want back is my cattle," she assures the Ranger.

"Little lady, that's going to take some doing," he says.

"But not impossible," Lillian tries.

Shaking his head, the Ranger expresses some thoughts. "Not impossible. I am a Texas Ranger. I do have some knowledge of the territory. There are some ways to cut some miles off the chase."

"Well?" Lillian smiles.

"Well, what?" The Ranger responds gruffly.

"Are we going to just stand here and argue about it or do we go after the train?" she offers.

"'We'?"

"The cattle are my responsibility and they're on that train, you know."

"I can't be taking care of you AND the train," he says.

"Don't worry about me," posturing herself in adding, "I can take care of myself. But I can't let my father down."

The Ranger stops to fit and adjust the armaments beneath that duster while thinking this thing through. He eyeballs the little lady, then the dimming electric lights — scratching his stubby five o'clock shadowed jaw with those dirty, gun-smoked hands, fixedly looking deeply into her eyes a moment as the flickering, frolicking lights finally falter, give up and fail.

"Okay, missy. But you best to be on your horse and keep up 'cause I can't be looking back once we take off. And if you hesitate or fall behind...." the Ranger nods.

Lillian interrupts, "I won't fall behind."

"Well then...," the Ranger says, "you best to get on your horse if we're going to catch 'em 'cause time's a-wastin' and once we take off, there's no turning back." Satisfied his words have hit their mark, he finishes by adding, "Let's get a move on."

Walking down the stairs of the hallway and through the lobby to the street, they notice that the lights have gone out throughout most of the town. Yet the bystanders are no less or more affected by it as they just step aside and open a pathway for the Ranger and Lillian to pass through onto the street. The town is almost in complete darkness except for some gas lanterns that light a few establishments.

Abner unties his horse and turns to Lillian, "Meet you at the edge of town." Lillian dashes off to the corrals as the Ranger mounts his horse and guides it down the darkened gravel roadway.

Lillian is quick to catch up with the high-spirited Appaloosa the Ranger is riding, as she pulls up next to him on her chestnut colored mare, while he adjusts the collar of that old, white duster of his. He ponders on his thoughts, fixing his eyes on the little cowgirl and her pony, while thinking it all over again.

"Are you sure you're cut out for this?" he asks, sizing her up once more.

"I don't have much choice," she says.

"You could...," the Ranger starts, before being interrupted.

"...COULD, recover the cattle on that train," she affirms with emphasis.

Spurring his mount to a trot, the Ranger pulls that old, white hat firmly down on his head and takes one more look at the lady who's moving up beside him on her horse while staying step for step with him. Kicking his horse up to a full canter, he takes one more look at her as the darkened town, and the vast barren wastelands ahead of him are touched by nothing more than a full moon and the gentle whisper of the cool lonely, winds.

The locomotive is pounding away like a rapidly-pacing heart, coughing and spewing blackened smoke from its internal organs out the smoke stack. It cries for relief from the strain as it races down those tracks towards its ultimate destination and freedom — through the moon-filled night — thirsting for that freedom only the Mexican border can offer. While the bandits celebrate the success of their hijack, Fierro interests himself with other matters of immediate concern. He looks over the engine cab. "Where's Mario?" he puzzles out loud.

"He's in the caboose," comes the reply from the bandit engineering the locomotive.

"Caboose?" Fierro is surprised. "What's he doing in the caboose?"

One of the scraggly men shoveling coal looks at the major and adds, "He is keeping an eye out for anyone who follows."

Startled and somewhat surprised, Fierro turns to the caboose, then back to his men in the cab. "Follows?" he wonders out loud, while fumbling and still wondering a moment, finally saying, "Aye, the lazy dawg." Grabbing his sombrero and looking out the cab towards the back of the train as winds from the on-rushing locomotive buck and push him back, he steadies himself a moment then leans back into the cab to say to the engineer, "I'll be back."

With the whole train vibrating, shaking, and whining to the strained engine behind him, Fierro climbs up to the coal car and makes his way through the blackened rubble to the first cattle car. He grabs a rung of a ladder and makes his way to the top of the car as the wind off that on-rushing rail buster almost blows his sombrero clean off. Grabbing the brim while the cattle moan and groan beneath him, he steadies himself and tops the freight car and begins a delicately-balanced walk over the rattling cattle cars like a high wire act without the benefit of a net to catch him should he fall from this speeding train. Though he's oblivious to the cattle stomping around the wooden floor of the cars under him, he continues to leap from car to car, carefully moving towards the end of the train and the caboose.

Coming to the last car and turning into the wind, Fierro grabs his sombrero and starts his climb down the ladder where he soon touches the bottom of the last cattle car and easily crosses links to the caboose. He opens the door to find that it's empty. Surprised, he enters the car and begins a search for his man, Mario. He looks under a seat, out the window, then behind some other seats, moving down the aisle bewildered and puzzled. Finally he looks up and checks a luggage hold where he finds a small cache of weapons under lock and key, which amuses him as he weighs over the stores with a smile.

Still confused over the whereabouts of his man, the major finally comes to the end of the car and opens the last door where he finds Mario eyeballing the fast retreating trestles in the Texas night.

Pulling his revolver from his holster, Fierro taps Mario on the top of his head, using the butt of his pistol. Surprised and instantly shocked, Mario instinctively reaches for his six-shooter, while spinning and drawing in one quick motion.

"Qué pasa, compadre?" Fierro questions his man.

Blinking several times in confusion and relief, and returning his attention to the open range and disappearing tracks, Mario holsters his weapon and confidently reports, "I sense something."

"We are a good hour out of that town. They could never catch us now. There's nothing but the border between us and Mexico now."

Once more gazing into the darkness as the steel rails fast fade at a furious pace, Mario squints outward and beyond the tracks saying, "Something's out there.... I don't know what it is, but I must keep a lookout."

"As you wish," Fierro says. "But we need you up front to shovel soon. Do what you must do, but be up front soon, eh?"

Mario simply nods.

Stars split the western sky into billions of blinking beacons except when they touch the horizon, where the warmed, baked surroundings respond to the fluctuation in cooled temperatures, by giving off the impression or illusion of little dancing lights in the skies. A full moon splashes light across these western wastelands, further outlining the desert rocks, boulders, vegetation, which gently sway to the wisps of winds just blowing the dust around.

Miles and countless miles of silent flatlands reach out there as far and deep as the eye can see — spreading so vast and wide, the curvature of the very planet can be seen just reaching up out there, like the great state of Texas was offering a hand shake to warm 'em up and make 'em feel right at home in their skies. While it might be dark, it remains the same tortured territory it is during the day.

Worn by the hard driving ride, Lillian and the Ranger cross these testy, darkened lands, hell-bent for leather, as step for step they go, neither fading nor faltering from their desire to sight and catch that hijacked train. Down one bend, up another, wind one curve, round another, and another, as the miles count down on this rush for justice. And yet, there is no train to be seen. Lillian's will and drive are as strong and purposeful as the Ranger's are sure, for though they are driven by a common cause, the chase is a hard one, especially under the grueling conditions of nightfall.

Concerned for Lillian's well-being, the Ranger glances over for a quick assessment but sees she's holding her own and completely focused on the road ahead, paying little attention beyond the hard, continuous, driving pace set by the Ranger and his Appaloosa. This ride is the supreme test of man and beast and though heavy breathing and sweat off the horses are a concern, they top a ridge and the Ranger is able to gain Lillian's attention.

Reaching level ground, he shouts to her over the sound of pounding hooves and grunts from these overworked horses. "We need to rest and water these horses."

Lillian nods, while grasping her hat at the top of the ridge and holding onto her lead and saddle horn. The Ranger points out a new direction and continues his lead while Lillian's mare follows step for step in this long-paced race.

Water is a rare and valuable commodity in this part of the country, and it requires a special kind of knowledge and experience of the terrain to locate it. But the Ranger displays that talent by finding a small water hole nestled between some rocks and boulders near a set of train tracks.

Slowing from the hurried race, the Ranger and Lillian approach the small pool and dismount. While the Ranger views the area, he walks his horse into the cool liquid, relieving the overburdened animal for the moment. Lillian isn't as gracious, as she kneels down in the water only to have the Ranger pause her with a word of caution.

"Don't drink it," he says. "Use your canteen."

Lillian looks at him a little puzzled but heeds his warning by going over to her horse and pulling the canteen off the saddle and unscrewing the top and drinking from there.

"It ain't safe," he goes on. "But it won't hurt the horses."

Wandering over to the railroad tracks with the labored walk from all those weapons under his coat, the Ranger straddles the rails, following their path with a keen eye on the far horizon. Lillian keeps an eye on the Ranger, not quite sure what to make of his actions. He squats down and takes his glove off and touches the rail line. Taking his hat off, he bends over to listen for any tell-tale signs. Standing up, he takes another gulp from his canteen and makes his way over to the water hole where he bends down and unties his bandanna and soaks it in the pool. He wipes his face and neck, prompting Lillian to follow his lead. The Ranger meditates while looking at the darkened night. Following a brief moment of analysis, he begins to splash his horse with some water, which quickly evaporates into steam off the overheated Appaloosa and dissipates into the moonlit night. He pats the horse a couple of times and walks him out of the water hole towards a large rock. He lets the reins go while taking a seat and taking another sip of his water.

"What are you doing?" Lillian asks, moving from the pool towards the Ranger with her horse in tow.

Relaxing for a moment, the Ranger says, "Well, from what I can gather, we're about fifteen, twenty minutes behind."

Puzzled, she asserts herself, saying, "This is a hell of a time to sit down and rest."

"Killing the horses won't get us there any faster," he assures the concerned little lady. "Missy, we'll make up some time across an arroyo I know. It's just up a stretch."

"You sure seem confident," she responds, staring at him as he casually sips from his canteen.

"Practical," comes the answer from this experienced lawman.

The moon reflects off the pulsating ripples of the watering hole, giving the faint presence of something that heightens an awareness in the Ranger. He reacts instinctively, unbuttoning his duster and looking around. Though he senses someone is watching them, Lillian is still in full conversation as she walks over to a rock near the lawman and sits down. "What's so practical..." she starts to say.

The Ranger motions silence as he swiftly moves from the rock to the watering hole and some other rocks for another perspective. Looking peripherally, using all his senses, he sounds a "shhhh" to his companion who sits there, completely baffled by these actions.

"What are you doing now?" she inquires in utter disbelief.

"Shhhh," repeats the lawman, this time motioning her to be quiet. He uses all his senses to determine where this feeling is coming from, or, is it just a hunch or some by-product of all his years on the trail?

Off in the distance atop a small hill, the Ranger's questions are answered as the outline of a figure appears and stands before them. Though quite a distance from the pool, the figure's white peasant clothing clearly defines the image of man—a *péon*, a native of these parts.

Relieved for the moment, the Ranger eases up and looks over at Lillian while pointing the man out. "A Yaqui," he informs the little cowgirl.

"A what?" she asks, confused.

Shaking his head, the Ranger makes his way back towards her trying to explain. "A Yaqui Indian," he repeats. Studying the Indian as though he were an endangered species, he continues with reverence and a certain respect, trying to further explain. "These Indians live in the southwest and Mexico."

Curious, Lillian asks, "What does he want?"

"Nothing I can think of," says the Ranger. "They aren't known for too much trouble around the white man, but they can be right smart, sassy and downright hell on the Apache."

Lillian leans over for a better look at the figure as the Ranger begins to brush off his duster while moving towards his horse to mount up. He motions Lillian to do the same. Bewildered, she moves to her mare in silence and caution while keeping an eye on the Indian.

Taking the lead to his horse, the Ranger maintains a view of the Indian as he mounts up and steadies his steed. The Yaqui moves to the side of the hill, then disappears from sight. "Gone," says the Ranger.

Before mounting her horse, Lillian turns for one last look but it's too late, the Yaqui has faded away as quickly as he had arrived. Saddling up, she takes her leather lead and looks at the Ranger as they begin to move from the water hole. "What's so special about a...a Yaqui?"

Picking up the pace, the Ranger replies, "They're supposed to be endowed with some pretty interesting powers."

Further confused, Lillian looks at the Ranger in earnest asking, "What kind of powers?"

Before spurring his horse to a trot, he responds, "Well, as legend has it, the men have the power to change into creatures of the desert."

"What?" Lillian asks in disbelief, catching up on her pony. "Why, I've never heard of such a thing. Are you teasing me?" she says, half amused.

Putting his glove back on and digging his spurs into the side of his Appaloosa, coaxing the critter into a canter, he adds, "Missy, there are lots of things I've been accused of, but teasing? No. That ain't one of them," he shakes his head.

"Why was he watching us?" Lillian wonders out loud.

"Danged if I know," responds the seasoned lawman. "Maybe it's his watering hole or something?" Pausing a moment, he adds, "Who knows? Who cares? Anyhow, don't we have a train to catch?"

With enough said, the Ranger whips his horse to a full run, leaving Lillian to shake her head in confusion as she looks back one last time. Spurring her mare in a race to catch up with the Ranger, they're once more dust in the wind.

Traveling at great speed, the cattle train hauls its freight towards the border town of Laredo, unhampered by any interference. As Mario makes his way over the wails and grunts of the Herefords packed in the cattle cars beneath him, he carefully advances towards the engine cab, jumping from car to car. Leaping to one car, he almost loses his sombrero but catches it just before it becomes track litter. The faint outline of two horsemen trailing them on the pre-dawn skyline touched by the fast-fading full moon in the distance, surprises him.

Alarmed, Mario finds himself moving even faster towards the engine cab, almost in total disregard for his safety. He leaps and jumps from car to car more hurriedly, looking back in confirmation of the suspicions he had warned Fierro of. Racing across the windblown freight cars to the coal car, Mario climbs through the black carbon and wades through it towards his compatriots. Fighting through the rock fuel he steps and sinks into in passing, he finally leaps into the engine cab and grabs Fierro by the shoulder.

The major is occupied with watching the tracks ahead. Pulling himself into the cab and refitting his hat, he notices a nervous, excitable Mario anxiously say, "We are being followed."

"What?" says an unbelieving Fierro. "Are you loco? Maybe it is the mescal that is speaking?"

Pointing towards their rear, Mario responds, "See for yourself!"

Driving as hard and loud as those steel rails can sing, the locomotive rounds a bend and the major turns back to take a look. The wind slams his hat against his head and drives him backwards with echoes of Mario's earlier fears. Looking over the engine cab and his men with more concern, he motions his men to continue to fuel the furnace as he re-evaluates the situation.

One of Fierro's soldiers has another concern as he nervously reports to his commanding officer. "Major, we must stop to take water or we'll overheat the engine and never make it to the border."

"How much further must we go?" asks Fierro.

"The next water stop is maybe ten miles or more," comes the reply from the coal-stained man.

"Keep shoveling," comes the order from the major. Looking back, he says to himself in mumbled calculation. "Ten miles to a water stop?" He shakes his head in disbelief. "Aye, *caramba!*" After another moment of digestion, he says to the engineer manning the controls, "Can't you make this thing go any faster?"

The driver looks at Fierro and says, "The load is too great a burden as it is, Major."

Confused and exasperated, Fierro orders, "Well...make it go faster!" Thinking this isn't enough, he continues, "I'm going back to check our rear. Grabbing Mario by the arm, he says, "Come with me. We might have to fight them off when we stop for water."

Mario is quick to follow his Major, as Fierro climbs to the coal car and quickly makes his way through the carbon rubble to the first cattle car. Grasping the ladder, he looks at Mario and asks, "How long will it take to fill it up with water?"

"I don't know," comes the reply from his man.

The major looks at the engine cab, the road ahead, then at Mario, and back to the ladder where he begins his climb. Topping the ladder and holding his windswept sombrero in hand, Fierro carefully begins his walk over the rattling freight car with Mario close behind. Leaping from car to car until they reach the caboose, Fierro goes to the luggage hold where all those weapons were locked up. Pulling his pistol out, he shoots the lock off the bar securing the rifles then rips the bar off and grabs a rifle and hands it to Mario. "Check for bullets," he tells his companion.

"Empty," comes the reply.

Looking further, the major finds a box of shells and gives them to his partner. Securing a weapon and a box of bullets for himself, both men move to the rear door of the car, open and exit it into the crosswinds trailing the train. The major looks down the tracks, then to Mario.

The Ranger and Lillian are still on the sprint as the lawman points a change in direction. Lillian guides her mare in chase. Coming to the edge of an arroyo, the race slows as they descend into the empty riverbed and across exposed rocks leading to a rise. Both riders dig in, and while Lillian is somewhat rattled by the sudden change in extremes, she grabs a hold of her saddle horn and hangs on while spurring her horse to continue. Topping the gorge, the faint touch of sunrise breaks up the skies, sending darkness into light and shades of purple, yellow, and finally into blue.

"We've got them if we can make it to that water stop," the Ranger shouts to Lillian.

"What do you think?" asks the exhausted cow gal.

"Missy," comes the reply from the beleaguered Ranger, "at this point I don't know what to expect. I don't know who's on that train or how many we're dealing with. This could get pretty ugly."

"I'm here to help," offers the courageous little lady, panting as heavily as her horse.

"Help?" spouts the Ranger. "You'll probably be a bigger hindrance than whoever stole that train. Look, I can't be watching over you all the time, so you're going to have to fend for yourself."

"Fine," says Lillian. "But I'll be there for you."

"We'll be at that water stop soon," shouts the Ranger, still kicking and whipping his mount to the charge. "You just stay out of this, okay?"

Lillian nods as they ride into the new day with dawn at their backs.

In a clearing of these vast wastelands sits the idling locomotive, steaming, hissing, and accepting water from an old wooden tower next to the tracks. Wheezing and whining as one man watches over the funnel leading to the engine, the desperados keep a watchful eye on the area while Fierro and Mario hold vigil on the caboose, surveying the terrain.

Hellbent for leather, the Ranger and Lillian see the train and veer towards some boulders within sight of the iron horse, shy of drawing attention. Arriving at the protected area unseen or noticed, they dismount and cautiously move for cover. The Ranger assesses the surroundings from behind a small boulder, opens his duster and pulls out his Sharp's Buffalo gun without taking his eyes off the freight train or the occupants he can now see.

Pulling several shells off one of the holsters crisscrossing his shoulders and breach-loading the weapon with one shell, while keeping the others close at hand on the granite stone hiding his presence, he once more takes visual inventory in deep concentration as all his long, hard years have taught him to do. Positioning himself and raising the rifle to his shoulder, he lifts the gun sight and takes careful, steady aim.

The crack of a pistol behind him rings out, startling him. Taking cover in protection, he recovers to see Lillian with a pistol in her hand. After gathering his senses, he looks at the gun-drawing lady saying, "What the hell!"

Pointing at a rattlesnake ripped apart from the bullet of her pistol she says, "It was coming at you."

Shaking his head in bewilderment and confusion, he looks at the lady saying, "You gave our position away!"

Looking at the dead reptile, he goes on, "You think a little critter like that could actually eat me or something?" Pausing to catch his breath and shaken nerves, he continues, "I told you to keep out of this. Now, you holster that little cap gun and let me get on with my business."

"I was just trying to help," she insists.

"Little lady, I've been bit so many times by them things, I'm immune to their poison. But I'm just gettin' a taste of your venom." Regaining his calm and composure, he says to the embarrassed little cow girl, "Now, stay low!"

Sighting the locomotive again, he wonders about the advantage of surprise that has just been lost. Slowly setting up again, prepared to get a bead on one of the men milling around the train, looking for a sign of where that gun blast may have originated. The sharp, quick blast from two rifles cut the silence from the train in the direction of the Ranger and Lillian. Though the shots fall short, kicking up dust and dirt between the two groups, the Ranger is distracted once more by the little lady as she taps him on the shoulder, throwing him off his concentration once again.

"What now?" he responds, pulling his weapon down and looking at her.

Pointing to their rear near a clearing, she wonders, "Is that the same...Indian?"

Astonished by her interruptions, he looks behind and beyond to see the remarkable resemblance of that Indian just standing there. After a moment the Ranger looks back at

Lillian and says, "I don't know for sure, but there appears to be some characteristics," as several more shots are fired from the caboose of the train.

"But how?" Lillian questions.

Following previous thought, the Ranger says, "Like I said, they're supposed to have some interesting powers." Thinking a moment more, after hearing several more shots from the train, he goes on. "Maybe he flew here or something?" Shrugging his already overburdened shoulders and looking at the snake, he says, "Who knows...maybe that snake was a cousin or something? Look, you want your train back or not?"

"I'm not so concerned with the train as I am with its contents," she reminds him.

"Then don't distract me," he says, after more rifle shots ring through the morning air. "Speaking as a man of some experience," he pauses a moment to allow his words to sink in on her, "if I were you, I'd take some cover."

Lillian sheepishly sinks low and moves to a rock next to Abner, somewhat concerned by the Yaqui on one side of her, the train on the other, and the Ranger slipping up and over the boulder to take aim in the middle of it all.

Focusing on one man working the funnel on top of the train, the Ranger gets a bead on the bandit and pulls off one shot that kicks him back and off the boulder. The shot reverberates and echoes all the way to and beyond the train, hitting its mark, sending one desperado spread-eagle over the side of the train, dead, before he's lost in sight falling behind the train.

Sighting the flash of the discharged weapon, Mario and the major return rapid fire from their disadvantaged positions.

Reloading, Abner takes steady aim again and lets go another well-placed round that thunders and shakes the earth around him, kicking him back again, while forcing Lillian to cover her ears.

Fierro and Mario sight and shoot, and sight and shoot, until a bullet off that buffalo gun rips right through the metal backplate of the caboose and carries through to the back door of the last car, rattling it and breaking the window.

The major looks at Mario who's examining the huge gaping hole in the metal sheet that was their protection and cover. He traced its path to the door. "What the...?" says Fierro, almost unbelieving.

Mario puts his finger through the hole and jerks back from the still-hot metal plate. "What kind of madness is this?"

Eyeing the plate, the back door, then thinking about it, the major says suspiciously, "I don't know...." Shaking his head and allowing his military intelligence to override what prior advantage he had held, with two rifles, he finally says to Mario, "...But I don't want to be on the other side of the next one."

Both hijackers rush through the rattled caboose door and exit the fire fight as another shell rips into the last car, leaving another huge hole. Mario and the major exit the caboose next to the last cattle car and jump to the side of the train and swiftly run towards the engine. One more round from that thundering buffalo gun smashes into the caboose, rattling the car and shattering a window.

Running unexposed by the side of the cattle cars, the major and Mario make a quick dash to the locomotive, passing the dead body of their fallen comrade as they approach the cab. Mario stops to cross himself in respect for his departed friend, but Fierro grabs him and pushes him forward saying, "This is no time for religion."

Boarding the train, the major yells, "Forget the water!"

Another bullet slams into the cab of the locomotive sending everyone sprawling for cover. The major raises his head and screams, "Get this train going...*Andalé!*"

The engineer looks at the major and says, "Major, the water?"

"You value water over your own life?" Fierro poses the question in no uncertain terms. *"Vamanos!"* he orders, waving his hand forward.

The engine starts to pitch and whine as it begins to bellow black smoke. The wheels spin, unable to grab hold of those steel rails beneath it. Another shot booms from behind some rocks, sending the passengers in the cab diving for cover. Mario rises and fires some desperate shots in answer, but the engine kicks in, finally grabbing and gripping those trestles and slowly struggling and gaining speed. It jerks as it collects its full load of cattle cars in tow.

Angered, the Ranger watches the train moving out. He stands up and advances from behind the rocks and sends one more bullet ringing through the air. Pursuing the train in an exposed march, openly aggressive and defiant of any personal harm, he continues to load and shoot, as the engine labors to pick up speed. Dropping his Sharps and reaching into his duster for the Winchester as he moves on the train, he pauses one moment, shoulders the repeater, takes aim, and fires. Some wild shots are returned from the train which is slowly building speed and momentum for the escape.

Another series of shots are fired from the train. As the bullets slam into the ground, dangerously close to the Ranger, he continues his steady walk, cock, aim, and fire assault on the fleeing engine. The gunplay is fast and furious. Bullets rip into the ground, closer and closer to the Ranger. Some finally spit dirt up and on him, temporarily blinding him. One lucky shot clips him near the knee, dropping him from his pursuit. Rising from the dust, he continues to crank off all his remaining shots as the train reaches cruise speed and begins to disappear from sight.

The Ranger buries his head in the dust and grimaces in pain, rolling over and grabbing his wounded leg. Lillian dashes from behind the boulders and rushes to the Ranger's aid but he won't have any of it. He reaches into his pants pocket and pulls out some chaw, rips off a portion and begins chewing the hardened pack.

"Hell of a time for tobacco," Lillian says, trying to tend to the injured lawman.

Seriously in pain and sweating, he removes his bandanna and says to the little lady trying to nurse him, "Missy? Didn't I tell you to lay low?"

Looking into the distance where the train is gaining speed, the sound of the train whistle allows the *banditos* a brief victory, as they hang from the side of the engine shouting, cheering and sending off a few more wild rounds of ammo, Lillian sadly confirms, "The train's as good as gone now."

Furiously grinding on the chaw and clutching his leg, the Ranger holds the pain, though somewhat wide-eyed. He looks at Lillian, then at his leg, out towards the tracks, the water stop and the one dead man next to the tracks—anything to disassociate himself from the obvious pain.

"What can I do?" asks Lillian as the Ranger pulls his leather chaps up to reveal a small wound just below the knee.

"You can pay no never mind," he says, gritting his teeth.

Standing up in a huff, Lillian backs off and says, "You make it sound like it was my fault!"

"Just leave it alone," he responds painfully, pulling his blood-soaked pant leg up for a better view of the bullet wound.

"That's a hell of an attitude to take," she responds.

Stopping a moment, the Ranger looks over at Lillian somewhat confused and surprised, saying, "Attitude?"

Angrily pacing before the downed-and-injured lawman, she goes on and on and on. "Big, tough, Texas Ranger...can't be doctored or tended to by a woman!" Making a shallow, narrow path where she's been pacing, she stops and puts her hands on her waist. Looking down at the wounded Ranger, she continues with the lecture, further adding insult to the already injured lawman.

"Weren't you the one who said, 'Once we take off, there's no turning back!'...and...and I'd better keep up, and all that manly Texas Ranger stuff you guys are supposed to be known for. Is this supposed to be some sort of display of your manhood right now?"

The Ranger counters the best he can under the circumstances. "It's the display of an 'ol fool man who's old enough to take you over his...good knee...."

"Violence! That solves everything," she rants and raves as the Ranger wipes the wound clean with his bandanna.

"When you're dealing with the likes of hijacked trains, shooting comes with the territory—like bein' thrown from a horse—you get back on," he says, pulling the tobacco plug from his mouth and eyeballing the wound.... With a precision that can only come from experience, the lawman lines up the wound and the wad of chaw and adroitly applies it with some skill and pain.

"Get back on the horse!" she exclaims, watching his first aid. "What kind of recommendation is that under circumstances such as this?"

Looking up at her in pain, he says, "Yeah. What else can you do?" He continues to attend to the wound by wrapping and tying the bandanna in place.

"Keep going!" she responds emphatically, almost uncaring.

Rolling his pant leg down and staring at her, he says, "You got any idea what you're talking about?" He attempts to stand up. "There must be a dozen guns on that train, and what are you packin'?" He points at her pistol. "All you got is that...that little, snake-shootin' pop gun."

"I can try to make it to Laredo before they cross the border and try to get some help there," she says out loud.

Steadying himself, Abner limps towards his Appaloosa and struggles aboard his faithful mount. Wheeling the steed about and pointing to his Buffalo gun, the Ranger says, "Well? Can you pick that up for me?"

"What?" she asks.

"Are we going to Laredo or are we going to discuss my tobacco problem?"

Surprised, Lillian moves towards the weapon somewhat unsure of his actions and motive. She doesn't say anything as she retrieves the heavy rifle and wipes it clean. Returning it to the lawman, she thinks this is the extent of her doctoring. She hands him the weapon a little sorry for her behavior then asks a curious question. "What are you going to do about that dead body over there?" She points towards the water tower.

"He wasn't much of a concern to them. Why let it concern you?"

"You can't just leave him out there to rot," she says.

"Missy, seems to me you got more concern for the dead than you do for the living," he tells her, favoring his leg a bit. "He ain't going to tell us anything that train hasn't already explained."

"Is that some sort of code of the west?" she asks.

"He appears to be part of the territory now," the Ranger responds, fitting his hat.

"Well, if you ask me, this territory can be pretty unmerciful," she surmises as she makes her way to her horse. She saddles up with some thoughts about the whole thing, but her concentration is disrupted when she sees the Yaqui Indian approaching.

"I believe I can help you," comes the unexpected offer from the slight, Spanish-accented Yaqui. He is wearing typical peasant clothing; white cotton top and pants, favoring buckskin moccasins over sandals.

Taking a hard look and an accounting of the Yaqui, the Ranger turns to Lillian, who doesn't really quite know what to make of the situation. Abner painfully gets off his horse and moves to a boulder and some shade from the early morning sun. He sits down on a rock, takes off his hat and nurses his leg, all the while sizing up the man in front of him.

Lillian dismounts and joins the Ranger. "I'm sorry I was so cold and indifferent to your wound." She stumbles for more words and sentiments as she goes on. "I've felt helpless since this whole thing began, and...."

Still eyeing the Yaqui as Lillian goes on, the lawman puts his hand on Lillian's shoulder and says, "You know, I believe this man can help us."

"What?" says Lillian, surprised.

"Let's hear what the man has to offer. He's a native of these parts—knows the place better than me. I just covered the frontier up north, did some work down here on a thing or two until my bounty work."

Looking the Yaqui over, he says, "It's his territory too. Maybe he has a thing or two to say?" He leans back against the hard granite boulder, favoring and running his hand over his wounded leg. "Let the man speak his mind. Even Texas Rangers take advice."

Lillian looks at the Indian with a degree of curiosity and suspicion before saying, "What do you have in mind?"

"My name is Juan and I am a Yaqui. That train is headed for the Mexican border," he says confidently. "I speak Spanish, and, I can cross the border to find out where they're taking the train."

"I don't care about the train," comes Lillian's reply to the unexpected offer.

"Hold on, now," says the Ranger in response. "Let's not be too hasty. He's offered some help I can't provide. I mean, he can cross that border over there and though I don't rightly know how he got here, I know he's here now and, he's right about crossing that border. My jurisdiction is the state of Texas. I ain't got no authority beyond that state line."

Still wondering, Lillian asks the Yaqui, "Do you have any idea why they'd steal the train?"

Juan joins the duo under the shade of the boulder and continues his thoughts. "The revolution in Mexico has been going on for six years now and the armies are running low on food, supplies and arms. I think I can pull off a deal."

"A deal?" asks the Ranger, a little surprised. "You mean like...arms for cattle?"

"Si," comes the immediate answer. I'll set up a deal for us to meet in Laredo," the Yaqui confidently assures the two weary travelers.

"How will you find us?" questions Lillian.

"I will find you," comes the confident response from Juan.

Lillian looks at the Ranger. The Ranger looks at Lillian. They both look at Juan.

Laredo is a large city compared to its neighbor to the west, Nuevo Laredo, on the opposite side of the Mexican border. Though that border town doesn't stretch very far from the American side, it seems to span a whole lifetime and century as the Texas town boasts electricity and plumbing, street cars, trucks and automobiles to ferry a very active populous through the cement-lined streets, while horses still provide a lot of the basic transportation for all the various horsemen, wagons, carriages and buckboards on the Mexican side of the border.

Blending Victorian and false-fronted buildings that are weather-worn under constant heat that strips and peels the old paint off the surfaces of these old wooden structures, the town still holds the charm of an active southwestern community despite any temperature change, or border dispute. Trains are still a vital part of the transportation and commerce of the area, and though the rails do pass into Mexico from this juncture on a map, the territory really reflects the spirit of the great state of Texas.

Lillian and the Ranger enter this city as it awakens to a new business day. A mild flow in traffic can be seen as stores are just putting their wares out for the coming day. Ambling along, the Ranger checks his right leg for the wound he got at the water stop, while Lillian views this border town just opening its doors for business. The clickety-clack of the horses' hooves on the paved roadway give a whole new impression on the modernity of this town and era.

Lillian looks at the Ranger favoring his leg, saying, "You should see a doctor about that leg."

Drawing his attention from the wound, the lawman looks over at Lillian with a slight smile saying, "It ain't no hill for a stepper. I've had worse."

Shaking her head in sympathy, she says, "No doubt." But after a momentary pause, she looks at him and sincerely asks, "Whatever made you decide to become a Texas Ranger, if you don't mind my asking?"

"It was just meant to be, I suppose," he halfway answers.

"What's that mean?" she responds, unsure that any real answer was provided.

Smiling and glancing over at her after checking his knee, he says, "You don't want to hear my old war stories now, do you? It'll only make me feel older than I already feel."

"Seriously," she goes on. "What made you become a Ranger?"

Guiding his horse to the side of the street, he says, "Why don't we pull over and get some grub?"

Walking to the boardwalk, he painfully dismounts and limps over to tie his Appaloosa to a hitching post. Lillian follows his lead, more out of exhaustion than anything else. They've pulled a long night and maybe a meal isn't such a bad idea. She gets off her horse and moves to the boardwalk to hitch her mare to the wooden pole and follows the Ranger up some stairs to a tiny restaurant that overlooks the just-awakening town.

The old eatery is littered with old newspapers as wallpaper, displaying all the highlights of the day; the sinking of the Titanic, the Olympics, Arizona statehood, etc. The two weary travelers wander in and find a table near a window, and sit down. Out of instinct, the Ranger sits with his back to the wall, protecting his back while he pulls the curtain of the window aside for a clear view of the street. He looks around the tiny establishment to find they're the only customers at this early hour of the day.

Over the years the Ranger has learned to absorb his surroundings while always covering his rear, as many a man not as alert had come to a final chapter in their lives from such a miscalculation, men such as Wild Bill Hitchcock who neglected that one standard code they'd all stood by that unlucky day.

A stout waiter exits the kitchen, sees the two patrons, grabs a couple of menus off a counter top and walks over to Lillian and the Ranger. He bids them a "Good morning," depositing the menus and standing before them smiling as he taps his foot impatiently. Lillian studies the menu while the Ranger is distracted by the waiter's uneasy pace. Looking up from his menu and trying to gauge the over-energetic little fellow, the Ranger gives him a fast hard stare which catches the tubby order taker by surprise. "I'll be back to take your order in a moment," he says, spinning and walking back to the kitchen only to turn once and look back in curiosity.

Physically drained and exasperated, Lillian places her menu down and looks over at the Ranger. She finally asks, "Why did you become a Ranger?"

Unmoved by the question, as he continues to survey the restaurant's list of digestibles, he finally replies, "Missy, I don't know if I should get into it. I mean, it's a long, dull story." Changing the subject, he asks, half nodding, while putting the menu down, "What about you? What brings you down here with all that cattle?"

Leaning back and fielding the thought, she looks him over and eventually explains herself. "My father's a pretty important man in Oklahoma, but he owns a spread down near Edna. Before he went on this business trip back east, I begged him for a chance to help in his absence. I sort of grew up on that ranch and I wanted to prove I could be of help to him. He never had a son, but I wanted to show him I knew my stuff."

"Yeah," responds the Ranger, unimpressed. "Just like them boys back in Bitter Creek I crossed paths with. Cattle rustling, train robberies, bank holdups, stagecoach jobs.... Yeah, some folks just know their callin' I suppose."

"What was your calling?" asks the concerned little lady.

Amused, the Ranger responds with, "Waiter!" calling to the back of the restaurant.

The waiter exits the swinging moth-winged doors towards the hungry duo, eager to take an order in this otherwise quiet little restaurant. Smiling, he asks, "So? What'll it be this morning?"

The Ranger looks at Lillian who looks up at the waiter and asks, "Can I have some bacon and eggs, and some coffee?"

"Double up that order on me," says the hungry lawman.

The waiter takes the menus in hand and says, "Comin' right up, folks." He spins and walks towards the kitchen with the menus under his arm.

Changing the subject, Lillian leans forward and asks, "How do you think Juan will find us?"

"Didn't bother him none," mumbles the Ranger, looking out the window. "Why let it bother you?"

"It's the cattle that concerns me, you know," says the little lady, tapping her fingers on the table nervously.

"Well," says the Ranger, turning from the window, "it seems to be pretty much out of our hands at the moment."

The waiter returns with a couple of cups of coffee. The Ranger takes the brew in hand and holds it to his nose and takes a serious whiff. He puts the mug to his lips and takes a sip. "Whew," he says, shaking his head in satisfaction. "That sure tastes good after a night on the open range."

Lillian takes a sip of her coffee and cringes as the effect shakes her down to the spine. She reaches for the sugar bowl and puts several generous spoonfuls of the sweetener in the mug and tries a sip again. Shaking her head once more in disgust, she reaches into her mouth with her fingers and probes for something until she finally pulls it out and stares at the alarming discovery. She shakes her head and sarcastically says, "Nice grind."

After taking a hearty swig of his hot, thick liquid, Abner responds with a smile, "Cowboy coffee! That's what they call it around these parts. Strong enough to defend itself," he proudly proclaims.

Wiping the discovery from her fingers on the side of her chaps, Lillian says, "I wasn't talking about the brew so much as the particles that came with it in my cup!"

Placing his mug of java down on the table, he leans forward and whispers to her with a grin, "Do you know how they brew this stuff?"

"I don't know if I want to know," she responds seriously.

Grabbing the mug and leaning back for another sip, he continues. "They fill up a coffee pot with some water and grind, and let 'er boil. Then, when they want to know if it's ready, they take a horseshoe and drop it in. If it floats, it's ready," he says with a certain pride.

"Enough with the jokes. Are you going to tell me about your involvement with the Rangers or do I have to go to your headquarters for answers?" she insists.

Ignoring the interruption, he goes on as if the question wasn't even asked. "Maybe you're missing some of the subtle, more interesting aspects of this brew." Holding the mug up and savoring it like a rare bottle of wine, he adds," Did you notice it had body?"

"Yeah," Lillian responds. "I hear it's strong enough to defend itself."

Changing his mood, the Ranger studies Lillian a moment before beginning to recount the unavoidable. "I was born in 1873 and lived with my folks down there near Houston. I reckon I was seven when our house got blowed down by a twister. I was the only one who survived as my folks were killed almost immediately. I was taken to another family to live with, but that didn't work out very well as the old man was a drunk and he kept beatin' on me for just about anything." Pausing to take a sip of his coffee and focus in on the darkened fluid rolling around in that cup like it was a crystal ball, he re-thinks his past.

"I'm sorry," says the saddened little lady, for prying into the man's private life.

"Well," continues the lawman, "after a year or two, I'd had enough, so I just ran away." He sips on the brew while reliving his past. "I eventually got caught and sent to an orphanage until I was thirteen. Found a job, lost it, drifted around and around until I found myself riding shotgun for Wells Fargo. I was on that job until we got held up so often, I almost knew them owl hoots by first names and the pistols they were a totin'. And dang if you don't grow weary of those guns bein' pointed at you all the time and them gettin' the draw on. So's I just up and quit and decided with all them outlaws out there, I'd just settle the score on my own." He laughs, then goes on, shaking his head, "Sure seemed like a lot of them were out there back then." Pausing to reflect a moment, he adds, "Anyhow, I reckon when the dust settled, I'd just been doin' it a long time."

"It must have been a very hard existence," Lillian sympathizes.

"I ain't got much I can compare it to, but I've seen my fair share of homes and jobs, and I reckon I just got accustomed to bein' on the open range so long it just became my home and a way of life." He takes another sip of that horse-kick coffee and continues.

"But one day this here feller approached me saying he was a 'Territorial Ranger' — that's what they used to call them back then — because they had so much territory to cover they were just called that, 'Territorial Rangers'. I learned the ropes from this old Ranger and he taught me most of what I know," he says, taking another sip of his coffee.

"You mean all those guns and rifles?" Lillian wonders from observation and recent history.

"Well, not exactly," comes the reply. "Some things I sorta learned on my own." Pausing to look her over, he goes on. "One thing you learn out there on the range is...don't be short of weapons or ammo."

After a moment of thought Lillian says, "So, it wasn't by design...your becoming a Texas Ranger."

"Naw, it just sort of happened," he replies, swishing the remaining coffee around in the mug and looking at the bottom of the almost empty cup while still reflecting on the past.

The waiter bursts through the swinging moth-winged doors of the kitchen with two plates in hand, making his way to the table. The Ranger puts his mug aside as the waiter places the plates down in front of these road-weary travelers.

Crossing the border unhampered, Fierro and his men celebrate. They've bluffed their way across into Mexico after sustaining only one casualty. The train slows down as it approaches another water tower, where the crew moves with efficiency as one man climbs aboard the engine and pulls the funnel down from the water tower to quench the great thirst the engine requires.

"Hurry," yells the major from the cab over the moans and groans of the cattle from the back of the train. "We've got to get the steer to the Colonel."

Puzzled, Mario asks, "What's the rush? We've made it to Mexico. They cannot touch us now."

Fierro sizes up his crew then shouts, "*Vamanos!*"

The locomotive staggers, twitches and whines as the freight cars line up for the tow. The wheels spin a couple of times before grabbing those steel rails, finally grinding towards speed.

Fierro looks at the engineer and asks, "How long to the Rubio Ranch?"

"Two hours at most," comes the answer from the man at the controls.

"Two hours it is!" comes the response from the major.

As the cattle train pulls away from the water stop, Juan is seen standing in the distance. He watches the train build up speed and move down the trestles towards that far horizon, as the engine builds up speed and bellows smoke in its trail. Juan's vision wanders far beyond the train to the skies above Mexican territory.

. Having completed his breakfast, the Ranger sits back in his chair and pulls out a pouch of tobacco and begins to roll a cigarette. Amused, Lillian looks at him and says, "Chaw? And now a cigarette?"

Abner doesn't even flinch as his eyes under the brim of his hat rise to meet hers from across the table. He finally pulls the rolled paper and leaf up to his mouth to lick the paper and twist it into a tiny cigarette. Still gazing at her, he pulls a wooden match out and lights it off his thumbnail. He blows out the match and puts it on his plate. "Little lady," he says with a smirk, "does anything else I do disturb you?"

"I was just trying to be sociable," she innocently counters.

Looking the establishment over, then back at her, he exhales before speaking. "Yeah. I guess you're right," he says, taking another drag off the hot boxed cigarette. "We are in a social sorta place, aren't we?" Exhaling again and taking another puff, he goes on. "Well, you're going to have to forgive my manners as I'm sort of this old coot and sorta set in my old ways."

"Like putting tobacco on an open wound?" she reminds him.

"What's it to you?" he says, a little disgusted. He puts the cigarette out on the plate where he has left the match. Looking her over, he finally softens and throws his attention elsewhere. "I reckon it's about time to look that wound over anyhow. I'm sure that chaw did the trick."

Reaching under the table and fidgeting a moment, he pulls the wad of blackened chewed tobacco up and looks around for a suitable place to dispose of it. Reaching for his napkin, he folds the remains of the chewed-up leaf into it then places the mess onto the plate next to the cigarette butt and match, shocking Lillian.

Unmoved by her reaction, he tends to his wound a moment longer, grimacing and grinding those tobacco-stained teeth of his, till he lifts his head and looks around. He grabs her napkin and continues his self-administered doctoring, shocking her even more. For a man in obvious discomfort, he holds his pain well.

"Aren't you going to see a doctor?" she asks.

Looking up at her after finishing with the first aid, he pushes the plate aside and nonchalantly says, "Never have time to. Anyhow, the bullet grazed me a good one, but that just seems to be another part of this here territory we're in."

"Is this more of that 'code of the west' kind of stuff or something?" she questions.

"No," he insists, "I'm just taking care of business the only way I know how to."

Sympathetically Lillian inquires, "But it must hurt?"

Staring at her while responding to her nagging, he says, "Missy, I think it hurts you more than it hurts me! Look, we're not here to talk about my medical history. We best to get something going before Juan gets to town."

Confused, Lillian asks, "What do you mean?"

"Well, figure it out for yourself. Juan has a deal going with those border bandits. You want your cattle back, don't you?"

"Of course I do!" comes her reply.

"Then," he leans forward for emphasis, "we best make preparation."

"How do we do that?" wonders Lillian aloud.

"Well," he surmises, "maybe we should get a couple of guns together."

"Why guns?"

"You don't reckon they'll just want to trade straight up on them pretty red locks of yours, do you?" he says. Getting up and limping towards the door of the restaurant, he looks back at Lillian still sitting at the table all confused. "Come on," he says. "We didn't come this far to stop now."

Lillian jumps from her chair and walks to the Ranger who's digging around in his pocket for some money. He squeezes an eagle and flips it on the table as they exit the tiny eatery.

Looking over the street while adjusting his hat and duster, he gazes at the blending of old and new centuries passing before him, as a bicyclist peddles by. He notices the wagons, buckboards, carriages, horsemen and automobiles pass and shakes his head. He pulls his hat down as a buzzing sound distracts him from above. He looks up and notices the telephone lines stretching all the way down the block and beyond, until he catches the glimpse of an aeroplane flying towards the Mexican border. Somewhat feeling lost he says to himself, "So this is the twentieth century?"

Six Mexican revolutionaries on horseback, led by Major Rudolf Fierro, wind their way through the desert heat towards the Rubio Ranch. Now armed with a full complement of rifles, pistols, and ammo belts crossing their shoulders, their horses kick up dust and dirt as they pull into the courtyard of this majestic hacienda and dismount.

There to greet the men is a small man with greasy black hair and a small outgrowth of beard. Strangely, he wears a pair of green battle fatigues, a sombrero, and an ammo belt with a sidearm. This is Private Juan Garza. He takes the leather leads of the horses as this small band of soldiers are met with much enthusiasm by Captain Isador Lopez, a tall, smart-looking officer with slick black hair and a sense of duty to match. Dressed and armed like Garza, he shakes hands with Major Fierro. Discounting a salute, in this loosely-knit outfit of revolutionary soldiers, there really is no military formality between the Captain and Major.

The palatial ranch is an unlikely place to be found in such a desolate region of this economically-distressed country. Hampered by revolution, it still resounds of old

Spanish architecture with origins that seem an unusual setting for such a meeting. But the Rubio Ranch is considered booty—one of the treasures of a war waged for over six years. It is strategically located and was ruthlessly confiscated from the wealthy land owner.

Encased by eight-foot adobe walls and cast iron fencing leading to an entrance gate, red tiles highlight the huge white house as if it were a mirage in the open desert. But it wasn't, as it had electricity, plumbing, telephone lines, and just about every other modern convenience to be found on the American side of the border. The arched doorway over the entrance of the main house was as large as some of the houses found in the general area, but it was simply an entrance to the larger prize. This house has passed from Diaz to Madero to Villa and his men. Now it serves another.

Fierro leaves his men by the gravel courtyard to attend to his business as he's escorted into the main house by Captain Lopez. Passing through a large entrance way to a lobby area, the Captain leads the major to a living room where he's met by Colonel Julio Cardenas, a clean-shaven, lanky man dressed in the same green fatigues as his men, while also wearing a holster and pistol. Though the Colonel is already entertaining his beautiful young wife, his graying mother and two infant children, he greets the major with a warm hug and firm shoulder embrace. The major wastes no time in reporting. "Colonel, our mission was a success."

"*Bueno, amigo!*" Cardenas smiles. "Well done! Well done, indeed!" he says with a broad smile. "It took some convincing, but I assured General Villa you were the right man for the job."

Embarrassed, the major admits, "I shouldn't have gotten drunk and messed up that train schedule for his ceremony. But I'm grateful you helped me, and I hope I have proven myself to be in his good graces once again."

"*Si,*" comes the reply from the Colonel. "You are to report to the General with my blessings and highest recommendation. And pass my thanks to him for these fine uniforms he has provided me and my men with."

The major wonders aloud, "These uniforms? They are most unusual wear, are they not?"

"Something to do with some sort of changeover in Europe that has effected the new century or something. Wearing a red or blue formal uniform makes for high ceremony in some places where rank has privilege. But now it appears such bright colors make for an easy target on the battlefields. The style is spreading through Europe, the Baltic states and throughout the Russias. They are being worn in France during this current conflict with Germany," says the Colonel, updating the inquisitive Major. Going on, Cardenas asks, "By the way, did you encounter any trouble?"

"I lost one man, but we cleared the border without incident," comes the major's reply.

"Despite your loss, you did a good job," commends the Colonel. "You should report to General Villa and tell him of your successful mission. I'm sure he'll be pleased to see you again."

"*Muchas gracias, Colonel*," responds the major as he shakes Cardenas' hand and exits the room. He passes through the lobby past Lopez to the courtyard where he assembles his men and horses. He orders them to mount, and like the wind, the small band of men departs the hacienda, leaving only Private Garza to watch them fade into the desert.

From a distant corner of the area, Juan sees the group of men exit the ranch. He waits until the dust in their tracks has settled, then he looks to the hacienda and begins the long, hot walk towards it.

Bursting through the double doors of the library and walking in angrily, Colonel Cardenas eyes the Yaqui sitting in a chair with his hands tied behind his back. Two of the Colonel's green-fatigued soldiers, armed to the teeth with

pistols and cartridge belts clipped to their shoulders, stand
guard over Juan.

"You..," almost half-surprised by the boldness of the
Yaqui, Cardenas goes on, "...you want to see me?" He looks
the man over, puzzled. He jerks his head up and steadies a
strong, hard look at his captive. "What would a *péon* want
with me?"

Looking up, Juan says, "A trade."

Stunned by the proposal, Cardenas laughs then looks
the Yaqui over suspiciously. "What have you to trade?"

"Guns," replies Juan.

Cardenas motions his men to untie Juan as he moves
to a desk in the room, seeking a cigar. Biting and spitting off
the tip of one, he eyes the Yaqui Indian very carefully.
Leaning on the edge of the desk, he asks suspiciously, "How
would a peasant like you have guns? Don't you know we're
here fighting for you?"

Massaging his wrists after being released from the
tightly wrapped rope, Juan gazes at the Colonel for a moment then asks, "An army without guns?

Lighting his stogie with a wooden match from the
desk, Cardenas eyes Juan thoughtfully through the rising
white smoke of his Havana-rolled tobacco. "What have you
to say?" Cardenas asks, offering Juan a cigar then walking to
the chair behind the desk to sit down.

Walking down the main street of Laredo, Lillian is
distracted by something that draws her attention from the
Ranger, whose funny little labored walk is now further
hampered by a limp due to the bullet wound in his leg. He
wanders down the boardwalk viewing the street, several
paces beyond the little lady, until the lawman turns, stops
and studies her as she gazes into the window of a store.

Standing before a dress displayed in the window, the
reflection off the glass almost places her within the garment
itself, but it's an illusion and she soon recognizes it, though

not before the Ranger doubles back and notices something. "You like that dress?" he questions her.

"What?" she asks.

Enunciating his words so they'll be more clearly understood, he asks, "Do you want that dress?"

Suspiciously she answers, "What do you have in mind?"

"Look," he says, "you go on in there and try it on. I'll be right back."

Somewhat bewildered and confused by his directive, she's unable to fully understand this unusual request, as he's already turned and limped down the block before she can question him further.

Watching the Ranger pass from sight, Lillian slowly walks to the entrance of the clothing store and opens the door. She takes one last look down the street, puzzled. She enters the establishment and slowly makes her way towards the dress display, examining and admiring it all at the same time.

Though a little scruffy from a very long night and day on the chase, she stands before a mirror and views herself in the dress. Loaded with frills, lace and shiny buttons, she sparkles in it. This is the first time in almost twenty-four hours she's shown any element of femininity about her. For the moment, she's no longer concerned about anything but the beautiful dress she's wearing.

A sales lady assists in putting her hair up, which only highlights her overall beauty. Lost in the moment, she's no longer on the chase.

The Ranger enters the store to find a completely different image of his riding partner. She sees Abner in the mirror, smiles, then turns around to pose for him. She's ravishing.

"Turn around," he says, almost unbelieving of the transformation from cowgirl to this beautiful young lady. She revels in the moment as she swings around and continues to model the outfit. For a brief moment she's a woman.

A very beautiful woman. The Ranger quietly looks her over, and after some serious thought, scratches his chin and says, "You know, this just might work."

Surprised, Lillian says, "What?"

"I'll explain later," he says to the little gal. Turning to the shop lady, he asks, "How much?"

"Forty dollars," she answers.

The Ranger pulls a roll of bills from his pocket that shocks Lillian and the sales lady. Peeling off forty dollars, he hands it over to the merchant and looks at Lillian, saying, "You need some shoes, too." Turning to the sales lady, he asks "How much are shoes?"

"They vary," says the surprised merchant, having never made such a quick sale before.

Peeling off another twenty dollars, which alarms Lillian, he says, "Will this take care of it?" The sales lady nods as Lillian looks on in confusion.

"Did you rob a bank or something?" she asks.

"Never mind where I got the money. You've got to get a bath and get all dolled up."

"Dolled up!" exclaims Lillian.

"Are we going to get into questions and answers again? Just do as you're told," he insists.

Concerned by all this sudden activity, she shakes her head and says, "I can't pay you back until the cattle are returned."

"Never mind about the money," the Ranger says as he gathers his thoughts and goes on talking to himself while studying Lillian in a curious sort of manner. "This IS going to work! Missy," he says, "I want you to get a bath and your hair all made up pretty, then meet me over at the hotel across the street...with that dress on."

"If I have to take a bath...maybe you ought to consider the same," she observes.

"Don't worry. I'll take care of my part," he says, pulling some more money from the roll of bills he's pocketing. "You just take this money and do like I say, and meet me in room 15 over yonder. Is that clear?" He hands her the greenbacks. Lillian answers with a sheepish nod. "Don't forget," says the Ranger as he turns and tips his hat to the matronly sales lady before walking out the shop door. Turning back, he eyeballs Lillian and reminds her, "Room 15. Across the Street." Stepping onto the boardwalk, he exits to the street and limps down the block.

The sales lady is amused but she's cut off quickly by Lillian. "About those shoes?"

Stepping out of the clothing store to the boardwalk with two packages in her arms, she's surprised to find Juan walking towards her in a white three-piece suit.

"Juan!" she exclaims, blinking her eyes in disbelief.

"We must find the Ranger," he says.

"No problem," she assures him. "He's across the street in the hotel. But where did you get that suit?" she asks.

Ignoring the question, Juan says, "Time is of the essence. We must see him now."

"Follow me," she answers, slightly dazed by the appearance of the Yaqui Indian. She never suspected that he could also transform his looks.

Taking one of Lillian's packages, Juan crosses the street through some moderate traffic followed by Lillian. They enter the hotel and make their way through the lobby and down a darkened hallway of this ancient old building until they come to room 15. Lillian knocks, still amused at her companion beside her.

The door opens to a clean-shaven Ranger sporting a plaid, three-piece suit and a brown derby to match. "Welcome," he says, opening the door wide for them and extending his arm like a doorman at some fancy restaurant or hotel. "Come on in."

Stunned, Lillian enters the room gazing at the Ranger and Juan, not completely comprehending all that's going on. She sees a wide array of weapons displayed on the bed and continues to sound her confusion over everything. "I don't understand all this. A dress. You guys. All these guns?"

"All part of the plan, if I'm not mistaken," says the dapper lawman, all decked out in the finest of threads. He looks at Juan for some validation and reinforcement.

"We must speak," says Juan.

"You've got my ear," comes the reply from the Ranger, admiring his well-dressed guest. "Sit down and tell me what you got...and," he pauses to size up the Yaqui, "those are some awfully nice clothes you got on, if you don't mind my sayin' so, though..., do you mind saying where you got them?" He asks sincerely.

Taking a seat in a chair next to the bed, both men engage in conversation while Lillian stands by the door holding her package, overwhelmed by the two. She puts her package down on a dresser and walks over to the bed to look at all the various weapons spread out.

"I met with Colonel Cardenas," Juan begins. "He will accept to meet with us later today."

"Here?" the lawman asks.

"*Si*, here," Juan confirms as Lillian continues to gaze at the suited men and the weapons next to them.

"What's this all about?" she interrupts them.

Ignoring the little lady, Juan goes on to say, "The Colonel is Pancho Villas' bodyguard," stunning the Ranger and Lillian. "He has been one for many years now," the Yaqui goes on, "He's the one who also purchases arms for the revolution."

"*Pancho Villa?*" a shocked Lillian exclaims.

Nodding, the Ranger gets up and starts pacing the room with a limp, thinking. "Now that's saying something. That explains all those guns on the train. I guess we're on the right track now." Thinking a moment longer while looking his partners over, he asks, "What do you expect?"

Juan lays out the plan. "They should be in town by five o'clock this afternoon. I told him I would meet them at a cantina down the street I know of. I'll bring them back here, shortly thereafter."

Looking at Lillian, the Ranger says, "We'll be prepared."

"Prepared?" Lillian responds. "What are you two talking about? What am I supposed to do?"

"You just keep quiet and look pretty," comes the response from the lawman. "You can do that, can't you" he says.

Lillian is further stunned as she has no idea what she's gotten herself into. "Where'd you get the money to buy all these guns? And...," turning to Juan, "where'd you get that suit?"

The Ranger looks at Juan to assure him she's their comrade. "You'll get used to it." Turning to the little lady he says, "Would you please stop asking questions and just play the part of a sweet, innocent bystander? Your appearance could take the edge off these desperados."

"Revolutionaries," Juan interjects.

Studying Juan a moment, the Ranger corrects himself. "Revolutionaries." Turning back to Lillian, he apprises her of her role in the charade. "They'll think you're a gun merchant's lady...if we're lucky."

Insulted, Lillian says, "Why, of all the...."

Before she can finish her sentence, Juan and the Ranger go over the weapons available to them. After studying them, Juan says, "I think everything is in order here. I'll go to the cantina and await their arrival." Juan nods to the Ranger and smiles to the confused and insulted Lillian as he opens the door and exits into the hallway.

"Don't just stand there gawking," says the lawman. "Close the door, would you," he requests. Lillian is completely dumbfounded by everything she's seen and heard.

Closing the door, she looks at the Ranger and asks, "How do you expect to get the cattle back by negotiating arms from this side of the border?"

"We just show them some samples of a supply we're supposed to have. We don't really have the authentic articles, we just put on a show for them. Just like I'm asking you to do."

Still confused, she continues her line of questioning. "But how do you get the cattle back on this side of the border?"

"We tell them the weapons are in a warehouse and that an exchange can be made there. Once they cross the border, they'll be ours."

"I still don't get it," Lillian replies. "What if...?"

The Ranger cuts her off. "Your part is to look pretty and not open your mouth, understand?" Limping from one side of the room to the other, then over to the window of the room, he puts his hands on the sill and says to himself, "Pancho Villa. The General, himself!"

He looks at Lillian then stares out the window to check the street. Cars, horses and carriages pass unknowing or caring of what plans were just discussed and initiated in this tiny room on the edge of the Mexican border. Meanwhile, businessmen in suits, cowboys, Indians, and Mexicans, all continue their daily activities in this town on the very edge of the Mexican revolution.

"Colonel Cardenas," the Ranger repeats as he gazes upon this active, peaceful town. "Villas' very own body-guard. This could become very, very interesting."

The smoke-filled cantina dances to the sounds of marimba music as cowboys down their bottles of red-eye, and Mexicans partner up to téquila. The room is totally unaware of Juan standing at the bar, nursing a half-empty bottle of mescal and a shot glass. He checks his pocket watch for the time, places it back into his vest pocket and looks over the room for anyone who might be suspicious.

Through the swinging butterfly doors of this crowded old bar, step three bold men: Cardenas, Lopez and Garza. Looking the room over carefully, it is Garza who first spots Juan and points him out to his companions. Cardenas sizes up the Yaqui before walking towards him through the crowd to embrace the Indian as if he were some dear, old friend or relative. *"Juanito! Compadré. Como esta?"*

"Prepared to do business,"replies Juan.

"Aye," says Cardenas, still looking Juan and the room over carefully. Finally he says, "Not even time for a drink with this impatient one," he says to Lopez and Garza. "You must be either in a big hurry to celebrate or go on to the next deal, eh?" Cardenas laughs. "But I will stop for a small drink. I conduct business better that way." Looking to his men, he asks, *"Amigos? Cervezas?"*

The Ranger is still looking out the window at the street traffic, hoping to catch a view of Juan and the men he's dealing with. He pulls a pocket watch from his vest and studies it. Replacing it, he turns to the little lady in the room and says, "They should be here by now."

"I'm scared," Lillian responds.

"You want your cattle back, don't you?" counters the lawman. "Stay calm and just try to look pretty. I'll do the rest," he says, trying to comfort her.

"What if something goes wrong?" she asks.

"What could possibly go wrong?" he replies, assuring her.

Three Dodge touring cars carrying five khaki-clad soldiers per automobile tool down the street. The soldiers hold carbines in their hands as the drivers follow the instructions of the ranking officer in the lead car: General John J. "Blackjack" Pershing. This is the Punitive Expeditionary Forces, Eighth Brigade, and they're returning from a scout across the border back to their base camp just inside the city limits. They're followed by a squadron of foot soldiers and high-prancing cavalry that have been in the surrounding area for several months since their departure from the Presidio in San Francisco. Though Fort Bliss, near El Paso, is their usual base of operation, the search for Pancho Villa has brought them south. The traffic in the streets part and stop as pedestrians take note of the stars and bars on parade down the streets of this southwestern town.

Rumors travel fast in a small town, and Laredo is no different, as word eventually hits the cantina where Juan and the *Villiastas* are meeting. Talk passes from table to table until it hits the bar and rebounds off the three revolutionaries. Shocked, Cardenas backs off the deal with Juan, giving the Yaqui the look of death as he suspects a set up. Staring at the Indian, the Colonel says, "Was this your plan, *Péon?*

"I had no idea!" Juan responds, startled and shocked.

"Catch us in the cantina. Keep the reward for yourself or something?" Cardenas growls in disgust.

"This has nothing to do with the Army," Juan insists.

"It does now!" roars Cardenas.

Grabbing his partners, the Colonel rushes them out the back door of the tiny establishment as Juan follows close behind in protest.

Stepping into the alleyway, Cardenas orders, "Garza! Go to the front of the cantina and bring the horses around back."

"*Si, Colonel*," replies the little private as he dashes through the backdoor of the cantina .

Still protesting, Juan pleads, "Colonel, I had no idea. The guns await your approval just down the street at the hotel."

"*Si*. No doubt with the barrel of a .45 aimed at my back," says the Colonel. "I don't deal arms when the whole United States Army is at the front door."

"Trying another approach, Juan says, ""Won't you at least come to the hotel from the back?"

Rounding the corner with three horses in tow, Garza hands the halters to his officers and awaits Cardenas' next order. Sternly looking Juan over as he mounts his steed and steadying it, he barks, "You want to talk business? Bring your arms down to the Rubio Ranch across the border. There, I know the U. S. Army won't be looking for me." As

Lopez and Garza get aboard their mounts, Cardenas spurs his steed and yells, "*Adios, Péon!*"

Kicking up gravel and dirt, the three horsemen round the corner of the back alley and head off towards the border. Distraught, Juan returns to the cantina through the back door.

Looking out the window of the hotel room, the Ranger sights the Eighth Brigade moving down the street in force. "Damn! Damn! Damn!" the lawman shouts, slamming his fists on the window sill. He turns from the window, shaking his head and thumbing to it for Lillian to see. Lillian is confused as she steps past the Ranger to see what's going on. Three touring cars pass in formation, throwing her into slight shock. Regaining her composure, she looks at the Ranger and says, "What can go wrong?" half mocking his self-assuredness on the deal they'd set up.

Clearly upset, the Ranger limps around the room like a caged animal about to strike. He instinctively knows they've lost their prey. A knock at the door alters his mood. He motions Lillian to answer it. Walking slowly towards the door, she hesitates before opening it with caution and fear.

Standing before them is Juan, who's in despair over the botched deal. Juan steps into the room and says, "The bird has taken wing. The Army has scared them off."

"Damn! Damn! Damn!" the Ranger says again, stomping his feet and setting that wound off in a world of pain for him. Grabbing the leg, he unfastens his tie and takes it off, throwing it against the dresser.

"What do we do now?" inquires the little lady.

Interrupting, the Ranger asks, "Did they say anything?"

Juan can only shrug and say, "If we want to do business with them, we've got to cross the border."

"Well, that does it," says the Ranger, taking his coat off and pushing the weapons aside on the bed. Sitting down, he tosses his jacket on one of the brass bed poles.

Surprised, Lillian looks at the lawman and says, "What do you mean, 'that does it'?"

He lifts his weary head and studies her a moment. "I can't cross that border. I'm a Texas Ranger. Texas. Not Mexico."

"You're not going to come this far to be scared off, are you?" she challenges him.

"I ain't scared," he mumbles, distraught and shaking his head. "I don't have any authority south of this town." Looking her over, he says, "Don't you get it? Even if I go into Mexico, my badge can't help."

Juan questions, "What if you were to take the badge off?"

"Look," the lawman says, "I've been upholding the law with this here badge a long, long time."

"But you can't cross the border because of a silly little tin star?" Lillian asks.

Angered, the Ranger peers into Lillian's eyes and says, "TIN STAR? Do you know what this TIN STAR means down there?" He waits for an answer from either of his companions. "A target!" he finishes.

"We can still meet with Cardenas. He told me where to come," says the anxious Yaqui.

"Well," says Lillian, "if *Mister* Texas Ranger can't go," she says, "I'll go it alone." She hesitates, then looks at Juan saying, "Unless you want to come along?"

"I will go," says Juan. "But it does not look good. No weapons, no cattle."

Leaning back on the bed, Abner reaches into his vest pocket and pulls out his tack of tobacco and begins rolling a cigarette. He studies the two as he lights it up and blows out some smoke, tossing his match to the side of the bed. He continues to look at them as he goes through some silent study, taking another drag off that stubby little smoke and exhaling.

Lillian stares at the Ranger with some studying of her own. She finally asks, "By the way? Where did you get all that money for all these clothes, guns, and hotel room? And everything else?"

Flicking an ash, he responds nonchalantly, "I had some money stuck away."

"Where?" she says, half laughing. "Where could you possibly hide any money?"

"Do we have to go through this all over again, Missy?" he says. "Look, where I got the money ain't no concern of yours."

"It is, if it wasn't legal," she answers.

"It was legal," he says. "All of it."

Wandering over to Juan's side as he leans against the wooden dresser, she asks the lawman, "So? What are you going to do now? Chase down some more of those outlaws in the Wild Bunch and The-Hole-in-the-Wall Gang? Butcher them all up and call that justice?"

"Missy," he says, grinding his teeth. "You're getting under my skin."

"DON'T call me Missy!" she barks at the old desert dawg. "My name is Lillian. L-I-L-L-I-A-N. I think you know how to spell, don't you?"

"Yeah...," he snaps back and goes on. "Damn it! I can spell. And, I can SMELL." Pausing before going on, he says, "And I can smell some big trouble when I'm near it...and, I'm almost knee-deep in it right now!"

Silence takes the room as the Ranger moves to the window and pulls the curtains aside and surveys the street outside. He takes one more drag of the smoke and tosses it out the window. He turns to Lillian and Juan and grumbles, "Okay, okay. What do you have in mind?"

Thrilled by the change in attitude, Lillian excitedly says, "That's more like it." Taking the lead, she asks Juan, "What did this Colonel Cardenas have in mind?"

Pausing for a moment as he searches the Ranger for a sign of assurance, he explains. "There is this hacienda about two hours ride from here. It is called the Rubio Ranch. This is where the Colonel apparently conducts business. He said he would deal with us down there."

Startled, the lawman interjects his thoughts on the matter before Lillian can question the reality of what's being said. "You mean, we've got to travel two hours in a hostile country filled with revolutionaries and you say I'm scared? Do you have any idea what they do to *gringas* down there if caught?

"I'll take my chances," she proudly announces.

"The Ranger is right," Juan says. "It is not safe for you."

"Well, if you won't help me, I'll have to go it alone," she says, a little upset by all the loss in courage. She begins to pace the floor in anger, stops and looks the two men in the eye and says, "And you call yourselves men?"

Moving to comfort Lillian, Juan says, "The Ranger is right again. These are desperate men fighting a desperate war. Why else would they cross the border to steal a train filled with cattle?"

"How did you know all this stuff to begin with?" Lillian questions Juan.

For a solemn moment, Juan looks skyward. He throws his companions off as he says, "Some people look and never see. Some people listen and never hear." Pausing, he looks at his two companions and speaks slowly and confidently. "I have my allies."

"Allies?" Lillian almost laughs. Looking at the Ranger for interpretation, she says, "What's that supposed to mean?"

Standing up and limping towards her, the Ranger puts his hand on her shoulder and says, "What he's trying to tell you is, he has information from a higher source than you or me."

Somewhat puzzled by the interpretation, Juan says, "Whatever you want to call it, I knew. I know. And, I'm prepared to go with you down to that ranch. That is what this is all about, is it not? Getting the cattle back?"

"Yeah, yeah, yeah," the Ranger says, limping back to the bed and sitting down. "I suppose so, but it ain't easy traveling."

"We've come this far," says the proud little lady.

"I reckon so," the lawman ventures, "and I honestly thought you'd have had enough before we hit Laredo."

"Well, I didn't," she immediately responds. "And the cattle are still a major concern that has to be dealt with," she adds as a reminder.

"I'm prepared to go," says Juan.

"I am, too," says Lillian.

"Well, hold on now," the Ranger responds. "Let me get these silly clothes off and back into my gear." He gets up and limps to the closet and opens the door. "I think better with them on," he says, stepping in and closing the door behind him.

"For the last time," Lillian nags, "will you tell me where you got all that money?"

"Abner, little lady. Abner's the name, and before you go yankin' my tail anymore on where I get my worth, you ought to know my name." A heap of rustling and rattling goes on inside the closet as the lawman makes his change.

Lillian looks at Juan somewhat puzzled and confused. "Are you going to tell me about the money or do I have to go to the Marshal?"

From behind the noisy interior of the closet comes, "Now, why would you want to trouble the Marshal? He wouldn't know anything about it."

"So help me...," Lillian threatens.

"Okay already," comes the word from the innermost depths of the closet. "I'll tell you, but give me a chance to change first, will you?"

Hearing mumbles, curses and complaints from the interior closet as the Ranger changes in the tiny cubicle, Lillian and Juan are somewhat amused, wondering what might be going on in there.

"Well?" Lillian persists.

The door opens and the lawman steps out, as he has left the remains of his suit, vest and pants on the floor of the closet, unconcerned for their well-being. Despite the clean shave, he's back to his chaps, duster, hat and armaments, and just as ornery as ever.

"If you must know...," he says, adjusting his clothes and looking his two companions over. "I've been out there on the range so long, I never had much call for any cash. So, I went to the Ranger station and cashed in all my chips. Over fifteen hundred dollars!" he proudly says, pulling the balance of the roll out and showing it off to them. "There!" he says. "Are you happy now? It was all legal and fair. Nobody got killed in the process." Looking at them for a moment, he goes on. "Can we go now?"

Reaching into his duster for a pocket, the lawman struggles to pull his badge out. He holds it up and does a brief study of it while giving it a slight polish against his canvas duster. Taking Lillian's hand, he drops the tin star in her palm, saying, "This won't stop a bullet, but it might save your life anyway."

Grasping the star, she looks at it a moment, then looks at the Ranger. She shakes her head, "I can't take this."

"We're not going down there, lessin you do," he assures her. "That's the only real protection I can provide. I mean, should something go wrong down there."

Embracing the star, she looks at both men and says, "You're both very, very brave men. I'll let everyone know about this when we get back."

"Lillian," the lawman says, "if my tin star don't mean nothin' down there...what do you think your politics are goin' to amount to?" Sizing up his two trail partners a moment, he finally says, "Let's hit the road."

Declining shyly, Lillian sheepishly says, "I can't."

Surprised, the Ranger says, "First, you're all a head of steam to go. Then you don't want to go?" He shakes his head all puzzled. "Would you make up your mind?"

"I can't go down there dressed like this! I've got to change, too!"

"I must do the same," says Juan, getting the full attention of Lillian and the Ranger.

Shaking his head and speaking to himself, the lawman mumbles, "Everyone's in a hurry, but nobody can go."

Moving down a dusty trail towards a makeshift tent-lined base camp of the Punitive Expeditionary Forces, three Dodge touring cars circle the perimeter of the parade grounds, leading the foot troops and cavalry. The Infantry marches to a clearing for inspection while the horse soldiers move to some corrals adjacent to an open field.

The touring cars circle the parade grounds once more, then peel off and drive towards some tents that overlook the field the soldiers are marching into. The impeccably-dressed General Officer getting out of the lead vehicle is Brigadier General John J. Pershing. He salutes his men and walks to a tent and enters it. The vehicles move from the area towards the soldiers lined up for inspection on the parade grounds. Although the khaki-uniformed troops are at ease, some waver in the afternoon sun from heat exhaustion as they stand prepared for review.

Two crusty old cavalry bluejackets stand at the edge of the corral viewing the khaki-clad foot soldiers absorbing the hot desert sun, as the horses are being moved into the corrals. One of the old coots leaning on the wooden corral posts sweating beads down his forehead to his thick mustache, shakes his head and looks to the other old soldier in similar condition. "Well, it looks like we're in for something now."

The other trooper, cross-armed and leaning on the same pole gazing out responds, "I hear tell they just came back from a border patrol. Couldn't find that Pancho Villa guy."

Removing his dark blue hat and wiping the sweat from his brow with a bandanna, the first trooper says with a slight laugh, "Francisco 'Pancho' Villa. Now, wouldn't that be something?"

Looking over at the first trooper a little confused, the second trooper says, "What?"

Putting the bandanna in his back pocket and placing his hat back on, he looks towards the Headquarter's tent and says, "Pershing and Villa."

The parade ground is being perused by a young officer wearing his khaki uniform buttoned to the collar and donning a matching campaign hat. He walks past the heat-beaten troops, carrying a swagger stick and a side arm holstering an ivory-handled pistol. It is his trademark and he answers to Lieutenant — Lieutenant George S. Patton. The six-foot, one-inch, spit-and-polish officer walks the ranks as the soldiers stand weather-worn, beaten, and prepared for the order to fall out.

Spotting an old recruit that captures his eye, Patton approaches with a discerning nature that prompts the old desert trooper to snap to attention. Looking him over, the young lieutenant says, "What have we here?" Rounding the old soldier in an on-the-spot inspection, Patton studies him closely then shouts, "You look like hell, soldier!" Focusing in on the trooper's uniform, he shouts, "Button that uniform. Wipe that dust from your boots."

The old soldier reaches for the button on his tunic, but the young lieutenant barks, "I didn't say move!" He eyes the weary but scared trooper adding, "I'm not done with you...."

"Sir!" says the confused recruit, still at attention. "We just...."

Cutting him off, Patton shouts, "What?"

Straightening up, the old trooper tries to explain. "We just marched in and all our uniforms are dirty."

Patton uses his swagger stick to draw a line across the dust-covered boots of the old soldier. "You call that dirty? What are you going to do when the lead really starts to fly?. If you don't take care of your uniform, maybe you can't take care of your weapon?" He studies the man further, then shouts, "Present arms!"

The soldier moves instinctively as trained and Patton grabs the carbine from the trooper and inspects it.

The old bluejackets at the corral catch an eyeful of the young lieutenant putting the old recruit through the paces and can't believe it. The mustached old cavalryman turns to his partner. "Boy, are we in for it now! What are they drummin' up over there in that Officer Corps these days?"

"I don't know, says the other trooper, focusing in on the inspection from a distance. "He looks like a West Pointer to me." All spit and polish, it appears. Foul-mouthed, son-of-a-gun, too! Must be all of twenty years old and beatin' on that old buzzard like that?" He shakes his head in concern and disbelief. "Why, the old trooper must be twice as old as that Lieutenant himself. Shameful, I say. Just shameful! This man's Army is about to change I do suspect."

"I reckon," says the mustached cavalryman next to his partner, reaching for his bandanna to wipe his brow again.

Brigadier General John J. "Blackjack" Pershing, emerges from the tent, housing Headquarters for the Punitive Expeditionary Forces and gazes upon the graded field substituting as a parade ground, while his road-weary troops are lined up absorbing the oppressive heat. Looking at a Captain standing near him for a command, the General once more surveys the field, then says, "Dismiss the men, Captain."

Snapping to attention and bringing his hand up for a sharp orderly salute, the Captain shouts, "Yes, Sir!"

Saluting back, the General pivots and re-enters the tent to his quarters.

The Captain does an about face as a Second Lieutenant standing next to him raises his arm in salute while receiving the order, "Dismiss the troops, Lieutenant."

"Yes, Sir!" He spins and marches towards the parade ground where the order is passed down the ranks and the men fall out. Most of the men move towards the shade of some trees near the corrals or reach for canteens, while other men just rush to the water trough near the corrals and soak themselves in the desert -warmed liquid.

The two old bluejackets by the corral view the activity that has just unfolded before them with some amusement as the ragged, khaki-uniformed soldiers make their way towards their designated areas and tents. Relief from the heat is their most important desire at the moment. Water and cover from the late afternoon sun is what's central to them now.

"Worn out, are you?" the mustached old bluejacket smiles at one young khaki-clad trooper who has just finished submerging his head in the wooden water trough.

"Yeah," comes the young soldier's reply, wiping his forehead with his shirt sleeve and gazing at the sun a moment. "It sure gets hot down here, don't it?" He shakes his head, wiping down his water-soaked hair.

Giggling, the old mustached bluejacket shakes his head as he points to the parade grounds. "Not as hot as that 'greenhorn' Lieutenant can make it on a man." He twitches his eyebrows for added enunciation.

"Oh, Patton?" replies the young trooper, not totally unfamiliar with what the old mustached cavalryman refers to as officer material. Turning to the parade ground then back to the old horse soldiers, he says, "Yeah, he's a real character, isn't he?" He pauses a moment to wipe his neck and brow with a bandanna. Rising to lean against one of the splintered wooden poles that acts as a temporary corral, he says, "Though rumor has it, he ain't really all that bad."

"That's what they said about John Wilkes Booth!" exclaims the stout bluejacket standing next tot he mustached cavalryman.

"Could be," says the young recruit. "But Patton runs in different circles." Pointing behind the two old coots and getting their attention, he says, "You see all them horses over there behind you? Some of those ponies are his."

"What?" says the chubby little bluejacket in surprise. "You mean...." he thinks for a moment, "he outright owns them?"

"That a fact?" comes the response from the mustached old cavalryman, scratching his sunburned head.

"Yeah," says the young soldier, informing them of more. "He plays polo."

Surprised, the two old troopers burst out laughing, doubling over. After they quit their giggling and slapping their knees and carrying on, the young recruit adds, "He's supposed to come from this pretty wealthy family out there in California. Apparently, they own the entire San Gabriel Valley."

"An entire valley?" the mustached bluecoat responds in amazement. "Can you believe that? Not just a hill or a mountain, but an entire valley!"

"That is something," confirms the other old coot, wiping his brow and shaking his head in wonder.

The young recruit goes on, now shading the sun from his eyes. "He's pretty political too. His father ran for office and George did some politicking for him—advertising, I think. But it wasn't enough. His father lost the election, proving that landed gentry can't always own everything, even a political seat."

"Now, don't that beat all!" responds the mustached old trooper. He goes on. "And that Lieutenant...Patton, is it...? He chose to come back to the Army?"

"Never left it," answers the young recruit. "Did it while still serving.... Connections is what they say. See, his grandfather was a colonel in the civil war—Johnnie Reb—it's gotten real deep in his blood."

"That right?" wonders the mustached old trooper out loud.

"Yeah," responds the young soldier, adding, "But he was killed. So Patton's carried this military thing with him his whole life. Couldn't get into West Point, went to this other military college – Citadel. I think. He's all military."

"I reckon," says the old trooper, wiping his brow. "Either that or he's plumb loco."

"He's a pretty dedicated and talented man for his age," says the young infantryman, continuing. "He's a first class marksman with a pistol at every fort he's been stationed at. And get this," he leans towards the old bluejackets for emphasis, "he even sword fights!"

The two old troopers, completely caught by surprise on that line, bust up all over again in uncontrolled hysterics and laughter. The tubby, squat bluecoat repeats, "Sword fights?"

"Who the hell sword fights anymore?" says the other mustached trooper, laughing out loud and reaching for his bandanna to wipe his brow again.

"Look," says the young ground recruit, "I don't make this stuff up. I hear it from the people who were with him at these other duty stations." He leans in again. "They say he might be the richest man in the Army!"

Laughing again, the two old coots can hardly contain themselves as the pudgy little blue-clad cavalryman says "Nobody gets rich in this man's Army!"

"Nope," confirms the mustached old bluejacket, shaking his head. "Not this man's Army."

"Anyone that owns that many horses better be rich," comes the analysis from the chubby old bluecoat as he leans on the corral post, sizing up the young soldier on his next question. "Does he race them ponies for money or something?"

"Naw," replies the young man. "Just polo. I suppose anything else would be frowned upon in that social circle of his."

Busting up again, the mustached cavalryman laughs his head off before saying, "Social circle! Now don't that beat all! We get sun, dirt, flies, lizards and snakes.... He gets champagne." The roaring laughter diminishes into a chuckle as he wipes his eyes clear of tears.

"You know what he once did?" continues the fatigued young man, wiping his brow of sweat as he is still affected by the late afternoon heat. "He actually paid his way to Stockholm, Sweden to represent these United States of America in them 1912 Olympic Games!"

Somewhat more seriously, the fat old cavalry horseman says, "Olympic Games? You mean that thing Jim Thorpe did?"

The young khaki-dressed soldier thinks a moment, then says, "Not exactly, but close. Thorpe did the Decathlon. Nodding toward the Headquarter's tent, he goes on. "The lieutenant over there? He did the Pentathlon."

Puzzled, the mustached old cavalry trooper scratches his head and says, "I hear tell 'bout that Jim Thorpe—Decathlon."

"Might a been the Indian's last hurrah," says the other old coot, standing next to the mustached horse hand.

"Well, could be. But the Decathlon is ten events while that Pentathlon is only five. And Patton," the young, informed recruit adds, "he actually won the fencing part of the competition."

"Fencing?" queries the chubby little bluejacket, confused. Somewhat unsophisticated, he seriously asks, "What did they do? Send 'em on out o put up barbed wire or something?"

"Fencing," explains the young man, "you know? Sword fighting! Marksmanship with a pistol, horseback riding and other things they consider sport, is what he really did."

Pointing across the open field, the unbelieving tubby little trooper asks, "And he even paid his way all the way over there to do all that stuff?"

"...And back?" asks the mustached trooper, reinforcing his partner's sentiments.

"Only from what I hear," says the young recruit, wiping his brow of sweat and shaking his hand free of excess fluid. He goes on, "I also heard he stayed on a yacht or some luxury liner anchored in the bay just off shore in Stockholm. Livin' it up and beyond the means of all the rest of the Olympic team."

The old bluejackets laugh it up but not before they see the young lieutenant exit the Headquarter's tent and make a bee line towards the corral.

Detecting trouble, the mustached old horse soldier pulls his bandanna out, wipes his brow and puts it back in his pocket. "Too bad he didn't come back on that Titanic."

Walking across the flattened terrain that serves as the parade ground, the young lieutenant walks past the infantry soldiers cooling themselves off by the water troughs and sitting under the shade of some trees. He walks towards the corral where he spots the two old bluejackets and shouts, "You two!"

Pointing to themselves, they snap to attention and shout, "Yes, Sir!"

Looking the two old cavalrymen over, then at the horses that have been unsaddled and left free to wander in the wooden pens under the heat, he says, "Brush down those horses and give them some food."

"Yes, Sir!" comes the reply from the mustached trooper and his sidekick as they both snap to attention and hold a salute, frozen by intimidation.

Looking at them standing there, Patton yells, "Well? What are you waiting for? A written invitation?"

Discarding the salute, both troopers dash for a wooden shack next to where the hay is piled up.

The young lieutenant crosses his arms and shakes his head as he views the old troopers run for duty and protection from the blistering heat.

Central Laredo is a bustling town at sunset as offices, shops, restaurants and saloons turn on the electricity, highlighting the establishments down the narrow streets where shadows grow long, covering the town in soft lightened tones.

The Ranger and Lillian view the proceedings of slight traffic, and, change towards evening. A horse-drawn street car rattles down some rusty old rails as pedestrians wait at one corner to board the city transportation service which seems to gain the horn of one impatient motorist. It startles one horse and rider as they pass from the other side of the shadowed street.

An energy surge flashes power to the street lights lining the boardwalk, dimming then rising to full brilliance, finally filling the town in diffused lights. From the rickety, splintered boardwalk in front of the hotel stands the Ranger and Lillian, watching the change in hour. Before them on the street are their horses and one mule weighed down with a canvas sack tied to it. Lighting a stubby little cigarette he's just rolled from a tiny pouch, the Ranger tosses the wooden match stick into the street and takes a deep draw of the smoke as he watches Lillian's displeasure with this action. Blowing smoke out slowly and deliberately, he takes another draw of the smoke, unmoved by her silent protest.

Rounding the corner, bareback, is Juan on a donkey, as he heels his sure-footed mount with those moccasins of his. Back in his white cotton pants and top, he rides up to the front of the hotel next to the other horses and mule and jumps off. Tying the lead of his Arizona nightingale to the hitching post, he turns and observes the western skies as they shift towards darkness.

"It's about time you got here," says the Ranger, limping to the edge of the boardwalk to toss his smoke off into the street. "I was startin' to wonder about that courage of yours."

"Lay off him," says Lillian as she walks down some steps to the street to greet the Indian. "He was more willing to help me than you," she says to the lawman, looking at him from the street.

Slightly taken aback by this, the Ranger says, "Yeah? Who brought you across the desert last night? And what about that shootout at the water stop?"

"You want a pat on the back or something?" she answers. "That's what you're trained to do. Juan's doing it out of kindness."

"Kindness?" says the crusty old lawman, readjusting his duster and searching for the dignity he's just lost.

Silent to all the nonsense is Juan, who's oblivious to it all. He recognizes their personality traits now and doesn't mix in, as in the course of half a day, he already understands them. He speaks from another place of experience and warns, "I don't think it wise to cross the border at night."

"Why's that?" asks the Ranger.

"Much confusion on the border," replies the Yaqui. "The Punitive Expeditionary Forces have drawn too much attention to the south, making it risky to travel when dark." He pauses so his companions can digest his reasoning. "The people are on edge and are already involved with a revolution, and the Army makes them nervous. Travel at night could draw unwanted trouble."

"What do you suggest?" asks Lillian.

"Spend the night here. Cross at dawn. It'll be cooler and less confusing," Juan says.

"Then why'd we get all worked up about going over in such a hurry?" the Ranger wants to know.

Looking at the Ranger, Lillian admits, "It was my fault. I just wanted to get this thing over and done with," shaking her head and going on. "I just wanted to get the cattle to market and get back home," she says, breaking down and crying from exhaustion and confusion. "I'm just so tired," she admits, wiping the tears from her eyes.

Trying to comfort her, the Ranger finally agrees. "Maybe a night of rest would be good for all of us," says the lawman, passing out some sympathetic justice from his usual book of law and order. " I've pulled a long day myself and I'm sure the little lady could use some rest, too. I still have the key to that room and maybe we should take advantage of it." Looking at the darkening western skies and the street lights paving the boardwalk and street, he says, "Let's call it a night. I'm sort of hungry myself."

"Me, too," smiles Lillian, somewhat relieved of the tension she's been under, as she wipes her eyes clear of tears.

Juan simply nods in agreement.

"I guess that settles it," says the Ranger. Looking at Juan, he says, "Why don't you take the horses, donkey and mule to the stable while I take the weapons back to the hotel room. We'll meet you at that café across the way." He points across the street to a small but comfortable little joint.

Juan nods again as the Ranger limps to the mule to untie the *aparejo* fastened to the back of the animal.

Unfastening the halters, Juan begins his walk towards the stables when three touring cars of the Punitive Expeditionary Forces, filled with khaki-clad army regulars, drivers, scouts, and advisers rush past Juan, kicking up dirt and dust in front of him and the mounts. The lead drop top sounds its horn, spooking the critters as it wheels its way down the block towards the border.

Chauffeuring the lead 1910 Dodge carrying General Pershing is Leonard Hudnall, a civilian assigned to driving one of these new motorized vehicles for army personnel. Seated next to Hudnall is that upstart Lieutenant Patton who's checking his ivory-handled pistol for cartridges. General Pershing, book ended by two other enlisted men takes notice of the ambitious young man, commenting with a smile, "A little excited about this scout, Lieutenant?"

Startled by the comment, Patton turns to answer the General. "Sir?"

"You can put that pistol away," says the General. "I don't expect too much action on this scout."

"As you say, Sir!" responds the young lieutenant, turning around and holstering his weapon and securing the leather strap.

"Patton," says the General, tapping George on the shoulder, "I'll send you down tomorrow," assures the General. "Maybe that'll satisfy your curiosity."

Turning back to the General officer, Patton responds with surprise, and a certain pleasure, "Yes, Sir!"

Juan watches the three automobiles move down the dusty street, until he turns, looks at a concerned Ranger and Lillian, then continues his labored walk towards the stables with the animals in tow.

Traces of electric light splash on the walls of the darkened hotel room as Lillian sleeps comfortably on the brass bed in the room, while the Ranger is cuddled up on the floor lying on an apishamore, still wearing his duster with his Stetson covering his eyes. Juan siestas in the corner of the room, seated at the Ranger's feet.

Beads of sweat roll down Juan's face as he twists and turns in his sleep until awakened with a start. Looking around the room, he recognizes Lillian on the bed and the Ranger at his feet; although his attention is more drawn to the moisture dripping down his forehead to his cheeks and dripping to the floor.

Reaching up to wipe his brow, he realizes his whole body is soaked in perspiration, but his simple movement has startled the Ranger from his slumber, who instinctively reaches for something in his duster. He stops when he recognizes his location and situation. Noticing the dampened Yaqui from the streetlight shining into the room, the Ranger whispers, "You, okay?"

Looking at the lawman, he whispers, "Yes, I am. I'm okay. I.... It was a vision," he says trying to calm the Ranger, as he wipes his brow and neck free of sweat. He looks at the Ranger, struggling to find the right words. "A vision of...much trouble."

"We're all a little nervous," says Abner.

"You don't understand," whispers Juan. "I've had visions since my childhood. They guide me. They reveal the future to me. It is an important part of my makeup, and, life."

"You aren't going to get into some medicine man stuff, are you?" responds the Ranger in a whisper.

Thinking a moment, he suggests, "Do you think your vision, could...might maybe guide you back to sleep again? I suspect we're going to be in for a long day tomorrow, and I reckon the rest could do us both some good."

Juan studies the Ranger a moment and whispers, "My vision guided me to you two, and the vision has returned to show me tomorrow," insists the Yaqui.

"Tomorrow?" says the lawman, blinking in disbelief.

The whispers have grown louder and have awakened Lillian enough that she rolls over, signaling Juan and the Ranger to be silent. They look at the bed, then back to each other. The lawman tries to complete the conversation in hushed tones. "Can we pick this up in the morning? Say, at about breakfast?"

Juan nods as he wipes more perspiration from his forehead and tries to steady himself. He looks around the room one more time before closing his eyes. But the vision is still with him.

Sitting at the same table next to the same window and facing the same street as before, the Ranger spreads the curtains and peers out the window at the morning traffic on the streets. Lillian and Juan are going through breakfast as impatience strikes the Ranger.

Seeing buckboards and automobiles gaining the day, he stands up and limps towards the waiter behind the counter working on his morning menu. Pulling some bills from his pocket and paying the tab, he grabs a toothpick, smiles and says, "That was a nice grind of coffee today." He digs away in his mouth with the tiny splinter while rolling a small discovery off his tongue and spitting it out. He adds, "The little lady thought so too!" Turning, he limps and lumbers—half in pain and half because of the weight of the heavy armament—past his two companions while walking to the front door, saying, "I'm going to check the pack on the mule.

Lillian studies Juan from behind her seat at the table, contemplating the best way to approach her question to Juan. After taking a bite of her buck cakes, she puts the fork and knife down, wipes her lips with a napkin and puts it down next to her plate. She looks at Juan seriously for a moment, then asks, "What was your vision?"

The Yaqui is startled. Still eating as he avoids her gaze, he simply says, "It was nothing."

"It woke the Ranger and me up!" says the curious little lady.

Unable to avoid the inevitable, Juan puts his utensils down and studies her a moment. After some hesitation, he finally relinquishes, saying, "It wasn't meant to awaken you. It was a vision intended for me."

Reaching beyond her grasp, she asks, "Is this some sort of Yaqui hocus pocus or something?"

Sitting back in his chair, he reflects upon what she can understand. "It was part of my apprenticeship under my...medicine man."

"Yeah?" says Lillian as if she has penetrated some deeply hidden mystical cavern of Yaqui power.

But Juan cuts her off. "It is nothing. It was meant for me and me alone."

Lillian looks into Juan's eyes for more of an answer. Surprisingly, Juan opens up a little bit more and explains himself. "I didn't just happen on the both of you the other night. My vision guided me to you! I've been aware of these visions since I was a boy. It guided me to my teacher. It guided me to last night. It now warns me of today."

"What was the vision?" Lillian inquires.

"Thunder and lightning," comes the reply.

Confused by the answer, Lillian asks, "What does that mean?"

Entering the café with that labored, limping walk, the Ranger accidentally breaks up the conversation just established by his two trail partners. He offers his two companions a couple of rifles he carries in his hands. "You might need it," he says.

The mood is broken as Lillian and Juan just shake their heads. "No," says Lillian. "Not me. I'll take my chances without it," she reasons. "Anyhow, you'll be there, right?"

"I'm trying to help you right now," comes the response from the experienced lawman. "I've been trying to help you since Bitter Creek," he goes on. "I don't know what'll happen down there, and I can only do so much. You should attempt to protect yourself. Don't always count on me."

Unable to raise a stir in her, he says, "Suit yourself." Turning towards the door to leave, he suddenly stops in his tracks, spins around, and looks the two over. "Then you best stay clear of me if something breaks out."

Lillian and Juan nod their understanding. The Ranger "Humphs," throws out his chest, barely seen through the duster, turns, and limps out of the joint. But he's stopped by the sight of three touring cars of the Punitive Expeditionary Forces tooling down the street towards the border. Stepping back into the restaurant, he announces, "Look, we best to get a move on. I just saw the Army leaving town with a complement of soldiers and arms. And they're a buildin' up a head of steam movin' south."

"To the border?" exclaims Lillian, somewhat surprised.

"I reckon so," says the crusty old lawman.

Rising from the table in a rush, Lillian and Juan push their chairs aside as the waiter approaches the table to clear it. Having overheard their conversation, he volunteers, "That wasn't the regular Army. They left at dawn. That must be a different group of detail...or, whatever they call it,"

Startled by all this, the three rush outside to their mounts. Untying the Appaloosa and the mule, Abner climbs aboard his steady steed and leads his horse and the mule into the street, as Lillian and Juan catch up on their rides. The lawman spurs his mount to a trot, dragging the mule behind, as all three move down the street towards the border.

The late morning sun begins to scorch the surrounding terrain as Lillian, Juan, and the Ranger make their way through the humbling, desolate expanse of Mexican desert with the henny and weapons in tow. Lillian reaches for her canteen to douse her bandanna with water as the Ranger checks the halter on the mule trailing behind him.

Juan turns to his two companions to say, "I'll ride ahead," gaining a nod from the Ranger, as he kicks his donkey into a trot in advance of the heat-worn duo.

"What's with him?" asks Lillian, wiping her face with the wet bandanna as she cradles the canteen. "You know, that vision and all...last night?" surprising the lawman as she ties the canteen down to the saddle and awaits a reply from the saddle-worn Ranger.

Taking his eyes off the trail and Juan, who's scurrying towards the horizon, he absently turns his attention to the little lady. "So you heard us?"

"I suppose so," she says. "You couldn't help it.... In a room that small."

"Well," pulling his Stetson back and wiping his brow with the arm of his duster sleeve and refitting the brim, he looks at the little lady and searches for some words to explain it all. Then shaking his head, he just says, "I don't have much of an answer for you. I don't come into contact with Yaqui very much, but they are a spiritual people and don't take much to fighting or aggression. They're supposed to be endowed with certain powers."

"That doesn't say anything!" says Lillian. "What kind of powers?"

"Like I told you back at that water hole," he says, "they have the powers of the desert."

"That's as clear as mud," she says. "I mean, that can mean almost anything."

Looking her in the eye the best a person can over a couple of heat-worn horses clomping along through desert sand and blazing heat, he says, "How do you think he kept up with us when we were chasing that train?"

Thinking a moment, she says, "He must have had a ride or something?"

"On that?" he points to Juan, and the donkey ahead of them on the trail. "Why, even you know that that old donkey would fall over dead from all the locoweed it would have to eat to get Juan through all that territory we covered. " Reflecting on it some more, he adds, "Think about that shootout at the water stop?"

"He..., he just appeared!" she says, almost not believing her own words.

"That's what I mean," he says. "He got there, but how? Well, that's another question."

Befuddled and confused, Lillian thinks about her conversation at the breakfast table with Juan, and offers, "He told me his vision brought him to us."

Shrugging those already overburdened shoulders and sizing her up, he says, "Could be. Then again, what do I know? Look, they say the Yaqui can be very mystical."

"Mystical?" she puzzles.

"I'm not a Yaqui, but I'm told they can change into...how can I say it? They can see through the eyes of another."

"What's that mean?" puzzles Lillian.

Stuck for more than an explanation, he says, "Well, you'll just have to ask him yourself, I guess." He spurs his mount to a trot, and with the henny in haul, he leaves Lillian to think it over the best she can.

After a little thought, she kicks her mare up to a trot to pull up beside the Ranger who's slowed his steed and mule down to a walk again. Lillian attempts some more questions. "What does 'thunder' and 'lightning' mean to you?"

"I don't know," comes the response from the Ranger who is a little irritated by all the queries. "Maybe it's a symbol or something? Look, the way I see it, vision or otherwise, I'm glad he's along. I'm already tense enough about that soured-out deal gone wrong back there in Laredo, and I'm just glad to have some help along. Anyway, his offer to help has gotten us this far, and that's a mite bit better than I could have done alone."

"But why would he get 'thunder' and 'lightning' out of a vision?" she presses on.

"Look," he brings his horse to a stop and addresses her the best he can. "You'll just have to ask him, you get it?" Kicking his horse back to a walk, he continues, "I'm trying to figure out where we are and what we're going to do when we get to where we're going."

Catching up to the Ranger, she goes on. "I still don't understand." Looking up as she continues, "I don't see a cloud in the sky. How can he get a vision of 'thunder' and 'lightning' out of a clear sky?

"Well, that's mystical now, isn't it?" The Ranger yanks on the leather lead to the mule and spurs his Appaloosa to a gallop as Lillian follows him through the desert heat and dust kicked up by his horse.

Atop a hill, overlooking a great expanse, Juan has come to a stop. He searches the horizon, turns back to see his companions coming, then gazes beyond the horizon to the clear blue skies.

Three 1910 Dodge touring cars filled with Army personnel and attachments armed and on the lookout, swiftly come down a musky roadway stirring up a lot of dust. Second Lieutenant Patton rides shotgun in the lead automobile driven by Leonard Hudnall. Spotting a hacienda in the distance, Patton points it out to the driver and says, "Go on to that ranch over there." Hudnall sees the lone habitat encased and surrounded by the vast Mexican desert, grinds the vehicle into gear and lead-foots it towards the large adobe structure as the other two cars pick up pace and catch up.

Turning to the back seat of the rag top, the lieutenant addresses E. L. Holmdahl, an ex-Villa soldier, now riding scout for the Punitive Expeditionary Forces. "All these years of training for combat, and the General has me looking for corn!" He shakes his head in disbelief and disgust.

"Armies have to eat," comes the reply from Holmdahl.

"But I was trained to fight," says the lieutenant.

Entering the main gate of this desert palace, an ornate Spanish sign reads: The Rubio Ranch. The last vehicle stalls before lurching forward in acceleration then backfires as it moves through the cast iron gates of this *ranchero*.

Carefully hidden between the shade and high grass of a *molté* Lillian, Juan, and the Ranger spot the three touring cars pulling into the hacienda. "Army!" curses the lawman, grabbing a handful of pebbles and dirt beside him on the ground, kicking and cussing displeasure at the untimely arrival of the khakis.

"What are we going to do now?" questions the little lady lying between the Ranger and Yaqui.

Totally transfixed on his view of the hacienda, Juan says, "Thunder!"

"What?" snaps Lillian, looking at Juan after overhearing his whisper. "What did you say?"

Slowly turning to Lillian, he clearly explains himself. "The 'thunder.'" Looking back at the structure, he warns, "It has arrived."

Looking from side to side, skyward, down and beyond, the crusty old lawman shakes his head and with a halfway smile says, "I don't see no 'thunder.'" Puzzled even further, he goes on to add, "I don't even see a thunderhead in the sky or on the horizon! All I see is a bunch of guys in uniform movin' right into that there *ranchero* up ahead."

Still transfixed on the hacienda, Juan squints, as he whispers, "It is him!"

"Well, 'thunder' or not," responds the old coot, "We have more than we bargained for now!"

"We must be patient," says the Yaqui, still gazing at the desert structure, giving some assurance.

"Patient?" answers the lawman. "Patient?" he repeats. "We ought to call this whole thing off, if you ask me. The revolution is one thing. The cattle is another...but, the U.S. Army? Well, we're talking a horse of a different color here now, aren't we? My instincts tell me...."

"Patience," Lillian sounds him down, sternly staring at the Ranger.

Confused and bewildered, the lawman questions, "Patience? Is that what you said?" He shakes his head and tosses the remains of the dirt and pebbles down. "I just don't get you."

"Remember what the waiter said?" Lillian tries to remind the lawman.

"The waiter?" the Ranger exclaims, totally shocked as if hit with whiplash. Shaking his head and mumbling to himself, "'Thunder'...'lightning'...and now, we've got a waiter! What did I get myself into?" Painfully struggling to crawl back from his overlook, weighted and wounded, cursing and cussing to himself, he's distracted by Juan, who motions him forward. Shaking his head, he sees Lillian motioning him forward too. Puzzled, he slowly crawls back into position in time to see the three touring cars exit the hacienda and move in a straight line towards the open desert.

"Patience," comes the word from Lillian.

Down the roughed out horse trail, the pack of Dodge touring cars bounce, dance, and sway on, kicking up a whirlwind of dust, dirt and grime as they pass through the desert while occupants hold on for dear life. Holding onto the door for leverage as the vehicles dart past pot holes and other obstacles, Second Lieutenant Patton grabs hold of his campaign hat with his free hand while turning to Holmdahl, who's wedged between two other soldiers. Patton says, "I saw something in that hacienda that just doesn't set well."

Holmdahl leans forward, holding his Aussie hat. "I think I saw something, too!" Looking back, he goes on, "A few of those men were Villa regulars when I was with them."

Patton looks past Holmdahl at the distant *ranchero*, wondering out loud, "Something else, though," shaking his head and going on. "Maybe just a hunch or something." Turning to the driver of the wildly steered car, Patton says, "Hudnall."

"Lieutenant?" comes the immediate reply from Hudnall, his eyes fixed on the road in complete concentration.

"When you hit the main road, I want you to double back."

"Yes, Sir!" responds the commander of the wheel of this whirling dervish.

Dancing and swaying their way over a hill, the three touring cars disappear beyond the sight of the ranch.

The sun has no mercy for those locked from the shelter of key protection, and as the intensity of the heat bears down on the ground until the dirt and sands sting, three riders and a pack mule move towards the only cover to be found in this Mexican desert wasteland—the Rubio Ranch.

"I've got a funny feeling about all this," says the experienced Ranger to his companions.

"What can go wrong?" Lillian asks. "The Army left. The 'thunder' is gone.... What more do you want?"

"Sorta confident, aren't you," sounds the lawman, still suspicious as he surveys the *ranchero* for signs of life.

"I don't see the train," comes Lillian's observation.

Though Juan appears tuned into something beyond the understanding of his companions, he warns, "I still feel the 'thunder.'"

Turning to her Yaqui friend and trying to reassure him, Lillian attempts to belie his fears. "You just saw your 'thunder' leave," she says. "There aren't any clouds in the sky. No 'lightning.' No 'thunder.' We only have to conduct business and get out," she says. "I'm supposed to keep quiet and look pretty, right?"

"One, two, three, huh? Simple as that?" answers the lawman. "Lillian, we're about to step into the belly of the beast!"

Confirming the Ranger's sentiments, Juan adds, "Yes, I agree. Our job has only just begun."

The three strangers approach the cast iron gates leading into the courtyard of the hacienda, slowly making their way towards the main house. Walking their mounts and the one drag mule deeper into the courtyard, they witness four unlikely men skinning a cow. Lillian is completely overwhelmed by the sight of these butchers cutting her bovine apart. She recognizes the brand on the dead carcass as one of her stolen stock. Holding her contempt, she grits her teeth and stares ahead as Private Garza exits the main house and makes his way towards the three to greet them. Juan and the Ranger note Lillian's mood at the sight of the butchered Hereford and realize what she must be feeling. They control themselves as they slowly move towards the green fatigued private.

Blazing heat so repressively weighted that even flies near the carcass of the hereford, seek cover of shelter as they cling to shadows of tiny crevices and holes in the adobe shack where the butchers are plying their trade. Garza seems unaffected by the heat, barely breaking a sweat as he smiles at the three travelers and says, "*Buenos dias, senor and senorita,*" waiting for the road-weary warriors to get off their mounts. The Ranger tosses the heavily-armed private the halter of the henny as he dismounts and painfully limps his way to a hitching post to tie his Appaloosa. Lillian and Juan follow the lawman's lead as Garza goes on to say, "Colonel Cardenas awaits you in the house."

Taking a sharp inventory of the surroundings, the Ranger turns back to the private and says, "I'll be needing something off that mule," walking over to him.

Lillian, a little frightened by the circumstances at hand, takes note of the beautiful grounds and main house of this luxurious hacienda, finding her only real comfort to be that of her two friends who've journeyed through the wastelands to arrive at this destination.

As the Ranger struggles to unload the canvas-wrapped weapons off the mule, Juan walks over to assist. Carrying one load apiece while Lillian still absorbs the magnificent grounds and housees, Captain Isador Lopez approaches them from the entrance of the house.

"*Buenos Dias*," says the smiling officer. "Welcome to the Rubio Ranch. I am Captain Lopez. Colonel Cardenas is expecting you." Showing them the way to the entrance, as Garza walks the rides towards the stable, the three weary travelers begin the long march towards the doorway of the main house.

Entering a large lobby, Lopez guides them down a hallway towards two large doors that lead to the library. Stepping into the large room, Colonel Cardenas is standing with a baby in his arms, while his beautiful young wife stands next to him with another child in her arms.

"One *momento*," says the Colonel as he hands his baby to Lopez and kisses his wife, scooting her out the door with Lopez. "Business," he says to his lovely wife.

Studying his three guests more carefully, he shakes his head saying, "I once more had deep concern for you people, as a small contingency of American soldiers were here just a moment ago. But they only inquired for some food." He approaches the trio and leads them further into the room. Sizing them up as Captain Lopez returns to the room, the Colonel clears a table and walks back to his desk for a cigar.

"You may rest your weapons on the table," says Cardenas as he eyes Lillian and the Ranger while he lights his cigar and tosses the extinguished match into a pot-bellied fireplace. He slowly exhales, further examining these guests. Pulling the chair from the desk, he sits down, leans back, places one boot on the lip of the desk for balance and takes another deep draw off the hand-rolled Havana cigar. Eyeing the canvas packs on the table, he cocks his head in wonder, prompting the Ranger to open it for examination. Carefully unwinding the packs, the lawman sweeps open the canvas to reveal the weapons. Twisting his head a bit, the Colonel puts his foot down and leans forward as his interest is piqued. Moving from his chair to the table, he looks at Juan, then back to the guns, ignoring Lillian and the Ranger altogether.

"New?" asks a surprised Cardenas.

"*Si*," replies Juan. "As I said they would be."

Picking up a Remington repeating rifle and looking it over, Cardenas inspects the weapon from barrel to butt, even taking a whiff from the barrel and saying in curiosity, "You have stocks of such weaponry?"

"In Laredo," says the Yaqui.

Grabbing a Winchester rifle, Cardenas resumes the inspection, pausing to re-examine the Ranger and Lillian but continuing his business. He hands the Winchester to Lopez for inspection. Cardenas reaches for a pistol from the second pack the Ranger has just opened. Feeling the weight and spinning the cylinders, then spot pointing the revolver around the room , he stops with the pistol pointed at the Ranger.

"*Muy Bueno. Muy bueno*," says Lopez, distracting Cardenas from the lawman. Eyeing the Ranger, he slowly lowers the pistol and returns his attention to the table.

"Very good," says Lopez.

"*Si*, good," Cardenas suspiciously replies.

Stopped at the main road, the three touring cars idle as they line up awaiting direction from the officer in command of the unit. Breaking from his deep concentration, Lieutenant Patton turns in his seat and stares into the wasteland, then to Holmdahl, then the driver, saying, "Double back to that *ranchero*. Something...I just can't shake." Turning back to Holmdahl, he continues, shaking his head. "Something's going on down there."

The lead car grinds into gear and suddenly jerks forward off road, bouncing and swaying as it makes its way back onto the pock-marked road in the direction of the hacienda they'd just come from.

"Cattle for arms, *Si?*" questions Cardenas, confirming the initial deal.

"As we had agreed," Juan answers.

"What about ammunition?" asks the Colonel.

"We have that too," interjects the Ranger, surprising everyone.

Uncomfortable and overcome by the Ranger, the Colonel backs off and moves towards his desk still puffing his cigar. He is still suspicious of the Ranger as he takes his chair behind the desk once again. He looks the three guests over more closely and finally says, "*Juanito?* Why bring *gringos* in on this?"

"They are my partners," replies the Yaqui. "They are the ones who own the munitions. I am merely the agent."

"The agent!" laughs Cardenas. Thinking a moment about his bargaining position as he draws on his smoke, saying, "There are fifty thousand guns strategically hidden near here at this very moment. One million, eight hundred thousand rounds of ammunition to go with them.," he adds, hoping to humble them.

"I've got eight million more rounds on delivery from St. Louis, and another three million rounds on order out of New York." His three visitors are startled. Flicking the ash of his cigar and exhaling, he says, "I worry about *gringos* that are out of their territory." Sizing Lillian up, he goes on. "Women? *Gringas?* Well, this is entirely another matter too, is it not?"

"Our warehouse is stocked with weapons," Lillian says, attempting to reinforce her position and defend her companions. "Where's the cattle?" she cuts to the chase.

"Cattle?" Cardenas questions. "Yes, I have cattle. I have a whole train load of cattle. But I am a bit confused."

He moves from his chair past the desk to study the three *compancheros* from north of his side of the American border. He studies Juan; the *péon*, in peasant clothing, though more curious about the small cowboy and his bulky appearance under that duster of his. Moving towards Lillian and sizing her up, he finally says, "I had heard they'd given the vote to women across the border, but I didn't know that gave them the political freedom to be gun runners down here."

"You just bring the cattle to Laredo and we'll make the exchange there," says the Ranger.

Instantly insulted, the Colonel turns to Juan and asks, "Who is this *gringo*?"

Thinking quickly, Lillian interjects. "He's the one who funded our purchases of arms. The weapons are in *my* warehouse near the loading docks."

"I see," says the Colonel, backing off for the moment. "Cattle for arms," he repeats himself. "Cattle for arms." He walks back to his desk and chair, flicking an ash into the fireplace, while examining and re-examining the trio with mixed emotions, as he sits down and puts his boots back up on the edge of the table, while taking a long drag off that Havana hand-rolled cigar.

With firm conviction, Cardenas says, "My cattle is good, strong beef, but I have reservations about crossing that border again. We just had a visit by the *Americanos*, but they were seeking corn." He pauses to assess these unusual guests before adding, "I don't take chances unless I have to. Going to Laredo is not such a good idea for me."

"We'll only make the exchange at the warehouse there," Lillian assures Cardenas.

"Not safe," rebuffs the Colonel, flicking his Havana and taking another deep draw.

Juan attempts to reason. "It wasn't safe for us to come down here, but we did. We have more of what you want, but we cannot transport such a load on mule through these hostile lands. You must come across the border to receive them."

"You say you have a train," interjects the Ranger.

Stunned by all the attempts to persuade him, the Colonel says, "The weapons are good. But I am a wanted man across the border. I could be in big trouble over there."

"Send your men," says the Ranger. "We'll take care of the rest."

Lopez interrupts to confer with the Colonel. Huddled together at the desk, they whisper to each other until the Colonel returns his attention to the edgy trio.

"My soldiers need food, too," states Cardenas.

Juan counters, "An Army without weapons wages a weak war."

Indignant by Yaqui logic, Cardenas snaps, "What do you know of war, Yaqui? Aren't you supposed to be a peaceful tribe? What do you really know? Do you even know who Felix Diaz is? Or how he was overthrown by Francisco Madera? And how this rid Mexico of French Napoleonic rule. Or how General Victoriano Huerta had the populist assassinated, causing the counter-revolution and forcing Huerta out of the country to rule from Barcelona?"

"Huerta ruled Mexico from Spain?" Lillian asks.

"*Si!*" Cardenas exclaims. "He installed Diaz, the previously disposed ruler, to ratify treaties from Mexico City with foreign countries, allowing counter-insurgencies, with a foreign agenda, for their own private revolutions." Cardenas eyes the gun dealers before him. "They say Diaz has made a deal with the Germans and Japanese."

"Japanese?" asks the Ranger, somewhat startled.

"Japanese!" affirms Cardenas. "Carranza leads the Constitutionalist, while Diaz, under Huerta's rule, ratifies treaties with foreign powers. Do you hear me?" He straightens up and searches for understanding from these people in front of him. "*Foreign powers!* Not just arms! Foreign powers to help impact a revolution and, Pasqual Orasco to administer a part or a portion of it—riding a red flag for the Colorados.

"Huerta died a month ago, leaving Villa the Constitutionalists under Carranza, but there is word of his involvement with a counter-insurgency group aligned to Germany and Japan right now. They have a different agenda and he now has these foreign advisors to counsel and guide him. Though he rides for Carranza under one flag, what flag does he really wave now?

"I know there are men of foreign flags around, as I have seen a Captain Marinelli of the Italian Army reporting to me," Cardenas explains. "While Huerta governed the country upon his return, Diaz had already made his pact with the axis powers: Germany, Japan, and just about anyone else who wants to play." Lillian and the Ranger are mesmerized.

"While Orasco raids the northern borders with expatriots, ex-Federales and bandits—raping, pillaging, and burning even those who are blind to flag or country, another more serious agenda is emerging." Cardenas pauses briefly for their reactions before going on. "It is Captain Borunda, the 'Matador,' of the Colorados, who is executing orders AND political prisoners on command from Mexico City."

"I heard tell that Major Fierro, 'The Butcher', is another one of those murderers," says the Ranger, adding, "But I thought he was one of Villas' executioners."

"*Si, si,*" says the Colonel. "They're all assassins. In the name of the revolution and all that. But on the surface, while these crimes against humanity go on, beneath it all, there are more devious things going on. Diaz entertains Germany in unloading munitions at Vera Cruz.... Japan? Four years ago they wanted to buy Magdalena Bay. You should see their coal stations for refueling their Navy in Santiago Bay right now, and that fishing village in Monzanillo Bay? Large enough to feed an army!

"But there are many flags that wave in Mexico these days," Cardenas pauses, eyeing them more closely as he goes on. "Some flags can't even be seen—if you count counter-counter insurgencies. What do you know of the Iron Cross

Society, or the Black Dragon Society? What do you really know about this revolution and what its real aims and goals are?

"In ignoring Villa's intervention, he sought other ways to influence the American people about this struggle, as in Santa Ysabel, where *Villiastas* murdered seventeen United Coal Miners, or that raid into New Mexico and Columbus, where another seventeen were killed."

"Yes," says Juan, surprising everyone. "I have heard of this Iron Boot on the border. There is word from my people that this boot steps into Cuba, Colombia, and Haiti, and that the Black Dragon Society eyes interest in Hawaii and the Phillippines."

"Interesting," says Cardenas, leaning back in his chair and gazing upon Juan with curiosity. "So you know of the three worlds?"

"I have seen the falcon," nods Juan as he reaches behind and pulls a medicine bag out and opens it. He pulls a shiny object out of the pouch and holds it up like a precious gem to be seen by all, "I hold the pearl."

Lillian and the Ranger are more than surprised by this curious companion of theirs as they gaze upon this unlikely object Juan now displays before all.

Leaning forward, Cardenas studies Juan a moment, then his companions. He stands up and wanders the room in thought. After a moment, he stops and studies the pearl in Juan's hand. "You are a curious people, Yaqui. Cunning, yet peaceful. A curious combination."

"Peaceful and reasonable," Juan corrects, and goes on. "We have what you need, you have what we want."

"*Si, si,*" answers the Colonel, pacing the room with his hands behind his back and puffing on the *cigaro*. He turns to the trio and eyes them. "The weapons are important for the revolution, but the trade?" he wonders, shaking his head.

High noon, when shadows barely trace ground and only the wind to break the oppressive heat. A small motorized division of the Punitive Expeditionary Forces races towards the Rubio Ranch.

As the small convoy approaches the main gate, Lieutenant Patton orders the driver to slow down. He grabs his carbine and leaps from the automobile. Directing the other vehicles to follow the lead car to the side of the hacienda, Patton signals to one soldier in one passing car to get out while pointing to one scout from the last vehicle to fall out.

Coming to a rest at the side of the *ranchero*, one armed, khaki-clad soldier from each of the cars, jump out and dash around the back of the house while the remaining troopers move into position from their cars by the roadway where they stand guard. Patton looks the area over and when satisfied everyone is in position, he nods to the private, his scout, Heaton Lunt. Moving forward, both men follow the young lieutenant into the courtyard of the hacienda.

The four Mexicans butchering the Hereford see armed troopers in passing and send one man to the house to advance word. The *péon* races towards the front door and informs Private Garza of the "*Americanos,*" pointing towards the main gate and alarming the small, well-armed *Villiasta*, who rushes into the main house to warn his commanding officer.

Walking towards the gateway with his carbine in hand, Lunt and the trooper next to him follow Patton. Patton stops and turns to the scout. "Did you see that Mexican come out of the house?"

"Yeah," Lunt replies. "He just came right out and went over to that cow and started butchering it with those other men."

"I know there's something going on in that house," says the Second Lieutenant, moving towards the arched entrance way.

The Colonel, flicking ash into the fireplace, firmly looks over these three people with deep suspicion. "This revolution calls for some curious bed fellows," he says. "While I might buy and purchase the arms for our wars, you *gringos* are totally unaware of why these arms are really in need."

The faint sound of footsteps grow louder as Private Garza rushes into the library to report.

"Colonel!" Garza interrupts Cardenas. *"Americanos!"* He points outside.

Surprised and alarmed, Cardenas says, *"Americanos?"*

"Si," Lopez confirms.

Angered beyond words, the Colonel turns to Juan, Lillian and the Ranger in contempt. Roaring at Garza, he orders.

"Get the horses!" sending the little revolutionary dashing down the hallway towards the rear of the hacienda.

Turning back to the trio and staring them down, Cardenas' demeanor goes from contempt to rage, as he spits on the floor before them, shouting, "Damned *gringos!* I spit on you and your *stupido* scheme!" throwing the butt of his cigar into the fireplace, and turning to Lopez, he motions towards the doorway.

Lillian and Juan are now further shocked to see the Ranger casually move his hand up to the front of his duster towards his neck and top button, to unfasten it, while being further distracted by a figure crossing the sun-lit window behind the lawman. The window shimmers in a burst of light like a lightning flash, reminding Lillian of Juan's vision.

Cardenas spins towards the window to see an Army regular signaling some troopers further back. The Colonel reaches for his pistol and backs up to a bookcase. Panic sets in and he begins to sweat. He looks about the room, thinking of who will be the first to catch his wrath. His eyes rest upon the Ranger who now has his duster open and at the ready.

Reaching for his revolver and taking aim, Cardenas is suddenly distracted by a ruckus breaking out down the hall of the library. Garza rushes through the lobby and down the hallway towards the library, yelling, "The front is covered!"

Lopez draws his pistol and covers the three, informing the Colonel, "We must exit through the rear!"

In disgust, Cardenas looks at the three strangers, finally saying, "I'm an honorable man, but I will not kill you in the house that my mother, wife, and children dwell, though I will come back to catch and skin you alive some day!" he seethes, as Lopez grabs his arm and drags him from the room while still holding aim on the trio.

"We must go!" insists Garza, as Lopez again tries to drag Cardenas out the door, where now, the Colonel's mixed emotions begin to simmer and rise with more contempt. "And you wanted me to cross the border for you? When I get out of this, I will cross the border. There is no border that can prevent me from crossing, to come after you! We will meet again, gringos, but the next time it will be at my convenience, and when you least expect it...then, I will crush you three like the three little, tiny insects that you are!" Ranting and raving, his voice trails off the interior walls into echoes heard throughout the house as Lopez drags him to the lobby and finally towards a rear door where the sound of hooves and slapping leather replaces the Colonel's cries of rage.

Mounted on their horses in the noon-day sun just beside a patio, the revolutionaries survey the area then lead their horses to gravel where they draw their pistols, un-holster rifles, and kick their mounts on a sprint for the arched gateway.

Restrained by Lillian, the Ranger reaches for a pistol from his *buscadero*. She says dejectedly, "Let them go. There's nothing more to do."

"What about the cattle?" the lawman asks.

"Killing them won't get the cattle back," she says, as she now becomes aware of children's cries and the weeping wife, and, mother. All the noise and excitement has caused great confusion in the house.

Moving from the library to the hall, they find Cardenas' family huddled in a corner of a room. Lillian and

Juan move towards the frightened family to comfort them, as the Ranger stands in the hallway gripping his pistol, helpless to do anything.

Cautiously walking towards the arched iron gate of the *ranchero*, the young lieutenant looks over to an unarmed Heaton Lunt. "Where are those soldiers I sent to the south?"

"Maybe they got lost," answers Lunt.

"They should have been here by now," says Patton, looking the grounds over for any sign of his men.

Steadily advancing on the main entrance as the sun bears down on them, Lunt says, "Remember what General Pershing said about shooting!"

Looking back and nodding, Patton repeats the order, "Not until 'hostile identity is certain,'" As he turns forward again, all hell breaks loose as three armed horsemen round a corner of the ranch house at full charge, right into the path of Lunt, the private, and George S. Patton.

"Halt!" commands Lieutenant Patton, standing his ground while brandishing his carbine before them. The three horsemen swing their rides in another direction and sprint off. "Halt!" Patton shouts again, reaching for his ivory-handled pistol as he races after the horsemen with rifle and gun in hand.

Doubling back to the rear of the hacienda, the three horsemen are staggered by six khaki-clad troopers waiting for them. Cardenas, Lopez, and Garza spin and dash off towards the lesser odds—Patton, the private, and the unarmed scout on foot. Charging past the four *peones* skinning the Hereford with guns drawn and ready, the three revolutionaries dash towards a freedom that only three men now prevent them from gaining.

The sharp crack of pistol fire and charging horses alerts everyone inside the hacienda that a fire fight has begun. The Cardenas family shudder and cower in uncontrollable hysterics, as a stray bullet smashes through a window of the room and slams into a wall, sending Lillian, Juan, and the

Ranger to the floor for cover. Juan looks at his female companion and says, "The 'thunder' has returned."

The shot of a different caliber weapon tweaks the ear, as an answering shot is returned, sending another stray bullet into the house. Again, everyone ducks for cover. Rising from cover, the Ranger reaches into his duster and pulls out his pump action shotgun and moves down the hallway. Seeing him take action, Lillian shouts, "Where are you going?"

Stopping a moment, he kneels with his back to the wall, shotgun pointed up, surveying the windows in the long hallway. He turns towards Lillian and shouts, "Where a man ought to be." He pulls his hat down and painfully limps to the opposite side of the lobby where he views the courtyard and a full-fledged gun battle in progress.

Lillian and Juan look at each other in concern as the outbreak of gunfire outside has another bullet slam into the room hitting a chandelier and shorting the electric charge, causing a shower of sparks to rain down from the ceiling to the floor. Lillian looks at the chandelier as it sputters and spits out electric flashes, then to Juan. She no longer questions his visions. The stark reality of the events have given her actualization over visualization. Another wild shot passes through the room, slamming into a wall above them, showering them with adobe dust.

"I think I just saw some of your lightning," Lillian tells Juan, dusting off the adobe dust.

Juan looks at Lillian, nodding. "Yes, a storm is gathering."

The three revolutionaries charge at Patton, shooting their pistols as the young lieutenant stands his ground and returns fire from that ivory-handled pistol while clutching his carbine. Lunt dashes for cover in one direction, while the trooper runs towards the gate to set up and take aim.

Patton stands upright and alone, pistol aimed. The sound of discharged lead swishes past him, wide and wild, as only one bullet finds dirt and gravel in front of the young lieutenant, kicking up dust.

"Why, you...!" Patton tightens his jaw and grits his teeth and takes aim. Squeezing off five rapid shots at all three horsemen, he's only able to hit one horse and rider in passing, but this breaks up their rank and charge, scattering them into a free for all.

A volley of shots ring out from behind the lieutenant, forcing him to dash for protective cover by an adobe wall that Lunt's already pinned up against. Looking behind him in confusion, Patton sees it's his own men shooting, but the move effectively scatters the revolutionaries to the four winds.

High noon on this thirteenth day of May, 1916, brings the ringing pitches of various caliber weapons and hoof beats. Hot lead zips back and forth, smashing into gravel, walls, and windows, while leaving little clouds of dirt and adobe dust kicking up everywhere. It may not be Thanksgiving, but it sure does look like a turkey shoot.

Recovering from a shell blast that rains adobe dust from above, the young lieutenant reloads his pistol. Looking at Lunt, he says, "I was looking for a good fight, but I didn't think it would be like this!" He pushes the bullet-filled chamber of his pistol back into place and grabs Lunt, pulling him to the side of the building as more shots continue to echo throughout the courtyard.

Rounding the corner of the adobe wall, Patton and Lunt are surprised to find the four *péones* still butchering the Hereford, untouched or even moved by all the commotion and shooting. They take notice of the two *Americanos*, but tend to their chores. Patton looks at Lunt in concern for these men and misses the wounded Cardenas driving his horse towards the red brick stairs of the house and smashing through the large double doors.

Falling off his wounded, bloody mount, the Colonel writhes in pain as he reaches for his chest and realizes he's taken a serious wound when he sees blood on his hands. He looks up to see the Ranger, as his eyes burn with anger. He pulls up his revolver and begins firing, hitting the wall and forcing the lawman back for cover.

"Hell fire!" exclaims Abner, grasping the barrel of his weapon and spinning around the corner. He leans against an inside corridor of the house, as sweat forms on his temples and drips down his face. He looks both ways down the hallway before sliding down the side of the wall into a painful crouch, listening to the various caliber weapons going off in the fire fight just beyond him, while recognizing a far more immediate danger in a wounded Cardenas just around the corner. "Pinned down," he says to himself.

Holmdahl and Hudnall, the other drivers, dash from the entrance gate across the courtyard towards the lieutenant and Lunt, distracting Patton. "Take care of them," says the anxious Lieutenant to Lunt as he rounds the corner of the shack with his pistol reloaded and ready to fire.

Studying the four *péones* cutting away on the bloody beef, undisturbed or bothered by all the gunplay going on all around them, Hudnall taps Holmdahl on the shoulder and nods in the direction of the butchers. Several shots ring out near them, slamming into the adobe wall above them. It sends Lunt, Hudnall, and Holmdahl to the ground for cover as particles of dust and adobe rain down on them.

Standing by the corner of the shack right in the line of fire, Patton prepares to meet the challenge from Lopez blasting wildly with his revolver on his charging steed. He squeezes off a couple of rounds from his pistol, hesitates and lowers his aim and fires several more times, as the horse and rider dash right past him. One shot hits the hip of the horse, crippling and downing it and the rider, in a tremendous cloud of dust. Squirming in pain, the horse pins the Captain in the saddle as Patton and several other troopers advance on him. Tangled up in the saddle of the pain-filled horse and out of bullets for one handgun, Lopez is unable to reach for his other holstered pistol.

"Shoot him! Shoot him!" Lunt shouts to Patton from the side of the adobe shack.

Hearing Lunt's shouts from the courtyard, Cardenas realizes how serious his situation has become. He is bleeding from his chest, short-winded from the bullet in his lung, with sweat pouring from his brow down his face. He vents his anger on the Ranger, emptying his few remaining bullets from his handgun into the wall where the Ranger is crouched in safety.

Abner dives to the other side of the wall in the tight corridor, as bullets slam through the wall, smothering him in particles of dust, adobe and a great big cloud of concern. He gathers his courage, the pump action shotgun, and, ignoring the pain in his injured knee, moves towards the lobby and peeks around the corner to see Cardenas' horse buck and kick erratically from all the commotion going on with guns discharging everywhere. But it's enough for the Ranger to make a move as he painfully dashes into the lobby to level a quick burst of fire from his shotgun, just missing the Colonel — who returns fire — sending the lawman on a quick dash across the lobby to another hallway where he's able to dive in as Cardenas' bullets trail him into the corridor.

Getting up, the Ranger dashes back to the doorway with his weapon pointed. Cardenas, still holding the leather halter to his horse, misjudges the angle on the Ranger as he comes up pointing the shotgun. A wild shot from the Colonel is enough to back Abner off as the Colonel abandons his horse and runs for his life down a corridor towards another room to rearm himself.

Echoes down a hallway alerts the Ranger of a retreating Cardenas. Straightening up and stepping into harm's way, the lawman shoulders that beast of a weapon and follows his instincts as he now moves on Cardenas.

Captain Lopez is finally able to clear himself from the restraints of his out-of-control horse and saddle. Staring at Patton, Lunt, and four troopers surrounding him, he pauses

to consider why he hasn't already been shot. Puzzlement
turns to reflex as he draws his revolver from his holster, but
the faster, more accurate Second Lieutenant Patton beats him
to the draw. The Captain is dead before he even clears
leather. The soldiers move on the dead revolutionary with
carbines aimed, looking for any tell-tale signs of life.

Hudnall turns from the action to inadvertently see the
four *péones* are still cutting away on the beef and unaffected
by the events. He turns back to the soldiers, who are now
inching their way closer to the already dead Lopez.

Holstering his pistol, Patton hears several more rounds
being fired from behind him. He spots Private Garza taking
some wild shots at the troopers moving on his dead captain.
Pulling up his carbine, Patton squeezes off three quick bursts.
Two of the other soldiers next to the lieutenant swing their
carbines up and take aim at the private, who now turns and
makes a run for it. He is downed by a hail of bullets, but gets
up and limps to a wall, next to some barrels, where he takes
cover. With the troopers advancing on the downed private,
Patton points to Lunt, Hudnall, and Holmdahl, to attend to
the dead aptain, thus relieving the troopers and him to
continue their advance on Garza.

Colonel Cardenas rushes to the room where his family
is huddled, but is shocked to see Lillian and Juan comforting
them. Sweating and bleeding uncontrollably, Cardenas is
unable to take a clean shot without fear of hitting one of his
family. But this doesn't stop his outrage and threats. "I will
most certainly die...," he coughs up blood, "but not before
I..." he takes steady aim and slowly squeezes the trigger, but
is momentarily distracted by the sound of the Ranger's pump
action shotgun being cocked. Turning towards the Ranger,
he points his pistol, but Lillian and Juan make a charge at
him as his shot flies wide of the Ranger into the doorway
where it backs the lawman back into the hall.

The Colonel is knocked against the wall and down to
the ground, pistol dislodged from hand. More shots crash

through some windows of the hallway, forcing the Ranger back into the hallway even further.

Rounding the doorway once more, the Ranger is knocked back by a fleeing Cardenas dashing down the hallway towards the library for more weapons. Dodging the trapped and panicked horse which is unable to turn around in the lobby, the Colonel is able to make it to the library.

The Ranger holds his load, unable to make any clean shot, as the horse blocks his sight. Turning, he sees Lillian and Juan rushing up to him. He leans his pump action shotgun against the wall, allowing them its use, as he reaches into his duster to pull out the scatter gun and one pistol. Tipping his hat to his friends, he moves down the hall towards the library and the Colonel.

"Check that guy out over by that wall!" orders Second Lieutenant Patton. Three soldiers grasp their carbines and dash towards Private Garza, who lets go a burst of shots that pin the soldiers down and force them up against an adobe wall.

Hoping for further orders from the lieutenant, one of the soldiers looks back at Patton, only to catch a glimpse of the four *péones* still butchering the Hereford, unmoved or distracted by the firefight. They hack, slice, and cut the beef apart, indifferent to anything beyond the work at hand. Puzzled, the soldier turns back to the action as more shots from Garza keep him and the other troopers pinned down.

Emptying his revolver of bullets, Garza pulls another pistol out and fires two shots, places the gun on top of the barrel, then sights the wall and distance between himself and the soldiers as he reloads his other gun.

Whatever temperatures did not affect him before, he now feels as the heat and sweat rolls down his forehead into his eyes, hampering his vision. Wiping his eyes clear, he measures his chances of escape over the wall. He opens the chamber of the one pistol, discharges empty shells, slips in new bullets from his cartridge belt one at a time. Grabbing the pistol on top of the wooden barrel, he lets go one shot from his reloaded gun as he assesses the wall and all the factors relating to his escape.

Five shots ring out in front of him, slamming bullets above, beside, and all around the pudgy little private, smothering him in a cloud of adobe dust and dirt. He is pinned down as he hides behind the wooden barrels for cover. "*Aye...!*" he says to himself, both hands triggered on his revolvers. Protecting and covering his head, he is wide-eyed. "...Damned *gringos!*" he curses.

Kissing his two revolvers, he drags himself up, screaming and shooting at anything that moves, but he takes a quick shot from a bullet to his left shoulder, spinning him back against the wall and down to the ground. He grabs the wound as blood flows down his green fatigued shirt and onto his fingers and revolver. Raging and spitting curses, he grinds his teeth, instinctively rising, screaming, and shooting again. Once more he is hit in a volley of shots from the soldiers, downing him. Grimacing in pain from three more bullet wounds, he climbs back up to the firing line and lets go with everything he has left until a flurry of bullets finally downs him. He lies in a puddle of blood, eyes open, no longer interested in gauging distances for an escape attempt. His dead, fixed stare is already focused on the cloud-free blue skies and the heavens above.

The Colonel is loading a revolver and trying to stop the bleeding to his chest as sweat pours down his forehead. So many things to juggle, one man approaching, more just outside, waiting. He looks to his left, where one gunman awaits him, and to his right, where he sees a window—his only two choices. Silence from outside indicates the shooting has come to a stop.

Pushing the horse out of the way, the Ranger walks down the hallway towards the library with his scatter gun and pistol ready. He finally comes to a stop near the side of the doorway where he takes one last look down the hallway at his companions, where he motions them back into the room. He turns back to the doorway in deep concentration.

Cardenas senses something as he pulls his pistols up and studies the doorway and the window. The sudden silence of the fire fight concerns him as he wipes his brow and once more checks his chest wound.

Having taken all the time he can, Abner takes a deep breath, then painfully runs through the room, blindly unloading his shotgun to one side of the room, just missing the Colonel, who dives for cover and comes up shooting recklessly. The Ranger, under a table where the weapons from the arms deal are laid out, drops his scatter gun and pulls up his pistol and returns fire in Cardenas's direction. The close action between gunmen sends Cardenas in a mad dash for the window, where he leaps through, smashing the glass and tumbling onto the gravel where he gets up and starts to run for his life.

Soldiers standing over the dead body of Garza hear the broken glass and spin to see Cardenas slam to the ground, pick himself up and begin to run. Shouldering their carbines, the soldiers shoot at the Colonel.

The Ranger drags himself up, limps towards the broken window, sees Cardenas on the run, and begins emptying his pistol. Dropping one pistol, the Ranger pulls out another one as bullets fly wildly around Cardenas in his dash. Sighting the soldiers near him, Abner waves them off as he steps through the window to the gravel road. Turning on Cardenas, the Ranger takes steady aim and lets go of one well-placed shot, spinning the Colonel and sending him staggering to the gravel. Cardenas drags himself up, fires some shots, and continues his run.

"Cardenas has escaped," Juan says to Lillian as the two move from the safety of the room, down the hallway towards the library.

"I don't think so," says Lillian. "At least not just yet."

Rushing over to the soldiers who have pulled up fire on the Colonel, Lieutenant Patton queries one soldier. "What's going on?"

"There's one running along the wall," the soldier responds, pointing him out to the lieutenant. "He's about three hundred yards south of here."

"Who's that?" Patton points at the Ranger standing near the line of action.

"I don't know, Sir," replies the soldier.

Examining the Ranger from a distance, Patton orders his men to go after the Colonel. "Take him out!" cries the soldier leading the charge with three other troopers.

Lillian and Juan enter the library to see the Ranger standing outside the broken window as four soldiers rush past him with their carbines, stop, shoulder their arms and shoot.

The Ranger reloads his pistol as Lillian leans out the broken window. "Is that why you need so many guns?"

"What?" asks the surprised Ranger as he slams the cylinder of his reloaded pistol back into place.

"You miss so much you need all that back up?" she asks.

Stunned to disbelief, he just stares at her, then reaches into the back of his duster to pull out a sixteen-inch Buntline Special. Reaching into another pocket, he pulls out a wooden shoulder harness and begins assembling it on the spot, without even batting an eye.

Lillian can't believe all the armaments this man carries.

The Ranger looks at one soldier beside him, turns to Lillian, and pulls the weapon up to his shoulder and takes aim. A soldier misses his shot, kicking gravel and a cloud of dust up beside the fleeing Colonel. "Take him out," shouts Lieutenant Patton, walking towards his men as he eyes the Ranger and the little lady standing in the library looking out the broken window.

Coming to a wall, Cardenas spins and takes some wild shots as he realizes there's no way over or around the wall.

He turns one way then another, stops and shoots back at the soldiers and the Ranger. Another shot rings from the carbine of a soldier, slamming into the wall above Cardenas and covering him in adobe dust and silt.

Taking his eye off aim, the Ranger studies Patton, the troops, then turns towards Lillian and back to his aim. He squeezes off a shot that hits the mark, smashing into the Colonel's chest and slamming the man against the wall where he buckles and slides down to his knees, then to the ground. The Colonel is dead before his green fatigued trousers even touch gravel.

Patton eyes the Ranger, as soldiers come out of position into the courtyard and move towards the Lieutenant. Holmdahl, Lunt, and Hudnall finally join the procession of men walking towards Patton. Hudnall looks back at the shack where the four *péones* are *still* butchering the cow. He shakes his head and surveys the fight area.

Looking the Ranger over while eyeing Lillian in the broken window of the library, Patton says, "Sharp troops," as one khaki-clad soldier approaches him. The lieutenant eyes the trooper and barks, "Get those butchers over here! I want those bodies identified."

Holmdahl looks over the quieted area and says to the young lieutenant, "I think some of Cardenas' men are still in the area. They could have heard the gunfight."

"How many men do you think he'd have?" Patton questions.

"I don't know for sure," puzzles the scout. "Upwards to thirty. Maybe forty. Hard to tell."

Patton studies the Ranger, who's now breaking down his pistol attachment. Shouting to his troops, "Get those butchers over here, now!" he turns to the Ranger, and says, "I don't know who you are, mister, but when I finish off this sweep, I've got some questions for you."

Using the four butchers as human shields, Patton, Lunt, and two soldiers move through the house in search of other bandits. They enter the library and see the arms on the table and Lillian and Juan comforting the remaining Cardenas family members.

"Who are you?" Patton questions Lillian and Juan. Picking up a weapon and examining it, he adds, "Whose are these?"

"Those are mine," the Ranger answers, entering the room.

"And, just who are you?" asks the lieutenant.

"Lieutenant, I can explain everything," Lillian interrupts.

"Well, somebody better," responds the young officer. Looking at the Cardenas family being tended to by Juan, he turns back to the weapons on the table before focusing on the Ranger again.

Three bodies, three cars. Strapped to the hood of each vehicle as if they were hunting prizes after some weekend hunt, the lifeless figures bloat up in the heat as flies circle. The young lieutenant attends to Lillian, Juan, and the Ranger as the soldiers and scouts recount their day's work. Hudnall looks at the four *péones* sent back to work on the Hereford, butchering it. He turns to the bodies strapped to the 1910 Dodge touring cars, then back at the butchers, and shakes his head.

"Texas Ranger?" Patton says, looking Abner over in surprise. "A little out of your territory, aren't you?"

Lillian interrupts. "It's all my fault. I asked him to help me."

Looking at Juan and sizing him up, Patton lifts his head to ask, "And you?"

Interrupting again, Lillian says, "He's the one who brought us here to set up the deal. He has nothing to do with that group of revolutionaries. He was just trying to help me get my cattle back."

Digesting everything, Patton looks the group over again before turning to the automobiles and the men with him. He turns once more to the three strangers, saying,

"Okay, you don't appear to be much of a threat. You're free to go, but as far as I can tell, you're all out of your territory down here, and you should be up north in the states."

Without hesitation, the Ranger automatically responds for all of them, "Then we'll just be on our way, Lieutenant." He tips his hat to Patton and grabs Lillian and Juan. "You can count on my getting these two folks back across that border by nightfall, Sir. I want to thank you for your understanding and we'll just be movin' along, thank you very much."

Whereupon he drags his two companions away from the lieutenant and, his detail of soldiers, scouts, automobiles, and bodies.

"I don't want to ever see you down here again. Is that clear?" Patton shouts to the trio walking to their mounts tied to a hitching post in front of the main house.

Lunt approaches Patton. "Lieutenant? We should be getting back, Sir. It'll take us some time to cross the border. And them bodies...? Well, we'll be downwind of them all the way back, if you catch my drift?"

"Okay, okay," Patton replies, walking to the lead car and pausing to examine his war trophies tied to the hood of the drop-top. Turning to his driver, he says, "Forward!"

Patton jumps into the lead Dodge and settles in. As the automobiles approach the entrance gate, they suddenly come to a halt.

In the distance, fifty heavily armed men on horseback top a hill, viewing the vehicles by the hacienda with the three bodies strapped to the hoods of the automobiles. Patton looks at the driver of his vehicle and asks, "Lunt, are those Cardenas' men?"

"Hard to tell from here, Lieutenant," the scout/driver responds.

After some thought, the lieutenant says, "Well, I guess we'll just wait and find out."

The horsemen keep their distance as the small detail led by the young lieutenant hold their ground. Clearly, it is a Mexican stand-off.

The Ranger tightens the ropes of the load to the mule, but stops to take his hat off and wipe his forehead. Lillian notices the automobiles at the front gate and says, "Trouble?"

Spinning around and seeing the automobiles idling at the arched entrance, he says, "What now?"

"I'll check," says Juan as he runs to the south wall. He climbs a ladder and looks at the developing scene. The Yaqui climbs down the ladder and rushes back to his companions. "It appears to be a stand-off — Revolutionaries."

"Great! Just great!" the lawman curses as he unties the weapons loaded on the mule. "First you tie 'em down, then you transport 'em, then you display 'em, then you tie 'em back up, and now, this," looking at Lillian and Juan, struggling with the load as Juan offers some assistance.

There's an exchange of shots from both armies, but no advance. Distance outguns them all and nobody wants to engage beyond some angry shots of protest. The drivers gun their engines as two soldiers fire some warning shots. The horsemen fire small arms and rifles but fail to charge. A show of power but little intent beyond that. For every shot fired, another is answered, as side for side, the guns are discharged with no real harm coming to anyone.

Handing Lillian a Winchester and Juan a Remington repeating rifle, the Ranger reaches for some bullets in a saddlebag draped over the mule. He unbuttons his duster, reaches in and stops, turning towards the south wall, when he hears the thundering hooves of horses departing the area. It stops him in his tracks. Looking at his partners, he says, "What now?"

"I'll go check," says Juan, rushing to the wall and climbing the ladder again. He peers over the top and sees nothing, waving back an all clear sign. The three vehicles at the gate lurch forward and onto the road leading them into the desert. Juan climbs down the ladder and returns to Lillian and the Ranger.

"They have departed," Juan says, handing his weapon to the Ranger.

The Ranger shakes his head. "Don't that beat all. Over already. You know what that means?" he says to his companions.

"No," says Lillian, handing him the Winchester.

"It means I have to string this bugger back up!" he curses.

"Yes," says Juan. "But it will be for the last time."

Struggling with the load again, the lawman says, "I hope so. I'm gettin' plumb tired of all this packin' and unpackin'." He stops to look his companions over. "Just give me that open range. About the only place I can ever find a little peace and quiet."

Juan nods. "It has been difficult for us all." He walks to the other side of the mule and lends the old Ranger a hand with the load.

Patting her mare and untying the halter, Lillian says, "Well, I don't know about you two, but I'm as ready as I'll ever get to crossing that border and finally facing my father. I'm sure he's going to be disappointed in me."

"Look, you just tell him you had to take on Pancho Villa and the United States Army...," the lawman says, trying to help.

"He won't care. It's all cut and dry to him. He just wants the receipt."

"Receipt?" Juan asks, unsure of what that means.

"The bill of sale," she elaborates.

"Well," says the Ranger, finally strapping the load to the mule and untying the lead, while taking the halter for his horse, "I can't help you with a receipt, but I can go along and vouch for what happened."

"I will too," says Juan.

Lillian walks over to Juan and the Ranger and gives them each a hug.

"Don't be going soft on me, now," says the Ranger. "We've got some miles ahead of us, and we're in the middle of a desert."

The three weary adventurers walk their mounts to the front entrance of the *ranchero* as the Ranger takes one last look back at the hacienda, noticing the four *péones* still cutting away on that Hereford. They mount up and ride towards the open desert with the henny in tow.

Three touring cars pull into the base camp with the bodies of the revolutionaries strapped to the hood of each car, while Patton stands in the passenger seat as the vehicles round the parade ground and drive towards the front of the Punitive Expeditionary Forces Headquarters tent. As the lead rag-top rolls to a stop in front of HQ, Patton jumps out and walks towards the main tent while soldiers in the base camp are drawn to the spectacle.

General Pershing exits the tent in curiosity with the young lieutenant next to him. The General shakes his head in disbelief, walks towards the vehicles and the bodies that are so boldly and blatantly displayed on the hoods of each vehicle.

Nodding his head, the General goes from one car to the next until he finally stops at the last vehicle and takes his hat off. He scratches and shakes his head. Looking at the young lieutenant, he puts his hat back on. "Colonel Cardenas, Captain Lopez, and... who's this last fellow?" He points to the small bloated figure on the last drop-top.

"Garza, Sir. Private Garza."

"You had a shoot-out with these men while searching for food?" the General asks, shaking his head and questioning how such a thing could have happened.

"Yes, Sir!" responds the young lieutenant proudly.

The General looks at Patton. "In my tent. Now!" he barks. Turning and walking towards his tent, he pauses a second and turns back to Patton. "By the way," he points to the vehicles, "do something about those bodies, will you? I don't want them stinking up the camp."

Patton turns to Lunt, who's ahead of the game.

"I'll take care of 'em, Lieutenant," the scout says as he reaches for a bandanna and covers his nose, signaling the other two drivers into their cars.

Patton nods, turns and walks to the headquarters tent.

Waves of heat off the desert roll like a tidal wave over the land, washing three riders and a mule in perspiration and exhaustion. Lillian keeps shaking her head. The Ranger looks over at her and says, "What's gotten into you now?"

"I just don't know what I'm going to tell my father," she says, totally worn out and anguished.

"He will understand," Juan says, trying to comfort the little lady. "All fathers do."

Lillian reaches into her vest pocket and pulls out the Ranger badge and studies it a moment. She hands it back to the lawman. "Here's your Star," she says. "I won't be needing it anymore."

The Ranger takes the badge and looks at it a moment. He polishes it up a bit on that old canvas duster, before taking another look at these two trail worn riders beside him on this lonely ride back to the border.

"You know something?" he says to them as he reaches into his duster to put the badge away. "It took me five years to find a good place to put this star...and I haven't taken it off until I met you two."

"I'm sorry," says Lillian. "I didn't mean any harm. I just did what I thought I had to do."

In his own unique sort of way, the Ranger tries to comfort her. "Lillian, sometimes you eat the bear, and sometimes the bear eats you," shocking the little lady and the Yaqui. Seeing that it comforted nobody but himself, he adds, "Look, we gave it an honest shot."

"This much is true," confirms the Yaqui.

Curious over Juan and what had passed between him and Cardenas at the bargaining table, the lawman says, "Speaking of bear, I could barely keep a straight face when you pulled that rock out of the bag and started talking about that lead foot and all...."

"Iron boot," says Juan, adding, "And, it's a pearl."

"I feel so bad," says Lillian. "I feel like I've ruined your lives. I mean, you both could have been killed. And all for me and my cattle."

"You did not ruin my life," says Juan, turning to both riders beside him. "That was ruined a year ago when Villa and Cardenas crossed the border in Columbus, New Mexico."

Startled, the Ranger asks, "What do you mean?"

"While it is true they raided the city and burned it, they also killed seventeen innocent people," Juan recounts, adding, "One of those people was my bride."

All at once, their questions they had about this Yaqui Indian are finally answered.

Juan continues. "I'd been following them a year or more until I saw you two in pursuit. You were my only opportunity to get to them—to have justice served."

Lillian and the Ranger are stunned.

"It does not bring my bride back," says Juan, "but they won't be able to harm anyone else now."

"I didn't know," Lillian says, ashamed of herself.

The Ranger tries to ease the little lady's burden of distress. "How the hell could you have known? We only just met the man a day ago!"

Shaking her head at the Ranger in disbelief, she turns to Juan. "Juan, that's such a sad story. I'm so sorry."

"It brings an end to my travels," he explains. "Justice has been served and there is nothing more I have need for."

Lillian looks down and shakes her head, feeling completely stupid and selfish. She turns to the Ranger. "How will the Texas Rangers feel about you and your crossing the border?"

"How would they know?" responds the lawman, almost unaffected by anything.

"You DID take a sizeable amount of cash from them, didn't you? They'd have some questions or suspicions, wouldn't they?" Lillian reminds the lawman.

"Nope," he says, hanging on to the halter and riding along, as if oblivious to anything but the trail ahead. "I'll just say I strayed across the border without knowing it—if they should happen to ask." He believes that if it sounded good enough to him, it ought to sound good enough to them. "Money?" He thinks out loud. "Well, that is mine, you know. They don't have any jurisdiction over that."

"You just don't know who grateful I am to you two," Lillian says. "The sacrifices you made. The heroic efforts."

"We tried," says the lawman.

"I am sorry it did not turn out better for you," Juan says.

"Well, we're a lot wiser now for the experience," the Ranger says. "I mean, we have no reason to be down there anyhow. It isn't our revolution."

"Well, maybe it does concern us?" Juan surprisingly answers.

"How's that?" Lillian asks the Yaqui.

"Wait a minute," interrupts the Ranger. This ain't going to be about that steel foot and some rock you carry in a medicine bag, is it?"

Ignoring the lawman's words, Juan explains. "Though it appears to be a revolution to us, it is actually a great struggle for democracy—like it was for the United States. The Mexicans don't want anything more or less than what we already take for granted on our side of the border. But there are other elements at play, and we are helpless to prevent that interference."

"But why would they steal my cattle?" Lillian queries.

"They need food, too, even if the way they get it isn't so democratic."

Totally missing the point but oddly touching on another matter that is close to the heart, the Ranger says, "Little lady, you can't take on responsibility, unless you know how to handle it. Isn't that what the cattle is really about?"

"I don't know anymore," says Lillian. "But I sure do feel awful."

"Cheer up," says the Ranger. "You're alive and we'll be back in Laredo pretty soon. It might not be as bad as you think in a day or two."

"He speaks the truth," Juan says, trying to comfort the little lady, who's probably more range-worn and depleted of energy by the desert heat than anything else.

"I may not always get my man," says the Ranger with his sagebrush philosophy, "but I always learn something, and I never make the same mistake twice. I think you're being a little hard on yourself. All in all, I'd think your Pa would rather have you back alive than all the trains he can ship his cattle on." He finally hits a chord with the little lady, thus lightening the heavy load she now carries on that mare she's riding.

"Now," he adds, "you straighten up and take it like a...a.... Well, you just keep your chin up. The rest will take care of itself," the Ranger attempts to comfort the little lady.

Photographers and reporters crowd around Lieutenant George S. Patton standing and posing for pictures under the shade of a tree. Next to him are the dead bodies strapped to the hood of the touring cars.

"This was the first battle ever waged from a motorized vehicle, Lieutenant," says one reporter from the local paper as photographers snap shots. "Do you think the days of the cavalry are over?"

"Wars may be fought by men," the lieutenant answers, "but they'll still need transportation to get to the front lines."

"New York Tribune, Lieutenant," another reporter announces his credentials. "Lieutenant Patton, where do you go from here?"

"I've been assigned to General Pershing's personal staff," he says proudly.

" Hold that pose, Lieutenant," requests another reporter, taking a shot.

"Washington Post, Lieutenant," another reporter identifies the newspaper he works for. "Any war souvenirs you want to share with us?"

"I was given Cardenas' silver saddle and saber," nods the lieutenant.

"Times," shouts a different reporter, pushing his way towards the officer, pen and pad in hand, ready to spill the ink all over the paper. "What do you think of the revolution down there?"

"I'm a soldier, not a politician," Patton says. "I carry out orders. Clear and simple."

Abner, Lillian and Juan make their way through the late afternoon traffic of the border town of Laredo, as they walk their worn-out mounts to the hotel they were in the night before. Dismounting, they tie the horses and mule to the hitching post. The Ranger steps behind the henny and makes sure the ropes are tight on the old mule, then turns to his companions and says, "How about some grub?"

Worn and weary, Lillian answers, "I am a little hungry."

"Me, too," says Juan.

"Well, why don't we go across the street to the little café. That waiter ought to remember us," the Ranger says, also exhausted.

The three find an opening in the line of passing traffic of wagons, buggies, automobiles, and trucks, as one automobile grinds its gears and lurches forward, backfiring. It startles the Ranger, who reaches into his duster and looks around. Lillian grabs his arm and shakes her head.

Getting to the other side of the street, the lawman takes note of three other cowboys down the block who sport the same type of western wear he favors—dusters. Recognizing these men, the Ranger says, "Excuse me a moment. I've got some unfinished business to attend to."

"But..," says Lillian, puzzled.

"You all go on in and order. I'll be in before long," the Ranger assures his companions as he starts his labored walk down the street.

The three men offer their hands to the lawman as he walks up to them. "Welcome back, Abner," one of the cowboys greets him.

"How was it?" asks another cowboy, who is also a canvas-coated Texas Ranger with a handlebar mustache.

Abner is surprised that they knew of his exploits. He shrugs his shoulders. "It was unexpected."

"What? The shootout or the cattle?" Another Ranger with a slight growth of beard standing between the other Texas Rangers asks.

Abner is even more surprised. Suspiciously and cautiously, he asks, "How'd you know about the shootout and the cattle?"

The third close-shaven Texas Ranger eyes old Abner and says, ""We keep tabs on our people. Especially ones like you, Abe."

"I didn't break no code or rule, did I?" asks QAbner.

"No," says the unshaven Texas Ranger. "We wanted to congratulate you. We think you did a pretty good job down there."

Even more suspicious, Abner squints at these lawmen, eyeing them. "Just what do you mean, 'a good job'?"

"We just got word out of Nuevo Laredo three hours ago," says the mustached Texas Ranger.

Lifting his jaw and pointing his chin to his fellow lawmen, while eyeing them"Yeah? Well, what was so good about the job I'm supposed to have done? I couldn't bring the cattle back!"

The clean-shaven Texas Ranger explains, "Without any care or interest to yourself or your well-being, you willingly went into hostile territory, intent on helping this lady get her cattle back. You know, that little lady you were with?"

"I reckon after almost two full days, yeah, I semi-sorta got a bead on her," Abner says, eyeing the three men in front of him. "What of it?"

"Her father's a very important man in Oklahoma," the mustached lawman says.

"Yeah, I heard all about it on the trail. What of it?" Abner responds in anger.

"He got in touch with the governor's office here, alerting us to everything," says the unshaven lawman. "But we did some other research of our own and wanted to inform you that, while you might have crossed that border to help out that little lady, you crossed another border we thought you ought to know about."

"And what border might that be?" asks the cranky, worn-out Abner.

"You're the first Texas Ranger to engage in action across the border this century! The last Ranger to do that was Lee McNelly, back in 1877!" says the mustached Texas Ranger.

"And before I forget," says the clean-shaven Texas Ranger, "the Army located the cattle train after that shootout and they're bringing it in now! The cattle were saved and the little lady will be able to receive the goods once it crosses the border."

Extending his hand, the mustached Texas Ranger says, "We just wanted to congratulate you for upholding the good name of the Texas Ranger. And we hope you don't mind if we talk to your two friends."

Relieved, the Ranger shakes all their hands. "Why sure. Just follow me. We were just about to get something to eat. Why don't you all join us a spell?" Abner turns and leads the men down the street to the restaurant.

Sitting at the same table next to the same window, facing the same street, Lillian and Juan are looking over the menu when the four Texas Rangers enter the establishment and approach them. Abner takes a seat and says, "These are some Texas Ranger that want a word with you," he tells Lillian.

The mustached Texas Ranger says, "Lillian? We've got some news for you."

"Yes?" Lillian answers.

"That train that made off with all your cattle?

"Yes?" repeats Lillian.

"It should be rolling into town any time now."

Surprised and greatly relieved, Lillian claps her hands and smiles. Thrilled by what she's just heard, she leans over and kisses Juan then grabs Abner's hands. "I don't know what to say!" She looks up at the three Texas Rangers, filled with joy and surprise.

"There really isn't anything to say," says the clean-shaven Texas Ranger, adding, "It's your property and you can expect it directly, after it crosses that border. We can't account for the condition of the animals, but we know the train is in transit."

"I just can't believe it," sighs Lillian in great relief.

"There is just one other thing," says the mustached Texas Ranger. "Because of the extreme nature surrounding this situation, we received word from the Adjutant General's office that you two," he looks at Juan, "are to be sworn in as Texas Rangers!"

Lillian and Juan are shocked.

"Texas Rangers?" Lillian gasps in disbelief.

"That is quite an appointment after what we have just come through," says the Yaqui, totally surprised.

"I reckon they'll be taking my place on the range, next," comments Abner who is in for a different kind of surprise himself.

"I'm afraid not, Abe," says the mustached Ranger. "We've got another assignment for you, but you'll have to come to the office for the wanted poster on that—he's supposed to be in the general area—so you can train these two new Rangers on the job."

"On the job?" Abner protests. "On the job? First of all, they haven't agreed to the swearing in. Second, I'm used to working alone. And...."

He is cut off by the clean-shaven Texas Ranger, "The report we got was good, Abe. You can't buck the Adjutant General's office, and you're just the right man to train the first female Texas Ranger and Yaqui Indian."

"If that train comes in with all the cattle, I could be tempted," says Lillian, sort of scaring Abner a bit.

"You can count on me," says Juan, scaring Abner even more.

"Now, guys," Abner pleads with the lawmen, "I was just helpin' the little lady out. You don't want me taking her out there to the badlands with me, do you? And Juan? He carries these strange things in that medicine bag of his, not to mention some of these thoughts about metal shoes and all...."

"By appointment," says the mustached Texas Ranger.

"Stop by the office for the swearing in after your supper," says the unshaven Texas Ranger. "We'll set you up with that wanted poster to get you started." Tipping their hats to Lillian, Juan, and Abner, the three Texas Rangers depart the little café, leaving Abner a bundle of nerves.

"The cattle returned. I'm asked to join the Texas Rangers," Lillian says. "It's like a dream!"

"I am very proud," announces Juan as he reaches over and shakes Lillian's hand.

"I'm scared," says Abner, shaking his head.

"Why?" asks Lillian, concerned, yet serious.

"Because I'm going to have to train you," says Abner. "And I've never trained anyone before...which, quite honestly, should be of some concern to you as well."

"Didn't you tell me an old territorial Ranger once trained you?" Lillian asks Abner.

"A long time ago."

"Well, you can start by training some new friends. Right, Juan?"

"*Si*," says Juan. "I agree."

"See here," Abner protests, unable to stop Lillian from leaning over the table and giving him a kiss, shaking the old coot up even more.

The electric lights flutter and dance a moment, startling everyone but Abner, who sits there looking at these two new trainees of his, very concerned about the job that has been imposed on him.

"It was only a power shortage," Lillian laughs.

Staring at the little lady and Juan, Abner just shakes his head as he looks beyond them to the electric lights. "You know, I just don't know if I'll ever get used to this new century."

"Well, you've made it this far. You might as well get used to it," Lillian says, smiling.

Shaking his head and squinting at the two new employees before him, Abner says, "Yeah, I reckon so.... I reckon I'm going to have to get used to a lot of new things, aren't I?"

"Don't worry," says Lillian. "We'll always be at your side."

"That's what worries me," says the concerned Ranger, eyeing the two. "Who'll cover my rear?" Lillian and Juan laugh.

A squat and tubby waiter approaches the table and asks, "May I take your order?"

Three touring cars filled with Army Regulars drive past the window down the crowded street towards the border. As they disappear into the busy traffic at sunset, as the city lights spark, fuse and ignite, where the sound of a train whistle clearly cuts through the early evening air.

FOUR WEEKS,
ONE DAY LATER

Hot as the underside of a skillet just off a burning stove and as thick with humidity as the stinging sensation off some splattered grease, is this June day, at the southwestern base camp of the Punitive Expeditionary Forces. Dust kicked up by a prototype armored vehicle rounding the corner and rolling towards a review stand near the makeshift parade ground, rises and falls so fast, it resembles exhaust.

Little cutout slats have replaced the front windows of this newly-designed armored car, and though the driver can't be easily seen or shot at during close military action, this mobile unit is clearly under the control of somebody as it races down that dusty road and adjusting to every bump and dip in the road. It zips along at almost twenty-five miles an hour.

The vehicle passes the review stand and drives around the target range once more, finally stopping in front of some bleachers. It backs up and comes to a rest, out of range of the weapons display and targets setup not more than one hundred feet from the review stand.

General John J. "Blackjack" Pershing, First Lieutenant George S. Patton, Captain Frederick M. Turner, and several other staff officers sit in review as Major Leonard Hutton addresses the assembly.

"In addition to this prototype vehicle, there are a new generation of weapons we will now be displaying for you." The major, dressed in a khaki uniform and tie, signals a trooper standing on a wooden platform in front of the target range. The soldier returns the major's signal, prompting Major Hutton to shout, "Fire at will!"

The trooper moves into action, by removing a green canvas tarp from an object yhen reaching for a round metal magazine case which he attaches to the top of a machine gun, mounted on a tripod which he begins shooting at a distant target.

"This is the Lewis machine gun," shouts Major Hutton to the military assembly in the stands, trying to be heard over the rapid firing of the automatic weapon. "It can shoot five hundred and fifty rounds per minute. It can be mounted to an armored car, aeroplane, or even a motorcycle side car!"

The trooper continues to spray shots from target to target, displaying depth and range on accuracy and effectiveness.

"It carries fifty rounds per magazine and comes in various calibers. It can be quickly reloaded and attached to any vehicle or..." Hutton signals the trooper again, "it can be held by hand."

The trooper removes the machine gun from the tripod, holds it at his side, and fires, spraying the various targets on the open range, once more showing the versatility of the rapid fire weapon. When the trooper stops firing, the echoes off the weapon reverberate over the testing range and review stand until it diminishes into sound waves that ring, flutter and die into a silence that clears the air of any other sound.

General Pershing nods to his staff in approval.

Major Hutton points to the trooper again, who returns the signal, now removing another canvas tarp, revealing another weapon.

"The next weapon is the clip-fed Maxim machine gun. It discharges three hundred and thirty-three rounds in thirty seconds. It also comes in various calibers," shouts the major. The trooper steps up to the tripod-mounted weapon, feeds and sets ammo, sits down and fires the weapon across the open target range, spraying bursts from target to target.

"It's only limited by the amount of bullets available to it," shouts Major Hutton to the officers in the reviewing stand.

Bullets rip through the targets and kick up dirt behind it. Close or long, the bullets shred their intended bulls-eyes, tracking the ground in aim.

General Pershing nods to his staff once more, impressed by what he sees.

Hutton turns from the target range, focuses on the general staff and pauses to allow the reverberation off the Maxim gun silence before going on with his next description.

"The final prototype weapon will receive a patent within a week and should be in general service shortly thereafter. This weapon was designed and perfected by General John Talliaferro Thompson and will revolutionize warfare for the common foot soldier," shouts the major, signaling the trooper on the platform.

The soldier walks over to a trunk and unlatches it. He reaches in and pulls out a Thompson submachine gun and attaches a round flat magazine to the underbelly, sets the bolt and steps up to the firing line. He holds the weapon to his shoulder and fires. He stops, lowers the weapon to his waist and shoots the lightweight weapon from there. Swinging the weapon from side to side, the soldier provides an excellent display of the weapon's lethal power and capabilities.

Turning to his staff officers, General Pershing nods once more.

"Each magazine holds fifty, forty-five caliber bullets and can be easily reloaded and serviced by the operator," shouts the major to the assembly. "We are certain this weapon will drastically impact the future of warfare as the machine gun has generally been used for purposes of defense. This weapon will now allow the freedom of mobility and offense.

Removing the empty magazine and reloading a new one, the soldier yanks the bolt back and braces himself as he continues firing at the various targets on range. It is an awesome spectacle of fire power and versatility as the soldier once more shows the speed and efficiency of reloading and firing.

The thundering roar of the automatic machine fire off the testing range diminishes into hushed rings and echoes as the major takes one step forward and shouts, "This concludes our demonstration for the day. Any and all questions should be answered in the report being handed out right now."

Three fatigued soldiers pass out folders to the staff officers. One by one, the pages are opened and reviewed by the general staff. When General Pershing stands, the rest of the assembled officers follow his lead. One by one, they make their way down the bleachers and walk towards the target range to inspect and review the targets for a final view on the impact of these various weapons.

"Lieutenant," General Pershing says to First Lieutenant Patton, who's making his way down the stairs for the review.

Patton salutes the General, who returns the salute.

"Sir!" sounds the lieutenant, snapping to attention.

"I want you to meet Captain Turner," says the General, introducing him to the sharp, well-trimmed officer standing next to the Brigadier. "Captain Frederick M. Turner of the 13th Cavalry."

The lieutenant offers his hand to the officer. "Captain." Patton is surprised by the firmness of Turner's handshake.

"Lieutenant," responds the Captain as he looks the young lieutenant over.

"George," says the General to Patton, "I'm assigning you to Captain Turner's command for three days. You'll be his assistant and obey his every order. The 13th has a long and distinguished history in the Army. I don't want to see you tarnish their fine reputation or tradition."

"Yes, Sir!" says Lieutenant Patton. "It'll be an honor and a privilege to ride with Captain Turner. I'm well aware of the reputation and history of the Buffalo Soldiers."

The gravel-lined streets of the small western town still carries an edge of the last century as cowboys, Indians, and Mexicans wander down the boardwalk. Carriages, riders on horseback, automobiles, bicycles, buckboards, and motorcycles pass at no great speed or in any special lane, as it looks more like a free for all as these vehicles vie for position in traffic.

Electric lights spot this active little border town on the edge of Mexico, but you'd be hard pressed to believe that, judging by the ragtime music sweeping from the saloons and honky-tonks the town openly offers in its night life. The film, "The Plainsman," is displayed on the marquee of a small storefront theater.

In the maddened pace of this little town on the edge of the new century, Abner Caleb casually rides through the dusty roadway on his Appaloosa, making his way past the maze of traffic until he comes to a boarding house. He dismounts and looks over the building, adjusting his floor-length duster. Walking over to a hitching post in a funny, labored sort of gait, he ties his halter to a post and proceeds up the rickety old wooden stairs in that curious walk of his. He turns and glances down the street in both directions, distracted by a street light that blinks continuously. Shaking his head and refitting that old Stetson of his, he enters the building.

Looking the lobby over and sizing it up, he's reminded that they all basically look the same after all the years he's been through: a couch, table, chairs, old peeling wallpaper that's coming unglued from the ceilings where that hot Texas heat always rises. Then there's the chandelier, a vase, another painting depicting the landscape of the area, a statue of little concern and the old wooden counter with the mail slots and room keys backing it up.

With no attendant there to keep an eye on the old register sitting on top of the counter, he wanders over to spin it around and read through it. Eyeing the mail slots and keys, he turns and continues that labored and curious walk of his towards the stairs where he grabs the bannister and pulls his way up, step by step.

Reaching the top of the stairs and looking down the darkened hallway, the Ranger adjusts that long canvas overcoat of his, grits his teeth and begins his walk that resembles a waddle more than a step by step advance, as he arrives at a door in the middle of the hallway and comes to a stop.

Taking off his hat and wiping the perspiration from his forehead, he removes his gloves and unbuttons the duster as he focuses on the door. He pulls out a double-barreled scatter gun and a Colt .45 from inside the duster. Blinking a couple times and studying the door, he takes a deep breath, shakes his arms to loosen up and help adjust to the different weights of weapons in his hands.

Another moment of deep concentration, another look down at the weapons in his hands, another look at the door and he's ready. He takes a small step backwards, lifts his weapons, and gritting his teeth, kicks the door open.

A fat old bald-headed man in a compromising position atop a beautiful lady in the bed cries, "Damn!" The pretty little lady screams as they both pull the covers over themselves.

"I knew my husband would find out!" shouts the terrified pretty little lady who is twenty-five years the junior of the chunk of fat lying on top of her.

"Excuse me," says the embarrassed Texas Ranger, apologizing. "I have the wrong room!" seeing the room number swinging on the door, minus one nail.

"I'll say!" says the chubby bald-headed man.

The Ranger stops the swinging metal number on the door with his gun, saying, "Yep," nodding confirmation in adding, "This does appear to be the wrong room."

The bald-headed man glares at the Ranger, then his bed partner. "What kind of boarding house is this? They don't even have room service here."

The gal breaks down as the bald-headed man looks down at her to add, "Oh, keep quiet."

The Ranger is unsettled by the mistake. He tries to shut the door and make an exit, but the lock is broken and it won't shut. He struggles with the door knob again and again, finally abandoning the effort. He tips his hat, says, "I'm...ah...ah...I'm sorry. I made a mistake." He quickly turns and exits down the hallway. Still shaking his head and mumbling to himself, he more closely checks the door numbers as he further walks down the darkened corridor.

Stopping at room number nine, he carefully checks the number, even reaching up with that Colt and pushing it a bit to check the waters for missing nails. Satisfied, he steps back, looks down the hallway and sees the chubby baldheaded man and lady peering out from their room. He shakes his head, motioning them back into their room, then lifting his foot, he puts it through the door, smashing it wide open. Another pretty lady lay in bed. She screams, pulling the covers over her.

A young Mexican man leaps from the other side of the bed, grabs his pants, and jumps out the open window.

The Ranger tips his hat to the woman peeking out from behind the covers. "Pardon me, ma'am," he says, entering the room and letting go the scatter gun and putting a hole in the wall next to the window.

Walking past the bed to the window, the Ranger sticks his head out in time to see the escapee leaping from the building ledge to an overhang, and down to the ground where he dashes across a busy street filled with traffic.

The Ranger pockets the scatter gun, pulls the Winchester out, and takes aim, but holds fire as too many people are in the way. He next sees the young man leap into the back of an automobile where a fight breaks out between him and the driver.

"Damn!" says the Ranger, pocketing the Winchester and turning around—tipping his hat to the lady—then dashing out the door to the hallway towards the stairs.

Rushing down the steps, the Ranger pushes his way past four cowpokes signing the register in the lobby, prompting one of the cowboys to say, "Hey! Watch it, dude!"

Stopping, the Ranger lifts his Colt to the cowboy's face, not realizing the weapon is scaring the living daylights out of the cowpoke, snarling, "You're going to have to excuse my behavior as I'm sort of in a hurry at the moment."

Wasting no time, Abner dashes out the front door, to the boardwalk, where he sees the young man has won the fight with the automobile driver and has now commandeered the vehicle, as the driver lay sprawled out on the gravel roadway in the middle of traffic.

Grinding gears, the young man guns the vehicle through the traffic, finally gaining freedom off the congested street, by accelerating out of town down a side street.

The Ranger opens his duster and holsters the Colt, as several people on the street are startled to see all this armament he's carrying under that floor-length coat. Completely oblivious to their stares, he squints and grits his teeth as he reaches for his gloves and walks towards his horse tied up at the hitching post.

With his attention on the escaping motorist making a turn off the main street and disappearing, the Ranger walks his horse towards the middle of the street before climbing aboard the high-spirited steed, he spurs after his prey.

The chubby little displaced baldheaded man comes rushing out of the boarding house with nothing on but a bed sheet covering him, shouting, "Come back here, you coward! Come back and fight like a man!"

The four cowpokes at the counter are startled as they gaze at this half-naked baldheaded man standing on the boardwalk cursing, ranting and shaking his fist at the now departed Texas Ranger.

The Ranger negotiates traffic, picking up momentum and a head of steam as he finally reaches the edge of town and makes a wide turn, where he drops the reins and lets his Appaloosa earn its keep.

Driving frantically, the young man behind the wheel of the Model T looks behind to see if he's free and clear in his escape from town. Incredibly, that long-coated man is on his horse giving chase and gaining on him! Scared beyond his wits, the young man grabs the stick shift and grinds the gear, flooring the gas pedal and kicking up some dust and dirt as the automobile jerks and lurches forward, going even faster now.

Seeing the gap between him and the escapee lengthen, the Ranger is angered. He reaches into his duster, pulls a Colt and takes aim, but shoots high as a warning shot instead.

The young man, scared out of his heebeejeebees, ducks behind the steering wheel, coming up, looking back and grinding more gears, in trying to find more speed in the tin lizzy.

The Ranger takes another shot from the Colt with zero effect on the motorist, except to scare him into higher breakneck speeds of almost thirty miles an hour.

The Model T gains considerable distance from the Ranger, as his bullets are ineffective in slowing the driver down. Turning back and seeing the gap he's advanced in escape, the young man grabs the wheel of the buggy, straightens up in the seat, and, begins to laugh.

Confidently, he reaches out of the vehicle and grasps the little hand horn, squeezing off a couple of few honks before laughing again. He's free and clear now. Taking one last look behind, the young man sees that the canvas-clad old cowboy is losing ground and is actually slowing down. It's a free ride now, thinks the young man.

Coming to a stop, the Ranger dismounts, reaches into his duster and pulls out a Buffalo gun. He kneels, takes steady aim, and squeezes off one thunderous roar of a shot, bucking him like a mule, and almost standing him up, where he was just kneeling.

The bullet rips through the rear of the vehicle, passes through to the front seat, through the dashboard, leaving a huge hole there, finally coming to rest in the engine, which now stutters, kicks, and whines as internal fluids splash onto the windshield and steam is forced out the side of the hood of the now disabled vehicle.

"Damned *gringo!*" shouts the young man, slamming his fist on the steering wheel and cursing. Realizing he's now one hell of a big target out there in this vast, empty wasteland.

The Ranger stands, puts the thunder gun in the inside pocket of the duster, then walks over to his horse and mounts the beast. Spurring it to a trot, he 's satisfied that this deliberate pace is all that's needed to catch the disabled vehicle and its occupant now.

The tin lizzy is puffing smoke from its exhaust, and, moaning in the engine area as it clinks, clunks, and finally collapses in loss of power. The motor has stopped hacking and coughing as sizzling steam releasing itself from a blown-out radiator is barely heard in the slight gust of wind and motion.

Looking back in panic, the young man leaps from the slowing vehicle and makes a run for it, deciding his foot power is faster than the disabled Model T's. Picking himself up off the desert sand and sighting the oncoming rider, he dashes into the vast expanse of desert as the tin lizzy finally rolls to a stop.

The Ranger maintains his steady pace on his trusted horse.

Running and looking back, the young man darts between rocks and plant growth, not really knowing what to do beyond attempting a desperate escape from the quickly advancing cowboy in the duster. There's nothing in front of him but the desert, and nothing behind him but his worst fears.

The Ranger pulls even with the young man, letting his horse do the rest. It knocks the young man down.

Scrambling to his feet, the young man dashes in another direction as the Ranger reins in his Appaloosa and pursues him from another direction. The beast knocks him down again.

Reaching into his duster, the Ranger pulls out his Colt and takes a shot. But the gun is empty. He looks into the chamber, shakes his head, and puts it away. He pulls out another pistol and fires one shot into the ground in front of the fleeing young man, stopping him in his tracks.

The young man throws his hands up and faces the lawman. He sees a serious old Texas Ranger approaching him on horseback with a Colt .45 leveled at him.

"Don't shoot! Don't shoot," he yells, scared out of his mind.

Advancing on him, the Ranger says, "Then you best keep those hands where I can see 'em."

"I didn't do nothing, mister. Honest!" pleads the young man as he watches the Ranger circle him on that horse of his.

"We'll see about that," says the lawman as he jumps to the ground. Keeping the Colt aimed on the young man, he reaches into his duster and digs around for some handcuffs. He finds them, pulls them out, and tosses them at the young man. Using his pistol as a pointer, he motions the young man towards the links and says, "You put those on and we'll just get all this straightened out." He smiles at the young upstart and adds, "Won't we?"

"But I didn't do nothing, mister!" the young fellow pleads, shaking his head.

Leveling the pistol at the fellow's chest, the Ranger says, "Then there ain't nothing to fear, right?" He twitches his eyebrows and smiles at the young fellow.

The young man bends down and picks up the shackles. "Honest, mister," he shakes his head and goes on. "You got the wrong man."

The Ranger lowers his Colt and lets go a shot at the young man's feet, kicking up sand and dust on him.

"Okay, okay, already. You don't have to kill me," the fellow says.

"Put those shackles on and be quick about it," orders the Ranger one last time.

Putting the handcuffs on and sounding them to lock, the young fellow stands before the lawman, asking, "What am I supposed to have done?"

"Well," says the Ranger, nodding at the Model T. "How about rustling that there automobile for starters?"

"He tried to run me down," says the young man, shaking his head.

"Ain't no excuse," says the Ranger.

"That's all you got on me," replies the young man.

"We'll see about that when we get back to town. There might be some other stuff regarding you, but there is that matter of a bank robbery I came after you for to begin with."

"Bank robbery?" says the young man, confused.

"Yeah," responds the Ranger. "You plugged a bank teller and made off with eighty-five dollars." He pauses a moment to study the young man. "That's eighty-five dollars you're going to be thinking about a long, long time."

Shaking his head, the young man says, half laughing, "You got the wrong man, Marshal."

"I ain't no MARSHAL boy!" roars the Ranger, insulted and angered. "I'm Texas Ranger! Now, I figure you got a long walk ahead of you, so, you don't want to put too much distance between the two of us." He opens his duster, revealing the armament under that duster of his. "Understand?" nodding.

The young man is set square on where he currently stands with the law. Seeing the fire power under that duster, he puts his head down and begins the long walk back to the town from which he has just tried to escape.

Horses, buggies, automobiles, and trucks pass each other on the graveled streets just outside the front door of this town jail, as two figures walk past the window to the door. Pushing the shackled young man into the office, the Ranger follows, surprising a deputy seated behind a desk, talking to Lillian and Juan.

Jumping to her feet, Lillian rushes over to grab the young man, saying to the Ranger, "You didn't have to handcuff him. He's just a boy!"

"Don't be fooled. He's man enough," replies the Ranger.

"He roughed me up pretty awful, lady," the young man says to Lillian.

"How could you?" Lillian looks at the Ranger accusingly.

"He fell," says the Ranger.

She lifts the young man's chin and looks him in the eye. "Did he threaten you?"

Twitching his eyes and jerking his head back, he says, "I'll say. He shot me!"

"I did not," says the Ranger. He looks at the little lady. "Look, will you just jail him?"

Grabbing the young man's shoulders and looking him in the eye again, she asks, "Where do you come from?"

"Chihuahua," says the young man, looking at the Ranger proudly.

"You're a long way from home," says Juan, looking at both the Ranger and the young man.

"Where are your parents?" asks Lillian.

"They're dead," the young man responds.

"Any brothers or sisters?" Lillian asks with some concern.

"Trust me," says the Ranger. "This is a one-of-a-kind."

"You keep out of this," Lillian says.

Two automobiles collide head-on outside the office, and it's just enough of a distraction to divert attention. The two drivers wearing dusters, goggles and hats, get out of their respective cars to inspect the damage and argue over it. Steam rises from both cars as the drivers attempt to pull the vehicles apart unsuccessfully, starting a push-and-shove match.

Shaking his head, the Ranger spins and walks out to the street to restore order. He separates the two men and inspects the damage. Turning to his left, he raises his hand to silence the crowd. Turning to his right, he holds his other hand up to calm everyone down.

Inside the jailhouse office, Lillian turns to the young man. "What's your name?" she asks.

"Francisco Arango," he replies.

Juan looks at Lillian strangely, then at the young man. "Francisco Arango? Isn't that Pancho Villa's real name?"

"*Si,*" says Frank. "We are both named Francisco Arango. But HE changed his name to Pancho Villa."

"What do they call you?" asks Juan.

"Frank," answers the young man.

"Do you have any brothers or sisters?" Lillian asks again.

"I had a sister," Frank says.

"Had?" questions Juan.

"She is dead now," Frank says, getting angry at all the personal questions.

"A casualty of the revolution?" Juan asks.

"The casualty of a Colorado Lieutenant," spits Frank in disgust. "He raped my sister and I killed him. If I go back and get caught, they'll kill me."

"Settle down," Lillian says, trying to comfort him.

"Why are you here?" Juan asks in curiosity.

Silencing himself, Frank suddenly turns cold and indifferent to the questioning.

Out on the street, the Ranger successfully prevents another scuffle between the drivers for the time being.

"We're only trying to help you," says Lillian, sympathetically.

"I don't need no help," Frank answers defiantly.

"We can't let you go," Juan tells him.

Throwing his head back and laughing as he looks the tiny jail over, Frank says, "My friends will break me out of here."

"Where will you go then,?" Lillian asks.

"Across the border," Frank responds confidently.

"You say you're a wanted man over there," Juan reminds him.

"I'm a wanted man over here," Frank says proudly, as if he was receiving an award or something. "What difference does it make to you?"

"We're here to help you," Lillian tries to assure him.

While out on the street, one of the drivers in the car crash takes a wild swing at the other driver, causing another fight. The Ranger tries to separate them but is unsuccessful. Shaking his head in exasperation, he reaches into his duster for the Buffalo gun. When they finally see the weapon, they stop their fight and back up with hands raised. The Ranger motions them back to their cars, which they're glad to comply with.

Back in the office, Juan asks the young man again. "Why are you here?

Frank stands silent.

"Do you want to go to jail?" Lillian questions him in exasperation..

"Do what you must," replies Frank.

"Who sent you here?" Juan now asks.

Lillian notices Frank's tension. She turns to Juan. "You struck a nerve." Turning back to Frank, she asks, "Do you want me to bring the Ranger back?"

Visibly shaken at that thought, Frank says, "Okay, okay, already." Looking around to see that no one else can hear him, he says, "Lujan. Pedro Lujan. He's an aid to Pedro Villa."

"Villa, again," Juan says, shaking his head.

Out on the street, the Ranger successfully coaxes the drivers into their cars and puts his Buffalo gun back into his duster pocket. To get a better view of the head-on-collision, the Ranger signals both drivers to back up.

In the jailhouse office, Juan says to Lillian, "I'll return." He steps out the front door to the street, walks past the Ranger who's still trying to figure out why the automobiles won't separate.

Lillian says to Juan, "We're only trying to help."

"Then let me go," says Frank.

Shaking her head, Lillian says, "I can't do that. But if you tell me why you came across the border, maybe there's something I'll be able to do later."

Outside the office on the street, the Ranger climbs up on the bumpers of the two automobiles, and starts jumping on them, trying to separate them from each other.

In the office, Frank thinks a moment, then turns to Lillian, finally opening up. "They are planning a raid into Texas."

"Like the raid in Columbus, New Mexico?" Lillian asks, alarmed.

"*Si,*" says Frank. "I am part of an advance group."

When are they going to attack? Where?" Lillian tries to encourage the young man to talk more.

After a moment's hesitation, Frank says, "I'm supposed to return with the information."

Juan walks in through the door with some papers in his hands. "I've got it," he says.

"Wait a minute," she tells Juan. Then staring at Frank, she waits for his response to her urgent question. "Where do they intend to attack?"

Biting his lip, no longer able to stall, Frank says, "El Paso."

"El Paso? Why El Paso?"

"This might help," Juan interrupts, handing Lillian the papers in his hand.

Lillian studies the sheet, flipping through the pages.

The Ranger is finally able to separate the two automobiles and waves them to back up. Stepping into the middle of the street, he directs one vehicle to go one way and the other vehicle the other way. Then he motions the rest of the traffic to move forward. Having finished doing his duty, he returns to the office.

Lillian is studying some papers in her hands as the Ranger walks in.

"What's that," Frank asks Juan, nodding at the papers Lillian is reading.

"Be still!" growls the Ranger.

Looking up from the sheets, Lillian says, "Abner Caleb, you lay off the boy."

"Boy?" the Ranger shakes his head, pointing at the young man. "This...boy shot a teller and robbed a bank."

"I'll take care of this," Lillian says to the Ranger, who's fit to be tied after having just stopped a fight between two crazy automobile drivers on a hot dusty street, then, coming in to the office to find this shackled punk sweet-talking the little lady.

"Did you say Lujan?" Lillian asks Frank once more. "Pedro Lujan?"

"*Si*," nods Frank. He sees the Ranger and lowers his head.

"What's all this?" asks the Ranger.

Juan looks at the Ranger and explains. "This is a communique I remembered filing. It says Lujan was at Columbus."

"Frank says they're preparing for another raid. This time on El Paso," Lillian informs him.

The Ranger studies the young man. "Frank, huh? That what they call you? Frank!" He peers directly into the young man's face, scaring him even more. "Well, Frank, we'll see about this El Paso thing." He opens his duster, reaching for a hog leg and waddles to the door.

"Where do you think you're going?" Lillian asks.

The Ranger stops and spins around. "I'm going to stop this Lujan character before he does any serious damage."

"You don't even know where he is, for goodness' sake! How are you going to find him?"

"I'll find him shortly," says the Ranger.

"No way, *gringo*," says Frank.

Pulling a long-barreled revolver out of his duster and slowly bringing it up and pointing it at Frank, the Ranger looks at the young punk, saying, "You want me to part your hair at the eyebrows?" cocking the pistol and squaring his aim. "Now, where is he?"

Startled, Lillian pushes the revolver up and shoves the Ranger back. "You go get something to eat down the street and cool off, Mister. We'll be down in a minute."

Uncocking the pistol, he holsters the weapon, closes his duster and glares at Juan, then the deputy seated at the desk. Turning, he stomps out of the office and down the boardwalk.

Exiting the jail and walking down the boardwalk like a lit fuse ready to go off, the Ranger bumps into the baldheaded man and that pretty lady from the hotel as they step out onto the boardwalk.

"Excuse me," says the man, finally recognizing who he has just bumped into, shouts, "You again. Why, I ought to...."

"What?" interrupts the Ranger, itching for a fight. "What are you going to do?" Shaking his head, he dismisses the baldheaded man and moves on past him. The little lady shies in passing. The Ranger stops, turns to the lady. "Are you sure this guy's better than your husband?" Tipping his hat to her, he takes one last look at the chubby baldheaded man and continues his walk down the wooden walkway.

Further down the boardwalk, the Ranger steps off the wooden planks to his horse that's tethered to a hitching post. He removes the saddlebags from the horse and walks back to the boardwalk and enters a small restaurant a little further down the street and finds a table. Placing the saddlebags over the back of one chair, he pulls up another one and straddles it.

As he looks out the window, checking his position from the street, a waiter wearing a white shirt, black vest, and, bow tie approaches.

"Sir? Our specials for the day are...."

The lawman cuts him off. "Just bring me a steak."

"But you didn't hear what our catch-of-the-day is," the waiter protests, shaking his head.

Looking at the order taker, the Ranger says, "Beef! Corn-fed beef! That's all! Just give me a slab of meat. You have that, don't you?"

"Well," says the surprised waiter, "how would you like it?"

"On a plate. In front of me," answers the Ranger.

"I mean..., how would you like to have it cooked?"

"Cooked?" says the lawman. He squints at the waiter then turns back to the window. "Rare," he finally says.

After the waiter leaves, the Ranger reaches for his saddlebags and pulls out a box of cartridges and places it on the table. Pulling a pistol out of his duster, he unloads the spent cartridges and loads new ones from the box. Completed with one weapon, he holsters it and pulls out another revolver. He unloads and reloads all his weapons with bullets, leaving spent shell·casings in a pile on the table.

Just as he's done loading the last gun, the waiter appears through the swinging butterfly doors.

"Something to drink?" the order taker asks.

"How about a tall, cool one?" says the thirsty lawman.

"I can bring you a fine imported wine," says the waiter.

Shaking his head, the Ranger says, "Coffee." The waiter nods just as Lillian and Juan enter the restaurant and see the ranger in the corner. "Two more," he shouts, as the waiter nods again and returns to the kitchen.

Lillian and Juan seat themselves, but seeing the spent casings and boxed bullets on the table, Lillian asks, "Why didn't you load those weapons when you were at the jail?"

"Because you chased me out!" he responds. Studying them, "Did you jail that little...."

"Boy!" Lillian finishes for him. "He's just a boy."

"You know, that boy winged a man who might have had a wife and family that depended on him," the Ranger tells the little lady. "What if he lost his life over eighty-five dollars? Do you think time in jail is ever going to repay that eighty-five dollars?"

"He's safely behind bars. The Deputy has control of him now," she says.

Three young Mexican men ride boldly down the center of the street on horseback. They are met by a fourth one as they approach the jail.

While one man silently walks to the side of the building as lookout, the three men on horseback get off their mounts, tie them to the hitching post in front of the jail, and walk towards the door of the jailhouse pulling their revolvers. The lookout changes his position and walks over to the front of the jailhouse, and stands watch on the street.

Lillian hands several sheets of paper to the Ranger, who puts his revolver on the table as he takes the pages and goes through them. "There's the information on that boy," says Lillian.

"Uh-huh," says the Ranger, flipping through the papers.

"He's part of Pedro Lujan's group," Lillian continues. "They operate across the border. Lujan's supposed to be an advisor to Pancho Villa."

"What else?" asks the Ranger, looking at Lillian and Juan.

"Lujan needs money for arms, so he sent some youngsters across the border to rob some banks. Since they're young, Lujan figured nobody would shoot them and they couldn't be held for very long as they're only teenagers."

"Bad guess," says the Ranger, going back to review the papers.

"There's more," says Lillian. "Word is, Villa is mounting another attack across the border soon."

"Like Columbus," Juan says in concern.

Turning the papers over and reading the other side, the Ranger finally asks, "How do they get this information?"

"Villa has several advisors, it would seem," Lillian says. "This document comes from an American aide," she adds, "and, he reports of a German officer of high rank being involved."

"German?" the Ranger says, putting the papers down and looking at Lillian and Juan for confirmation. "Villa has a German advisor?"

"Since the government requested the removal of German military attachés from the embassy in Washington, they just went on down to Mexico."

Handing the papers back to Lillian, the Ranger picks up the revolver from the table, thinking. Spinning the cylinders, he holsters it, pulls out another revolver and does a quick check of the cylinders, and puts it back. When he looks up at Lillian and Juan again, it is with concern.

"We must stop the assault," says Lillian.

"It isn't our job," Juan responds, shaking his head.

Studying the two, the Ranger finally says, "Let me determine that."

"I think we should turn the boy over to the Army and let them question him," suggests Lillian.

"I agree," Juan says. "Three people cannot stop a raid."

Pulling his badge out and studying it a moment, the Ranger says to his two companions, "You know, it only took one Texas ranger to stop a town riot once."

The waiter appears from the kitchen through the swinging butterfly doors holding a plate. He's startled by the revolver in the Ranger's hand. Carefully placing the steak on the table, he backs away.

The Ranger spins the cylinders on the pistol, satisfying himself that it's fully loaded and ready. Grabbing the box of bullets from the table, he puts it back into the saddlebag and settles back in his chair. He gives his two companions a brief look before turning his attention to the steak.

As he picks up his fork and knife, the waiter appears with a cup of coffee which he carefully puts down on the table before backing away again. The Ranger takes a bite of his steak and grabs the coffee for a sip. Cringing at the taste, he holds the brew at arm's length, studies it, then puts it down, shaking his head.

"The Army must be notified at once," Lillian insists.

Chewing on the tough steak while cutting off another chunk, the Ranger swallows the beef and says, "Of what?" He puts the fork and knife down and looks at Lillian and Juan. "A possible raid?" Picking up the fork and knife again and slicing away, he adds, "Who? Where? When?" With a slice of beef on the fork, he asks, "Don't you think they already have the same information?"

"But we have one of Lujan's men!" Lillian exclaims.

Looking at Lillian in puzzlement, the Ranger says, "Not too long ago, he was a boy. Now he's a man." Shaking his head at the little lady in amazement, he puts the slice of beef in his mouth and chews, before slicing another piece.

"It's our responsibility to get that..." Lillian pauses to correct herself, "...young man to the proper authorities," barely gaining a glance from the Ranger, who chews on it.

A 1915 Dodge convertible driven by one khaki-clad soldier accompanied by another in the passenger seat, pulls up to the boardwalk just past the jail.

"I shouldn't be stopping," says the driver, nervously.

"Don't worry," the other trooper says, opening the door and stepping out. "I'll be right back. I'm just going to get some tobacco."

"Well, make it quick," replies the driver, holding the car in neutral while idling. "Don't forget, this is supposed to be some mighty important cargo we've got here."

The passenger trooper holds his hand up, nodding. He turns and walks into the store.

Frank and three young Mexican men walk out of the jail to horses, followed by the lookout. Taking the reins of their mounts and getting on, the trio guide their horses down the street while Frank and the lookout make their way by foot. Recognizing the Ranger's horse, Frank quickly leads his friend Jesse in a different direction, looking for a means of escape.

Jesse points to the 1915 Dodge idling beside the boardwalk. Frank nods. Cautiously they approach the automobile from the rear. Frank grabs Jesse and whispers something into his ear. Jesse nods and moves down the boardwalk towards the car while Frank rushes to the rear of the automobile and slips around to the side, crouching.

Coming up to the passenger's side of the car, Jesse stops and waves at the driver. *"Sénor Soldier?"*

The soldier stops tapping his fingers on the steering wheel and looks at the young man on the boardwalk. "Yeah, What do you want?"

"Do you know what time it is?" Jesse inquires.

As the soldier reaches for his pocket watch, he's grabbed around the neck from behind and wrestled out of the idling car. Lacking any leverage, the soldier falls onto the street as Jesse jumps into the passenger seat and Frank kicks the soldier before jumping into the car behind the steering wheel.

The soldier struggles to his feet and reaches for Frank, but Frank fights him off and puts the vehicle into gear. Hitting the gas pedal, Frank sends the car lurching forward, making it impossible for the soldier to get a good hold on any part of the auto. Sensing the car gaining speed, the soldier makes a last desperate lunge for the car but falls short.

Smoking a cigarette as he comes out of the store, the other soldier is shocked to see his partner sprawled out in the middle of the street and the Dodge gaining speed down the street.

The automobile grinds gears, backfires, then leaps forward again as Jesse stands up in the passenger seat, yelling at the fallen soldier, "Time to get a new car!" One last backfire, and it's nothing but tail end, exhaust, and the fading clamor of an engine growing distant.

The backfiring of the old buggy startles the Ranger. He reaches for a pistol in his duster instead of the beef.

"Relax," says Lillian. "It's probably nothing."

"I'll go see," Juan says, rising from his chair.

Unnerved, but not for long, the Ranger picks ups his fork and gazes at the slice of beef. He puts it in his mouth and chews. Swallowing, he looks at Lillian. "Why would Villa use foreign advisors? Especially German advisors. Don't they already have a conflict in Europe of their own? Do they want to expand the war to America?"

"That is curious, isn't it?" Lillian agrees.

Deep in thought, the Ranger puts down his fork and leans back. Shaking his head and reaching into an inside pocket of that duster, he pulls out a cigar and match. He ignites the match off the bottom of the table and brings it to the cigar, puffing. Looking up at the ceiling as he puffs, he tries to put everything together.

The waiter returns to the table with a glass of water he places before the Ranger. "We generally prefer our customers not smoke in here," he advises the Ranger, hands on waist, tapping his foot.

Studying the waiter, deep in thought, the Ranger leans forward and drops the cigar into the glass of water the waiter has just put down. "Do you mind if I fume?" he asks, blowing smoke into the fellow's face. Perplexed, the waiter exits in a huff.

"This isn't just a border skirmish if internationals are involved," comments the Ranger. "There must be a bigger plan a-brewing."

"But what could that be?" Lillian wonders.

Juan rushes into the restaurant, out of breath. "He's escaped."

"Who...? Frank?" Lillian responds.

"Who else?" says the Ranger, standing up and reaching for his saddlebags. "He said his friends would spring him." Tossing the saddlebags over his shoulder, he digs into another inside pocket of his duster.

"He's probably making a run for the border," says the little lady, rising from her chair as well.

"Then it's time to take him down." The lawman tosses an eagle onto the table.

"We should telephone the border station and warn them," Lillian thinks out loud.

"You do that," says the Ranger, walking to the door of the restaurant. He makes a sudden stop, causing Lillian and Juan to bump into him. Returning to the table, he wraps the uneaten portion of his steak in a napkin and puts it in an outside pocket. Lillian and Juan step aside as he waddles back to the door.

Moving down the boardwalk in his labored way, the Ranger comes up to his horse. He steps off the wooden walk onto the graveled street and tosses his saddlebags over the horse. Untying the reins from the hitching post, he struggles to board his trusty mount. "I'm going after that boy...man... whatever you want to call him. You take care of it your way, I'll go about it the old-fashioned way." Tipping his hat to the two, he spurs his mount to a direct run.

Lillian turns to Juan. "You call the border guards. I'm going with him." Juan nods as Lillian boards her mare and kicks it to a direct run as well.

A double column of cavalry blue-clad soldiers winds its way through the Mexican desert, led by Captain Frederick

M. Turner. This is the M-Troop, 13th Cavalry. Riding in line next to him is khaki-clad First Lieutenant George S. Patton.

Though the desert conditions are harsh, this outfit, more commonly referred to as the Buffalo Soldiers, are up to it. The sharp and smartly-dressed troops are armed and prepared for any combat situation astride their horses.

"What do you think of my troops, Lieutenant?" the Captain questions Patton, sitting tall in the saddle.

"Outstanding group of men, Sir. Outstanding."

Looking back at the fine disciplined soldiers behind him and looking forward again, the Captain says proudly, "I'm not concerned about them, I'm consumed by them."

"Yes, Sir. They do have a long and distinguished history, Sir."

"And, I don't intend to see that reputation fall from grace," the Captain says emphatically.

A few of the bluejackets riding behind lead, hearing what the Captain said about them, nod to each other and pass the word down the ranks. But one private strikes a discordant note when he says to a corporal, "I ain't got nothin' against no Mexicans."

"Jackson," says the experienced corporal to his trail partner, "neither do I. But this is the first time the United States has been attacked by a foreign power this century. We can't allow that to happen again."

Private Jackson eyes the corporal. "Do you think America really cares about us? We're still nothing but colored to them. Do you know why I joined the Army? This is the only decent living a black man can make in these United States. Besides, where else would a negro be taught to read and write as a matter of course?"

The corporal turns to Jackson. "Fifty years ago, we were nothing but slaves. Great strides are being made for negroes these days."

"Like that film, 'Birth of a Nation,' by D. W. Griffith? Glorifying the Ku Klux Klan?" Jackson laughs. "You call that great strides?" Some of the soldiers behind in line nod and silently agree.

Staring Jackson down, the corporal informs him, "Did you know a hundred and nineteen coloreds protested that movie in San Francisco? When could a negro man ever do something like that before?"

"That ain't enough," responds Jackson, raising more attention from the soldiers in front and behind him.

"They just organized the National Association for the Colored Peoples just a few short years ago," says the corporal. "Give them a chance. It might work."

"I just don't know," Jackson says, shaking his head and tightening his grip on the reigns, a more physical reaction to his frustration than anything else.

"Well," says the corporal with total belief, "I do."

"What makes you so sure?" Jackson asks.

"The corporal turns to him, studying him a moment. "You know, I ain't a Christian, Jew, or Muslim. I ain't a Buddhist or a Hindu. And I don't reckon I know if there's one God better than all the rest. But I'll tell you one thing I do believe in. And that's our Constitution and the Bill of Rights. Yes, sir. I do believe in that." Thinking further on it, the corporal concludes, "I guess that would make me a Constitutionalist. Yeah." He nods affirmatively. "Yeah, I like that. I'm a Constitutionalist."

"Yeah. Okay, Jefferson," the private addresses the corporal by name. "Come off that high horse of yours and smell the Twentieth Century. The only thing a black man can do with any respectability these days is to shine shoes, bell hop, or be a conductor on a train. What kind of a life is that?" The disgruntled private shakes his head.

"You got it all wrong," says Jefferson. "Look at what George Washington Carver did."

"That's one man," replies Jackson, shaking his head.

"That's where it starts," Jefferson says. "Always with one man. With all those new-fangled automobiles going around more and more these days, do you think those drivers know a negro man invented the traffic light?"

"Do they care?" comes the instant response from Jackson.

"This is the dawning of a new age and you don't even recognize it," Jefferson says. "Black people are making a contribution. Before too long, integration will happen."

Shaking his head in defiance, Jackson asks, "What makes you think that's the answer?"

"Marcus Garvey talks about that," Jefferson answers.

"What makes it right for one man, don't make it right for the next," responds Jackson. "I want to be my own man."

"Some day we might all blend together by something as common as, say, a baseball game."

Laughing and shaking his head, Jackson says, "Now, I know you've been out in this Mexican sun too long. "Do you really think they'd let a negro man play professional baseball?"

"They just began that American League a few years ago, and a lot of folks are supporting it,"Jefferson replies. "Maybe somewhere down the line, one of those teams will open up the door for a Colored."

Not believing Jefferson's prediction, Jackson asks, "How do you figure a colored man's really going to ever make it in America?"

Without hesitation, Jefferson says, "The contributions are being made right now. Maybe someday it'll flow into the culture by other means."

"What's that mean?"

Taking a moment to think about it, Jefferson looks at the young soldier. "Ragtime! There you go. Music. Scott Joplin, Ferdinand 'Jelly Roll' Morton, Ben Harney. That's popular right now. That counts. That counts a lot. Almost like equality itself."

"Equality?" questions Jackson, raising some stir in the ranks in front and behind him. The bluejackets listen intently as the horses' steady hoof beats pound the desert ground.

"Yeah, equality," repeats Jefferson. "But the kind of equality that effects Asians, Mexicans, Blacks, Indians and all the other folks that come to America."

"Then why do I feel like a foreigner in my own country?"

"Because you allow yourself to feel alienated," says Jefferson. "But this is the only time you feel accepted. When you're in uniform."

"Speaking of uniforms," Jackson points to the front of the marching procession of horses. "Who's that uniform?"

"That's the lieutenant that saw action a couple of weeks ago with some of Pancho Villa's men," says Jefferson.

"Maybe we'll see some action too," Jackson remarks.

Jefferson looks at Jackson and points at Patton. They promoted him for his action."

"Then why is he riding with us?" Jackson asks.

"It's an opportunity for him to see the best cavalry unit in the U. S. Army!" Jefferson affirms with complete conviction.

The blazing heat bears down on the men and horses as they advance further into the Mexican wastelands. Captain Turner briefs the young lieutenant on the three-day assignment. "From the Civil War to the Indian Wars, to Cuba, these men have served gallantly," Turner says, turning to Patton. "Mexico is just another campaign to them."

"They appear to be a tough and able group of men, Sir," responds the young First Lieutenant.

"That they are, Lieutenant. That they are." The captain takes a moment to look over his new recruit. He spies the fancy pistol Patton has holstered. "I hear you're pretty able with that pearl-handled pistol of yours."

"Ivory, Sir," the young lieutenant says with some disdain. "Ivory-handled pistol. Only a New Orleans pimp would own a pearl-handled pistol."

"What?" asks the Captain, unsure of what he has just heard.

"Ivory-handled revolver, sir. That's what it is," the lieutenant repeats.

"They're still shooting irons, and not government-issue, Lieutenant. Studying Patton, the Captain says, "They tell me you're quite a marksman, Lieutenant. Just how good are you?"

A rabbit suddenly dashes out from some underbrush and hightails it towards safer ground.

Patton looks at the Captain and points at the wild rabbit on the dead run. "With your permission, Sir?"

"Have at it, Lieutenant," nods the Captain, laughing. "I want to see this."

Patton spurs his horse to a trot, in going after the scared little bunny leaping and bounding over obstacles in its flight. The First Lieutenant unfastens the leather hold on his holster and pulls out the ivory-handled pistol. At first shot, the hare falls dead before it even hits the ground.

"Expert shot, Lieutenant," congratulates the Captain, as Patton returns to formation.

"Thank you, Sir," says the young lieutenant, holstering his weapon, as the Buffalo Soldiers riding in line behind, nod their approval of this new officer accompanying them on this desert expedition.

Hurtling down a desert road, Frank grinds the shift to the 1915 Dodge, forcing a shift while gassing the engine, causing a backfire.

Jesse, pinned in the passenger's seat gripping the door with one hand and holding onto his seat with the other, turns to look at Frank, totally scared out of his mind. The vehicle is rattling down the dusty road at almost thirty miles an hour.

Frank looks at Jesse. "Don't worry, I've got everything under control," he says, as the vehicle weaves around a turn, hitting a dip in the road and continuing on without breaking speed.

"Whoa...a...a...!" shouts Jesse, grabbing the side of the windshield and the side of the seat simultaneously. Terrorized by the road ahead and Frank at the wheel, he turns around looking for his three companions on horseback following close behind.

Grinding gears again, Frank gets the stick shift into place. The car leaps forward, pinning Jesse to his seat again. Almost losing his hat on a turn, Jesse sees a trunk in the back seat and desperately tries to climb back to see what's in it. Bouncing and finally falling into the back seat, he puts his hat back on and tries to open the container. When he gets all the latches, he flips open the lid. Four Thompson submachine guns are in there.

"What's this?" Jesse wonders, reaching in and pulling one out. Looking into the trunk, he comes up with a round magazine which he fits into the weapon. He plays with it a bit and pulls the bolt action back. A series of shots throws him deep into the back seat, scaring Frank and scattering the horsemen following close behind.

"Wow," says a wide-eyed Jesse in amazement.

Frank turns back and eyes the weapon. "A Gatling gun?"

"A miniature Gatling gun!" replies Jesse with a huge smile. "This will come in handy," he laughs to himself, studying it more closely.

"Are there more back there?" Frank asks as the Dodge hits some bumps, forcing him to look forward and take the wheel again.

Jesse looks again. "*Quatro..*"

"Any ammunition?" Frank asks, looking over his shoulder again.

"*Si,*" replies Jesse. "But not enough for the revolution."

Frank smiles with a gleam in his eyes, taking a firm grip of the steering wheel. "Pedro will be pleased."

Lillian reins her mare to the charge, closing the gap between her and the Ranger. Coming to a wide turn, she pulls even with him and they dart for the border through the desert wastelands.

A uniformed border agent hangs up the ear piece to a small wind-up telephone next to a door, as he exits the building to approach another agent at a gateway.

"Pull that gate down," says the office agent. "We've got a whole lot of trouble coming our way."

Curious, the agent pulls a wooden plank down and obstructs the roadway. "What's up?" he asks.

"We'd better get our rifles," the office agent suggests, spinning around and returning to the door and into the interior office followed by the other agent.

Handing the gate agent a Winchester repeater, he points outside the door and says, "You take that side."

Delighting in his newly-acquired weapon, Jesse smiles and cradles it in his arms as if it were a new-born child, despite the fact the weapon is cold steel and still warm from the few shots he got off by accident.

Almost at the border, Frank sees the two agents taking aim with their rifles in front of the obstructed gateway. He raises his hand and signals the horsemen to follow him as he guns the engine. Turning back to Jesse, he says, "Shoot them."

Smiling, Jesse doesn't have to be told twice. He stands and braces himself between the front and back seats of the Dodge and lets go a quick burst of fire that kicks him back. Repositioning himself and leaning into the automatic weapon, he fires again.

Bullets rip into the station, tearing the wood siding apart and blowing out all the windows. The two border guards dive for cover and roll out of harm's way.

The wooden plank is no match for the speeding Dodge as it breaks apart, splintering into a thousand pieces. Riding close behind are the three horsemen who take some wild shots at the agents, keeping them out of position to fire back.

Jesse looks back at the border station as the vehicle continues to bounce and weave down the Mexican roadway. Waving at the horsemen behind him to move aside, Jesse lines up another aim on the border guards and lets go another burst of fire.

"How many bullets does it have?" Frank asks Jesse in curiosity.

"I don't know," Jesse replies. Taking aim again, he pulls off a few more bursts, then pulls the weapon down and examines it once more.

"Well," Frank says, looking back at Jesse. "Save some for Pedro." Grabbing the steering wheel and holding on, he makes a wide turn, causing Jesse to fall into the back seat. He just sits there, admiring the weapon.

"Pedro will be proud of us," smiles Jesse.

"Not if we run out of bullets," says Frank, as he grinds gears and hits the gas pedal.

The Ranger and Lillian cross the border as the two border agents recover from the assault, completely dazed by the swiftness of the firefight and the weapon that overwhelmed them. Looking at the remains of their border shack, they can only shake their heads in astonishment, as the Ranger and Lillian charge into Mexican territory after Frank and his gang.

Dusting himself off and looking at his partner, the gate agent asks, "What kind of gun was that?"

Shaking his head, the other agent responds, "I don't know. But it's Mexican now."

Driving deeper into the Mexican desert with Frank at the wheel of the 1915 Dodge, Jesse climbs into the front seat. The horsemen close ranks and follow the Dodge, heading for the distant mountain pass ahead. Not too far behind them is the Ranger and Lillian, pushing their mounts to the physical limits on this desperate chase.

Silent is the vast expanse of wasteland as Juan walks in the desert. Deep in the middle of nowhere and far from where he has been, he stops to take notice of a hawk gliding above him. Sitting down on the sand, he studies the bird as the winged creature leans into the gentle breeze and steadies itself, as if it were studying the Yaqui below.

Riding the gusts of wind sweeping up and down, another hawk suddenly rises from below and joins the first one in the thermals.... It peels off and heads towards the distant mountain range.

As heat bakes the burning sands into waves that distort the distant horizon, ripples of hot air rise off the ground towards the only living creature in sight—the one hawk—gliding over the empty wasteland.

Jesse sees two riders just beyond the rear of the three horsemen in the gang, alarming him. Tapping Frank on the shoulder, he points them out. Jesse signals his *compadrés* to move aside as he levels the Thompson to get a gauge on the weapon's range between him and the two distant riders.

"Save the bullets," says Frank, calming his partner down.

Jesse signals one of his *compadrés* on horseback to shoot at the two horsemen behind them.

Bullets zip by the Ranger and Lillian as they spur their mounts to a full charge. The Ranger motions Lillian to ride wide of him as he stands in his saddle, reaches into his duster and pulls out his Winchester, firing three rapid shots in succession.

The bullets hit the front windshield of the Dodge, alarming Frank. He shoves Jesse while keeping his eye on the road as they approach a mountain pass. "Shoot them," he shouts.

"What about the bullets?" Jesse asks.

"Damn the bullets! Shoot them!" Frank insists, leaning forward, steadying the steering wheel, and giving the car gas.

Jesse stands, steadies himself, then lets go with a barrage of shots, sending the Ranger and his horse off the road but still on the chase.

Making his way back to the road and on even ground, the Ranger stands in his saddle again, cranking off three more shots from that Winchester of his. Lillian rides wide and even with the Ranger, just off road.

Two of the Ranger's shots rip into the cab of the automobile while one bullet hits a tire, disabling the vehicle.

Swerving left and right on the road, Frank struggles to maintain control of the Dodge as it approaches a curve just inside the mountain divide. But as it hits the first rise and turn past the mouth of the mountains, Frank is unable to control it, forcing him off the road and into a small hill, where the car comes to rest

The three gang members on horseback, rush past the vehicle on the run, suddenly pulling up, spinning, and returning pistol fire. Jesse jumps from the vehicle with the Thompson, with Frank right behind him, taking cover behind some boulders near a hill. The three other men jump off their horses and rush over to join Frank and Jesse.

The sharp crack of pistol fire fills the air as the Ranger and Lillian pull up and run for cover. The Ranger fires some return shots with the rifle. Checking Lillian while forcing the rifle back into his duster, he pulls out a pistol and reaches over the granite, fires six rapid shots. Coming back down and holstering the pistol, he pulls another out. He leans over and fires two more shots, then ducks.

"What now?" asks Lillian.

"Stay down," says the Ranger as he leans over the rock and fires twice more before coming down for cover. Pulling some bullets out of his shoulder holster, he opens the gun chamber on the pistol, empties four spent cartridges and reloads. He puts the pistol on the rock, removes the pistol that's empty and opens the chamber. He empties the casing and reloads. Looking around, he pulls his hat down and tells Lillian, "Stay put." He dashes for higher ground under the protection of the boulders they're behind.

Bullets whizz by the rock as Lillian watches the Ranger move towards a better vantage. More bullets zip by. Other shots slam into the rock in front of her. Falling back, Lillian rises with her pistol in hand. "Enough is enough," she says. Crawling to the rock, she leans over and pulls off three rapid shots and takes cover. Pulling some bullets out of her holster, she lays them on the ground next to her and gets the shock of her life. A hand grabs her shoulder from behind. She spins around and finds Juan.

"Where'd you come from?" she asks in astonishment, rolling her eyes and looking at him like he's an illusion. "How'd you get here?" as more bullets rip through the air again.

"I came as fast as I could," says Juan, crouching, almost indifferent to the gun battle. He studies Lillian, the field of fire, then back to the lady Ranger, saying, "I have a plan."

"Be careful," Lillian says, blindly reaching for the shells she's left on the ground as she watches Juan dash across the road towards some hills on the other side of the divide. He draws machine gun fire but safely disappears behind some rocks, leaving Lillian to her bullets in hand, as another barrage of pistol fire slams into the rock she's hiding behind for cover.

"This is ridiculous," says Frank. "We have them outnumbered." A bullet smashes into a rock next to him, sending him sprawling to the ground. He gets up on his knees, crawling back to the rock for cover.

One of the young men stands and starts thumb-busting his pistol only to take a shot to the chest, spinning him to the ground, dead.

Frank's eyes widen at the sight of his fallen comrade. He looks at Jesse in confusion. Jesse looks at the dead man, then back at Frank. "The numbers are going down."

Taking a deep breath and another look at the Thompson, Jesse stands up and fires a burst of shells towards the rock behind which Lillian takes cover.

Taking a bead on one of the bandits behind the rocks, the Ranger squeezes the trigger of the Buffalo gun, setting the mountain divide a-tremble as the thunder of that weapon echoes throughout the tiny valley and beyond.

Hearing the distant echo of thunder in the direction of the mountains, accompanied by the crisp sound of small pistol fire, the 13th Cavalry, led by Captain Turner and his first officer, Lieutenant Patton, turn the column of Buffalo Soldiers towards the gunfire and file through the desert at a paced trot.

A round slams into a rock, shattering it and, sending the young man sprawling for cover, counting his blessings. He sweats profusely as he hugs the rock he's hiding behind. Cheek to rock, the young man looks at Frank and Jesse with fear in his eyes. Jesse nods to the young man, shows him the Thompson, then stands and fires the machine gun until it runs out of bullets. Standing there, wide open to fire and struggling with the empty weapon, Frank reaches up and pulls him down.

"Damn!" says Jesse. "Out of bullets!"

Eyeing the car, Frank looks at Jesse and says, "Well, go to the car and get some more."

Unexpectedly, Jesse hands Frank the Thompson and makes a dash for the Dodge. A shot from the Buffalo gun stops Jesse in his tracks and sends him back to the cover of the rocks.

Topping a hill behind the bandits, Juan goes unnoticed. He sees the Dodge, the young men, Lillian, and the Ranger in their positions, as well as the road in the mountain divide. Studying the surroundings and using his senses, he takes inventory of everything. Seeing a small stone, he walks to it and picks it up. He kneels with the stone in his hand and pitches it underhand a few feet away. It lands on another small stone, which causes it to roll into some other stones, soon generating a small landslide which grows large enough to draw the bandits' attention, sending them running.

The Ranger takes one of the bandits out with the Buffalo gun. He stands and reloads, taking aim again. Lillian fires some shots from her position as the remaining three bandits make a run for the horses, with one of them returning the Ranger's fire.

Jesse jumps onto the back of the horse Frank's riding, cradling the Thompson in one hand and grabbing Frank and holding on with the other for dear life. Two horses leave the scene, one horse carrying two men as they dash around the face of the mountain. One horse, one automobile and two fallen outlaws left behind.

Rising and firing his reloaded Winchester rifle, the Ranger lets go a series of shots but misses his intended target as the bandits and horses make their escape. Pulling his weapon down and eyeing the escape, the Ranger pauses a moment. "Damn!"

Climbing his way down past Lillian, he reaches for the reins of his Appaloosa and climbs aboard. He sticks the rifle in his duster, looks at Lillian and says, "Can't let them get away." Reining his horse on a spin, he adds, "You keep an eye on that buggy." Digging in with those spurs, he sets his horse to the challenge.

"Where will I find you?" shouts Lillian.

"I will find him," Juan startles Lillian as he walks up from behind her.

Riding into a small village, Frank, Jesse, and the other horseman pull up to a small cantina and dismount. They enter the establishment, not bothering to tie the horses to the hitching post. Jesse cradles the Thompson as he follows Frank and the other man through the swinging moth-winged doors leading into the little shack. A trio of *campesino's* play *huapango* music at a feverish pace as the young men look the area over.

In a corner, a card game is being played while a *senorita* serves drinks to various customers. Some people are eating tortillas and *menudo* at a table, while at another, a group of curious men sit. One man, dressed in slightly better *campesino* attire while sporting a tooled *bandillero*, is Pedro Lujan. The other man, well-groomed, dressed in a white suit and fedora, is General Heinrich Schmidt of the German high command. He carries a very serious scar across his face. Two other *Villiastas* share the table dressed in the whites and tans of the desert with soft high boots. One of these men favors a *Bandilleros* with shotgun shells and small bore carbine revolver ammunition. The other man wears long cartridges of the seven MM Mausers, of the Mexican army. They drink mescal and talk as Frank and his compatriots make their way towards the table.

"Of course we need arms," Pedro says to General Schmidt. "How do you wage a revolution without them?" We need men and soldiers to use the arms as well."

"Pedro," says Frank, interrupting.

"Silence," Lujan says, waving him off and continuing. "...not boys...and juvenile delinquents." Looking at Frank, Jesse, and the other young man, he says, "like these."

Pointing at the Thompson submachine gun Jesse is cradling in his arms, General Schmidt asks, "What is that?"

"A Gatling gun," Frank answers, turning to Pedro.

"A what?" Pedro asks, staring at the weapon .

"It shoots...*rapido*," says Jesse, handing the weapon to Lujan, who examines it more closely. Looking at Frank and Jesse, he says, "*Rapido?* From such a small weapon?"

Weighing and balancing the gun in his hand, he asks, "Where do the bullets go?"

"Allow me," interjects the German General, reaching for the weapon. Pedro hands it over to him.

"Where did you come by such a weapon?" Pedro asks the young men as General Schmidt looks the Thompson over.

"In the back of an automobile I stole," Frank answers.

Pedro laughs a moment, then asks, "Were there more?"

"*Si,*" answers Frank. "Four, total."

Looking up from the machine gun in surprise, General Schmidt says, "Four?" He turns to Lujan and says, "I must have one. My government would be most interested in a weapon such as this." He weighs the gun in his hand and studies it as he goes on. "This is robust, compared to the M96 we issue some of our officers."

"My country needs it more, right now," responds Lujan, looking at the young men. "Where is this automobile?"

"North of here. But," says the worried young man, eyeing the stucco walls to his side and thinking of things much worse than an abandoned automobile. "There are *Americanos* near."

"They're all over," Pedro remarks, unconcerned. He turns to the German General. "They killed Colonel Cardenas a month ago." He shakes his head and reaches for his drink. "Why don't the *Americanos* go back to their side of the border and leave our revolution to ourselves?"

"It is important you distract the Americans, as great strides are being made in the Rhineland right now," says the German General. "The promised territories will be duly assigned by the Kaiser when we liberate Europe and come to your aid."

Pedro looks at Frank, Jesse, and the other young man, saying, "Get yourselves something to eat and drink. You've earned it. What I further discuss with the General is not for your ears."

As the young men make their way to a table, Lujan takes a sip of his mescal and turns to the German General. "General, promises of California, Texas, Arizona, and New Mexico are just that. Promises. Further rewards of Oklahoma, Kansas, Colorado, Utah, South Dakota and other lands are nothing more than...words." He looks at the Thompson Schmidt is still handling. "I can wage a greater war with weapons such as this. And that is more of an immediate concern to me and my countrymen now!"

"We have the means to duplicate such weaponry," states the General. "It would strengthen your efforts many times over."

"But we need the arms now," says Lujan. "Not in a month, or a year."

"You must give me one of the four," insists Schmidt, still examining the weapon. "I'll speak to Pancho Villa about it."

"We'll see," says Lujan. "We must recover the weapons first. I'll make my decision then."

"This is most urgent," the German General insists once more. "You'll be generously rewarded."

Shaking his head and taking the weapon back from Schmidt, who resists at first, but finally relinquishes the Thompson, Lujan says, "Rewards from Germany concern me little."

"If the Colorados should get them," Schmidt ventures, "it would be most disastrous to your war effort."

"If the *Americanos* get them," Lujan replies, studying the weapon again, "it becomes disastrous."

Frank returns to the table to speak to Pedro as he's clearly upset. While he addresses Pedro, his eyes search the north, sensing something serious is about to happen. "Pedro," he interrupts. "A gringo from Texas has been chasing us."

"So?" Pedro asks, totally unconcerned. He continues to examine the weapon.

"He must be near," says the worried young man.

"One man does not concern me," Pedro responds.

"He's a Texas Ranger," Frank explains, still eyeing the north side of the building. He can almost sense the arrival of his greatest fear. He looks at Pedro and the Thompson. "He knows of this weapon. He must be stopped."

Thinking a moment, Lujan weighs the machine gun for balance. Eyeing the German General, he speaks to Frank. "Francisco, you will accompany my men to this automobile and return with the rest of these weapons."

Backing away from the table and shaking his head, Frank declines Pedro's suggestion. "But the Ranger is after me!"

Pedro simply says, "You will do as you're told and that is final." He waves the young man off and reaches for his drink, shaking his head at the insolence of youth these days.

Indifferent to the young man and Pedro's order, the General eyes the weapon, then looks at Pedro. "I will send a telegram off to Herr Zimmerman in Germany. He will prepare the necessary papers guaranteeing the land appropriations. I'm sure you'll be quite satisfied."

"A telegram from your *Sénor* Zimmerman is worth no more than the paper it is written on," says Lujan. "But I know why you offer such treasures," he assures the German General, quite confident of his information.

"And," says Schmidt, "why is that?" He smugly leans back in his chair, crossing his arms and legs, while lifting his chin awaiting an answer.

"Your struggle in Europe is drawing too much American opinion. You sank the Lusitania. You blew up a munitions dump in Delaware. You declared war on Russia, England, and France. And you've seized the Atlantic. The ploy you're designing here, in Mexico, is to distract attention of America from the conflict going on in Europe. They are a giant you don't want to awaken. And you think raids across the border will disillusion them."

He takes another sip of his mescal, eyeing the General. "You are mistaken about these *norté Americanos*, General.

They prepare for your conflict as we speak." The German officer offers in confidence.

"I'm only an advisor," he informs Pedro, reaching for his drink. "I don't set political policy. I only carry out orders and report my findings." He sips on the aguave drink and places the shot glass back on the table.

"General," Lujan says, as he examines the foreign officer. "It is only through the good graces of Pancho Villa, I even tolerate you. But the American Congress just signed the National Service Bill, meaning an additional one hundred and seventy thousand men will be conscripted for military duty as well as another half million men on reserve."

He eyes the General, giving him time to let his words sink in. "There are already twenty thousand Americans on our borders. Do you think they prepare to invade Mexico with a force like that? President Wilson has tried to stay out of the war, but you're backing him into a corner and he'll turn and strike out at both Mexico and Europe." Reaching for his drink, he takes a hard swallow and places the glass back on the table, studying Lujan, before going on.

"The Americans are too diffused with troops in Haiti and Santa Domingo.... They can't even locate Pancho Villa down here with that Punitive Expeditionary Force. Do you think America can prepare for a war with Germany?" the German officer offers. "We are sabotaging any taste they might have for war. They'd rather read accounts of it in their newspapers, or read dime novels about Cowboys and Indians. This is the Twentieth Century and America is still in the nineteenth," General Schmidt informs Pedro.

"This is a subjective thing, General," Lujan counters. "Much confusion in Mexico these days. Diaz is disposed. Madero assassinated. Huerta exiled.... We've had ten Presidents in four years, one holding office for a full twenty-eight minutes. There are Constitutionalists, Pacificos, Colorados, Rurales, Federales.... Carranza controls one portion, Orasco another, Zapata to the south, Villa to the north, and...," he studies the German General, grinding his teeth, "the Germans dictate policy?" Reaching for the bottle, he pours himself a drink. He puts the bottle down and leans back in his chair. "This is no longer a revolution for the people. It's a power struggle of war lords."

"Are you saying you're a prisoner of war?" the General questions Lujan.

"With an agenda like that," Pedro advises the German General, "we are all prisoners of war...here and abroad. Tell me, General, you've been around this country. Have you ever seen a prison camp?"

"No," answers the General, almost indignant at such a preposterous question.

Peering in on the General, Pedro asks, "Do you know why?"

"Enlighten me, Pedro," Schmidt plays along as he reaches for another shot of mescal and really not expecting much of an explanation.

"Economics," Lujan informs him. He studies the General more carefully. "A simple bullet is cheaper than housing, feeding , and guarding prisoners. If you let them go, they can return to fight you—so you kill them! This is why Villa has Major Fierro, 'The Butcher'. He should really be called 'The Judge,' as he sentences and executes the prisoners. I hear Orasco has such a man himself." He eyes the General, reaching for another shot of his drink. Sitting back and taking a quick shot, he grits his teeth, places the glass back on the table and continues. "Life is cheap down here, General. But with such atrocities such as all this needless killing, we're all prisoners." He lets his words sink in, then adds one last important thought. "I take orders from Pancho Villa, *Sénor General*. But I'm a Mexican, not a politician. You feed General Villa empty promises while my country starves to death. I no more hunger for war. I say, Mexico for Mexicans."

"Get me one of these weapons," General Schmidt says, as if he'd never heard one word of what Lujan has said. "...And you can—"

Rising from his chair in anger, Lujan stares unbelievingly at the General. "What? Have more promises of more land? What will you offer next? The White House?" Grabbing the Thompson and holding it in the German General's face, he says, "All for one of these?" Taking a moment to control his emotions, he looks at the German officer. "Before you offer any more land in the Americas, maybe you should check with President Wilson."

"If you can't honor my request," says Schmidt, unmoved, "perhaps General Villa will have something to say about it."

Lujan shakes his head in sadness, not knowing how to explain himself better. "One rapido rifle? All this for one rapido rifle?" He stands firm and in command. "Let me get them first. I will decide then."

Lillian looks on as Juan inspects the contents of the trunk in the back seat of the 1915 Dodge. Juan sees something in the distance, distracting him. He closes the lid, baffling Lillian. "What's wrong?" she asks, following his line of vision as he looks towards the open wastelands.

"Trouble," says Juan.

Lillian steps back from the automobile and shields her eyes from the sun. She stares at the horizon for a minute. "That's the Cavalry," she says, looking at Juan in surprise, then turning again for another look. "Those are American troops. They're black!"

"Keep quiet," says Juan as he jumps down from the back seat to Lillian's side, waiting for the closing column to ride up.

Trotting towards Lillian, Juan, and the Dodge, the two-lined Cavalry separate as they approach the group, finally surrounding it when they come to a halt. The whole contingency of Buffalo Soldiers look at Lillian and Juan silently. "You seem to be having some difficulties, I see," observes Captain Turner.

"Nothing we can't handle," says Lillian.

"Don't I know you?" asks Lieutenant Patton, taking a moment to recall where he'd seen these two people. Finally registering, he says, "Shouldn't you be on the other side of the border?"

"Actually," Lillian responds quickly, "there isn't any reason why we can't be here, Lieutenant. There aren't any official diplomatic relations between America and Mexico, you know."

"All the more reason to be in the United States," Says the Captain.

What seems to be the problem here," asks the lieutenant, surveying the automobile.

"Flat tire," answers Juan.

"That shouldn't be too difficult to repair," Patton says. Looking to his Captain, he asks, "Do you mind if I take a look, Sir?" Turner nods.

The lieutenant dismounts and walks over to the right rear tire, kneels down and examines the rubber tire. "At first glance," he says, "that does seem to be a nasty hole. What did you pick up?" he asks Lillian and Juan as he looks around the edge and reaches for something, struggling with it a moment.

Examining it more closely, he finally says, "This tire has been rendered disabled by...." He holds up a small lead object to show Lillian and Juan. "...What looks like a very large forty-five caliber bullet."

He stands up, tossing the 300-grain chunk of lead in his hand. "Now, he says, studying Lillian and Juan, "I wonder where you picked up one of these?" He looks at Captain Turner a moment, then walks to the front of the car. "What about your spare tire?"

"Haven't gotten to it yet," says Lillian.

Pausing in seriousness and addressing the Captain, the young lieutenant says, "Captain? This looks like a Government-issue automobile."

"Check it out, Lieutenant," orders Captain Turner.

Patton leans into the vehicle and inspects the front seat and dashboard, finally rising. "I believe I've got proof of ownership, Sir."

"Well, Lieutenant," says Captain Turner, "don't keep me in suspense."

"U. S. Army."

Looking at Lillian and Juan, Captain Turner says, "you two have some explaining to do."

Patton continues to search the vehicle, finally making his way to the back seat where the trunk is sitting. He opens it and is perturbed by what he sees. "There's more, Captain," he says.

"What is it, Lieutenant?" Turner asks.

Patton pulls up one of the machine guns and holds it over his head. "This is the prototype weapon General Thompson invented that we saw demonstrated at the testing range." Looking at Lillian and Juan the young Lieutenant asks them, "Where did you come by this?"

"Lieutenant? Captain?" Lillian tries to explain. "We're Texas Rangers. We chased the bandits who stole this vehicle across the border. We stopped the car but the bandits got away." She reaches for her badge while Juan reaches into a pocket and holds his badge up.

"Sergeant major!" Captain Turner barks.

A single horseman moves from formation and walks his horse over to the captain and salutes. "Sir!" he says, holding the salute.

Returning the salute, Captain Turner says, "Call some troopers up here, change that tire, see if this car will run, and either drive it or drag it back to base camp."

Saluting again, the sergeant major shouts, "Yes, Sir!" The Captain returns salute and the sergeant major reins his horse towards the automobile, shouting orders to some men in Cavalry formation. "Johnson, Jackson, Jefferson, and Burrell, front and center!"

Four men drop from rank and rein their horses towards the sergeant major who lifts his head and gives the order, "Change the tire and let's get this automobile back to the base camp by one means or another!" Without hesitation, the troopers dismount and walk past Lillian and Juan to the car.

Placing the weapon back into the trunk, Patton gets out of the car and walks over to Lillian and Juan, studying them with some curiosity. "Texas rangers?"

"Yeah. Texas Rangers," Lillian responds, showing the young lieutenant her star as Juan does the same.

Patton examines the badge in Lillian's hand, as she finally just hands it to him to inspect. After a moment he hands it back and shakes his head, looking to the Captain. "It's authentic, Sir."

Captain Turner dismounts and walks over to Lillian, Juan, and the young lieutenant. Looking at the badge a moment, he asks, "Isn't it unusual for a woman to be a Texas Ranger?"

"By appointment of the Adjutant General," she responds.

"The Adjutant General and Texas Rangers have no authority on this side of the border," Captain Turner observes.

"Maybe not, Captain," says Lillian. "But we stopped the vehicle before it could go any farther." She adds, "And we did save the guns."

"Most of the guns," Patton corrects her. "One is missing."

"How do you explain that?" Captain Turner demands.

"Another Ranger is in pursuit of that right now," Lillian explains. "With your permission, we'd like to find him."

"Where is he?" Turner inquires.

"We think he's just south of here," Lillian points as Juan nods in agreement. "Captain?" she goes on, "We certainly didn't steal the automobile, nor did we intend to keep any weapons we find in the car. We want a youth who escaped jail."

"This isn't your territory," says the Captain. "And I can't be responsible for you."

"We're not under your jurisdiction and you have no right to deny us our duty," Lillian insists.

"I can't let you go until you've been questioned," says the Captain.

"We are not the enemy," Juan finally speaks.

"Sir?" Patton suggests, "what if we all accompany them to the next town? We can question them en route."

"That is irregular, Lieutenant," Turner answers.

"This is an irregular weapon, Sir," Patton reminds his commanding officer.

Walking his trusted mount down the middle of a gravel roadway in a small Mexican village, the Ranger cautiously surveys the town for any danger. As he ambles along, looking form side to side and up ahead, a young lady with a baby in her arms approaches him.

"*Señor*, you have food for me?"

He ignores her and continues his cautious pace down the street, even more alert to danger.

Dropping her peasant blouse, exposing her shoulder, she says, "I trade you for some food." The Ranger reaches into his duster and pulls out a coin, handing it to her.

"Bless you," she says, turning and dashing back to the side of the building and disappearing down an alleyway.

Riding up to the side of the only cantina in town, he gets off his Appaloosa and ties it to the hitching post. He dusts himself off, wipes his brow and takes a deep breath. Adjusting his duster, he walks to the swinging butterfly doors and peeks in from the side. Some dogs bark in the distance. Inside the cantina, a musical trio completes a song. The Ranger sees several Mexicans seated at the bar drinking. Next to a hallway, a card game with five serious gamblers is winding down. It is the group at the table with the machine gun that most holds his attention. Moving towards the alleyway, the Ranger rounds the corner and moves towards the side entrance.

Coming to the side of the open doorway, the Ranger opens his duster and pulls out his scatter gun and one pistol. He slips into the doorway and silently moves towards the main room of this small but packed establishment.

"This is a curious weapon," Pedro says, examining it once more and looking down the barrel, twisting the weapon around in his grasp.

"Krupps can re-tool it so it'll be better," says General Schmidt quite confidently.

Frank returns to the table from the bar with a drink in his hand. He is no calmer than he was before as he insists to Pedro. "He must be getting closer."

The General interjects, somewhat annoyed by the constant interruption of the youth. "The Texas Ranger?" He looks around the room and tries to buck up the young man's courage. "A single man against so many?"

"This is no ordinary man," Frank says on the edge of tears.

"You say you escaped from him twice and you're still afraid of him?" the General remarks, trying to reassure the young man. "He sounds like a buffoon."

"Perhaps the General has not heard of the legend of the Texas Rangers?" Lujan tries to explain to Schmidt.

"This is absurd," remarks the German General in amazement. "This is but one man. You must be kidding me," he says, not believing what he hears.

Moving slowly down the hallway towards the main room of the cantina, the Ranger takes his hat off while still gripping his pistol. He peers around the corner for a quick spot check. He sees Frank at the table where the Thompson lies between four men in conversation. It is enough for what he needs to know. Slipping back into the hallway, he braces himself.

"...And he isn't in Texas, anymore," the German General speaks volubly and overconfidently. "He's fair game for the revolution, if you ask me. Give me a gun and I'll go after him."

Exhaling, the Ranger takes a bold step into the cantina, the revolver pointing at the table and the scatter gun covering everyone else. Seeing the guns, the customers flee, leaving only the bartender and the men sitting at the table with Pedro Lujan, who are frozen by the weapons pointed at them. "You ain't going after nobody," says the Ranger.

The General stands in defiance.

"Sit down!" snarls the Ranger, taking dead aim on the white-suited, foreign advisor. The General complies with care.

Eyeing the Ranger a moment and steadying himself, General Schmidt looks at Lujan and Frank. Sticking out his chin, he turns back to look at the Ranger. "So, this is what's supposed to have tamed the West?"

A little befuddled, the Ranger responds. "Now, I don't know what part of Mexico you hail from, Partner, so you just settle in a bit while I piece all this together." Looking at Frank and scaring him, the Ranger nods and says, "You! "Bring me that gun."

"Sénor Ranger," says Pedro, reasonably. "This is the silly act of a child."

"Well," responds the Ranger, "this child tried to take my head off with that gun." Motioning the young man, the Ranger goes on. "Now boy, you bring that gun over real slow and easy and we'll be moving right along."

"You're not going take that boy across the border, are you?" Pedro asks the lawman in a reasonable voice.

Nodding, the Ranger says, "That is my job."

"Your job doesn't extend down here," Schmidt says, asserting himself.

"It does today, Mister," the Ranger replies. "I don't mean you fellas any harm.... So you just let me attend to my business and I'll be moving on."

The General looks at Pedro. "You can't let him leave here with that weapon. It's a fortune of war."

"I don't reckon it belongs to anyone but the United States Government, and I aim to return it...and...this boy. Now, you can raise a ruckus all you want, but I'm leaving with them both. I ain't got no quarrel with any of you, so let's leave it at that."

Turning to Frank who's made his way to the Ranger with the Thompson in hand, the Ranger says, "Now, boy, you move on out to the street."

"Do as he says," Pedro nods to the young man.

"This is ridiculous," says the General in exasperation. "Somebody, do something."

Pedro looks at the General and says, "Let it go. There is nothing more to do, unless you want to get shot."

"This is preposterous!" shouts the General ineffectively. "You're allowing one...cowboy to waltz into this cantina and just walk off with that gun!"

"Mister," says the Ranger. "This isn't anything personal between the both of us. So, let's just keep it that way." Looking the group at the table over and backing up with both weapons leveled, the Ranger says, "I'll be moving on...and you can attend to your revolution as you see fit. Until then, don't interfere."

In desperation, the General looks at Pedro and orders him, "Do something!"

"Sit down, General," says Lujan, trying to relax the man. "This has gone far enough. I will not sacrifice more lives on your account. I've no taste for spilt blood anymore."

Growing more anxious as he watches the Ranger backpedaling, the General pleads with Lujan. "This weapon can help the revolution."

Pedro turns to Schmidt, looking him over. "Were you in Juarez when the *Maderistas* took control? Did you hear the cries of '*Viva Revolución*' from the peons as they finally had a bit of hope when Diaz was ousted after thirty years of dictatorial rule? This is a human struggle that has lost perspective," Pedro tells the General. "Let the Ranger go. I want no more trouble."

"I will not stand for this," says the German General.

From beneath the counter of the bar, the bartender pulls up a shotgun and cocks the weapon, pointing it at the Ranger's back, catching the lawman completely by surprise.

The General sees this and stands up with a smile on his face as he gauges the distance between the bartender and the Ranger and between the Ranger and himself. Seeing the Ranger closing his eyes for a moment, General Schmidt reaches into his coat pocket and pulls out a Mauser pocket pistol, taking steady aim at the Ranger.

"As they so quaintly say," says the General, slowly walking to the Ranger with the pistol pointed at the lawman's head, "we've got the drop on you."

Reaching for the Ranger's shotgun, he says, "I wouldn't do anything rash. He places the weapon on the bar, then removes the pistol from the Ranger's hand and places that on the bar as well. Motioning the bartender to back off, he circles the Ranger, sizing him up. "This is where the Old West comes to an end for you, Texas Ranger."

Coming face to face with the Ranger, still pointing the gun at his face, the General speaks to Pedro. "See? There's nothing to fear, Pedro."

"Lujan?" the Ranger questions, as the General motions him to raise his hands.

"*Si, Sénor*," says Pedro, smiling. "At your service."

"I came for that gun," says the Ranger.

"It's ours now," the General smiles. "It'll be taken to Germany where the Krupps will produce it in mass quantities using superior German engineering," he says. "We'll sweep through Europe with every foot soldier carrying one of these. Within one year, we'll take control of Europe, then we'll invade the Americas. There'll be no stopping us."

"Why would you invade the Americas?" the Ranger asks. "Isn't Europe enough territory for you?"

Insulted, the General takes a step towards the Ranger and slaps him in the face. "Insolent dog! We'll take whatever we see fit to take."

"Mexico, too?" the Ranger asks, as blood begins to run from his lip.

"If need be," replies the General, adding confidently, "Yes." The General raises his pistol and takes aim again. "There will be no stopping the German people from their destiny with a weapon such as this," he says pridefully. "We are the Aryan race!"

"Aryan race?" the Ranger wonders out loud. "Is that anything like the Kentucky Derby?" It gains him another slap from the General, who backs up and levels the pistol into the Ranger's face.

"Fool!" shouts the German General, looking at the Ranger as if looking at a clown. "We'll rule the world!"

"I've got to tell you," the lawman says, shaking his head slowly as more blood drips from his lip. "I don't generally like being slapped around."

Stepping forward, Schmidt slaps him again. "Get used to it, American scum. This is just a preview of what's to come in the future."

The Ranger shakes his head, recovering. He looks over at Pedro. "Lujan? Do you hear what he's saying? That weapon isn't for your cause. He has a different plan for it. I'd say it was a master plan." With his hands raised, he studies the German General and nods, smiling. "Well, that don't cut no mustard with me, Mister."

"Mustard?" repeats the General. "Cut mustard?" He looks at Lujan. "You don't cut mustard!" Stepping forward, he hits the Ranger with his Mauser, staggering the lawman where he stands. "Don't worry about the blood. You'll be dead before too long."

"Does that mean I don't get the gun?" asks the Ranger.

"You're about to die and you worry about the gun?" the General shakes his head in wonderment. While holding aim on the Ranger, he speaks to Pedro. "You see? This is an example of the American value system. He stands before you, about to die, and he wonders about this weapon."

"Is it necessary to kill him?" Pedro asks.

"He's worthless to us," says the General. "The weapon is more vital."

"To whom?" questions the Ranger. "You, or them?" he looks at Lujan.

"It shouldn't make any difference to you," the German General says. "I'm about to write the last chapter in your sordid dime novel life."

"General?" Pedro says. "There may be more coming."

Startled, the Ranger eyes his captor and questions, *"General?"*

Proud that the ranger recognizes his title, he claps his heels and introduces himself. "General Heinrich Schmidt. German military attache to Mexico."

"You are a ways from home, aren't you," the Ranger notes, shaking his head.

Pointing the pistol straight-armed and aimed, the General says, "The Rhineland is my home, but Germany will rule the world."

Looking at Lujan, the Ranger asks, "Is this the best you can do for advisors?"

"Shut up, ignorant swine!" shouts General Schmidt.

Uncomfortable by everything, Lujan interjects. "There's been enough killing, General. His death serves no purpose in our revolution."

"He's right," says the lawman, standing there with his hands up, surveying the room. "I'm only after a weapon that rightfully belongs to the U. S. Government."

"As long as I have control of such a weapon," the General says, eyeing the Ranger, "it belongs to the German Government."

"What about the revolution?" Lujan questions Schmidt with concern.

"There's a greater battle to be waged in Europe," says the German officer, advising Lujan. He steps back and holds his aim, chuckling. "You won't object if I back off before shooting you, will you? I'd hate to get blood on my suit."

The Ranger examines the German General from head to foot, causing the General to ask in exasperation, "What are you looking at?"

"I was just looking at those boots of yours," says the Ranger. Are they iron-toed or something? I mean, I've heard about them."

"Boots?" inquires the General in complete astonishment, looking at the Ranger.

"You wouldn't deny a man a final request, would you?" ventures the lawman, staring at the General with the Mauser leveled on him.

Still perplexed, Schmidt asks, "And what would that be, Texas Ranger? The name of my boot maker?" he laughs.

"Well," says the Ranger, looking up and square into the eyes of the German advisor. He smirks a little, saying, "I ain't all clear on all this German engineering stuff you've been going on about," he says, shaking his head, "but I am familiar with what they call, 'American ingenuity.'"

Dropping his right hand, a wrist-activated palm pistol slips into his hand as he takes a quick shot at the General, catching him completely by surprise, squarely wounding him in the gun hand. The astonished General drops the revolver and grabs his blood-stained hand with the other.

Spinning and dashing for cover behind the bar counter, the Ranger lets go another shot, hitting and dropping the bartender. The two *Villiastas* next to Lujan and Schmidt whip out their pistols and blast away at the bar counter as Jesse and his friend bolt for the cantina door as the hot leads fly.

From behind the counter, the Ranger puts his palm pistol back in place, grabs a bottle beneath the counter and tosses it in the direction of the gunfire. Reaching over the top of the bar, he pulls down the scatter gun, crawls to the end of the bar, stands and lets go with both barrels, blowing both men back.

Two other *Villiastas* enter from the hallway with guns drawn and start shooting wildly at the Ranger, as the German General, Pedro, and Frank make an escape out the front entrance of the cantina. But the Ranger drops down and comes up on the other side of the counter with a pistol in hand, thumb-busting the revolver empty, catching the two men and laying them down.

Moving from the back of the counter towards the front door of the cantina, the Ranger hears the sound of horses passing down the alleyway towards the rear of the establishment. He turns in unison with their loud pounding hooves. Reaching into his duster and pulling his pump action shotgun out, he faces the back wall of the cantina and lets go with five rapid shots, putting a hole in it large enough for him to walk through.

Walking towards the smoke and dust left over from the hole in the wall he just blasted, the lawman steps into the sunlight and onto the hot gravel, only to see Schmidt, Lujan, and Frank in a mad dash on horseback headed towards the open desert.

Opening his duster, the Ranger puts the shotgun away and pulls out his Winchester, cocks and shoots, cocks and shoots and finally lowers the weapon. He puts it inside the duster, pulls out the Buffalo gun, takes aim and lets go a thundering blast, slamming into the horse Pedro is on, downing it and sending the rider flying free of the downed animal. Frank reins his horse to a stop as Pedro gets up and dashes to the horse and grabs the saddle and Frank at the same time, dragging himself aboard. Frank kicks the horse to a full run, with Schmidt just ahead of them.

Just as he is pulling the Buffalo gun up again and taking aim, the lawman gets tapped on the shoulder, startling him. Turning, he sees Lillian. "Did you ever consider hitting them with the butt of the gun?" she asks. "You'd save bullets that way."

"Where'd you come from?" asks the surprised Ranger.

"With a ruckus like this, how could we miss you?" says the little lady.

Unamused by her jokes, the Ranger pulls up the gun, takes aim and lets go another thundering shot that bucks him up and back. The shot misses the three fleeing men. "Damn," he says, shaking his head.

"What are you going to do now?" questions Lillian.

Giving the little lady a hard look, he turns, walks back into the cantina through the hole in the wall and picks up his scatter gun from behind the counter. He moves towards the entrance of the establishment to exit into the street where he sees Captain Frederick M. Turner, Lieutenant George S. Patton, Juan, and the 13th Cavalry, mounted and waiting.

Slipping his scatter gun into his duster while looking at these men, he continues to the hitching post and unties his horse. He climbs aboard, takes the reins, and spurs his mount in chase.

"You!" shouts Captain Turner to the Ranger, as Lillian exits the cantina with the Thompson in hand, helpless to stop the lawman, as he rounds the corner into the alleyway, on the chase.

Lillian approaches the Captain and hands him the submachine gun. He looks down at her, accepting the weapon, saying, "Where did you come by this?"

"In the cantina," Lillian responds.

"Who was that man?" asks the Captain.

"That was the Ranger I told you about," she reminds him. Turning to Juan, she says, "That must have been Lujan." Juan nods in agreement.

"Who?" asks the Captain.

"The man the Ranger's been after. Pedro Lujan. One of Pancho Villa's advisors." Walking to her mount and getting on, she takes the horse's reins and leads it towards the alleyway. "That must have been the man he was shooting at."

She spurs her horse as the Captain shouts, "Where are you going?"

"To follow him," she says. "He might need help."

Juan gets on a horse left behind from the mountain shootout and follows Lillian towards the open range.

"Patton," the Captain orders his First Lieutenant, "prepare to move the troops out."

"Yes, Sir," says the young lieutenant, saluting his commanding officer and riding to the formation of Buffalo Soldiers. The young lieutenant approaches the sergeant major, for salutes and orders exchanged.

"Prepare to move out!" shouts the Captain, as Patton returns to his side on horseback. Checking his Cavalry formation once, the Captain raises his right arm and shouts, "Forward!" motioning the advance.

As the horses move down the gravel towards the alleyway, Captain Turner looks at Patton. "Lieutenant?"

"Sir?" responds Patton.

"You've been designing a new saber for the Army, haven't you?"

"Yes, Sir," the lieutenant replies with curiosity.

"Perhaps there will be something to be learned from this that'll be helpful to you on those plans," says the Captain, as they pass through the alleyway towards the wide, open expanse of desert.

Two horses, one carrying General Schmidt, the other laboring under Frank at the reins, and Pedro holding on for dear life, slow down as they approach an arroyo and move through the hazard of the dry creek bed, then racing for higher ground.

"He's right behind us," shouts Pedro as he grips the young man, pushing him to go faster.

Driving hard on the trail and oblivious to anything but the two horses and three riders ahead of him, the Ranger gives that Appaloosa free reins and spurs his mount for all it's got.

Coming to a rise, the General pulls a rifle from the saddle scabbard and attempts a shot as Frank and Pedro's horse tops the ridge. "That'll only anger him more," says Frank, looking back while gripping his horse between his legs.

"Not if I get him first," says Schmidt, trying to sight the Ranger on a full charge.

"Don't anger him!" Frank shouts. "Don't anger him!" The General squeezes off a shot that spooks his horse into bucking. He misses his intended target. Concerned over control of his horse, the General drops the rifle and fights the beast until he's able to guide it back on course of the retreat, following Frank and Pedro just ahead of him.

On a full charge, the Ranger reaches into his duster and pulls out the Winchester and cocks it. Standing in the saddle, he takes a shot at the fleeing men and misses. Coming to the edge of the arroyo, he pulls up his horse, jumps off, puts the Winchester back into his duster and pulls out the Buffalo gun. Loading the weapon with a bullet from one of the holsters crossing his chest, he kneels, snaps up the long distance vernier sight, and squeezes off one shot as Lillian gallops up behind him

The echo of that thunder gun gains the attention and respect of Schmidt, Frank and Pedro as they hear the bullet whiz by them on their dash around a bend.

Wide-eyed and scared, the General shouts, "We've got to stop him!" He digs his heels into the belly of his beast, snapping his reins on the neck of the horse and forcing every ounce of energy the horse can muster into the escape.

Pointing ahead while holding onto Frank, Lujan shouts, "Over there! Over that way!" He continues to shout and point, gaining the eye of the General. "My *hacienda* is just ahead. I have weapons there," he yells, hanging on tight to the young man guiding his ride as he looks back to see if the Ranger has rounded the bend yet.

"It'll be my pleasure to kill him," yells the General as he kicks his horse for as much as it can sustain under the blazing heat and circumstances of the moment.

Rounding another bend leading into a small valley surrounded by some hills, the riders dash towards a hacienda where they leap off their horses and make a mad foot dash for the front door and enter.

Following Pedro into the living room where a variety of rifles are mounted on a wall, the General reaches for a Sharps, desperately shouting, "Give me some bullets, quick! I'm going to get him before he gets us!"

Lujan goes through some drawers of a desk, finally handing a box of bullets to Frank, who dashes over to the window the General has just opened. Schmidt takes the box of shells, opens it and grabs a bullet to load the weapon. Reaching for two more bullets, he puts them between his fingers and kneels at the window, sticking the rifle out and taking aim. "This will be the last time he comes to Mexico," the General says out loud as he eyes the open area before him for the first sign of the Ranger.

Climbing aboard his Appaloosa, Lillian grabs the Ranger, fighting him off the charge. "Stop!" she pleads as he tries to control his horse while the little lady is tugging and pulling on him.

Lillian continues to shout, "Will you just stop! The Cavalry is just behind us!" Unable to give chase with the little lady clinging onto him and the saddle of his horse, the Ranger looks at her, then behind him to check his rear.

Looking down at Lillian with fire in his eyes as she's being dragged across the ground, the Ranger pulls up on the reins, halting his horse. Shaking his head, he says, "This ain't just a Ranger thing anymore...it's personal."

"Abner," Lillian pleads. "You just sit still and let the Cavalry take care of it."

"Not while I've got bullets in my guns," the Ranger stands firm.

Bucking that mount and fighting the Ranger back, she pleads again. "You've got to stop this right now! This is a military action now."

Hesitating a moment, the Ranger stares down at the little lady as fiercely as a man has ever done, then yanking those reins up and spurring that horse to the edge of the arroyo until he's free of Lillian, he stops when he hears her cry, "I don't want you killed!"

Before he edges up to the roadway leading to the dried out river bed, he stares at Lillian and assures her, "The only killing going to be done around here will be by my hand."

"Not if they get you first," she reasons, walking towards the lawman and his horse.

Pulling his hat down, the Ranger says, "It won't make a difference now. I have to stop them. There ain't no other way."

Close enough now to grab the reins of his horse and fight him off the chase again, she says, "Whose life are you taking anyhow? What about Juan and me? Don't we count?" Staring up at the Ranger, she says, "You know we count on you a lot. If you get killed, we won't be worth a lot to the Rangers."

Staring at her and shaking his head, the Ranger says, "Do you have any idea what they have planned?"

"Whatever it is, the Cavalry can take care of it," she insists, noting the rising dust on the distant horizon formed by the columns of the 13th on the advance. "Look!" she shouts. "They're almost here. You've done your job. We've recovered the guns."

"What about that little jailbird?" he asks, still fighting for control of the Appaloosa's reins.

"The Cavalry will bring him in," she answers.

"He won't give up easy," says the Ranger, realizing the Cavalry is closing in on them, prompting more fight from the cantankerous old Ranger who is dead set in his ways of frontier justice.

"Do you think two men and a boy can stand against that?" Lillian asks, making her point. The sound of the thundering hooves are now clearly audible in the distance.

"I ain't asking you to come along," he says, trying another approach.

"I'm begging you to stop this obsession," she pleads, still trying to reason with him.

"Obsession?" the lawman says, rankled. "You think this is an obsession?" He grinds his teeth and yanks on the reins of his horse. "This is a pursuit of armed criminals," he emphasizes. "It's our sworn duty to uphold the law."

"Not when the Cavalry is here to take over," she insists. "Look, you've done your job, Mister. You stood off a whole saloon with desperadoes. Isn't that enough killing for one day?" she asks, finally letting go of the reins as the Cavalry is close enough to take over. "It'll be over soon enough," she assures the lawman as Juan rides up to the two and dismounts to join Lillian. "Pack up those irons, Mister. You earned your pay for the day," she says, turning to Juan and the Cavalry.

"The Cavalry will take over now," Juan also assures the Ranger.

"What's the situation here?" Captain Turner asks, coming to a halt.

"This is Abner Caleb. He's been tracking the bandits," says Lillian, somewhat relieved.

"Where are they now?" asks the Officer in Command.

"Just ahead," says the overruled and defeated Ranger.

"How many?" the Captain inquires, looking at the three.

The Ranger says, "Two men and a..."

"Boy," Lillian finishes for him, looking at the Ranger.

Squaring off with Lillian in an eye-for-eye confrontation, the Ranger lifts his head to face the Captain. "I wounded one, but I want that boy. You can do what you want with the rest, but the boy is...ours," he says, catching himself and returning to his stare-down with the little lady.

"We'll survey the area and see what we can do about it," the Captain says, all duty and order.

"That little hoodlum held up a bank, shot a teller, escaped from me twice, and I can't let that go unpunished," says the Ranger with conviction.

"We'll see about that," says the Captain. "Until otherwise indicated, this is now an official military action and your services will no longer be needed."

"We understand, Captain," Lillian acknowledges.

The Captain turns to his Lieutenant and orders, "Tell the sergeant major to split the column on our advance."

"Yes, Sir," salutes the lieutenant, holding it while inquiring, "Will there be a charge, Sir?"

Returning the salute and eyeing the lieutenant as he thinks about the question, he responds, "If need be." Looking at Lillian, Juan, and the Ranger a moment, the Captain returns his attention to the lieutenant. "Give the order, Lieutenant."

"Sergeant major!" shouts Lieutenant Patton, drawing a tough-looking old trooper forward on his horse.

The sergeant salutes the young officer. "Yes, Sir!"

Returning the salute, Patton says, "Break ranks and send one column to each side of the road when we come up off the arroyo."

"Yes, Sir!" salutes the sergeant.

"Sergeant Major?" Turner cuts in with a question.

"Sir?"

"Do you have a forward point man?"

"Finest in the Cavalry, Sir," the sergeant responds without hesitation.

"Send him forward with another man to give us a report on what's just beyond that bend off that rise," the Captain orders. "And I'll need six of your best horsemen for another assignment."

"Yes, Sir," the sergeant major responds, saluting. He rides down the Cavalry formation.

Two troops dart out of line and move down the arroyo to the other side, where they climb to the rise and ride towards the bend and disappear. Six other troopers walk their horses up to the Captain and Lieutenant as the rest of the troops begin the ride down the side of the arroyo, over the dried river bed and towards the other side of the rise.

"Lieutenant," says the Captain. "If reports come back of a fortification of any kind ahead, I want the troops to dismount and flank it from rifle distance."

"Yes, Sir," says Patton, saluting.

"And George," says the Captain, "send these men off for message relay back to us, then, have them form up with us following any troop displacement." He salutes the lieutenant.

"Yes, Sir," says the young lieutenant, saluting his commanding officer and waving the six Buffalo Soldiers to follow him into the arroyo.

Lillian is impressed by the swift action. "Captain? May we accompany you?"

"Only if you stay out of harm's way," nods the Captain. "I understand your need for the prisoner, but this is our action now."

Pedro approaches the General at the window, peering into the clearing leading to the hacienda as he checks for any sign of the Ranger in the surrounding hillsides. "The Ranger must be drawing near by now," he says to the General. "I can sense him." Perspiration beads at his temples.

"He'll never penetrate this house," says the General, reassuring Lujan. "I'll make sure of that. He'll come around that corner and I'll shoot him before he's a heartbeat from here." He sights the Sharps he has shouldered.

"I wouldn't underestimate the Texas Ranger," Pedro warns his new house guest. "He is very resourceful.

"So I've heard," says the General, turning to Lujan and showing him his injured wrist now tied with a handkerchief. Returning to his firing line and taking aim again, he says, "But reputations can be gained or lost in moments."

"You are too certain of yourself, General," Pedro says.

Turning once more to Lujan, the General says, "This isn't the frontier, Pedro. I'm not a savage Indian or some...desperado." Taking up aim, Schmidt goes on. "I'm not afraid of any reputation. I can stand man to man with him."

"Then," responds Pedro looking directly at the General, "why do you seek protection behind a window?"

"To see from which direction he comes," says Pancho Villa's tense German military advisor.

"There's only one way in," comments Pedro.

Angrily, the General turns to Lujan, shouldering his weapon. "Allow me to deal with this man in my own fashion. We'll see how he deals with the element of surprise."

One trooper jumps off his horse with a rope in hand and ties one end to a tree and unrolls the line to tie the other end to another tree. The rest of the troopers dismount, tie the leads to their horses to the line, pull their carbines from the saddle scabbards and rush into position behind a hill overlooking the hacienda. The sergeant major moves down the line as his troops take up arms and aim.

"Stand steady," the sergeant major repeats as he makes his way past the men.

One trooper looks to the man next to him. "This won't take long."

The other trooper takes a bead off his weapon, responding, "It'll be a duck shoot."

"It'll be murder," observes another trooper, taking aim.

"What do you think they'll do?" asks the first trooper.

"Speaking from experience," says a corporal next to the first trooper, taking his eye off aim and looking the troops over, "we'll attack from the front and flush them out. This is going to be a shooting gallery before too long and they won't stand a chance."

The first trooper says, "We know the lieutenant can shoot at rabbits...let's see how he stands up to men that shoot back."

The sergeant major walks down the line repeating the same order to the pride and joy of this enlisted man's career. "Steady men. Stand ready. Don't shoot until ordered."

Peering out the window with a steady aim on nothing, General Heinrich Schmidt says, "That Texas Ranger is about to get a belly-full of German diplomacy."

Shaking his head, Pedro says, "I don't think this is such a good idea, General."

Angrily, the General turns to Pedro. "Leave that up to me. I'm the advisor."

Frank takes cover behind a desk and peeks over the top. Pedro follows his lead, joining the young man behind the heavy wooden desk and backing off the General.

The General, looking for Pedro and Frank, takes his eye off aim. He sees them huddled behind a desk. "Are you going to hide like that little boy?" he asks Pedro.

Peeking over the top of the desk, Pedro says, "This is now your battle, General."

Shouldering his weapon and turning back to the window, Schmidt eyes the only road in. "I'll shoot him when he's in the open. If I miss, he'll have nowhere to run."

"Firing positions," orders the sergeant major. His troops crawl forward on their stomachs and clear their line of fire. They level their carbines, taking aim.

"Don't fire until ordered to," commands the sergeant major as bluejackets square off and take aim across the flank position. They have the hacienda surrounded and out-gunned.

"Stand ready," he repeats to his men. "Stand steady."

With his troops firmly in place, armed and aimed, the sergeant major sights the area, looks towards Captain Turner, Lieutenant Patton, and the other six Buffalo Soldiers just around the bend and signals them from his position behind a hill, just out of sight of the hacienda below him.

"There's the signal," First Lieutenant Patton informs his commanding officer, pointing to the hills and drawing the attention of all the soldiers on horseback.

Turning towards the hills for a look on his own, the Captain sees the sergeant major waving. "Return his signal, Lieutenant," says the Captain as he looks his troops over. Walking his horse forward a few steps, he takes another view of the surrounding area, finally turning back to the troops behind him. "Positions, Gentlemen."

Lieutenant Patton and the six Buffalo Soldiers rein their mounts up to Captain Turner and come to a halt next to him. The Captain looks to his left, then his right, then down to his scabbard belted to his uniform. Reaching for his sabre, he pulls it up and out. The cold steel weapon sounds a pitch as it slides out of its confines. Raising the glistening sabre in the afternoon sun, the Captain orders, "Sabres!"

In unison, the soldiers withdraw their weapons, steadying their horses, who are galvanized by the sound of the blades being raised by their riders.

Placing the sabre on his right shoulder at rest, the Captain says, "On my order, prepare to charge." He reins his horse to a slow walk. "Forward!" he orders.

The troops pace their horses to his. The small formation of eight men increase their march to a trot as they round a bend leading to the hacienda. Coming to a canter, then a gallop, the soldiers hold steady as they round the bend and see the distant hacienda.

Lowering his sabre and pointing it at the structure, Captain Turner spurs his mount, shouting, "Charge!"

Lieutenant Patton and the six Buffalo Soldiers lower their sabres and instantly join in the attack.

The hard pounding hooves of the racing horses on the desert floor are drowned by the blood-curdling yells of the riders on the advance.

With one eye closed and the other sighted down the long barrel of the Sharps aimed on open desert and hills before him, General Schmidt pauses to wipe his forehead then return to the firing line. He pauses again at an unusual sound that breaks up the silence from his position at the window. The mysterious sound reaches far into the room, puzzling Pedro. "*Que pasa?*" he asks, peeking over the desk at the General.

Leveling the weapon and sighting once more, the General fingers the trigger, bracing himself. As he pulls the hammer back he sees a horse round the bend at full charge. No, two, four...eight soldiers on a charge! Wild-eyed and beyond surprise, the General goes limp in astonishment. Putting the weapon down and slamming the window shut, he backs up to the desk where Frank and Pedro have taken refuge.

Pedro looks at him shaking and transfixed by what he's just seen. "What position of German diplomacy does this fall under?" Pedro asks.

Looking at Pedro with contempt, the General dips for cover behind the desk as the blood-curdling shouts outside the hacienda grow stronger. Pedro looks at Frank huddled in the corner, then towards the window, before taking cover himself.

The eight soldiers with sabres lowered, yelling and charging on horseback, come to an immediate halt outside the dust-filled hacienda, unable to advance any further.

Captain Turner turns to Lieutenant Patton. "Well? Where are they?" The horses snort and shuffle their feet on the gravel just outside the front door.

Lowering his sabre, the Captain stands in his saddle and looks around. He turns to his men who are just as surprised. "We did get a signal, didn't we?" he asks.

"Yes, Sir," says the also-surprised Lieutenant.

"Well, then," demands the Captain, "just exactly where are they?"

"I don't know, Sir."

Shaking his head in exasperation and frustration, the Captain says, "Well...go knock at the door."

The young lieutenant dismounts and walks up to the door and knocks. No answer. He knocks again. Still no answer. He turns and shrugs his shoulders, not knowing what else he can do.

"Try again, Lieutenant. Somebody's got to be home," Captain Turner remarks, looking through some windows of the hacienda from his horse. The other men also look for any signs of life from their positions on horseback.

Huddled for cover behind the desk, Pedro, Frank, and the General hear a sharp knock on the door. They look at each other in confusion. "Anyone in there?" someone shouts from the outside. The knocking grows louder and heavier, eventually becoming a weighty thump.

Looking at the Captain, Patton shrugs again. He turns to the door once more, lifts his sabre and pounds the butt of the handle into the hard wood door, leaving deep indentations. "Open up!" the lieutenant shouts. "OPEN UP, NOW!", he repeats, lifting his foot and kicking the door. After a momentary pause, Patton knocks, kicks and slams the butt handle of his sabre into the door, yelling, "Come on out!"

Lillian, Juan, and the Ranger round the bend, leading their horses in a slow walk to the hacienda, as it appears the Cavalry are already there and in control of the situation.

"Don't worry," says Lillian to the disheartened Ranger as he lolls along just shaking his head in disappointment. "They said they'd give us Frank," Lillian assures the lawman who's unable to express the deep personal failure he appears to have suffered from this experience.

Turning to the little lady, the Ranger says, "It's that German General I'm concerned about now."

"The Army will take care of him," responds Juan.

Shaking his head in deep disgust, the Ranger says, "You know he actually slapped me!" It does not even approach the contempt he has for Heinrich Schmidt, German General and advisor to Pancho Villa.

"Is that what you're so worked up about?" laughs Lillian who thinks it is a minor thing.

Rubbing his cheek, the Ranger grits his teeth and says, "You know, nobody's ever slapped me before." He eyes the hacienda up ahead. "I owe him for that."

"But the threat of the raid is now over," says Juan.

"We've stopped it," Lillian corroborates. "Isn't that enough?"

"NO!" says the Ranger, bringing his horse to a stop and looking his fellow Texas Rangers over.

"What else do you want?" Lillian asks in frustration, bringing her horse to a stop as Juan pulls up for an explanation as well.

"That General was talking about world domination. Not just the war in Europe, but America too," the Ranger says.

"He doesn't seem very dominant now," remarks Juan, pointing towards the hacienda where Lieutenant Patton is continuing his assault on the front door.

"This is a direct order of the U. S. Army! Open this door immediately or we will...." Lieutenant Patton turns to Captain Turner, shrugs, turns back to the door and yells, "...burn the house down!" Still no answer at the door.

Exhausted and frustrated, the First Lieutenant pleads, "Please open the door."

"I'd say the General's plans won't get very far now," says Lillian as she finally spots the rest of the Buffalo Soldiers dotting the hillside with weapons aimed at the hacienda.

Unmoved by all the firepower he sees outlined against the hills, the Ranger spurs his mount forward. "You allow people like that to go free, they'll come back to haunt you someday. You mark my words."

Lillian and Juan pull up next to him. "He might have diplomatic immunity," Juan thinks out loud.

"Then they'll send him back to Germany and he can make some plans on the war that's already being waged over there," says Lillian, trying to reason with the lawman. "Are you going to track him all the way over there?"

"It don't hold well—him beating on an old man like me, then talkin' about world domination," the Ranger gripes, rubbing on that cheek of his as he shakes his head. He looks at his fellow Texas Rangers. "Where's the justice in all that?"

"His failure will be punishment enough," says Juan, the voice of Yaqui wisdom.

"You'll just have to accept what the Army gives us out of this," says Lillian, confident that justice will be served.

"You mean that little...," the Ranger snarls, reacting to Lillian's solution to the whole matter.

"Boy!" she breaks in. "He's still a boy!"

Lieutenant Patton steps back as the door opens and Frank steps out with his hands over his head. The young officer looks over at Captain Turner. "Where are the others?"

"Inside," says the scared young man, looking at Patton and the troops on horseback. "They won't come out."

"Well, go get them. And be quick about it," Patton says in frustration.

Frank backs into the house and drops his hands, rushing down a hallway towards a room. Lieutenant Patton turns to Captain Turner and sees Lillian, Juan, and the Ranger approaching. The Captain turns and sees them too.

As Lieutenant Patton turns back to the hacienda, Frank, Pedro, and the General exit with arms raised. The lieutenant directs them to the gravel road in front of Captain Turner.

"I have diplomatic immunity as a German," shouts the General. Seeing the Ranger, Lillian, and Juan approaching on horseback, the General's voice rises a pitch. Pointing at Abner, he fairly squeaks. "And keep that man away from me!"

Curious, Patton, Turner and the other six troopers turn around as Lillian, Juan, and the Ranger ride up and come to a stop.

The Ranger stares at Schmidt. Finally coming to a decision, he reaches into his duster. Lillian puts her hand on his, pressing it down. "Let it be," she says.

"He's unarmed," says Juan, concerned at what the Ranger was about to do.

"I was just going to wing him," says the Ranger, yanking his arm out of the duster and rubbing his cheek, all the while eyeing that German national with a look that could kill.

The mounted troopers get off the horses and approach the captives as the Ranger, Lillian and Juan decide to move forward and take their prisoner. Dismounting, they walk over to Captain Turner and Lieutenant Patton as Frank, Pedro, and the General are pushed against the wall and frisked.

"Is that who you're after?" Patton nods towards the young man, addressing the Texas Rangers.

Still rubbing his cheek, the Ranger eyes Schmidt. "For the time being."

Patton looks at Lillian and Juan for corroboration. Lillian smiles and nods. The Ranger moves past the soldiers towards the German General who is against the wall of the building like his fellow captives. He stops in front of

Schmidt, looking him over. Grabbing the man's injured right hand in a handshake, he applies just enough pressure to make the General buckle at his knees.

"This here is General Heinrich Schmidt, a German advisor to Pancho Villa," Abner tells the soldiers. Slapping the General's wounded hand, Abner releases the handshake. He admonishes the soldiers, "You take good care of him, now. You see, he's got some serious big plans for the future." Schmidt grimaces in pain.

Moving towards Pedro, the Ranger eyes the man up and down then slaps him on the shoulder, gripping it like a tight wrench. Pedro cringes with pain. "And this here is Pedro Lujan," the Ranger says, removing his vice grip and shoving him back. "He is a direct advisor to Pancho Villa himself."

The Ranger steps back, nodding at the Captain and the lieutenant. "They're yours now," he says. "But watch out for that General there. He's got some big designs on the world."

Lieutenant Patton says, "Seems he has problems just answering a knock at a front door. You can have the boy," he tells Abner. "We have what we want." Then he looks sternly at the three Texas Rangers. "You get back across that border before I change my mind about everything. Is that clear?" It sounds more of an order than anything else.

"Thank you, Lieutenant," says Lillian. "We can take it from here."

Fitting that old hat firmly down on his head, the Ranger nods. "Yeah. Let's get a move on before I have a change in attitude."

Lillian leads Frank to one of the horses he rode in on. The young man turns to take one last look at Pedro and the General, but he catches a glimpse of the Ranger opening his duster, which is a reminder to him of their previous encounters.

Mounting their horses and spurring them to the open range ahead, the three Texas Rangers and Frank head back for the border and the United States of America.

In a double column riding in from the open range towards the Headquarters of General Pershing's Punitive Expeditionary Forces base camp, the 13th Cavalry parades through the campgrounds with their captives Pedro Lujan and General Schmidt.

General John J. "Blackjack" Pershing emerges from his tent on advance word and watches as the Buffalo Soldiers march their captives towards him. The group halts in front of him. Returning the Captain's salute, Pershing says, "Turner? Explain this."

Motioning the captives forward under guard, Captain Turner turns to General Pershing. "This is Pedro Lujan, advisor to Pancho Villa. And this is General Schmidt, German Military Attaché."

"German?" remarks General Pershing in surprise. He turns to Patton for confirmation. "Lieutenant?'

"Yes, Sir," says Patton. "We charged them, but they wouldn't fight"

The General eyes the captives. "Take them to the stockade," he says. "We'll deal with them later." Looking at the young lieutenant, he says, "Patton. I want to speak to you right now." As the young lieutenant dismounts and walks towards General Pershing, he addresses Captain Turner. "And would you get somebody to stop that man from bleeding?" pointing to Schmidt.

"Yes, Sir," says Captain Turner, saluting. Spurring his mount towards some tents beyond the parade grounds, he shouts, "Forward, march!" The 13th Cavalry follows their commanding officer while holding guard on the two prisoners.

As Patton walks up to General Pershing and salutes, the General returns the salute and smiles. He shakes his head. "You may be a Lieutenant, but you're my bandit."

The three Rangers and Frank ride into town as the city awakens to another night of action. Automobiles, bicycles, wagons, and carriages pass. Ragtime entertains cowboys,

Indians, and Mexicans. Making their way through the traffic
to the jail, they dismount and enter the building.

The Deputy stands up from his chair behind the desk
as the group walks in with Frank. "Throw away the key this
time," says the Ranger, pushing the young man towards the
Deputy.

"He's just a...," Lillian begins, before she is cut off.

"What?" snarls the Ranger.

After taking a moment to think, she says, "Juvenile,
okay?" Turning to Frank she says, "You'll be all right," as the
Deputy escorts the young man to his cell in the adjoining
room.

While Juan sits down, the Ranger pulls out some
pistols to reload as he eyes the street, Lillian asks, "If we're
Texas Rangers, why do we spend so much time in Mexico?"

"The call to duty knows no boundaries," responds the
Ranger, pulling some shells from his holster and still looking
at the passing traffic. After a moment of thought, he turns to
her. "And that's part of the territory."

"That territory has just expanded," says Juan , tilting
his head and looking at Lillian and the Ranger.

"Just what does that mean?" asks Lillian, exhaustion
having caught up with her.

"Germany is not Mexico," Juan says.

"Nor is Texas, Arizona, California, New Mexico or any
other land that General can offer up," says the Ranger,
turning from the window and moving towards the desk. He
holsters one pistol and pulls out another, leaving the empty
casings on the desk.

"Do you think the revolution will ever end?" asks
Lillian, walking over to a chair.

"Not as long as they can't mind their own politics,"
says the Ranger, slipping cartridges into the cylinders of
another pistol. Holstering the revolver, he leaves more
casings on the table. "And using children and foreign
nationals will only prolong it."

A woman enters the jail, looking at everyone. "There's a young boy painting something on the side of your building," she says.

"That does it!" says the Ranger as he quickly sidesteps the lady at the door to the boardwalk and out to the alleyway.

A young man finishes his last stroke, puts the brush into a red paint bucket and steps back to admire his work, when he sees the Ranger jump off the edge of the boardwalk. Dropping the can, he dashes down the darkened alleyway.

"Come back here!" shouts the Ranger, reaching inside his duster and pulling out a long-barreled revolver. Lillian and Juan rush up to him just as he stands erect, levels and points it at the fleeing youth. Lillian grabs his gun hand and pushes it up, spins the Ranger around and confronts him.

"Let him go!" shouts Lillian, seriously concerned about this man before her.

Yanking his arm free, the Ranger says, "You can't allow them to do that. They'll come back...and before you know it, it'll be on everything."

"You have no right to shoot him," says Lillian.

"I reckon that depends on which side of the revolver you're standing on now, don't it?" he eyes the little lady. "Anyway, you know me, Lillian. I'd probably miss him anyway."

Holding the revolver up to her, he looks at her dead serious. "You think a shout from me is gonna be more effective than the rumble of one of these? Are you kidding? Why, that boy would have something to brag about the rest of his days. 'A Texas Ranger shot at me.'" Shaking his head, he puts the revolver back into his duster and backs off from the little lady and Juan chuckling.

"What?" asks Lillian, blinking her eyes.

"You think I can't tell the difference?" he says, shaking his head in disappointment for the little lady. "Now I gotta pull out the paint remover and get it all off and that's one part of the territory I don't like."

"Look," says Juan, pointing to the wall.

Lillian and the Ranger turn to the wall. They read the words above the red paint running to the ground. *VIVA REVOLUCIÓN!*

SEVEN DAYS LATER

The clear blue skies, untouched by any clouds, are disrupted by a buzzing sound on the distant horizon, growing louder by the moment. In the distance, a gray object pitches and dips as it finally rises and levels off. Racing over and past an open field as it banks, a Sopwith Camel continues its turn towards an approach and landing.

First Lieutenant George S. Patton stands next to a 1914 Ford convertible with Sergeant Simmons sitting behind the steering wheel of the vehicle. Two other touring cars sit idling behind the Ford drop-top with two drivers and two khaki-dressed soldiers standing by each car.

"General Pershing will be pleased by the arrival of the aero-squadron," Lieutenant Patton tells the sergeant sitting in the vehicle.

"Do they actually expect to see action?" asks Sergeant Simmons.

"I don't make out the orders, Sergeant," says the young lieutenant to the khaki-clad driver. "I just carry them out. They say 'Bring General Scriven in'...and I'm here to bring him in. Simple enough." Turning back to the aeroplane, the young lieutenant watches as it levels off and sweeps the open field.

With the wind racing past them in the open cockpit of the dual-winged aircraft, the pilot adjusts his goggles and scarf. Gripping the throttle with one hand and cupping his mouth with the other, he yells to his only passenger in the front seat. "Brace yourself, General!"

The one lone passenger has his hands already clutched to the fuselage. He's frozen in place, his scarf blowing in the wind as he stares straight ahead through his goggles.

"Wouldn't you want to do that?" asks Lieutenant Patton, arms crossed while admiring the freedom of free flight. "Fly like a bird?" He shakes his head at the wonder of it all.

"I got enough with just trying to drive one of these here automobiles," replies the sergeant. "I don't think I'm ready to take wing just yet."

"It's one of the marvels of the modern world, Sergeant," says the lieutenant, shaking his head in amazement. "You know, it was only one short decade ago that they actually had the first powered flight. And look at 'em now. Look how far we've come in such a short time." Patton continues to watch the aeroplane bank, level , and slow down for the landing.

The whirling engine roars in its descent onto the flat graveled roadway that's being used as a landing field amidst the vast expanse of wasteland in the desert. As the aeroplane finally touches ground, it bounces up and down, again and again, racing to the end of the makeshift airfield, where it slowly turns and rolls towards the three automobiles waiting by the side of the field. The pilot cuts the engine as the lieutenant and Sergeant Simmons run to the plane.

Unbuckling his seatbelt, the pilot climbs out of the cockpit and jumps to the ground. After saluting Lieutenant

Patton, he lifts his goggles and rests them on top of his leather flight helmet. He notices Lieutenant Patton still holding his salute for the General.

"General?" says Lieutenant Patton, still holding his salute. "We've been awaiting your arrival. General?" Looking closer with concern at the silent General, he turns to the pilot with questioning eyes.

"He's probably just a little fatigued," says the pilot diplomatically, taking off his helmet and goggles and dusting himself. "It happens on the first flight...sometimes."

"General?" the young lieutenant tries once more, still holding his salute. Peering closer at the General, Patton gets a better view of the passenger. He finally drops his salute and turns to the pilot. "You call that fatigued? He looks like death warmed over."

Turning to Sergeant Simmons, he points to the soldiers at the other touring cars. "Get those men over here!"

Simmons turns and yells, "Phillips, Jones, Morris—"

Covering his ears, Patton interrupts. "I said get them. I didn't say yell to them."

The sergeant salutes the lieutenant and dashes off to meet the three soldiers approaching the aeroplane. Simmons signals the driver in the last car to join them. All five men walk towards the plane.

Viewing the General in the cockpit, whose hands are locked in a grip on the fuselage as he stares forward, Lieutenant Patton steps up to the wing of the plane to get a better look.

As the other soldiers reach the plane, Patton organizes them. "Two of you men get on the other side of this plane. You two get over there." He points to the other side of the Sopwith as he jumps off the wing and walks over to the pilot. "We're going to have to pry him out," he says, shaking his head.

Oblivious to everything around him, the General, in charge of the aero-squadron, has a death grip on the side panels of the Sopwith Camel. The soldiers get into position on First Lieutenant Patton's command. They look over at the young lieutenant, waiting for further instructions.

"Get him out!" Patton says.

Leaning over and looking in, the sergeant says, "How?"

Frustrated, Patton shouts, "Carefully!"

Totally frozen in place, the General's grip on the rails of the fuselage is impossible to break. The soldiers struggle to pry open his hands one finger at a time as the General holds his fixed stare on the distant horizon.

One soldier leans over into the passenger seat and unbuckles the General's seatbelt while the other soldiers get toeholds on the side of the plane and climb up. Bracing themselves, they reach in and try to lift the General, but he's too heavy and can't be budged. The soldiers try again.

Patton walks over to the aeroplane, calling the men off. He peers in and takes a worried look at the General, studying him closely. Finally he says to Sergeant Simmons, "He looks like he's alive." That gains a confirming nod from the sergeant and the other men.

While Patton is speaking, one soldier moves between the passenger and the pilot's seat, attempting to lift the General from that position. He finally gains a hold under the General's arms and gets enough of a lift for the other men to reach in and lift the General in unison.

Carefully rotating the General in his fixed seated position, the soldiers lower him to two other soldiers on the ground, who turn to Patton. "What should we do with him now, Lieutenant?" one recruit asks.

Frustrated, Patton says, "Put him in the vehicle. And get those other men to help ease him into place." Turning to Sergeant Simmons, he mutters, "Don't want General Pershing upset over this."

"No, Sir!" agrees Sergeant Simmons.

Four men carry the frozen General to the 1914 Ford and struggle to put him in the back seat of the vehicle in the same way they struggled to get him out of the plane.

Walking towards the car and directing the soldiers back to their vehicles, Patton jumps into the passenger seat of his Ford. "Let's get him back to camp without causing any further damage to him," he says to Sergeant Simmons behind the wheel of the car.

Turning to the back seat where the General sits in his fixed state, the lieutenant says, "We'll be in camp soon, General. You just take it easy back there." Turning to Simmons and shaking his head, he motions the driver forward. The sergeant throws the vehicle into gear and steps on the gas pedal, leading the other two touring cars down the road towards the wide open expanse of desert.

A young boy in overalls and bare feet carries the reins of a horse in hand as his younger sister sits atop the old lumbering beast. They walk down an old flat gravel road as a backfiring motorcycle passes them. As the engine of the vehicle grinds into a lower gear, it spews fumes from its exhaust, then speeds up after passing the two children and the horse.

A horse-drawn wagon passes the two children going in the opposite direction. At a road junction, the young boy hesitates, then steps to the side of the road as he watches a 1914 Dodge truck drive by, kicking up dust and dirt, as the driver sounds the horn. When the dust settles, the faint outline of a single horseman can barely be seen in the distance. The children cross the road as the figure on the horizon becomes more recognizable as a cowboy on horseback.

The quiet little town is just awakening to a new day as a man unloads some supplies to a dolly from a 1915 Ford truck parked in front of a little store. The store merchant, standing on the boardwalk, looks on. Street lights flicker and die as the little boy, a little girl, and a horse, pass through town. A banner draped across the gravel-lined street reads: HUGHES FOR PRESIDENT.

The cowboy on horseback, wearing a large, canvas duster and a low-propped hat, passes just beneath the banner and walks his Appaloosa to a hitching post in front of a two-story hotel that proudly advertises itself as the TEXICAN HOTEL.

The rider dismounts and studies the sleepy little town as he waddles over to the hitching post in an unusual gait that appears to be labored. He ties his leather halter to the post and climbs the weathered stairs to the boardwalk, taking a moment to view the town, before entering the old hotel.

Abner sizes up the lobby a moment, then seeing that no one's behind the guest counter to help him, he slowly walks over to the hotel desk and turns the registry around to study it. He spins the book back around and looks at the mailboxes behind the counter, then turns to the stairs leading up.

As he waddles over to the stairway and grabs the bannister, the lights of the chandelier start to flicker, dance, fade, and finally go out, leaving the cowboy with a moment to think. Hesitating as he looks at the chandelier, he grabs the rail and begins his labored unusual climb up the stairs.

The Ranger's silhouette enters a darkened hallway and passes into shadows as he walks down the hall towards a specific door. He stops and takes a deep breath. Taking off his gloves, he wipes his lips with his wrist and slides it down the front of his duster. Opening his duster, he reveals his buscadero and two additional holstered revolvers crisscrossing his chest. He reaches into one of the inside pockets of his overcoat, pulls out a sawed-off scatter gun from his right and a revolver from the left side of his waist rig. He studies the two weapons in his hand.

Stepping closer to the door, he takes a long look at the room number, even taking time to reach up and see if the metal number is firmly in place with nails. He steps back, takes another deep breath, levels his weapons as he lifts his right foot....

He kicks the door open and steps into the room aggressively. There's nobody there. Puzzled, he looks around. Walking to the window, he looks out. He steps back and looks under the bed. He looks at the closet, but before he can walk over to it, the door across the hall opens and a man peeks out, startling the Ranger. Spinning around, he levels his weapons, scaring the man, who quickly closes the door.

As the Ranger looks back at the closet, curious, the door across the hallway opens again, revealing four tough-looking cowboys with their rigs on and shootin' irons within grasp. One of the cowboys reaches for his pistol as the Ranger instinctively swings the scatter gun to his side and lets go a shot, pinning the gunman up against the other cowboys. The cowboy's pistol goes off in a last twitch reaction before the other cowboys push him out of the room and slam the door.

The Ranger recovers and braces himself, then moves towards the door without hesitation. He automatically unloads the last shell in the scatter gun into the door lock, shattering the door. With a revolver blasting indiscriminately at anything that moves, the Ranger advances, dropping his scatter gun and reaching for another pistol inside his duster as he continues the assault on two men.

One last cowboy leaps out a window, taking a wild shot before diving. The Ranger drops a pistol and reaches for another, but the escaped man is free. Abner walks up to the window and looks out, as the cowboy jumps from the second story ledge to the ground and dashes across the street. The Ranger pulls his pistol up and takes a shot, missing the man now on the run.

Shaking his head and gritting his teeth, the Ranger rests one hot iron on the window sill as he holsters the other pistol. He pulls his Winchester out of the duster without batting an eye and pulls that long gun up to his shoulder. Taking aim, he lets go with one shot that downs the fleeing man in his tracks. He pulls his weapon up and carefully places it back into an inside pocket of his canvas overcoat and picks up the revolver cooling on the window sill.

A stirring on the floor behind the Ranger alerts him to turn and take aim. He sees one of the downed cowboys in the room reaching for his head with a wounded left arm. The pain in his arm overwhelms him instantly as he now remembers the gunshot he's taken. Moaning in pain, he grimaces when he looks up and sees the Ranger with a weapon trained on him.

"Don't shoot," he says, holding up his bloodstained hand and wounded arm. "I give up."·

Several people from down the hall are at the door of the hotel room, looking and gawking at the devastation. The Ranger pivots, pointing his pistol. Recognizing them as just curious people, the Ranger pulls up his weapon. "I'm Abner Caleb, Texas Ranger. These men are wanted by the great state of Texas."

The cowboy on the floor rubs his sore head. Turning to him, the Ranger kicks his pistol out of reach and holds his revolver on the seriously wounded man . He turns to the few people at the door. "Somebody get a sheriff."

"Texas Ranger?" says the downed cowboy.

"Yes, sir. Texas Ranger," Abner responds, keeping the revolver aimed and looking the man over in curiosity. Reaching down and grabbing the outlaw, he drags him to his feet as the outlaw groans and grabs his wounded arm.

"Well, get up," the Ranger says, straightening the man up and shoving him against the wall. "All you got was an arm wound. What are you belly-aching about?" He peers at the outlaw for a closer examination. "What did you do? Bang your head?" The outlaw stops rubbing his head and covers his wound.

"I must have knocked it against that dresser," the owl hoot says, pointing to the only other piece of furniture in the room other than the bed.

"Well," says the Ranger, "it could have been a lot worse."

Recovering, the owl hoot focuses in on the Ranger. "Being a Texas Ranger don't give you no right to break in on us like that," he complains, holding his arm.

"Yes, it does," replies the Ranger, reaching into his duster and pulling out a handful of wanted posters. He tosses them on the dresser next to the outlaw. "That's my license. You just pick on through them till you get to your picture and that'll be my license on you." He grins. "Same with the other boys. But since you're still standing, I'll just escort you over to the jail myself. How's that for license?"

He motions the man forward with his pistol. "Now, get a move on 'fore I just take in nothing but those posters and the fond memory of the conversation I had with you before you died." Scaring the hell out of the outlaw, the Ranger knows the owl hoot has no doubt the Ranger would carry out his word.

"Okay, Mister Ranger," the owl hoot says as he makes his way towards the door. "I don't aim to die over any misunderstanding. I reckon those posters do say, 'Dead or Alive.'" Grabbing his wounded hand, he shuffles to the door. "I do prefer bein' alive, so I'll go peaceful like." He raises his one good arm and exits the room ahead of the Ranger. The Ranger picks up the posters from the dresser and stuffs them into his duster as he follows close behind with his pistol aimed at the owl hoot .

Shuffling his feet, the outlaw slowly walks down the hallway towards the stairs.

"Think you can get those feet of yours steppin' a little quicker, Mister? The wound was to your arm," the Ranger reminds the outlaw as he cocks his pistol, putting some new spirit into the captive's deliberate slow pace. "Get a move on."

The wounded outlaw stumbles through a door into an office followed by the Ranger. Lillian and Juan are seated at their desks going though some wanted posters. Lillian is startled as the wounded cowboy collapses on her desk in obvious pain. "You gotta do something about this guy," he says to Lillian, holding his injured arm. "He just flat out killed three of my friends."

Standing up in a rage and staring at the Ranger, Lillian asks, "Is that right?"

"It was in the line of duty," says the Ranger, staring right back at the little lady, then at Juan, who puts his posters down and eyes the Ranger and the outlaw.

Walking towards the outlaw to examine him, Lillian turns to the Ranger. "It's always in the line of duty, isn't it? What is that, an excuse or something? Don't you ask questions first?"

Surprised at her outrage, the Ranger says, "Weren't no question about it."

"He just shot in the door and then started shooting at us...and we returned fire." The outlaw nods to himself. "Yep. That's what it was...self-defense." Turning to the Ranger, he asks, "Why'd you come gunning for us, lawman?"

The Ranger reaches into his duster and pulls all the posters out and tosses them onto Lillian's desk. "Darnel Adams," he points to the posters and goes on. "It says so right there. 'Dead or Alive.' You're a dangerous man," he says, walking over to the owl hoot and grabbing him and staring him in the eye. "Do you want me to finish the job?"

Lillian steps between the two men. "Hold on now. We can be more civilized about all this. Let's all calm down and gather our senses." Looking at both men, she leans over and picks up the wanted poster. She reads it. "Uh-huh. I see. Bank robbery, murder, and rape...RAPE!" she says, repulsed, looking at the outlaw with different eyes.

"Why are you leaving this scum by my desk?" she asks the Ranger. "Shouldn't he be in jail?"

Sitting on the edge of Lillian's desk, Juan picks up the wanted poster and looks it over. He looks at Darnel and shakes his head. "Now I know you don't want to alienate me.... Looks like I'm your only friend." Standing up and suddenly reaching for Darnel Adam's collar, Juan starts to pulls him towards the jail with the outlaw resisting.

"Okay, okay. Go easy," Darnel says, raising his one good arm and trying to fight Juan off.

Sitting down again, Juan studies the owl hoot a moment. "What were you doing here?" he asks. "Not enough money in the banks to rob?"

Lillian looks over at Juan with a slight smile of amusement at his subtle but effective tactics.

"Okay. Okay, already," Adams says, looking at the three Rangers and stalling for time. "Can I have some water?"

Reaching into his duster and pulling out a revolver, the Ranger says, "I'll give you the butt of my pistol across the head," he offers instead.

"Alright...alright. Forget the water," says Adams. "Just don't let that guy near me."

The three Rangers wait for his information.

"We were gonna run some liquor across the border," Adams finally unburdens himself.

"Now where would the Mexicans get money to buy liquor," asks the Ranger, lifting his pistol and taking a step closer to the outlaw.

"No. No," shouts Adams in alarm, fearing he is not being completely understood. "The liquor's made in Mexico. We were going to transport it over to this side of the border and sell it here," he says, looking at the three Rangers for a sign of understanding. "The money was supposed to help fund the revolution over there."

"You mean, you're traitors?" Lillian clarifies.

"Not exactly, ma'am," says the outlaw. "We offered our help...but it was turned down."

"Help?" questions Juan.

"Yeah," says Adam, trying to explain. "We had this convention a couple of years ago in Denver. All the boys in the Hole-in-the-Wall Gang and the Wild Bunch...Butch, Sundance, Harry Tracy...."

Amazed, Lillian shakes her head. "A convention of outlaws?"

"Yeah," Adams nods. "About twelve hundred men... and assorted women."

"Get on with it," the Ranger says, wanting more.

"Well," Adams says, looking them all over. "We sent a letter to the President of these United States his-self. We said if he'd give us amnesty we'd go down to Mexico and get Pancho Villa ourselves." He hopes his story is making sense to the Rangers.

"And?" Juan asks, wanting more.

"The President said he could take care of both us and the Mexican Revolution." He looks pathetically at the three Rangers and goes on. "So, like Butch and the Kid, we took off. That about did the Hole-in-the-Wall Gang and the Wild Bunch in. They disbanded after that," says the dejected outlaw.

"So you looked to make a quick buck off all this?" the Ranger inquires.

Looking up, Adams says, "A guy's got to make a living."

Shaking his head in disbelief, the Ranger sits down on the edge of Juan's desk. "Would you put this...owl hoot in jail?" he says. "I don't know if I can stand any more of this."

"Just a second," says Lillian, studying the outlaw a moment. "Where were you going to get the alcohol?" she asks.

"From some General in Carrizal," Adam says, rubbing his wound and shaking his head. "Trevino. General Trevino. He has an army surrounding him, but he was expecting us."

Lillian looks at the Ranger and says, "We've got to talk."

"Put him away," says the Ranger to Juan, pointing to the jail, while turning his attention to Lillian.

Juan grabs Adams by the good arm and takes him to the cell as Lillian waits until Juan has Adams safely behind closed doors. She turns to the Ranger. "That must be how the liquor is getting in," she says. "It's smuggled across the border."

"So?" says the Ranger. "You want me to guard the border or something?"

"Don't you see?" she tries to explain as she lays out her thoughts to the lawman who still isn't quite clear on it. "We cross the border in their place, find out how they do it and put a stop to it."

"Just like that?" answers the Ranger. "Cross over and...plug the leak?" He shakes his head, shrugging his shoulders.

"Something like that," Lillian says, looking back at the cell area then back at the Ranger, thinking that if an old coot like Adams could do it, she could do a better job of it.

"Tarnation...that's dumb!" says the Ranger as he reminds her of the hard facts and of the odds against them winning. "Didn't you hear what he said about that army?"

"They won't know what we're going to do with the liquor," Lillian says. "We'll just say we're there to smuggle it across the border to fund the revolution.... *Viva Revolución*," she finishes.

"Did I miss something?" says Juan as he enters the room and hears Lillian's statement.

The Ranger points to Lillian. "Now she wants to join the revolution." He gets up from Juan's desk, shaking his head, and waddles to the door where he braces himself against it. "You talk some sense into her," he says, gazing at the mildly trafficked street.

"Is this necessary?" Juan tries to reason with her. "You've only been a Texas Ranger...five weeks."

The Ranger turns from the doorway and walks back towards Lillian and Juan. "No. No. No," he says. "She wants to smuggle liquor."

"To plug the leak?" Juan asks.

"See!" Lillian exclaims. "Even Juan agrees with me."

"What is this?" asks the Ranger. "A conspiracy?" He looks both of these new recruits over.

"You must stem the problem at its source," says the enlightened Yaqui, siding with Lillian.

"Mexico has a lot of problems," the Ranger says. "Liquor is one of their charms and biggest products. Let them figure it out for themselves. I ain't crossing no border to ferret out no liquor," he says, crossing his arms and shaking his head.

"Temperance is our job," Lillian reminds the old Ranger who is set in his beliefs.

"It is?" questions Juan, to whom this was news.

"It is now," Lillian assures him. She looks at Juan and the Ranger confidently.

"You can't be delegating authority like that," says the Ranger.

"It's better than kicking in a door and killing men before breakfast," Lillian reminds him.

"You can't very well know...," the Ranger tries to explain these things to the new Texas Ranger on the block.

"NOT our responsibility," Lillian emphasizes, as the room goes quiet from any counter response.

After a moment's thought, the Ranger insists, "Mexico ain't Texas!"

"And Texas ain't Mexico," she reminds the lawman, adding, "but the liquor still passes across the border. We've got to stop it!"

The Ranger squints at Juan, trying to size him up. All the Yaqui does is simply nod in agreement with the little lady.

General Scriven of the aero-squadron is seated in his chair behind his desk still frozen in position as he stares wide-eyed at the wall on the other side of the room, not really focusing on anything. His arms and hands remain locked in position as if they were still gripping the rails of the aeroplane he's no longer in. Totally unaware of anything going on around or about him, he still has the look of fright on his face as he sits motionless.

Lieutenant Patton places some files on the desk in front of him and steps back. "If there's anything else you need, sir...," he says, coming to attention and smartly saluting, "I'll be in the outer office." He pauses a moment before dropping the salute. He peers at the General's face a moment, then leans back and finally completes the salute. Spinning around, he exits the office and closes the door behind him. The General remains frozen in position.

Shaking his head after closing the door, Lieutenant Patton just stands there in thought for a moment, then walks over to his desk and sits down. He rummages through some documents, turns towards the office, but shakes his head and goes back to his chores.

A Buffalo Soldier in Cavalry blue rides up to an office building on a military dispatch bicycle with a leather pouch over his shoulder. He gets off the bicycle and leans the bike against a hitching post. Taking off the leather bag, he makes his way up the stairs and enters.

Walking up to Lieutenant Patton's desk and coming to a stop, the Buffalo Soldier raises his hand in salute as the young lieutenant casually meets and returns it. The soldier opens the pouch, hands some papers to the First Lieutenant and steps back to await orders.

"What's this?" asks Patton, looking down and studying the papers a moment. When he looks up, the young Buffalo Soldier snaps to attention and salutes. "Uh-huh.... Okay, Private," says Patton, returning the salute and standing up. "That'll be all."

The soldier completes his salute, spins and exits. Patton studies the papers once more before walking over to the General's door and knocking.

Lieutenant Patton opens the door and looks in. The General is still frozen in position, blankly staring at the wall. Tapping at the door a few more times before entering, Patton

sheepishly approaches the desk and salutes, saying, "Sir?"
Peering at the General's face again, he steps closer to the
desk and holds out the papers.   "I just got this
communique.... The forces are marching to Carrizal," he
informs the General who is still totally oblivious to everything.

Leaving the papers on the General's desk, Patton backs
up and adds, "I'll...I'll keep you informed of further developments." Coming to attention and saluting, the young officer
does an about face and exits to his office, stopping once more
to examine the General before closing the door. He returns
to his desk and sits down, going through some papers on his
desk.

A sergeant passing his door, stops to ask him a
question. "Has the General come out of it yet?"

"No," says the young lieutenant, shaking his head.
"And I'm stuck here with him while our troops advance in
Mexico." He turns to the General's closed door, then back to
the sergeant, shaking his head again, helpless to do anything.

The khaki-clad Punitive Expeditionary Forces are
riding their government-issue horses through the hot, barren
Mexican wastelands as a Fokker aeroplane banks on a turn
over the Mexican desert and flies over the troop columns.
Colonel Hart, Major Watkins, and Captain Leeman look
skyward as the Fokker returns and flies high overhead.

"Who does that belong to?" asks Colonel Hart,
shading his eyes and trying to make out any identification.

"It's a Fokker," responds the major. "German made.
It shouldn't be here, Sir."

"Who do you think it is?" inquires the Colonel,
watching the plane move through open air space away from
the march.

"I don't know," the major shakes his head. "Maybe it's
an observer plane."

"Then they can chart our position," says the Colonel.

"But they're too far out of distance for us to stop them," says the major.

"Can they do us any harm?" asks the Captain.

"I don't know," replies the major, shaking his head.

Taking a deep breath and exhaling, the Colonel finally says, "They used balloons in the Civil War to chart the enemy's position. But that," he nods to the aeroplane, "would give a better perspective today."

The pilot banks the Fokker on a turn as the one passenger in the front seat looks up from the ground and smiles. He leans back in his seat and takes his goggles off to wipe the lenses clean. It is General Heinrich Schmidt, German military advisor to Pancho Villa and a member of the German High Command. He turns to the pilot and shouts, "I'll have something to report upon arrival at Carrizal," he smiles, pointing to the troop formations and advance.

The aeroplane banks on another turn and sweeps the open air for the Mexican highlands.

Colonel Hart addresses a lieutenant on horseback who's taking notes on a small pad next to the office staff. "We are moving on Carrizal and General Trevino," dictates the full bird Colonel. "Get that off to headquarters immediately."

The lieutenant salutes and says, "Yes, Sir!" as he places the pad in his pocket, reins and spurs his horse to the rear on a gallop.

Deep in a corner of a darkened, wooden warehouse, stands a small table where some pink boll worms are crawling over themselves in a glass jar. A thin nail is hammered through the top of the metal lid, while General Schmidt's eyes glitter as he studies the contents of the bottle in wonder and glee. He pulls the nail from the lid and places it down next to the hammer.

Lowering the bottle to the table, the General rubs his hands and smiles to the man next to him, Japanese Imperial Navy Admiral Itichi "The Tiger" Yamagato. The white suit and white uniform of both men are a stark contrast to the heavily-shadowed warehouse, as the only real light that penetrates the building comes from a large double door behind them.

Shaking his head and taking a closer look at the contents of the bottle in amazement, the white-uniformed Admiral asks, "These innocent little creatures of nature?"

"Yes, Admiral," General Schmidt answers. "These hybrid worms supplied by Professor Heinrich F. Albert, our German scientific attache to Mexico, projects that when they're released across the border, they will destroy the cotton crop from Texas to Georgia."

Amazed, the Admiral lifts the bottle and examines the worms more closely. "Such a small and yet devastating weapon," he says, shaking his head and smiling. He hands the bottle to Schmidt. "Those stupid Americans will never figure this one out."

General Schmidt takes a glass cutter and scores the side of the bottle, then walks over to a wagon and reaches for a wind-up clock. He removes the two metal bells from the top and sets the time from the back. The clock's hammers vibrate from side to side. He stops the alarm and rewinds the clock, resets it, then carefully inserts it and the bottle in a false bottom of the wagon and covers both with a piece of wood.

He steps back and looks at his pocket watch. "In twelve hours, the United States will be invaded by a power they never even knew existed...and there is very little they can do to stop it." He smiles at the Admiral and laughs.

"Here are the morning reports and duty roster," Lieutenant Patton tells the General as he places the sheets on the desk and stands back, studying Scriven who's still frozen in position gazing at the wall. Patton peers at the officer, shaking his head. "If there's anything more...," he adds, pointing to the adjoining office, "I'll just be outside this door." Turning and walking to the door as he steps into his outer office, the young lieutenant grabs the door knob and says, "You needn't hesitate in calling...." He slowly closes the door. Taking his seat behind his desk, Patton attends to the paperwork laid out before him.

A Buffalo Soldier on a bicycle rides up to the building with a message pouch around his neck and shoulder. He pulls up to a hitching post and leans his two-wheeler against it and rushes up the stairs of a building and enters.

Approaching the Duty Sergeant seated behind a counter, the Buffalo Soldier takes his leather pouch off and says, "I have an urgent message."

The sergeant studies the blue-clad soldier before saying, "I'll take that."

The bluejacket hands the pouch over to the sergeant and stands at ease as the noncom pulls the contents of the pouch out and looks through the papers. Looking up at the Buffalo Soldier, the sergeant nods and says, "Thank you. That will be all." The bluejacket spins and exits the office as the sergeant once more studies the papers before walking around the duty counter and making his way down the long hallway.

"These reports just came in, Lieutenant," says the Duty Sergeant standing in the doorway, catching Patton going over some documents.

Looking up, the young lieutenant motions the sergeant into the room. "Thank you," says Patton, looking down at the sheets he's just been handed and automatically saying, "that'll be all." Then quickly reminded of a question he had, the lieutenant asks, "Sergeant, wait. Is the surgeon on post?"

"I don't know, Sir," responds the sergeant.

Nodding, the young lieutenant says, "If so, find him and bring him here." He turns to the office door behind him, shaking his head, then looking at the enlisted man in front of him. "We need to try to revive the General."

The sergeant slowly nods, turns to his right and walks on down the hall towards his office. Patton stands up and walks over to the General's door, softly knocking. Opening it to look in on the General, he finds the General still locked solid and frozen in the same position.

Shaking his head, he enters the office and salutes the frozen General. Placing some more papers on top of the other papers he'd left on the desk earlier, he backs up once more. "More word on the advancing troops, Sir," he says, bending over, tilting his head and squinting at the General, trying to catch a glimpse of any sign of the General coming out of his frozen state. Leaning back, the lieutenant informs the General. "They say additional reports will be forthcoming."

As there is no answer from the General, Patton finally steps back. "If there's anything else I can get you...a cup of coffee, some brandy, a cigar...," the lieutenant backs up to the door, stops and says, "...and I'll keep you advised on further developments in Mexico." He closes the door behind him.

The heat rising off the Mexican desert floor is more like an oven than anything else as hot waves of warmed desert dirt and sand rise towards the skies. Mixed in, is the dirt and dust kicked up from a double column of ground-pounding, khaki-clad soldiers marching towards some mountain highlands.

One soldier in the middle of the march reaches into his pocket and pulls out a letter and opens it. He turns to the man next to him and says, "I just got some mail from home," he laughs. "It took three months to get here."

"That's how long we've been down here," replies the private next to him.

"No accounting for time these days," laughs the soldier with the letter from home. Shaking his head and opening his envelope, he pulls some pages out to read.

"I know what you mean," says the other private, adding, "They just passed the eight-hour work day, but look at us." He nods up the line at all the soldiers in the march.

"Yeah," says the first trooper. "Eight hours. Ha! I'd look forward to a simple twelve-hour day." He shakes his head. "Eight hours. Well, we're on government time now."

"And it isn't even any more than the thirteen cents an hour my sister makes working at that sweat shop in New York," says the private, trudging along the desert path being broken down by the soldiers ahead of him.

"But what are you going to spend your money on down here?" asks the first soldier, looking around the wastelands.

"Nothing I'd particularly care for," says the recruit. "All I want to buy is one of them Model Ts."

"You know, they've already sold one million of them and they cost a thousand dollars," says the first soldier.

"And you can get it in any color you want," informs the knowledgeable private

"As long as it's black," says the first soldier, sparking a laugh from both recruits. "The soldier finally pulls his letter up and starts reading it. Pausing, he says, "My sister says the Ziegfeld Follies has a cowboy who has them rolling in the aisles every night. Will Rogers. This guy from Oklahoma." He puts his letter down and shakes his head. "You know, I never heard of any cowboy ever being funny. What can a cowboy say that's funny?" he asks the private next to him.

"Well, there is a fascination with the West," the private says. "Zane Grey and all those other writers. Fascination with the west? This is sort of the reality of it, isn't it? Sand, scorpions, snakes, beans and more beans. Fascination—my butt." He looks down the line, then up ahead, finally back at the soldier next to him. "It sorta makes sense. I guess it was only a matter of time before a cowboy hit Broadway. Coming in off the range to a big city like New York is sorta funny in itself."

The first soldier lifts his chin. "I once saw me a professional drowner in Coney Island once. Yes, sir. That was the most remarkable recovery I have ever seen. If you got to drown somewhere, Coney Island is the place to be. Four life guards pulled this guy out, revived him...and, no less than fifteen minutes later, he was on a stage juggling at a side show. Fields," says the soldier, nodding his head. "W. C. Fields. Professional drowner *and* the World's Greatest Juggler—he told me that himself."

He looks down at the letter and makes another comment to the private next to him. "But New York is growing in a lot of other ways, too. They're building these enormous buildings they call...," he looks at the letter and points to two words, "*sky scrapers*, and they don't see an end to it." He lowers the papers and looks around. "With all the room this country has, why would anyone want to build a fifty story building?"

The private looks around and says with some assurance, "I don't think they'll ever build 'em out here. Look kind of strange coming across the desert and seeing one lonesome town filled with buildings like that. It would be a case of spent, and, lost wages. Anyhow, I don't see how they can get much larger than that. Fifty storys is a lot of storys." He shakes his head, then nods in agreement with himself.

"With people like Rockefeller, Vanderbilt, Morgan, Westinghouse, Carnegie, Edison, and Ford running around out there..., I guess it's 'sky's the limits,' anyhow," says the first soldier, folding the letter and putting it back in the envelope and stuffing it in his pocket.

"I suppose so," answers the private. "But what about us little guys? Do you think they even consider us?"

"They have to, don't they?" answers the first trooper. "I mean, we're the ones who buy all their stuff."

"Well," says the private, "I don't buy this marching through Mexico. Who came up with that idea?"

"Pancho Villa," comes the reply from the first soldier. "He crossed the border and killed seventeen people in New

Mexico and that's part of the United States, our homeland. That's reason enough."

"Well, then," says the private, wiping his brows and looking over the vast expanse of desert wasteland, "when I get a chance, I'll just have to write that Mr. Villa myself and thank him for letting me tour Mexico on foot." Both men laugh as the private looks around again and squints at the horizon, shaking his head in disbelief. "Wonderful! Join the army and see the desert. Maybe catch Pancho Villa if he can be found to begin with. I suppose he's as good a reason to be down here as anything else. This is his country, isn't it?"

"It appears so," says the first soldier, nodding and shifting the backpack on his back as he hunkers down for the long march ahead. "It would appear to be so."

Ambling through the desert heat on horseback, Lillian, Juan, and the Ranger slowly make their way through Mexican wastelands at no great speed or pace. The Ranger has an eye out for any possible trouble that could occur, keeping one hand inside his partially unbuttoned canvas duster.

"There are reports out of Houston that there's a Japanese Army in Mexico right now!" says Lillian, trying to make some conversation on the open trail.

"It is also reported that the Japanese Navy is off the Pacific Coast," Juan adds.

Taking his eye off the desert, the Ranger turns to his riding partners. "Why would the Japanese Navy be here?" They're supposed to be our allies," he says, shaking his head.

"They've become quite dominant since defeating the Russian Navy a few years ago...and there does seem to be a problem with Japanese immigration right now," Lillian explains. "The loss to the Japanese caused a small revolution in Russia that failed, but they say the dissension is still prevalent."

"It isn't enough Germany was involved...now we've got the Japanese?" the Ranger says, going back to his lookout duty. "What's this world coming to?"

"Dangerously close to a war of world-wide proportions," Lillian surmises.

"A world war?" Juan questions.

"The papers report the war in Europe is spreading to the Middle East," says Lillian with concern. "They say the Sultan of Turkey is calling for a holy war." She shakes her head. "Something's going on over there."

The Ranger turns back to Lillian and Juan. "Well, if it don't have anything to do with temperance or illegal liquor crossing the border, I don't much care one way or another. It don't give me no never mind, 'tall," he says, nodding.

Shocked, Lillian responds, "It's your duty to care. You're an American."

Reining his horse to a stop and staring at Lillian who also pulls up, along with Juan, the Ranger says, "Texican, Lil." The lawman spurs his horse back to a walk as he defiantly looks ahead of him. "A product of mesquite and armadillos...not a naval maneuver in the Pacific, or a showdown with Germany in Mexico. I chase border bandits and owl hoots. I don't much care about no revolution in Mexico, Russia, or anywhere else, as long as they don't spread it to Texas. Lillian and Juan rein their horses and keep up with him.

"But they've already come across the border once," says Juan.

"And we stopped another attempt before it could get launched a week ago," replies the Ranger. "But this is about the flow of illegal liquor, isn't it? I don't see how this can possibly be linked to a war in Europe!" He shakes his head.

"Well," says Lillian, "the Germans are bogged down with the French in Verdun. They need something to inspire an offensive."

"You can't get more offensive than that German General from a week ago," says the Ranger.

"Schmidt?" asks Juan in concern.

"Yeah," says the Ranger, shaking his head. "Can you believe the Mexicans would support such a thing as that General?"

"They've convinced the Mexicans through manipulation," says Juan.

"Is this about the three worlds Colonel Cardenas spoke about a month ago?" Lillian asks the Yaqui.

"You aren't going to reach for that medicine bag and pull out that marble and try to convince me it's a gemstone now, are you?" asks the Ranger.

"The triad?" Juan asks. "Mexico, Germany, and Japan?"

"What do you know?" Lillian asks, attentive and eager to know more.

"The world navies are converting from coal to oil," Juan explains. "Mexico supplies oil for one fourth of the world and almost all the oil for the navy of the United Kingdom. It holds value beyond land. While Japan and Germany exploit Mexico, Germany is also exploring Guatemala, Salvador, and other republics of Central America for other oil reserves."

"You mean oil, Mexico, *and* promises of American territory beyond the United States?" the Ranger asks.

"*Si,*" Juan responds. "Mexico wants territory returned to them."

"Returned?" says Lillian in surprise.

"They haven't gotten over the Alamo," says Juan.

"The Alamo?" says the Ranger, unbelievingly. "The Alamo? That was thirty years before I was born...before Texas even became a state."

"Mexico is persistent," Juan explains. "Santa Ana rose and fell from power seven times."

"He might have had persistence," nods the Ranger, "but ol' Sam Houston caught him with his pants down in San Jacinto."

"You mean...'The Yellow Rose of Texas?" Juan inquires.

"What?" Lillian asks, confused.

"Yeah," says the Ranger. "His army was at siesta when Houston attacked. Took out all the officers so there wasn't any command for the troops. Sam only lost one man, and they say it was from a stray bullet. But they caught Santa Ana in a...," he looks over at Lillian as he tries to find the words, "shall we say, a love nest, with a mulatto woman."

"For whom the song is written," adds Juan.

Astonished, Lillian says, "'The Yellow Rose of Texas' is based on an affair Santa Ana had with a mulatto girl?"

"So it would seem," says Juan as Lillian shakes her head and grips the reins of her horse, not totally believing what she's just heard.

A *péon* approaches the trio from a distance with a burro in tow. The animal carries bags of corn draped over its side. A *ristro* of dried chiles is draped over its neck like a necklace. A young girl sits atop the corn as her mother walks close behind with a baby in her arms.

"What about the Mexican?" Lillian asks.

"They simply want freedom from whoever offers it," Juan says, looking at the group approaching him in the hot desert sun.

Juan, Lillian, and the Ranger stop as the *péon* and his family walk up and stop beside Juan. With concern for these people, Juan bows slightly and says, "*Buenos tardes.*"

"You must go back," says the *péon*, looking at Juan with deep concern and sincerity.

"Why?" Juan asks curiously.

"*Americanos* are driving on Carrizal. General Jacinto Trevino has taken over the city and we escaped with our lives." Turning back and looking towards the vast wastelands they have just come through, the *péon* turns back to

Juan. "There is nowhere else to go but up the mountain. They prepare to engage the enemy."

"How big is the army?" asks Juan.

"Large," says the *péon*. "The trail back is safest for you, " he says, pointing behind them.

"*Gracias*" says Juan. "...And a safe journey to you." The old *péon* stops and turns back and studies Juan a moment. "*Gracias.*"

"What was that all about?" asks Lillian with concern.

"General Trevino lies in wait for the Punitive Expeditionary Forces advancing on Carrizal," he explains. "It seems they prepare to wage war."

Shaking his head and gritting his teeth, the Ranger spurs his mount forward. "I don't know why you talked me into this. You know, you're like a divining rod...for trouble," he says.

Lillian spurs her mount up to the Ranger and flashes her badge at him. "By appointment, Mister. And don't you forget it!"

"Well," the Ranger says as Juan catches up to them, "Ma Ferguson has been handing out a lot of those lately. Almost like a shingle for a lawyer."

"You got something against lawyers?" Lillian asks, all headstrong and looking for a ruckus on these overdone wastelands that keep raining blazing sun down on them.

"No," says the Ranger, shaking his head. "Some of my best friends are lawyers." He halts his horse as Juan pulls up. "Some of the early Texas Rangers were lawyers, doctors, real estate people, even judges," he tells her. "A lot of really good men went down for the good of Texas. You remember that, cause you're wearing that badge now, just like they did. As the country became civilized another breed of lawman was needed to take over." He spurs his mount forward as Lillian and Juan ride to catch up.

"Other than holding up the law," Lillian inquires with sincerity, "what are your politics?"

This draws a laugh from the Ranger. He turns to Juan. "What about you, Juan?"

"Democrat," responds the Yaqui without a moment's hesitation, surprising Lillian into a laugh as she does not expect an answer from her trail companion.

"What's so funny?" asks the Ranger.

"Somehow, I never thought you had any political leanings," Lillian honestly remarks.

Tilting his head and studying her a moment, Juan says, "Just because I don't talk much doesn't mean I don't have thoughts or emotions."

"Of course you have thoughts and emotions," Lillian tries to apologize. "I just....".

"I'm for the people," Juan explains. "That's democratic."

"Well," says Lillian, trying to take her foot out of her mouth. "I'm a Republican. Abraham Lincoln was a Republican...and a lawyer, too, come to think of it. He was a common man who worked his way to the top."

"Lincoln was hardly 'common,'" says the Ranger. "He was a new breed of lawyer, specializing in corporation. And he never won an election until he ran for President. You might want to check this out, but he was the first Republican President, and that party was only about ten to a dozen years old before he won that election. Mind you, the man wasn't even on twelve of the southern ballots at the time of the election, and it wouldn't have made a difference anyhow, since he'd already won the election before the south had a chance to vote."

"That says something about your politics," says the little lady. "Who are you going to vote for, anyhow? Wilson or Hughes?"

"Neither of them," says the Ranger, holding tight to his secret.

"You mean you're out on the range so much you don't even know when to vote?"

"Nope," says the Ranger. "I reckon it really depends on how important it is to you."

"That doesn't tell me anything about your politics," she says, getting frustrated.

"What business is it of yours, anyway?" asks the Ranger, looking Lillian over like his privacy is being invaded.

"I'm just asking," says Lillian. "It isn't the inquisition. What difference does it make, anyhow? Juan is comfortable enough with it." She looks at Juan, then back to the old coot riding shotgun on his politics. "Did I penetrate some hidden corner of your mind or something?"

After a long pause and some consideration, the ranger finally opens up. "Bull Moose."

"Theodore Roosevelt?" she asks, shocked. "Muckrakers and all that stuff?"

Stiff-lipped and firm on his politics, he looks over at the little lady. "I never quite thought of it that way. I just sorta thought Teddy earned my vote when he charged up that hill in Cuba."

"That's a heck of a way to determine a vote," laughs Lillian.

"What's wrong with that?" asks the Ranger, looking at the little lady over, affronted. "Hughes or Wilson never charged no hill."

"You should vote for the best candidate," Lillian tries to clear things up. "Just because they run on a third ticket doesn't make it the best platform."

"Third ticket?" says the ranger, looking over at the little lady. "Teddy. Theodore Roosevelt. Bull Moose. How's that for third ticket?" He pulls his old hat down and pulls his collar up, trying to salvage his pride. Looking over at her and eyeing her, he goes on. ""He made a damned good President before. He won a Nobel Prize, was the chief of police of New York City, a great writer, Secretary of the Navy...and...and...he cleaned up football!"

Lillian shakes her head, laughing. "Cleaned up football? That's a hell of a reason to vote for him."

"What's wrong with football? It's a great American sport," he says with a little aggressiveness. "It's just got a little rough...that's all. He sort of...."

Juan interrupts, "He encourages the forward pass."

"What!" shouts Lillian. "This is preposterous!"

The Ranger looks over to Juan. "I guess women wouldn't understand."

"What's to understand?" she protests.

"America," says the Ranger, proudly.

"America?" Lillian responds in confusion.

"Yeah, America," says the Ranger. "Look at American sports: baseball, football,...that new game...basketball. They're all hand-based sports. You use your hands. Not like that sissy kick-the-ball-with-your-feet-or-your-head game, soccer. You know, where you just kick the ball around." He tries to explain the sport to her in the most simple way he can.

"What?" says Lillian again.

"America was built with hands, not kicked around like a ball," says the Ranger, shaking his head and hoping she understands.

"You'd base your vote on something like football?" she inquires incredulously.

Turning to Juan, the Ranger says, "Women just got the vote...they don't know how to use it just yet. Someday there'll be a politician that just...looks good or something. A shiny knight out of Camelot...and he'll win on looks alone or something. And it'll probably be the women that put him in office."

He shakes his head and eyes Lillian a moment. "Politics don't work that way. It's like that cracker barrel on on your hip. It's good for snakes and other critters you want to scare off. But now, you're about to step into a hive of bees with their stingers out, and you're holstered with a pop gun." Reaching for his peacemaker inside his duster and holding it up, he says, "This has power."

"Well," Lillian responds. "Juan doesn't have a gun."

Reaching into his duster and holstering the weapon, he says, " That's his choice. What do you think you can do with that?" He points to her pistol.

Lillian pulls her pistol out and examines the small revolver a moment. "It doesn't look like much," she admits.

"See that cactus?" the Ranger points at a prickly pear cactus standing alone on the desert floor not far from where they're passing on horseback. "Shoot it," says the much-experienced lawman, lifting his jaw and watching what she can do with the weapon.

"Why should I shoot that?" she demands.

""Don't ask me why. Shoot it," he orders.

"It doesn't pose a threat," the little lady responds.

"It never poses a threat until it's too late," he informs her, shaking his head at her stalling. In an attempt to appease her, he finally says, "Just shoot it. It's a target."

" As a target?"

"Yeah," says the Ranger whose patience is running out. "Let's see what you can do with that."

Cocking her pistol and looking at the Ranger, she turns to the cactus and lets go a shot that rips through the heart of one of the flat ears of the plant, shaking it from the repercussion. Five rapid shots follow the first shot into the cactus. Pulling her weapon up and opening the chamber of her pistol, she discharges the empty shells on the trail, looking at the Ranger, still mystified by his request to target a plant on the open road.

"Good," says the Ranger, impressed. "That was good." He refits his hat and nods. "I hope that taught you a lesson."

Reloading, Lillian asks. "Lesson? You just had me destroy an innocent plant and you say that was a lesson?"

"Ah...yeah," says the Ranger. "You just don't want to get too close to those.... They've got stingers, too."

"Stingers," Juan interjects, not quite understanding what is going on.

"Needles, okay?" the Ranger answers, flustered. "Just be careful around them."

"That's the lesson?" Lillian asks, holstering her pistol and turning back to the Ranger. "I waste six good shells on the open trail for advise on succulents?"

Pulling his hat down and answering, he says, "Yeah. It's part of the territory." He spurs his mount to a trot, leaving Lillian and Juan bewildered as they watch him ride off.

"Where are you going?" shouts Lillian.

"To stop a war," the Ranger shouts back as he puts a gap between himself and his two trail mates.

Looking at Juan, Lillian says, "He can't do that, can he?"

Juan shrugs and shakes his head, grabbing the reins of his horse and heeling it into a trot after the lawman as Lillian follows his lead.

Riding a bicycle through the blazing heat of a wind-free mid-morning, where the humidity is so thick, the blue-clad Buffalo Soldier looks like he's covered from head to foot in sweat as he pulls up to the Punitive Expeditionary Forces Headquarters. He gets off his bike and leans it against the hitching post, huffing and puffing as he walks towards the steps leading into the building. Taking the leather pouch off and stopping to take his hat off to wipe his forehead, he moves toward the steps and puts the hat back on.

The Duty Sergeant behind the counter looks up from some papers and sees the soldier and the pouch he's carrying in his hand.

"I'll take that," says the noncom. The soldier gladly hands over the whole pouch to the Duty Sergeant and stands by for the next order. The sergeant opens the pouch, removes some papers and looks them over a moment. Looking up at the soldier, he hands him back his pouch and says, "Thank you... That will be all."

The soldier puts the empty pouch over his shoulder, spins around and exits the building as the sergeant rounds the counter and walks down the hall, shuffling through the papers as he walks.

Standing at the office door of Lieutenant Patton, the sergeant notices the young officer going over some papers on his desk. Tapping lightly on the door, he gains Patton's attention. "Here are the latest reports on the troop advance."

"Come in," says the First Lieutenant as the soldier walks over to his desk and hands him the papers. After a very brief study of the material, Patton looks up in anticipation. "Have you found the surgeon?"

The sergeant shakes his head.

"Well, keep trying."

The sergeant spins, exits the office and turns down the hallway and disappears.

The young lieutenant reads the papers as he stands up from his desk and walks over to the General's door and knocks. After a moment, Patton opens the door and takes a glimpse inside. He finds the General is still frozen in position. Patton steps through the door with the report and approaches the General's desk. He salutes and lays the papers down on top of the other papers he'd previously put down.

Unmoved, unchanged, and unaware of anything around him, the General's gaze is still on the wall in the same fixed position, oblivious to anything and everything.

"These are the latest reports out of Mexico, Sir," says Lieutenant Patton, peering into the eyes of his commanding officer. He examines him with concern. Extending his hand and passing it in front of the General's face several times, he snaps his fingers. Not getting any response, Patton backs up to the door, grabs the knob and says, "I'll update you as I receive word, Sir." He salutes and leaves the office.

Seated at a desk wearing his formal khaki uniform and playing with a wooden cane that oddly resembles a golf club, General Jacinto Trevino entertains German General Heinrich Schmidt, Professor Heinrich Alpert, and Japanese Imperial Navy Admiral Itichi "The Tiger" Yamagato.

"Everything's in place," says General Schmidt. "The cotton will decline little by little and they'll be unable to stop the destruction. "We'll get across the border and blow up some oil fields at Spindle Top and that will solidify our efforts in distracting the Americans. Remember, a war with Mexico will absorb munitions going to the allies."

Professor Alpert adds, "Other insects are being developed right now for other infestation."

"Don't let them loose down here," says an alarmed General Trevino, placing his cane down and looking at his guests for more information.

"Relax, General," says the Professor. "Our efforts are aimed at the United States." He turns to Schmidt and Yamagato. "They are cross-breeding moths and bees as well. Caterpillars will attack the food chain...and they believe a new strain of bees can actually be able to attack in groups when provoked. We are currently exploring the possibility right now."

"This is all fine and well, Professor," says General Schmidt, "but will the Pink boll worm give us the desired results?"

"Ya, Ya," nods the Professor as a knock interrupts the conversation.

"*Si,*" answers General Trevino, reaching for his cane again and turning to the door.

A khaki-dressed soldier enters, salutes and hands some papers to Trevino. He grabs the papers and salutes the soldier, motioning him out the door, simply adding, "*Gracias.*" as he studies the material just handed him.

"We've had George Sylvester Viereck and other propagandists working for Germany, seeding the American press with misinformation, while Edgar Held and Louis

Hess are petitioning Teddy Roosevelt to go to war with Mexico...even so far as to have Robert Lansing, the Secretary of State, fall under pressure, by planting rumors against him in newspapers designed to supplant him while we establish a U-boat base just south of Vera Cruz near the aeroport for our new aero-squadron."

"I have talked to Admiral Yashiro, the Grand Admiral of the Japanese fleet," says Yamagato. "He's aboard the battle cruiser, *Asama*, maneuvering in Turtle Bay just off the coast of lower California with three other cruisers and supply ships. He has assured me that the troops will be landing in Mexico and then marching on to California on what we now call the 'Plan of San Diego."

He smiles. "Plan two calls for an invasion through the Mississippi Valley, splitting the United States into two."

"Precisely," answers General Schmidt. "We need not defeat the United States all out. We simply divide and conquer."

The Professor pulls out his pocket watch and looks at it. Standing and looking the military men over, he says, "I must get to the wireless station to collect the messages from our agents. Mexico can only receive messages these days, so, Sweden secretly sends them through Herr Folke Cronholm."

Putting his watch back in his vest pocket, he goes on. "Since I am also the paymaster for German undercover activities in the United States, I'll need to see General Maximilian Kloss for some supplies. He's now the Director General of Mexican munitions and ordnance manufacture. There are commercial agents, wireless operators and newspapers to subsidize, you know. The thirty million dollars we've already funded the revolution with, needs to be portioned out appropriately.

"Indeed," remarks Schmidt. "This is why they've sent the German banker, Frederico Stallforth out. Revolutions are costly these days."

"Before I go though, I must remind you of the other channel you must use for coding messages to the Rhineland."

"Yes, Professor," Schmidt nods. "I won't forget.

The Professor walks to the door, turns, smiles and nods before exiting the office and closing the door, leaving the three military men·alone in the office.

General Schmidt looks at his two counterparts and lays out his plans. "Next week, we will blow up another munitions plant in New Jersey, so close to New York City itself, it'll light up so much of the sky, it'll strike direct fear into the very population of New York City itself."

"Yes," adds Admiral Yamagato. "We also have plans of our own on the east coast. This Hearst film company has made a serial about a Japanese invasion starring Irene Castle. It is about the Emperor's secret service, which concerns us. We think there'll be some changes in that area near Los Angeles they call Hollywoodland." He smiles and crosses his arms. "I don't know if it's Mary Pickford or Lillian Gish I most prefer, but one of them will be mine. I think I will prize one of America's sweethearts."

"No wonder they call you 'The Tiger,'" smiles Schmidt, seeking more information. "But what do your spies in the United States report on military conditions?"

"Mexico has a network of railways that meet the American border at regular intervals and terminals from the Pacific to the Gulf, a perfect system for moving troops and supplies," the Admiral answers. "What other plans have you designed?"

"Maybe someday, we'll even blow up what they now call...skyscrapers...." General Schmidt answers, nodding. He looks at the Admiral and General Trevino. "Done ever so precisely, it could very well cause a chain reaction...not, unlike dominos...all lined up. A whole city could be leveled if the proper estimates were made." The military men in front of him nod approvingly. "But back to the worm. First things first. We must not endanger our plans to transfer the insects."

General Trevino looks at Schmidt and Yamagato. "While Pancho Villa might appreciate the plans you have made for Mexico's part in the invasion," he looks down at the papers before him. "The *Americanos* are advancing on us."

"Yes, yes, yes," says General Schmidt, almost impatiently. "Four fifths of the Army of the United States are currently down here right now. They've shown themselves to be totally inefficient, and Carranza should know better, as he has fifty naturalized German officers commissioned in his service."

"And about fifty thousand soldiers from the Japanese Imperial Army about to land and march on the United States," Admiral Yamagato interrupts.

"Gentlemen, gentlemen," says Trevino, shaking his head. "While Mexico is not a wealthy country by any stretch of the imagination due to our current revolution, we have contributed in our own little way. We have fomented strikes among Mexican laborers in Arizona and California, disrupting harvest and train transport. And while these might be minor things to industrially-developed countries such as yours, it has an effect."

He stands up and looks at the papers in his hand, shaking his head. "Before all else, I must make arrangements. For I will strike a great blow for the revolution by attacking this American force advancing on us."

A knock on the door draws everyone's attention. "*Si,*" says Trevino to the khaki-clad soldier entering and saluting.

"The *gringos* are here," he addresses his commanding officer.

"I'll attend to them," says Admiral Yamagato. "I want to meet the unsuspecting people who will be delivering our little time bomb."

"Show him the way," Trevino says. The soldier salutes before exiting with the Japanese Admiral.

"This must not fail, Admiral," General Schmidt says, studying the Admiral.

"The timer is already set," says Yamagato. "And you already scored the bottle, have you not?" Schmidt nods. "Then you need not worry, General. The plan is ingenious. It's fool proof."

"What fool talked me into this?" asks the Ranger, looking around the wooden warehouse as he tips his hat back and shakes his head. Lillian, Juan, and the Ranger hold the reins of their mounts as they stand in the middle of the warehouse.

Mexican soldiers with rifles, run by an open door to one side of the building as a different platoon of soldiers do double-time from the opposite direction. There is a tenseness in the air as soldiers line up along a wall and raise their weapons. Two soldiers with a wooden cart unload shells to the men at the wall, moving down the line. Soldiers pass and stack more shells next to a machine gun, as another man loads and aims it.

A soldier and Admiral Yamagato pass by the frenzied-paced soldiers at the firing line to make their way into the warehouse to meet the newcomers. "I see you've found your way here safely," says the Admiral.

Although surprised, the three Texas Rangers neither flinch nor react to the formal white dress uniform of the naval officer in the midst of an obvious Mexican Army action in preparation for war.

Shaking his head as he looks around and about him, the Ranger says, "It don't look very safe around here."

"There's some trouble they're preparing for," replies the Admiral. "You don't have any great loyalties to the United States, do you?" he questions his three guests. "Because they are about to be engaged by this army," he says, smiling.

The Tiger recognizes Lillian to be a fair-haired beauty, prompting him to raise his head and study her more closely. "I had no idea female outlaws could be so attractive," he smiles with a chuckle, eyeing the beauty.

"I'm much less appealing with a Smith & Wesson in my hand," she tells him, concerned about the activity going on outside the warehouse.

"Ahh...yes," the Admiral says. "Very well, then. Over to the wagon." He escorts his three guests to the four-wheeler in the corner of the warehouse where the wagon stands prepared, filled with hay.

The Admiral taps the wagon. "Outward appearances mean nothing. This is more than a simple hay wagon destined for some obscure ranch with a supply of hay," he says. "Underneath the false cargo hides the real treasure." He bends, reaches under the wagon and knocks on the false bottom. It gives a slightly hollow sound. "You simply remove the hay, slide the panels out and the alcohol is at your disposal," he smiles. "You deliver the liquor to our contact in El Paso and you will be properly rewarded."

"Who's the contact?" asks the Ranger without wasting a moment.

"We'll get to that before you leave," the Admiral smiles. "But first, we must team the wagon." Leading the Rangers away from the wagon and out of the warehouse, the Admiral passes the soldiers manning their positions at the wall. The soldiers check their weapons and look over the terrain. Other soldiers pass bullets to other men taking positions at the wall. Admiral Yamagato leads the three past all the activity towards another building.

"This will give you an opportunity to refresh your-selves before your long journey across the border," the Admiral smiles, opening the door and escorting them in. "I'll take you to a room."

Admiral Yamagato, Lillian, Juan, and the Ranger walk through the building until they come to a door. The Admiral opens it and allows the trio to enter. Stepping in after them, 'The Tiger' closes the door.

Rounding the corner of the hallway and swiftly walking down the hall past the room the Admiral and the three Texas Rangers have just entered, General Schmidt and

General Trevino carrying his cane, walk towards the exit of the building. "The Americans will be at our mercy if we attack now," says Schmidt, all business and eager to get things started.

"They will be devastated," remarks Trevino, gripping his cane tight and ready for a good fight.

"They are completely in the open and their only retreat is a long one across the border," says Schmidt, recognizing the advantage. Turning to Trevino, he adds, "You will send a direct message to their President Wilson, by routing them."

"*Si*," responds General Trevino. "Our advance on the United States could be made easier on the heels of a retreating army."

"Precisely," acknowledges General Heinrich Schmidt, German General of the German High Command. "Good fortune is ours," he adds, as they enter another building and close the door behind them.

Admiral Yamagato opens the door and stands in the doorway. "I'll call on you in a couple of hours. Until then, rest. A meal will be prepared for you, then you can be on your way. I'm going to see to the wagon." Closing the door, the Admiral walks away, leaving Lillian, Juan, and the Ranger in marked bewilderment over the current situation.

"Now what?" asks the Ranger, looking his two friends over. "We're stuck in the middle of a battle that's gearing up and we can't even prevent it."

Shaking her head in concern, Lillian says, "How could we have known?"

"That's not the point," exclaims the Ranger, looking around the room, then stepping over to the window to look out and gaze at the troops outside preparing for battle. Turning back to Lillian and Juan, he says, "A lot of innocent men are going to be killed and there's very little we can do from here."

The Punitive Expeditionary Forces march through the difficult terrain, made even harder by the constant heat burning down on the already exhausted troops as they pound along the path in the desert dirt and dust on horseback.

General Schmidt and General Trevino put their binoculars down after gauging the Punitive Expeditionary Forces' advance. Sizing up the situation and point it out, General Schmidt says, "Machine guns could scatter the advance and displace the American forces."

"*Si,*" answers General Trevino, nodding in agreement. "That could really disrupt communications between troops, and we can attack with our infantry.

"Berlin will be happy with this," says Schmidt, smiling.

Colonel Hart calls a halt to the troop advance as Major Watkins and Captain Leeman ride up and pull alongside the commanding officer.

The captain pulls out a map and looks it over. "Carrizal, Sir," he says, responding to the Colonel.

"Wiping his forehead and putting his hat back on, he glances up at the sun. "Does it hold any strategic significance?" he asks, more out of duty than any personal need to know.

"Not really," answers Major Watkins, reaching for his canteen. "Beyond the fact it's supposed to be under the command of General Jacinto Trevino." He takes a sip of the warmed liquid. Tilting his head for a better look at the town that seems quiet enough, he says, "Though he has some Mexican regulars, we shouldn't anticipate any trouble."

The Colonel reaches for his binoculars and pulls them up to his eyes just as machine gun fire from inside the town sweeps the ranks of the Punitive Expeditionary Forces, scattering the troops. Rifle fire breaks out from behind the walls of the little town while several soldiers lie dead and

260   R. W. Turner

wounded from the attack. With the troops on the run for cover, more machine gun fire pins down the unprotected troops, wounding and killing more soldiers.

There's mayhem in the field as the staff officers on horseback are caught in the middle of blood-curdling screams of retreating men looking for cover, to return fire from carbines. They are out of rifle range. Smoke and dust rise off the desert floor as more machine gun fire sweeps the field.

The machine gun fire unnerves the Ranger as he stands in the room, helpless to do anything. "That does it," he says, shaking his head and walking over to the door.

"That does what?" exclaims Lillian, just as concerned.

"I came here to prevent something from happening...and I aim to complete what I started."

"There are two armies out there. What are you going to do?"

Shaking his head and gritting his teeth, the Ranger opens the door. "I don't know. But I'm not going to stand by and allow those boys to be killed!"

"You'll be killed!" warns Lillian, not knowing what else to say or do.

"Then I won't have to worry about the liquor now, will I?" the Ranger says, eyeing the little lady and Juan. He steps through the door and walks down the hallway.

"Stop him!" shouts Lillian to Juan.

"He will be protected," Juan assures Lillian rather calmly, despite the sound of machine gun fire and the sharp cracks of rifles going off, clearly indicating a major battle is being waged.

"This is a hell of a time to be philosophical," shouts Lillian eyeing the Indian with derision. "You think Yaqui magic can stop bullets?"

Juan simply nods. "He will have allies with him."

"He has Mexican and American forces in a pitched battle, and you think he's safe running around in the middle of it? And you think you can just reach into that little leather pouch of yours and...and...," she stumbles, looking for the words, "...pull out that...that...marble, and convince everyone to just call it all off?"

"He will be protected," Juan repeats himself, eyeing Lillian curiously as she nervously walks to the window and looks out at the war being waged right before her eyes.

The door to the building opens amidst smoke and various caliber gun fire. The Ranger steps onto the gravel and into a war zone. Soldiers run towards the wall to set up position while others resupply ammunition. Reaching the warehouse through all the commotion, he opens the large wooden double doors and steps in, casting a long shadow leading right up to the hay wagon which has been repositioned for the harnessing of horses.

General Schmidt puts his binoculars down as Trevino shouts some orders from his position on a balcony to a Captain standing below the structure. "Use more machine guns!" he yells as he pulls his binoculars up to view the action again.

Schmidt looks down at the Captain and catches a glimpse of the Ranger in the warehouse. Gathering himself, he lifts his head and tells General Trevino. "I must attend to some unfinished business."

"Si, si," says General Trevino, waving Schmidt off, not taking his eyes off the action before him.

Schmidt exits the balcony as General Trevino shouts more orders to the Captain below. Grasping his binoculars and looking down, he yells, "Set up field infantry and prepare to fire and advance on my command!"

Machine gun fire hits the lines of the Punitive Expeditionary Forces as more rifle fire pins down the American soldiers. Troopers dash for cover in all directions as their ranks are devastated. Four troopers run for protection in one direction, drawing a trail of rifle fire. More machine gun fire kicks up dirt and dust, as a group of other soldiers dive behind some rocks for cover as bullets hit just to the side of the men. When the dust settles, two men lie dead, one injured, and one attending to the wounded.

"I'm hit! I'm hit!" shouts a private, clutching his stomach in agony.

"Take it easy," says a corporal as he crawls over to the wounded soldier amidst the falling rocks and dirt. He examines the wounded soldier, not knowing what to do.

"Where do I start?" the trooper says, horrified at the sight. He reaches out to his fallen comrade as bullets rain on them. When the dust clears this time, there are two dead troopers.

Looking over the warehouse in desperation for anything that might help him, the Ranger grits his teeth and moves towards the wagon filled with liquor. He walks up to the side and kicks away one wooden stop from behind one wheel, then walks over to the other side, prepared to do the same to the other wheel.

"That will be all...Texas Ranger," says General Heinrich Schmidt, stepping in front of him with a pistol aimed at the lawman. Casually lifting the weapon and sighting it on Abner, the General says, ""I don't want to see any quick moves.... So just stand still. Any move will result in your immediate death." Aiming the pistol and slowly walking towards the Ranger, the General says, "Your friends will be along directly." He motions the Ranger away from the wagon with his other hand as he walks to the wagon and stands beside the precious cargo.

The battle has grown to new heights beyond the warehouse as Lillian and Juan enter the building with two soldiers aiming their rifles at them. Admiral Yamagato follows close behind the soldiers.

"Oh, here they are now," says Schmidt. The Admiral unholsters his firearm and nods at General Schmidt. "Careless of you, Admiral. The shipment might not have reached its intended target."

"Target?" questions the Ranger, looking over at Lillian and Juan, then back at the German General.

"Disarm that man...carefully," General Schmidt orders the two soldiers as Yamagato holds his pistol on Lillian and Juan.

The two soldiers approach the Ranger with caution as they unbutton his duster to reveal all his weapons. The lawman can only stand as the soldiers take his holstered revolvers and Buntline pistol.

"You might as well take that coat off him," says Schmidt. "...And keep an eye on that right arm of his. He might have something up his sleeve," the General says, massaging his bandaged right hand.

The soldiers remove the Ranger's palm pistol after the duster is removed. That Ranger stands before the German General totally unarmed. The soldiers place his weapons aside, pick up their rifles and point them at the Ranger. Admiral Yamagato cocks his pistol leveled at Lillian and Juan. Outside the warehouse, more rifle and machine gun fire fill the air.

General Schmidt places his pistol down on the wagon and takes off his coat. Eyeing the Ranger, he takes off his tie and unbuttons his shirt cuff. As he rolls up his shirt sleeves, he slowly walks toward the Ranger. "I think it's time I bring you in touch with the twentieth century, Texas Ranger."

Schmidt studies the crusty old lawman without his duster or the armaments. "You see, we have...shall we say...a new attitude in Germany. Though they call us anarchists, we're really National Socialists. Far above your archaic democracy and that...'All men are created equal'...sort of thing."

The Ranger eyes the General with contempt. "You couldn't attack head-on like the British in the revolutionary war, or try to push through the underbelly like in 1812. Germany has to go through the mid-section and use Mexico. Not really cheating, just a different approach to war. One we hadn't thought of before," he says, turning to Yamagato. "What did he promise you?"

"Wyoming!" smiles the Admiral.

"He can have Oklahoma, Kansas, Nebraska, Utah or even South Dakota," says the German General. "You see, the Japanese will control the West Coast of America, Germany the East Coast...and Mexico will possess the breadbasket, or...as you like to say in the United States...the heartland."

Circling the Ranger and looking him over, he goes on. "You see...your government isn't as secure as you'd like to believe. We've already blown up your Senate reception room in Washington, D. C. And chased your William Jennings Bryan from his seat as Secretary of State. When we had Archduke Ferdinand assassinated in Sarajevo, we already had set up a sequence of events which would ultimately lead Europe to war. When Pancho Villa crosses the border this time, the United States' outrage will be directed at Mexico, not Germany."

The German General smiles. "Our designs go beyond simple attacks on property and infringements of borders. While America waltzes from the cotillion to the two-step... and views the world through the eyes of nickelodeon...we will have a Socialist firmly planted in a high office in Washington. We have one there now even as we speak at this very moment."

Coming around face to face with the Ranger, Schmidt says, "Little by little, our message will get across. There are people in the wings ready to assist him once he makes his move...and before you know it, there'll be a Nationalist Socialist in the White House, and he'll be taking orders from Berlin!"

"America, controlled by Germany!" says the Ranger, shaking his head in disbelief.

"I think you're getting the picture, Texas Ranger. We'll move through Canada, Central and South America...Africa, India, China...."

"China?" questions the Ranger.

"Oh, yes!" says General Schmidt. "The Boxer Rebellion is being waged right now, or...haven't you grasped the delicate intricacies of reading yet?"

Eyeing the German General, the Ranger says, "I generally just read the sports page."

"Sports page?" laughs the General. "You read the sports page? Turning to the Japanese Admiral, Schmidt says, "How simply delightful! This man epitomizes your typical American. He reads sports and thinks he's Wyatt Earp...somewhere out in the old west." He turns to the Ranger and slaps him across the face. "Well? Texas Ranger? What's the score now?"

Rubbing his face and shaking his head, the Ranger looks at the German General. "You know? I'm plumb tired of you using my face to stop your slaps with. Now, I'm certain we can come to a better understanding about that."

"Understanding?" Schmidt asks. "Understand this, Texas Ranger. Within one year, America, the Constitution and your Bill of Rights...as you know it, will be nothing more than a quaint, distant memory."

"You think America is asleep?" asks the Ranger.

The General eyes the Ranger from head to toe. "Catatonic is the appropriate description.

Staring at the office wall, General Scriven is still frozen in place since before his landing earlier that morning. He doesn't respond to the knock on the office door.

The door opens and Lieutenant Patton enters with some new reports. He is accompanied by Sergeant Simmons carrying an array of bottles and tins on a tray. The First Lieutenant salutes the General, steps closer to his desk to pile more papers on his desk that have yet to be reviewed, and steps back.

"Our forces are under heavy attack in Carrizal, General," says the young officer, looking for any kind of response from his senior officer. "Do you have any orders?"

Completely frozen and alert to nothing, the General is hopelessly lost in his own world.

"Shouldn't we send reinforcements?" asks the lieutenant. "A lot of good men are losing their lives, General.... With your approval...I'd like to...."

Shaking his head and giving up, Patton motions the sergeant to put the tray down on the desk. Stepping forward and leaning over to peer into the General's eyes, the young lieutenant politely says, "I'd like to try something, Sir," he says.

He reaches for a bottle on the tray, looks at the label and puts it down. He chooses another bottle, reads the label, opens it, then hands it to the sergeant. Here, hold this under his nose. Do the same with the rest and see if any will shake him up. I've got to update the General's order to the battle group at Carrizal."

Patton leans in for one last look at the General, then backing off and saluting, he exits, as the sergeant walks over to the General's side at the desk.

The noncom takes a whiff of the bottle and shudders, cringing. Holding the bottle at arm's length, he leans towards the General and brings it up to the General's nose.

The Punitive Expeditionary Forces take a ferocious beating in the open field amidst the flying dirt, dust, and debris from machine gun fire and rifle bullets zipping through the air. The American troops are hopelessly pinned down.

Colonel Hart, Major Watkins, and Captain Leeman recover from a spray of bullets from behind a rock where they've found some protection. They had abandoned their horses for cover. "We're pinned down," shouts Major Watkins, looking around the battle field.

"We can't advance or retreat," Colonel Hart shouts back as bullets zip by, forcing him to dive down and take cover again.

"The men are taking a beating," shouts Captain Leeman, coming up from the rapid rifle fire and onslaught.

A corporal dashes towards the commanding officers, zigzagging across the open field. Finally diving over some rocks and crawling to the officer staff, he stops a moment to salute. "Twelve dead, Sir," he reports, holding his salute. The Colonel returns the salute, horrified.

"Evacuate the dead and wounded," shouts the Captain, drawing attention from the Colonel.

Saluting the Captain and looking around him as bullets zip by, the young corporal asks, "To where, Sir?"

"Are you disobeying a direct order, Soldier?" asks the major, dusting dirt and dust off him as he comes up after cover.

Holding a salute to the major and addressing him, the corporal says, "No, Sir. I'm just wondering where you'd like us to take them?"

The Colonel sees a young sixteen-year-old boy behind a rock fifteen feet away who's sighting and returning fire. "Private!" shouts the Colonel, gaining the young soldier's attention.

Surprised, the young man falls behind for cover and sees the Colonel. Juggling his rifle while sitting, he attempts a salute. "Yes, Sir?"

"Help this corporal attend to the dead and wounded," shouts the Colonel, disregarding the salute.

The young man struggles to his feet, looks towards the firing line and dashes for the command staff taking cover behind some rocks. The corporal salutes the Colonel, grabs the young man as they dash into the open battle field towards their men.

Shaking his head, the Colonel looks at his staff. "We can't take much more of this."

General Trevino walks down the front line encouraging his troops and cheering them on as more bullets are passed, loaded, and fired. Using his cane to clear his path through spent rifle casings, he stops and looks down at one piece of stucco shot off the wall, the size of a small golf ball. He looks ahead of him, then down at the piece of debris at his feet, thinks and wonders a moment, finally shakes his head and moves on.

General Schmidt circles the Ranger as the discharge of small and large weapon fire goes off outside the warehouse. General Trevino enters the double doors to the building and sees the wagon, Schmidt, Admiral Yamagato and two his soldiers leveling their rifles on Lillian, Juan, and the Ranger. The German General sees Trevino walk in from the glare of the sun piercing through the doorway. He nods at the Mexican General and turns back to the Ranger.

"I'm going to give you an exhibit of what we have to offer the world," Schmidt tells the Ranger, smiling. He kicks the Ranger in the stomach, doubling him over. Schmidt smiles at General Trevino. "That's '*Savat*,' he says, "something I took from the French."

Lillian and Juan tense, helpless to do anything. Yamagato is holding his weapon on them as he nods and smiles.

Schmidt continues pacing around the Ranger. "At the moment, Germany is in Verdun, waging war with France," he says, throwing another vicious blow at the Ranger. The Ranger doubles over, bringing him to his knees, trying to catch his breath. "That's something I learned from our allies," Schmidt says.

Lillian flinches, looking at Juan and wondering what he's thinking now about the protection the Ranger is supposed to have. Admiral Yamagato stands with his big smile and pistol directed at them.

"The Japanese," Schmidt goes on, "call that *Ju Jitsu*."

Catching his breath and rubbing his neck, the Ranger struggles to his feet. He looks around the warehouse, hearing all the weapons going off just outside the open doors of the warehouse. He sees soldiers setting up a cannon as others take up position and fire rifles, as even more soldiers supply them with bullets and shells. He turns back to Schmidt and takes a deep breath.

Schmidt walks up to him and flagrantly pummels him with a series of rapid punches to his face, sending him backwards. "That," says the German General proudly, "comes from the Marquis of Queensbury...or what you call... boxing. Germany has assimilated many cultures, many styles...Texas Ranger," says the German General in contempt for the lawman who now stands before him without weapons to back him up. "We will even assimilate you into our society," Schmidt finishes, kicking the feet from beneath the Ranger.

The Ranger drops to the ground, and while he is down, the German General kicks him repeatedly. "It is pointless to resist," says the General.

Bleeding from his nose and mouth, the Ranger looks up at the German General, then over to Lillian and Juan.

The Punitive Expeditionary Forces continue to take a beating. More men fall, wounded, as rifle fire mounts and machine gun fire escalates, filling the battle zone with smoke, dust, debris, and the smell of discharged black powder. The once calm desert is now marked by huge holes left by bullets. Cries of pain and agony are heard under the crack of rifle fire. More and more soldiers huddle for cover with no relief from the constant barrage.

The Ranger tries to roll over but the General's boot catches him square in the back of the head and he collapses. Confident and affirmed by his bullying and beating of the Ranger, Schmidt rolls down his sleeves and buttons his cuffs. He nods to General Trevino, who jerks his cane up, holding

it out to get a firmer grip on it. Trevino turns and exits the
warehouse to attend to the troops at the firing line.

The Ranger stirs a bit but Schmidt pays no attention.
He rubs his bandaged right hand that reminds him of a
previous encounter with the Ranger. Yamagato and the two
soldiers smile as they realize that the Ranger has been
defeated. Schmidt walks over to the Ranger and gives him
another kick, then backs up to look at the toes of his boot,
wondering if maybe he's dirtied them.

Despite the great battle being waged outside the
warehouse with machine guns and rifles firing, a crow flies
into the warehouse and lands on a ceiling rafter, surprising
everyone, except Juan—who sits down. Startled, Lillian
looks at Juan at her side. He reaches behind him and pulls
out his medicine bag, causing Admiral Yamagato to step
forward and point his pistol down at the Yaqui.

"What are you doing?" asks the Admiral.

Juan dips his fingers into the little leather pouch and
searches for something as Lillian watches him.

"What's going on over there?" asks Schmidt, finally
buttoning his last shirt cuff.

"Get up," shouts the Japanese Admiral. "Get up
now!"

Juan pulls out the pearl and holds it up to the Admiral,
who's stunned at the sight of it.

"What is it?" demands Schmidt, looking at them.

"He possesses the pearl," says an astonished
Yamagato, turning to the German General. "But that's
impossible!" he says, shaking his head. Turning back to the
Yaqui, he asks, "How did you get that?"

Juan looks up at the Admiral, as he twists the shiny
pearl in his fingers, studying it. Finally he looks up at the
Japanese Admiral. "I have been to the fourth world," he
says cryptically, shifting his fingers and causing a reflection
of the sunlight creeping into the building to flash a spark of
light into the Admiral's eye off the pearl.

Crawling over to the wagon and dragging himself to his feet with the help of the large wooden wheel, the Ranger notices the last wooden chock under the wagon wheel. He kicks it out from behind the wheel and the wagon begins to roll forward towards the open doorway.

The wagon rolls into a cannon placement and rolls over, causing the bottles of alcohol to break and spill freely over the entire area. The liquid flows to another cannon, where a spark ignites a fire, soon spreading rapidly to Mexican soldiers who abandon their positions. The fire is still small enough for the soldiers to put out, but when a shell ignites, it causes a chain fire explosion from the stacked shells against the wall, leaving a huge, gaping hole. Firing stops on the firing line as the fire expands in strength and power.

The huge explosion at the front wall of Carrizal catches the attention of the Punitive Expeditionary Forces. Captain Watkins sees the confusion behind the wall of Carrizal and quickly turns it to his advantage. He shouts to a soldier down the line. "Sound the charge, Soldier!"

Saluting and complying with the order, the soldier picks up his bugle and sounds the charge.

Hearing the bugle sound the offensive, troopers rise from cover with a renewed spirit and courage. They grab their carbines and charge the town.

The soldiers breach the wall and engage in close quarter battle, hand to hand. The Punitive Expeditionary Forces advance and engage the enemy face to face.

Colonel Hart stands amid the flames and smoke giving orders to his men. "Secure the entry!" He points to a gate as three soldiers grip their weapons and charge for position as ordered. "Cover that wall!" He directs three other soldiers entering through the gap in the wall to another area of the town.

A Mexican soldier approaches Colonel Hart from the rear with a rifle and bayonet, but the Colonel spins around in time, drawing his Colt .45 and shoots. He lets go another round at another Mexican soldier who has come closer.

Mexican soldiers advance on the invading Punitive Expeditionary Forces who have just gotten a foothold in the town. "Stop them!" shouts Colonel Hart as fresh Mexican troops round a corner and move on the American troops.

Colonel Hart stands firm as he raises his pistol and lets go with three rapid shots. Three American soldiers advance to the Colonel, kneel, and fire at four Mexican soldiers, downing them.

"Advance!" shouts Colonel Hart as the three soldiers rise and move forward, discharging their carbines on a shoot-and-advance tactic. "Take that building!" he issues another order. The soldiers move on it.

General Trevino is shocked to see the tide change in the battle from his view on the balcony. He looks at one side then the other as the Punitive Expeditionary Forces advance through the gap in the wall. The fire has spread to other parts of the wall, encircling and setting the cannons on fire, raging completely out of control.

Stunned, the General spins and enters the room off the balcony. Just below him, his troops are engaged in hand to hand combat. More and more American forces enter the town through the gaps made in the burning wall. Trevino returns to the balcony with a pistol and takes some wild shots at the American soldiers below him without doing any damage. He returns to the room adjoining the balcony and disappears again.

Four Punitive Expeditionary Forces soldiers move through the entrance of the building where General Trevino is situated. One trooper kicks in the door as the second man enters with rifle and bayonet on the offensive. He turns and calls for the others to follow him, motioning them forward. One by one, the four troopers advance through the building, covering their backs and flanks in this close-action, room-by-room assault.

General Schmidt is incensed as he turns from the fire raging uncontrollably just outside the warehouse. Admiral Yamagato rubs his eyes as two Mexican soldiers hold aim on Lillian and Juan. Juan gets to his feet, holding the pearl in his hand. The weapon-bearing soldiers seem hypnotized by the pearl. Lillian watches Schmidt's advance on the Ranger.

"That...is going to cost you...," says the German General as he moves in on the Ranger, "your life...Texas Ranger." The General throws a punch that sends Abner falling into one of the Mexican soldiers holding aim on Lillian and Juan.

The Ranger grabs the soldier's rifle and shoots the other soldier. He pulls the weapon from the stunned soldier and knocks him out with the steel butt plate, as Lillian and Juan rush Admiral Yamagato and wrestle the pistol from his hand, pointing the weapon at him.

One soldier is dead, another is knocked out. Admiral Yamagato is still rubbing his eyes as Lillian keeps him covered, leaving the German General standing before a battered, beaten Texas Ranger.

From the ceiling rafters, the crow caws and spreads its wings as it free-falls towards General Schmidt. It swoops past him and flies out the doorway of the warehouse and into the open desert. Juan watches the bird fly away into the distance before he puts the pearl back in the leather pouch and places it into his pocket. He turns to the Ranger and nods.

The Punitive Expeditionary Forces advance through the town, building by building, door by door, as fewer gun shots are fired from either force in this close action where the flames from the fire have spread beyond the walls to some of the smaller buildings inside Carrizal.

General Trevino back pedals, ordering his few remaining troops to fire on the advancing American soldiers who drop, level their carbines and return fire, forcing Trevino to duck into a building for protection.

One American soldier belt-feeds a Browning machine gun mounted on a tripod as the gunner lets go with some precision bursts outside the town, allowing more soldiers to advance through the opening in the wall. "Feed me! Feed me!" yells the gunner as the other soldier continues to unwind and belt-feed ammunition from a box.

Lieutenant Patton enters General Scriven's office with some new papers, brimming over with enthusiasm. He halts in front of the General's desk and salutes. "They've taken the advantage, Sir."

Frozen in his seat and focused on the wall, the General remains oblivious to anything and everything as the young lieutenant drops his salute and rushes to his side of the desk, laying the new papers on top of the stack of other papers already there.

Looking at the General then at Sergeant Simmons beside him, Patton says, "The forces are about to breach the walls of Carrizal!" The young officer exclaims excitedly, smiling broadly until he stops, looks at the frozen General, where his high spirits drop.

"This is the biggest battle being waged in the campaign and I'm stuck here, unable to take part in it." He scowls at the sergeant who can only shake his head. "Sergeant, let me attend to General Scriven a moment.

He walks to the other side of the General's desk and leans over to the General as the noncom looks on from the other side. "Sir, the surgeon is off base right now and this is all we have at the moment." Patton looks at the sergeant and head motions him out of the office.

After Sergeant Simmons leaves, the lieutenant reaches for some boot polish and unscrews it. Speaking to himself, he shakes his head. "My destiny is to ride a desk?" he asks of no one in particular in despair. Then looking skyward, he pleads, "Come on, give me a chance...." Moving into a better position, he brings the tin of black polish close to the General's nose. Too close. A knock at the door startles him. "Yes?"

Sergeant Simmons opens the door and looks in. "Any response?"

"Not yet," Patton replies, shaking his head. "Anything more on the troops"

"No, Sir," answers the sergeant.

"Well, keep me posted."

"Yes, Sir," says the dutiful Sergeant, saluting and closing the door.

Returning his attention to the rigid General, Lieutenant Patton looks at the tin of polish in his hand. Thoughtlessly, he sniffs it. The smell makes him shudder and cringe. He reads the ingredients. Rancid duck fat, chimney soot, rotten carnauba wax, and a few other unidentifiable things.

He finally notices the smudge of black shoe polish on the tip of the General's nose. Reaching for his handkerchief, he looks for the best approach to wipe off the smudge without making it worse. "Would a solvent work?" he wonders out loud. After a lot of thought, he steps back from the General's desk and salutes. "You rest easy, General," he says. "I'll be back momentarily."

He shuts the door, leaving the General in his petrified state, unchanged, except for a spot of black shoe polish on the tip of his nose.

Admiral Yamagato rubs his eyes as Lillian aims his pistol at him. Juan studies the Ranger and the German General as soldiers from the Punitive Expeditionary Forces rush past the warehouse entrance on their advance. Turning from Lillian and Juan, the battered and bloodied Ranger looks at Schmidt who raises his head arrogantly as he looks at the people surrounding him.

Staring at the German General from head to toe, the Ranger takes a deep breath and looks at the rifle in his hand. He looks at the German military officer once more, the man who had given him a terrible beating when he was down.

Dropping the rifle, he shakes his head. "It's time I give you an education, General."

The General laughs smugly. "Is this going to be about 'Save the Alamo,' or some other drivel like that?"

Walking towards the General slowly, the Ranger wipes some blood from the side of his mouth and shakes his head. "Remember the Alamo?" he asks.

Unbuttoning his cuffs and rolling up his sleeves, the General snickers. "I'll tell you what I remember about the Alamo. It fell!"

Getting closer and closer to the General, the Ranger lifts his chin. "Well then, let's see how many times you can rise and fall." He steps in front of the General and swings, catching the General in the jaw, sending the man sprawling to a wall of the warehouse. Moving in on the General, the Ranger grabs him and drops him with another punch that floors him. The General grabs his jaw, looking at the Ranger, wonderingly.

Slowly he stands up, takes a stance and throws a punch at Abner. Abner catches the fist before it lands and holds it, surprising the General. Schmidt throws a jab with his left fist. Abner also catches that hand. Holding the General's two fists, the Ranger pulls them down and slams his head into the man's face and knocking him down again.

Wasting no time, the Ranger moves in on the downed General with new energy. Schmidt throws a kick at the Ranger, but it's caught in the Ranger's grasp. He spins the General around like a calf about to be roped and tied, and throws him a few feet away. Schmidt scrambles to his feet and stares at the Ranger.

Wiping blood from his mouth, the General says, "You surprise me."

"...No surprises here, mister. What you see is what you get," says the Ranger.

"Nothing between the lines?" inquires the General, buying time as he tries to catch his breath.

"Nothing but the truth, buster," says the Ranger as he moves in on the General again, smacking him on the side of the head. The General gathers himself as if to throw a swing, but dashes to the warehouse door instead, catching Lillian and Juan by surprise.

"Don't let him get away," shouts Lillian, still holding aim on Admiral Yamagato who's still rubbing his eyes.

The Ranger walks over to his duster and weapons spread out in a corner of the warehouse and puts his gear back on. "I'll take care of him, my way." Looking at Lillian and Juan, he pulls his hat down and heads for the building's exit in pursuit of General Schmidt.

Outside, the balance of power has changed as the Punitive Expeditionary Forces storm the town. Fighting breaks out on the street as troops battle hand to hand. The Ranger pushes people out of the way as he pursues Schmidt.

Schmidt dashes into a building as the Ranger approaches. Three quick bursts of gunfire splinter the door as Abner reaches for the door knob. The Ranger takes cover at the side of the building, pulling out his pump-action shotgun. Stepping forward, he pumps four successive shots into the door, blowing it apart. He puts the weapon away and pulls out a sawed-off shotgun and a revolver. Stepping back and taking a deep breath, he steps through the door, prepared for anything. He answers a shot from the corner of the room with both barrels of the scatter gun.

Schmidt takes cover when the shots ride high against the wall behind him. He dashes to a hallway as bullets from the Ranger's pistol follow his retreat. Pocketing the scatter gun and his empty pistol, the Ranger pulls out two other revolvers, still in pursuit.

Coming to the end of the hall, Schmidt enters a room. Overcome with panic, he checks his Mauser broom-handle pistol. He pats himself for stripper clips, satisfied, he looks the room over for an exit.

The Ranger moves down the hallway, fiercely determined on rounding up this man. As he approaches a doorway, he leans against the wall beside it. Reloading both shotguns, he hears Schmidt's voice from inside the room. "There are provisions for my escape, Texas Ranger. You alone, can't stop me."

"Stop you?" asks the Ranger. "Hell, I'm going to kill you!"

"Big words for an old man," replies Schmidt from inside the room.

Grabbing the pump action shotgun, the Ranger slips it back into an inside pocket of his duster and holsters one revolver. He reaches for the scatter gun with one hand while holding the other revolver in the other hand. Taking a deep breath, he enters the room with both weapons leveled and ready to fire.

Stepping through the doorway of the empty room, the Ranger circles it with the weapons, ready to let go with whichever one that needs to be used to finish the job.

"It isn't as simple as that, is it?" The General's voice fills the empty room, but the man himself is nowhere to be seen.

The Ranger keeps circling the room from his position. He squints and keeps a sharp eye out for the General. "You can run, but you can't hide," he says, listening for a hint of the General's whereabouts. Getting no response, he looks the room over carefully. He walks to a wall , rubbing his gun hand over it, feeling, looking for something that can help him.

Noticing a seam in the wooden floor, he steps back, holsters the pistol, and trades shotguns. Kneeling and tapping the tip of the pump-action shotgun on the floor, he draws three rapid shots from beneath the floor, splintering it. The Ranger stands up and points his shotgun at the floor and lets go with three successive shots of his own. It blows a giant hole in the floor, leaving only the hinges of what had been a trap door. Even that finally falls into the chasm below.

Stepping back, the Ranger rapidly reloads the shotgun and comes up with it aimed. He reaches into his duster and pulls a shotgun shell out and tosses it through the hole in the wooden floor. Hitting the ground below, it draws gunfire from Schmidt. The Ranger steps to the other side of trap door and lets go two more blasts, then steps back.

"Clever, but not clever enough," comes General Schmidt's voice from below. Several shots follow, one comes dangerously close to the lawman. Coolly, he steps back to the wall. He hears several clicks from Schmidt's gun below. Schmidt has run out of bullets.

The Ranger methodically trades shotguns as he moves to the gaping hole in the floor. Looking down, he steps onto a stairway leading to a basement.

He enters the room below with his scatter gun and pistol leveled. It's a distillery, he discovers. Sidling up to a wall, he takes inventory of the room.

Schmidt's voice cuts through the silence. "Now you know where we make the whiskey." Moving towards the voice, the Ranger keeps his senses alert.

"There are a dozen distilleries such as this throughout Mexico, Texas Ranger. So even if you destroy this one, you'll never find the others...and the alcohol will continue to cross your border."

Moving silently towards the voice, the Ranger pauses beside some stacked barrels. "You think you can defeat America by getting us drunk?" he asks, silently counting the wooden casks.

"You ever hear of the Opium Wars, Texas Ranger?" asks Schmidt in his disembodied voice. Tracking the voice, the Ranger advances once more.

"Numb the public?" the Ranger responds. "Is that the strategy?"

"Something like that," Schmidt laughs dementedly. "We like to call it...public apathy."

The Ranger is finally able to locate Schmidt's position. But a wall separates them. Looking over the seam in the wall, he rubs his gun hand over it. You'll never leave here alive!" he shouts, throwing his voice to the far corner of the distillery.

Silently walking back towards the stacked barrels of whiskey, he pushes one off track, starting a chain reaction. The barrels roll towards the wall, smashing an opening as several wild shots ring out from inside the battered room.

Slowly moving on the opening in the wall as alcohol flows freely from some broken barrels, the Ranger pulls up his scatter gun and pokes it through the opening, blasting one side of the room then the other. He quickly puts the weapon in his duster, pulls out two revolvers and boldly steps into the darkened room. It is faintly lit by a fire at a processing still.

"You'll never be able to find me," taunts Schmidt. "We planned for such a possibility. I'll escape and finish my assignment."

"Pretty confident for a man on the run, aren't you?" answers the Ranger, still searching for the German General.

"I'm confident of my mission and the role Germany must play in the future," replies Schmidt. "It is our destiny, Texas Ranger." A shot rings out suddenly, unnerving the Ranger. Instinctively, he returns several rounds in the direction of the gun blast. "I thought that bullet would stop you," Schmidt's voice sounds surprised.

The light from the distillery shines a light on the Ranger, clearly showing a hole at the waistline of the duster. The Ranger grits his teeth and reaches into the duster and comes out with blood on his fingers. He opens the duster to look more closely and discovers that the stock of the Buffalo gun took the full impact of Schmidt's bullet. Pocketing the long rifle, he exchanges one pistol for another and holds both guns ready.

"You're gonna need more than that!" shouts the Ranger.

"Then try this!" comes Schmidt's voice, as more bullets are fired at the Ranger who stands bold and at the ready, returning fire from his two revolvers.

One of Schmidt's bullets sparks, setting one of the ruptured whiskey barrels on fire. Several bright flashes from different parts of the room suddenly burst into flames, lighting up the room. The Ranger looks around and sees some very large boxes and crates he hadn't seen before. He is curious, but he catches a glimpse of a door opening and shutting quickly. Moving towards the door, he realizes the flames are spreading throughout the room and igniting the wooden crates. His only escape is the one Schmidt has taken.

The Ranger hurries to the door to open it, but the door's locked. He backs up, pulls out the pump-action shotgun, cocks and shoots. He cocks and shoots again. Nothing! Cocks and shoots again. Again, nothing! He curses the weapon as he looks at it. Despite the huge hole the first shot put into the door, now nothing.

"Damn!" he mutters. "I just reloaded it." Shaking his head, he puts the shotgun back in his duster and reaches into the hole of the door and struggles to open it. The fire burns dangerously closer. He backs up, pulls the sawed-off shotgun out and blows off a hinge in the door with one shot, the other hinge with the second shot. Putting the weapon in his coat, he pulls out a revolver and steps forward, and kicks the door in.

The Ranger steps past the splintered door into a room filled with more large crates. Stepping to the side of the lit room, he opens his duster, pulls out the scatter gun and discharges both spent shell casings. Digging into the duster for two fresh shells, he reloads the weapon with them. He packs the scatter gun and pulls out the pump-action shotgun and reloads with more cartridges from his duster.

"You are wise to reload, Texas Ranger," General Schmidt's voice taunts him. "This is going to be long war."

"Not the way I see it," says the Ranger, digging for bullets to reload one pistol while he cradles the pump-action shotgun in one arm. "Do you hear that battle out there?" he shouts, holstering one pistol and slapping leather for another. He comes up with it and begins reloading.

Cries and screams along with gunfire is heard as the war still wages between both armies. "Those are American guns," says the Ranger, slipping the pistol into a holster and pulling another out to reload. "You're about to see the score change."

"Score?" responds Schmidt with curiosity. "Is that the education you were going to give me, Texas Ranger? Box scores?" He laughs.

Slamming the revolver's cylinder back into place, the Ranger hoists the scatter gun in his hand and readies himself. He takes a deep breath and looks around the room, trying to get a gauge on Schmidt's position from his voice. "I said I read the sports page, but I never said I followed any sport," he says, standing and listening attentively for a response.

"What did you do?" General Schmidt's voice sounds from a distance away. "Add up the scores?"

Slowly moving towards the voice as he sidles along the wall, the Ranger throws his voice to a far corner of the room, keeping his eyes peeled in the direction of Schmidt's voice. "No. I read what an old friend of mine has to say."

"You have friends who can write?" General Schmidt's voice taunts him again. "When did you ever meet anyone who could write?"

Instinctively moving by sound alone, the Ranger again throws his voice away from him. "A long time ago, back in Dodge. A guy named Masterson. You probably never heard of him." He senses Schmidt is close. "He used to partner up with Wyatt and this dentist guy named Holladay, who had a bad case of consumption or something."

Flames from the distillery are starting to creep into the room. He senses another approach to the situation and pockets the shotgun and pulls out a long-barreled revolver. Opening the cylinder to check his rounds, he slams it back into place. He cocks the pistol and holds it up. "And, as a rule, Bat never took as much abuse as you seem to enjoy handing out. But we have a code out west, and though it might be reasonable not to expect a diplomat like you to understand, it works in Texas."

Schmidt fires a shot, immediately returned by the Ranger. "But we're not in Texas, are we, Texas Ranger?" Schmidt responds.

Moving swiftly towards where the bullet was fired, the Ranger says, "And this ain't Germany."

"Is that how you got your men?" asks Schmidt from further away. "Did you bore them until they surrendered or something?"

The Ranger reaches some stacked boxes and sees a crowbar. He picks it up and tosses it across the room. The General steps from behind some other boxes and fires three rapid shots in the direction the crowbar fell. Seeing Schmidt, the Ranger fires several shots in his direction, ripping holes into some boxes. Recovering from the blast off the Ranger's long gun, Schmidt makes a dash across the room for another door.

The Ranger runs for the door, opens it, as a bullet rips into it from Schmidt's Mauser. The Ranger steps to the side of the door and holds his revolver up, reaching for the door-knob and carefully opening it. He takes a deep breath and steps through the door to a staircase leading up.

Carefully climbing the stairs, the Ranger approaches the top to another door. He opens the door slowly and cautiously, as three bullets rip into it. Staggering, he backs up to the side of the wall and pulls out his pump-action shotgun. He takes three steps down the stairs and fires four successive shots that rip the door apart. Taking a moment to replace the shotgun and pull out a Colt, he rapidly counts and inventories the number of shots he has taken and which

{284}

{R. W. Turner}

guns are still loaded. He takes one more breath, then steps through the door boldly.

The well-lit room clearly shows two bullet holes in his duster as blood stains part of the coat from his side. Despite the shots, he shows no ill effects. Carefully listening for any sign of Schmidt, the Ranger reaches inside his canvas duster and winces as he pulls out a large splinter of wood from his side, a remnant from the butt of the splintered Buffalo gun. He pats his coat down, shakes his head, and takes a deep breath before he slides behind a large box. Looking the room over as perspiration rolls down his temple, he sees a small window and two doors on the far wall, and a room full of more wooden crates and baskets.

"Let's make a deal, Texas Ranger," says Schmidt as he levels his pistol and aims at the closed door in front of him, anticipating a blind shot. "I have diplomatic immunity. I can reveal all the plans we have. I can be most helpful to your government."

The wall near Schmidt blasts wide open from the Ranger's Winchester, as the bullet keeps on going through a line of wooden crates from one to the next, until it smashes into an adobe wall above Schmidt's head, covering him with dust and debris.

Dashing for the small window, Schmidt stops when another blast from the Ranger's Winchester shatters the window frame. The General looks at the doorway only to see the Ranger standing there with the rifle pointed directly at him. He drops the pistol as the Ranger motions him towards the door. "Now we're going to take a very serious walk," says the Ranger.

The Punitive Expeditionary Forces round up prisoners and march them off as other Mexican soldiers hold their hands over their heads while American troops search them. Smoke is all that remains of the charred cannon emplacements as General Schmidt walks towards the warehouse where Lillian and Juan have Admiral Yamagato. Seeing the

Ranger pushing Schmidt forward at gun point, Lillian asks, "What about General Trevino?"

The Mexican General rounds a corner of the complex with his hands up as two troopers have weapons placed at his back. He passes the warehouse and sees Schmidt, Yamagato, Lillian, Juan, and the Ranger for the last time in his life as he's led to the command staff of the Punitive Expeditionary Forces.

Lieutenant Patton and the Duty Sergeant attend to General Scriven with assorted nostrums, cold remedies, and food items ranging from onions, garlic, cheese, perfumes, to other curious items not easily recognizable, from the tray on the desk. But nothing works. The General is still rigid even though traces of garlic are stuck in his mustache and his nose still has a smudge of shoe polish on the tip.

Shaking his head with deep concern, First Lieutenant Patton looks at the sergeant. "He has to come out of it!"

"What about cold water?" Sergeant Simmons offers a suggestion.

"I'm not going to soak my commanding officer," says the young lieutenant.

"Well," says the sergeant, peering at the General. "You can't leave him like that."

Frustrated and tired, Lieutenant Patton says, "I'm not leaving him in any way at all! I'm trying to help!"

A blue-jacketed messenger riding a bicycle, passes the window near the entrance of the building.

Spotting the soldier riding by, the Duty Sergeant says, "I'll get that, Lieutenant." Quickly saluting Patton, he exits the office.

The young lieutenant Patton looks at some of the items on the tray that he hasn't yet tried, and reaches for one. He looks at the label and opens it as Sergeant Simmons returns with the message just received.

Patton takes the papers and hands the sergeant the open bottle. He goes over the information then looks at the

General. "They've secured Carrizal, Sir. The enemy has been defeated." He goes on when, as expected, the General does not answer. "We sustained twelve losses. They were unable to locate Pancho Villa, however. Any orders?" He backs up and comes to attention, saluting the General. "With your permission, Sir, I'd like...to review the troops upon their return. If you need anything, the sergeant in charge is at your disposal." He looks at Sergeant Simmons. "Take care of him, will you?" He turns, opens the door and exits, closing the door behind him.

Four figures riding horseback through the desolate area dot the open wastelands. The day has grown old, and the shadows of the cactus grow long. While the sun still rides the skies close at horizon, the heat still rises off the desert floor.

"You may have me," says German General Heinrich Schmidt. "But you'll never be able to stop the movement. You're too heavily infiltrated to stop that now, and your army won't get anything out of Admiral Yamagato as their prisoner, either."

"What did you expect to accomplish by dragging America into a war?" asks Lillian.

"Europe will soon fall to Germany and the Central powers. By distracting the United States, the war could continue unabated by American influence," responds Schmidt.

"What about the Japanese? Aren't they our ally?"

"The United States has prevented the Japanese nationals from purchasing property in the Americas," the General explains. "They've even restricted immigration of Japanese laborers, so the Japanese sought other means of acquiring land."

"Acquisition through war?" asks the Ranger.

"Precisely," Schmidt answers. "The Turks are about to join our effort, thus involving Islam in a Holy War."

"It is not a Holy War," says Juan, eyeing the German General.

"It can still be," says Schmidt, confidently. "The Sultan is calling it that, and in underdeveloped countries where industry and technology have yet to find a foothold, a rifle is a very important commodity."

"Are you trying to thrust the world into a war?" asks the Ranger with concern.

"We're trying to keep it in order," responds Schmidt.

"Order through anarchy?" Lillian asks, not totally understanding such logic.

"Whatever means available to us. America is an isolationist country," says the General. "It's gearing up industrially and is a possible threat. These terrorist actions are specifically designed to off-set the balance of power. Better the United States focus on Mexico than on Europe."

"Mexicans have been oppressed by Europe since Cortez landed," Juan address the General with concern. "You're manipulating good people."

"Don't fool yourself," says the General. "They are as interested in the United States as anyone else. With the influence of a dominant power like Germany, it didn't require much convincing. If America won't sell her precious land, it can be had by other means."

"America is not for sale, mister," says the Ranger. "You've underestimated the people, and it's the people that make America great. If you happen to drag America into your...world war, it will be a major mistake on your part. Despite what you might think, America is a very proud country. It doesn't need the Germans, Japanese, or the Mexicans to tell them how to run it."

"Change is inevitable," says Schmidt, looking the three over with contempt. "We're only trying to help it along. This is the dawn of a new age. A modern age. Telephone calls can be made across the Atlantic and the Pacific. Automobiles that can travel one hundred thirty miles an hour. Zeplins, aeroplanes, motion pictures where little tramps like Charlie Chaplin reach popularity of world proportions. Synthetic materials are being created from petroleum products.... The treasure of the war, is the United States itself!"

Marching into the Punitive Expeditionary Forces camp, wounded and battle-torn soldiers head towards the parade grounds, too weary and worn out to complain or even talk. The troopers shuffle their feet, rather than march, to the tune of exhaustion.

Standing proud with his hands on his waist as the troops walk past him, Lieutenant Patton clutches a swagger stick, admiring and envying the dirty, blood-stained soldiers as they trudge past him completely oblivious to the silver bars of the lieutenant observing their return.

"How did you escape?" Lillian asks the German General, slowly keeping pace on his horse between Juan and the Ranger.

"Diplomatic immunity," Schmidt answers. "I didn't escape. I was deported. I simply transferred to a German U-Boat in the Gulf of Mexico and made my way to Carrizal via one of our aeroplanes to continue my duties. Though you might have stopped me, there are others who will take my place and continue the effort." Looking at the trio, he shakes his head. "We will not be denied."

Eyeing the General and shaking his head, the Ranger grits his teeth. "It's a wasted effort, General. You drag America into your war and you'll regret it."

"That remains to be seen, Texas Ranger," says the smug German General. "Your country hasn't engaged a foreign power in almost a hundred years—a full century. You don't have the military experience for a war overseas. Your officers lack abilities for modern warfare, and they are emotionally and militarily immature. Just another example of your ignorance."

Looking at Juan, then at the Ranger and Lillian, Schmidt says, "Your whole country is littered with loudmouthed, do-nothing people. They are mostly uneducated, undernourished, barefoot and in need of hygienics. That's why the United States is such an easy target. We can give it structure."

"We have this saying in America...'If it ain't broke, don't fix it,'" says the Ranger, eyeing the General and making himself clear. "The United States ain't broke."

Entering the compound of the Punitive Expeditionary Forces, Lillian, Juan, General Schmidt and the Ranger pass the review of Lieutenant Patton. Recognizing the German General, the young lieutenant drops his hands from his waist and lifts the swagger stick and furiously shakes it in angered direction.

Walking aggressively towards Schmidt as visually upset as any man can get, the lieutenant shouts, "You! What are you doing here? I sent you back to Germany last week.... You are not supposed to be here, mister. " He senses the German Officer's responsibility in all this and it makes him furious.

Still shaking the swagger stick, Patton yells to the Ranger. "Get that son-of-a-bitch back to Germany so I can personally go over there and kick his ass!" the young lieutenant demands, just about fit to be tied. "Better yet, get him off that horse and we'll settle it right here and now.... You son-of-a-flophouse Hun...whore!"

Schmidt is startled and shocked as they continue their slow pace into the camp with Lillian, Juan, and the Ranger doing nothing about the ravings of the lieutenant as he shakes the swagger stick menacingly closer to Schmidt.

"You pick the weapon, you bastard. Pistols, swords, knives, fists...teeth. You will not lay claim to this country while I'm alive!" Flushed in the face, the lieutenant cannot be calmed. "We've got you now and we'll send you back to Germany again, but if you ever breach these borders again, there won't be a safe place on the planet for you to hide. I'll turn it all over, looking for you, do you understand? I'll chase you to every corner of the globe, all seven seas...."

The lieutenant stops walking and shouts as the group continues its paced ride further into camp. "Nowhere on God's green earth will you find shelter from my wrath! You're mine, mister, do you hear me? I'm going to be all over you like bark on a tree.... Take that man to the brig, cause I've got some serious questions I'm going to ask him later."

The Ranger eyes the General as they pass beyond the furious young lieutenant still waving that swagger stick. Smiling, he pulls his hat down and says, "Looks like you made yourself a real friend there, General." Lillian, Juan and the Ranger continue to escort the German General into camp as Patton stands there shaking the stick, still raising hell.

Carriages, horsemen, automobiles, wagons, bicycles, and motorcycles crowd the busy city street as the beat of a single drum cuts through the air. Vehicles and animals part as dozens of women carrying axes and pickaxes march in time to the lone snare drum. Henrietta Primm leads the marching crowd down the middle of the street towards the Half Moon Saloon. Several of the women carry pickets with various slogans that read, NO MORE BOOZE. TEMPERANCE NOW. STOP THE FLOW OF WHISKEY. WOMEN'S CHRISTIAN TEMPERANCE UNION FOREVER. Waving the cards around as if they were banners, they seem to be begging anyone to deny them their right to protest.

The women halt as Henrietta tops the old wooden stairs in front of the saloon entrance. She is one of Carrie Nation's most ardent supporters. Turning to the other women standing in the street, she raises one hand to silence the women and gain their attention.

"Women of Texas, we are in a unique position. We've only just realized the power women now have with the right to vote. Today, we shall exhibit the power women have with the right to might." Henrietta raises a pickaxe over her head and the women on the street begin to cheer. She places the axe on her shoulder.

"Alcohol is the devil's own creation!" she proclaims. Turning and pointing at the swinging butterfly doors of the saloon, adding, "And this is the devil's playground!" The women cheer.

Several curious men within the saloon watch from the doors and windows, sipping their drinks, turning to each other and shrugging their shoulders, unaware of the momentous events unfolding before them.

"If we can't temper them with common sense," Mrs. Primm goes on, "then we'll get their attention another way." Pulling the axe off her shoulder and spinning around, she barges through the door of the saloon, leading the ladies on a charge up the stairs and into the saloon.

Pushing past the customers at the door, Henrietta walks to the bar. The few paying patrons back up and move aside, eyeing the women who have just entered their drinking den. Standing in front of the counter, Mrs. Primm addresses her sisters in protest. "If the owners of this establishment can't stop the flow of alcohol...."

"Now just a minute lady," interrupts the bartender. "We don't want no trouble around here."

"...Then maybe we can convince them another way!" Henrietta says, ignoring the saloon keeper and addressing her sister suffragettes.

"Look, ladies...," pleads the bartender. "We pay our bills and our taxes. We are a legitimate business and that means we're here legally."

The bartender's mild protest irks some of the ladies as they knock over some tables and chairs and step closer to the bar.

"Hold on, ladies!" says the barkeep, holding his hands out, trying to stop them from tearing up his place.

Henrietta pushes her way past some patrons at the bar and walks to the end of the counter. Turning to face the ladies, she raises her axe, turns around and slams it into a whiskey barrel next to the mirror behind the bar. Alcohol gushes out all over the floor. Ripping the axe out of the wooden container and turning to her sisters as the bartender and patrons look on in shock, Henrietta declares, "Ladies, let the lesson begin!"

All at once the saloon turns into a madhouse as the women attack everything in sight. There is obvious enjoyment in their act as the women break bottles behind the bar, axe other barrels and generally wreak havoc everywhere. Men are shoved out of the way, as there's no stopping the onslaught.

Several men are pummeled by women's purses while other men are manhandled by various women. One lady with a picket sign hits a cowboy who falls to the ground. Another woman kicks the downed cowpoke as he tries to take cover. The bartender stands up on the bar and tries to maintain control of the saloon. "Stop it! Stop it!" he shouts. A lady with a picket sign sweeps his feet right out from under him, effectively silencing him as he falls behind the bar and out of sight. There's no stopping the frenzy.

Three khaki-clad troopers jump to attention as General Schmidt is pushed through the door of the brig by Abner, while the General, in mid-sentence, continues. "...And it was John Locke who said, 'Life, liberty, and the pursuit of property – which your Thomas Jefferson so conveniently adjusted to fit your Constitution...'" says Schmidt, looking at the Ranger, Lillian, and Juan.

"John Locke was a subject of the British Empire," Lillian reminds him. "He was not a citizen. Subjects are just that...subject to the whims, rules, and laws of the land and of their rulers. Property is important to those who aren't allowed to own any, because a king, queen, tsar, sultan, or whatever, won't stand for such freedom." Eyeing the German General with deep contempt, she goes on. "The

American spirit won't stand for such tyranny anymore, and it can't be imposed upon the will of the people."

The Ranger interrupts. "You get it, bub? An attack on one citizen is an attack on every citizen."

"Freedom, Herr Schmidt," Lillian goes on. "That's what it's all about in the United States. Freedom from the oppression you'd try to forcibly lay on this country and its people. Freedom from cultures that arrogantly think they have the right to impose their beliefs on a free nation or the citizenry of that country."

She stares him down. "Freedom for anyone who seeks a free and open society, where every voice is heard and counted, not just of the few or the privileged. We vote. Even women can vote now. And we elect our officials, Schmidt. We put them in office to serve us. They are public servants, and they help us. Not like royalty or whatever dogma you're serving up or offering."

"We are a very civilized society," responds the German General. "You could learn something from us."

"I doubt it," says the Ranger, pushing him towards the three soldiers. "Lock him up. There's a Lieutenant who wants some words with him."

Looking at the young soldiers holding him, the German General says, "I want to make contact with my consulate."

"Better make it a telegram," says the Ranger. "Don't think we want to see this guy get an answer too quick."

The Ranger, Lillian, and Juan exit the brig to see more troops marching in. Looking down the road, they see Lieutenant Patton walking over to them. Suddenly Patton stops beside a building, surprised to see General Scriven leaning over the side of the railing, throwing up. Next to him is Sergeant Simmons, patting him on the back and shaking his head. Lieutenant Patton salutes the General, using his swagger stick and resumes his walk towards the brig.

The young lieutenant slows down as he approaches Lillian, Juan, and the Ranger, as all three are now on horseback and reining their horses. Just as he's taking a moment to look at them sternly, he hears a commotion and turns to check it out. When he turns back to the trio, they've already heeled their mounts to a walk out of camp.

Climbing the stairs and walking into the brig, the three soldiers come to attention, saluting. Patton returns the salute with his swagger stick. "Where's that prisoner who was just brought in?"

"He's in the brig, Lieutenant," responds one soldier with a bewildered look on his face.

"What's wrong with you?" snaps Patton, looking the soldier over.

The soldier reaches for a note on his desk. Handing it to Patton, he shakes his head. "I'm a little puzzled , sir."

Taking the paper and reading it, Patton says, "That damned German General is as dyslexic as I am. Send it. He's just asking for the consulate to put some pressure on for his release because he thinks we're stalling. Now where's that prisoner?"

One soldier picks up some keys and opens a door, allowing the lieutenant to enter. The other soldier looks over to the one with the note. "What's it say?"

Shaking his head in puzzlement, the trooper responds, "I don't understand it. He's German, but he wants the message sent to the Finland Station. ...And it says, 'Lean on - stall in.' I guess he wants to stick around awhile."

The other soldier says, "Do as the lieutenant ordered."

Cars, wagons, and horsemen are stopped in front of the saloon to watch the suffragettes. Exiting the Punitive Expeditionary Forces camp and walking their horses down the gravel street, Lillian looks at Juan with mystification. "Juan? You explained the three worlds as being a triad. What is this fourth world you've visited?"

Juan studies her. "It is the world of shadows," he finally says, though the Ranger is more curious about the traffic congestion in front of the saloon.

"What?" asks Lillian, perplexed. "Is this more Yaqui mysticism?"

"It is a spiritual world," he acknowledges. "It can be as simple as a shadow cast under a full moon or off a street light at night, or, it can be as complex as shadow governments or organizations with secret plans or agendas."

Shaking her head, Lillian studies Juan more seriously as his words have penetrated her understanding in a mysterious way.

The Ranger interrupts them. "I'll take care of this," he says, walking his horse up to a hitching post in front of the saloon and getting off his mount.

The Half Moon Saloon is in a complete uproar as several women grab the bartender, who is now back on the counter, being dragged along it by some women. They hoist him off the edge and throw him out the front window to the boardwalk.

The bartender lands at the Ranger's feet. Looking down at the man all sprawled out and knocked out on the ground in front of him, the Ranger asks, puzzled, "What's going on in there?" He peers through the broken window in curiosity as a bottle of whiskey flies past him onto the street.

Inside the saloon, a man is thrown off the stairs to a table below, smashing it to pieces. An old, whiskered desert rat covers his head as a woman hits him in the stomach with her purse. As he reaches for his stomach, she hits him in the face. He covers his face, only to have her hit him in the stomach again. He recovers and raises his fist at the lady, but another lady hits the sourdough over the head with a bottle, knocking him out.

Stepping through the swinging butterfly doors right into the frenzied brawl, the Ranger looks around as Lillian and Juan come up behind him. "Do something!" she says.

A bottle flies over the Ranger's head and smashes into the wooden wall, breaking to shards. Holding a cowboy in a headlock, a woman rushes past him, beating on the cowboy's head.

Shaking his head and looking the place over, the Ranger says, "What can I possibly do?" as another bottle flies past his head. The lawman doesn't even flinch.

"You've got to stop it!" demands Lillian as the Ranger stands there, completely befuddled.

The Ranger spins around as a man is thrown out the window on the other side of the bar. More bottles and glasses slam into the walls near the trio.

Shaking his head, the Ranger pushes past Lillian and Juan and exits the saloon into the street, barely escaping another bottle as it slams into the door jamb following his last steps outside the bar.

Lillian looks at Juan; who shrugs, spins and follows the Ranger, leaving Lillian to shake her head, take a deep breath, turn, and walk out.

Outside the saloon, people still crowd around to watch the action as the Ranger looks the town over, studying Main street. A chair flies out through the window of the saloon into the street, followed by a man.

Shaking his head, he steps down the stairs and walks over to his horse. He unties the lead from the hitching post, mounts his horse, and reaches into his duster, pulling out a pocket watch. Flipping up the cover, he checks the time. Satisfied, he puts it back into his pocket as he gazes up at the sky, noticing the day creeping towards sunset. The street lights start to spark, flicker, and light up.

Walking to her horse and getting on, Lillian asks excitedly, "What do we do now?"

As Juan gets on his horse, the Ranger shakes his head. "Nothin'," he says, looking straight at her. "We don't do nothin'." Nodding, he reins his mount around. Addressing Juan, he says, "Why don't you go on down the street and see if you can raise the Sheriff and see if he can come on over and quell this civil disturbance."

"The Sheriff?" Lillian asks. "Is that all?"

The Ranger looks at her a little puzzled as he spurs his mount down the street. Lillian catches up with him on her horse. He looks over at her and says, "Desperados, bandits, *pistoleeros*, rustlers, owl hoots, bank robbers, goat ropers, murderers, claim jumpers, assorted nefarious types, and even your basic embezzlers...yep." He nods. Then shaking his head, he says, "A saloon full of crazed women.... Sounds like a local problem."

"What?" says Lillian, perturbed. She rides up to the lawman. "That's all? Abner Caleb. You mean to tell me you'd allow such a thing?"

Pulling his hat down and collar up, he says, "'Taint my doin' to begin with."

"What kind of attitude is that?" she asks querulously.

"A safe one," responds the lawman.

Slapping her chaps and acting surprised, she looks the lawman over. "As I live and breathe, you mean to tell me there's a safe way to do things? We don't have to kick in doors, shoot people, beat on little kids...?"

"The 'little kid' was a teenager," interrupts the lawman.

"...Manhandle wounded prisoners, chase down foreign nationals...," she pauses a moment to look the Ranger over. "What about that territory you're always talking about?"

The Ranger spurs his horse to a trot. "That territory just ran out for the day."

Juan rides up beside Lillian as she catches up to Abner. "Wait a minute. I think I'm just getting the hang of this Texas Ranger stuff," she says. "We go after Pancho Villa again, right?"

"Only if he comes across that border again," says the Ranger.

"Then, can we go after him?" she asks eagerly.

Fittin' his old hat down and grippin' the leather lead, the Ranger adjusts his duster and says, "Yeah, well, we'll see...."

Leaving the sound of the saloon brawl behind, Lillian, Juan, and the Ranger disappear into cross traffic as three touring cars filled with khaki-uniformed soldiers armed with carbines, cross a corner and turn down a street, headed towards the Mexican border.

In a little over one year
later—thirteen months—the
Punitive Expeditionary Forces
land in France and engage a foreign enemy in open trench warfare.

A FINAL NOTE....

The Americans lost the battle of Carrizal.